THE PLUNGE

THE PLUNGE

A NOVEL

LILA RAICEK

PARK
ROW
BOOKS

ISBN-13: 978-0-7783-1060-0

The Plunge

Park Row Books
22 Adelaide St. West, 41st Floor
Toronto, Ontario M5H 4E3, Canada
ParkRowBooks.com

HarperCollins Publishers
Macken House, 39/40 Mayor Street Upper,
Dublin 1, D01 C9W8, Ireland
www.HarperCollins.com

Printed in U.S.A.

26 27 28 29 30 LBC 7 6 5 4 3

in memory of James,
scarlett, golden, and bright

Perhaps, perhaps this would be the one
to pull me out of my plunge.

—SYLVIA PLATH

The difference between false memories and
true ones is the same as for jewels:
it is always the false ones that look the
most real, the most brilliant.

—SALVADOR DALÍ

When I asked him once how to kill someone, he said without hesitating that he would sprinkle a diamond into someone's drink like salt, and let it lacerate their internal organs. There was also cinnabar, of course; the toxic inhalation of scarlet sulfide. Or even a bar of gold, which can easily bludgeon and then be melted down into a different shape, an untraceable weapon. But the way he'd kill me, he said, was with a branch of coral: a spiny crimson spike that could slice open a vein.

I can't remember now why I asked him. But when the body was found, bloody and limp near the water, I thought back to his answer.

That was the summer I learned about rocks and stones and gems. Their sparkle, their earthiness, belied their potential danger. That's what I grew to like about them, about him, and the world he moved through.

How could I have known where it would end, or even begin? That's not true: how could I not have known. I wanted to be distracted by the brilliant glare of things, like everyone else, obscuring the black inclusions at its core like little rotted seeds. I was distracted by so many things but mostly by the two of them, together. Which is how I met them both when I walked into the party.

PART I

1

The first invitation arrived without warning while I was lying in bed in the maid's room.

My phone rattled against the rim of the bathtub, a few feet away, but I didn't get up. It was almost dark out, thin blue threads of light streaming down the cracked walls. Outside, I could hear the rain pounding against the window air conditioner like a steel drum, the atonal chords of early spring. There was no one who would be calling me, I thought, at least not at this hour. But when the phone rang again, I crawled over to the bathroom to check it.

The number was blocked, a strange relic of anonymity. I don't know why I answered, but I hadn't spoken to anyone all day—or was it all week—so on the last ring I picked up.

"What are you doing right now?"

I stared at the screen, forgetting how to breathe. Slowly, the disembodied male voice returned to me, deep and soft, like a haunting refrain I'd heard once yet couldn't recall until now. He was someone I'd known briefly in the distant past—a neighbor from an apartment I no longer lived in, inhabiting a life that seemed impossibly far from where I was now.

"I'm lying in bed in a maid's room," I said.

“What are you wearing?” he continued.

I hesitated, pressing my back against the cold tub. I thought about saying something normal, such as: nothing, or red lace panties. But then I looked down at my faded, unwashed Led Zeppelin T-shirt with a wine stain purpled like a bruise, a stale trace of cigarette smoke from the last time it was worn by Graham, and reconsidered my answer.

“All black,” I said finally. “I’m in mourning for my life.”

“Do I have to come over there and bathe you?” he said.

“That would be nice, but my suitcase lives in the bathtub.”

And it was true. When I returned to New York, after two years away, it was November, and the leaves seemed to have spitefully refused to change. I moved into a maid’s room on East 89th Street, in an apartment that belonged to a seventy-six-year-old man, for lack of anywhere else to go. It wasn’t ideal, but then again, what was—in the real estate sense, that is. I arrived in the middle of the night with one carry-on suitcase, having left the rest of my life behind, and planted it in the mold-encrusted bathtub as that was the only available space. The maid’s room was the size of a closet—barely six feet wide by eight feet long—between the kitchen and service entrance, with no door separating the tiny bathroom. It fit a thin, mildewed single mattress on the floor, and cardboard boxes of rotting poetry books and cookbooks stacked up in the corner, hiding the shells of dead roaches. The faded floral yellow wallpaper was peeling off, revealing a web of cracks in the plaster, with a water-stained brown carpet to complete the interior portrait of decay. One small window looked out on an airshaft like a sunless prison, but it was blanketed in a thick coat of grime, so you could barely see through it at all.

“It’s like you finally escaped Germany,” a friend had said, referring to Los Angeles, “only to hide in an attic when you got to the other side.” But I preferred it here, invisibly co-cooned from the outside world, tending to my desolation. I liked its false sense of security, as if I didn't deserve to occupy any more space than it offered.

The seventy-six-year-old man was Samuel Shear, a staggeringly handsome former poet laureate who had been my mentor in college. During seminars, the female students would illicitly imagine his private life while we studied his striped Italian socks and listened to him read "Hymn from a Watermelon Pavilion" in a gravelly, baritone voice. Back then, he was widely regarded as the literary Clint Eastwood. Over the past decade, we had formed an unlikely friendship; he would dole out romantic advice, while I'd tag along on odd errands, like shopping for minimalist light fixtures in SoHo. But Sam had recently gone into cardiac arrest, followed by major heart surgery, so he was finally consigned to becoming the old man he had spent his life refusing to be.

As November bled into December, then into a new year, I barely left Sam's apartment. Sometimes we made collages with brightly colored paper cut like thin slices of tropical fruit. He taught me how to make risotto ai funghi and spaghetti alla puttanesca. We drank heavy Italian reds, Barolos and Montepulcianos, though mostly I would drink alone because he was on too much medication. We listened to jazz records and watched old thrillers. *Elevator to the Gallows. La Piscine.* He told me stories of his youth. About his depressive mother in Maine. About what it was like to fuck a Bond Girl. To fuck two Bond Girls. To live for a year on a hilltop in Rome. Sometimes he would translate a stray line of Spanish poetry aloud: *And you, smallest of lost stars that opens for me . . . never shut off your light over all the bedrooms we slept in till dawn.*

This continued through the raw depths of winter, one cold day fading into the next. Sometimes I would see friends, though most had left the city or felt like distant strangers now. Sometimes I would force myself to go on dates out of fear I would never date again. There was a CTO of a glasses start-up—also an investor in an ethical chocolate company, he frequently reminded me—who liked getting head in public hotel bathrooms. I gave him head at the Mark, the Lowell, the Crosby, and the Greenwich Hotel. He treated it like an action item on his to-do list that he could now satisfactorily check off. There was an agonized divorced novelist who would accept FaceTimes from his kids in Scarsdale while we were in bed, then analyze his guilt for hours afterward until he was too flaccid to do anything else. There was a contemporary art dealer who offered to Venmo me half a year of rent if I watched him jerk off in the back of an Uber. (I considered, then declined.) There was a biotech investor who revealed over dinner that he had spent the day with a secret elite group of visionaries at a secret elite conference, where they each had to share their most painful trauma. I asked, in my most empathetic voice, if he was willing to share his with me. He took my hand beneath a tower of oysters and said gravely: "When I realized I was losing my hair."

I stopped dating after that. I mostly stopped seeing anyone at all. I went back to watching old thrillers with Sam. *Purple Noon. Leave Her to Heaven.* The more time I spent alone with him, the more I, too, felt like an old man, as if I had already lived enough years of love, of loss, and could now accept the morbid solitude that precedes the coming of death.

But I wasn't a seventy-six-year-old man; I was a thirty-one-year-old woman.

Most nights, though, I cried silently in bed until I fell asleep, and I'd awaken in the dead of night, my teeth clenched from violent dreams. I was thinking of Graham, of the last night I saw him before he died, two weeks before our wedding date.

Somehow, half a year had passed like this, and it was May.

I got up from the floor and looked out the window, the phone still pressed to my ear. The light had changed, a silvery mist drifting across the faded column of bricks. I couldn't tell if it was from the weather, or the acrid plumes of smoke that rose from the rooftops beyond my enclosed view. I tried to calculate the last time I had washed my hair.

"Get dressed," he said before hanging up. "I'm sending you the address of a party."

I couldn't possibly go. But another sleepless night stretched before me, the dark hollow of hours waiting for dawn to come. I pressed my cheek against the cold glass until I could see a gray slab of sky, and wondered if his call was the portent I'd been too afraid to ask for.

An hour later, I was walking downtown on the unlit edge of Central Park. The rain had thinned, though it swamped the sewers and subways, leaking through the scaffolding that shielded the buildings like corroded armor. My hair was getting wet, the ribs of my cheap bodega umbrella buckling in the crosstown wind, but I was too nervous to care. My mind racing through anxious projections of what the night might hold.

I had not been to a party since my return, not really. In the early days of moving back, in a numb coma of shock, I was quick to interpret any invitation as some proof of normalcy: I was still included, even after what happened, even without Graham. But I had been wrong. Everyone just wanted a glimpse of me, to brush against the dark glitter of scandal. As though I were a wounded butterfly under microscopic observation, exposing the veins in my wings while they beat against the glass.

Until gradually the invitations dried up, and I was forgotten. It was easier that way, I justified, to resign myself to the fate of fading, to retreat into my dark cavern of grief. If I treated my own life as a half-remembered story, then maybe it would become true.

But that hadn't been the case.

I approached a revolving door on the corner of 59th and pushed my way inside. A doorman directed me to a discreet brass door, marked with a *D*, which opened to reveal a red throat of stairs, like a passageway into some infernal underworld. I wondered which of the nine circles I was entering—hopefully one with an open bar. The mirrored walls distorted my reflection through metallic-painted stripes, and I imagined that I was someone else: another pretty girl slinking into a party, nameless, without context. But then I caught a glimpse of my face, shiny with sweat, as if a visible shame coated my skin like a bad aura, or a disease.

Downstairs, I handed my soggy leather jacket to a coat check girl and grabbed a glass of white wine from a tray. I drifted toward the edge of the party, holding the glass close to my face as if it could obscure my presence. The room was an assault of red: red carpets and red floral walls and red velvet banquettes, reflected in chrome-plated ceilings. It was like a nightclub left over from a hedonistic decade the city was no longer in. I didn't even know what or who the party was for, then deduced it must be Cinco de Mayo based on the painted skull centerpieces next to bowls of loose cigarettes. And, evidently, it was the date.

I anxiously scanned the crowd, a minefield of faces. A group of women were thrusting their bony hips beneath a disco ball, their leather bondage dresses giving off the whiff of fresh divorce, while a few gay men in sockless loafers debated the merits of ketamine at the bar. "It's the new sober," one said. I exhaled, a small rush of relief that no one recognized me. But as I took a little shrimp taco from a passing tray, then immediately regretted it, I became acutely aware that I couldn't find the man who had invited me tonight. And maybe he wasn't here at all.

It was not normal to have come alone, I realized. Desperate, even. A desperation I had carefully buried, even from myself, like a bulb planted during a colder season that was now breaking the surface, a blighted bloom.

I took a large sip of wine, worried other people could sense it on me. I tried to call up a time when I liked parties, or at least was somewhat good at them. With Graham, our life had been consumed by a stream of parties, across cities and nights, slurring together like the memory of water. At his side, I was defined by the power of his presence, protected by the gilded constraint of it. *One hand on your glass and the other on me,* he would whisper, half joking, as all eyes in the room tracked our movements. Now, alone again, I felt the outline of his absence. I glanced at the couples here, carrying the pain around like a phantom limb, an invisible amputation. As if it weren't real, and at any moment I would feel his hand on my lower back, his face beaming to introduce me, our love breathing its own rarified air, on the precipice of some shimmering future.

No one knew what happened when the party was over, when the darkest hours set in. If only I had known all those parties would end in a graveyard, a dream left to rot below the earth with his mangled body. My nights now tinted with slow decay.

"You're still here?" a woman cried out.

Her shrill voice pierced the air. I knew who it was—a publicist with the tact of a minor dictator. I quickly sought an escape route but was marooned between two clusters of people with nowhere to turn.

"In New York, that is," she clarified, in case I thought she meant in existence. "No one knows where you've been hiding all this time."

"I guess they haven't deported me yet," I said, turning toward her. Her face looked as frozen and glassy as an ice-skating rink.

"That's right, your wedding was supposed to be here." She

frowned. "I even bought a new dress for the occasion that I still haven't worn."

"So did I," I said, though the irony seemed lost on her. My wedding dress, hanging in an abandoned closet like a suicide rope. I swallowed hard, looking down at my feet. I couldn't recall why she was invited to my wedding, then realized she wasn't—it must be something she told people to impress upon them her personal proximity to the tragedy, a fraudulent token of social currency. Everyone loved to peer through the glass of others' misfortune, as long as the pane of separation was airtight.

"Of course, it was horrible what happened, devastating, really." She arranged her features with pity, scanning my forehead like a barcode. "My god, just look at your poor face."

I touched my cheek, confused for a moment. Then realized she meant my scar, a raw red slash, snaking down my forehead above my right eye.

The night of the accident, on our final drive home, the windshield shattered like a mirror, splitting my skin with thick shards of glass. The surgeon had been young, in training, and looked at my face as if it were ruined before bothering to stitch it closed. Not the nerves or the tissue that held it together, but the composition itself, which, like a cubist portrait of a girl, contained a fearful asymmetry that no longer lent itself to beauty. I would never have my face again, but in its place a marred surface, a jagged bisection of pain.

I tried to readjust my side bangs, but they stuck to my hairline prickling with sweat.

"I mean, don't get me wrong. It must've been humiliating for him to be disgraced like that, so publicly," she went on. "But to try and take you down with him? As a fellow woman, I feel for you."

"Thank you," I said dumbly.

Instead of punching her, I bit the inside of my lip until a

piece of flesh tore. I didn't want to think about this, not here, not now, but unbidden flashes from our final night erupted like a fever: *the party, the fight, the cliff, the gun.*

"Trust me, it's better he killed hims—" She stopped. "Better it happened before the wedding than after. No one deserves to be a *real* widow at your age."

What about a fake widow, I wanted to say, but she had already pivoted away to fawn over the third wife of a producer who had started an evil eye jewelry line. I drained the rest of my wine, but the blood in my mouth made it taste metallic. I pushed my way over to the bar and tried to flag down a mustached bartender for a glass of water, and also a tequila. But I felt another pair of eyes boring into me like a drill.

Across the bar, a man nursing a whiskey was staring in my direction. He had a distinguished swoop of silver-white hair, a red pocket square poking out of his tweed blazer. When I met his gaze, his mouth twisted into a sly grimace of recognition that made my stomach turn. A lost night flickered behind my eyes, and I was filled with a strange unease that I had met him before at a party with Graham. I blinked a few times, hoping my vision was short-circuiting, that he was a glitch of my fractured memory.

But when I looked over again, the man was still staring.

I could suddenly sense a sea of glances darting around me, a tailwind of whispers trailing me like my own elongated shadow. *This is why you no longer go to parties,* I told myself. *This is why you deserve to disappear.*

I had to get out of this stupid party immediately. I headed in a direction I prayed was the exit, but the room started to spin, the ceiling churning with a gyre of disco-ball light, the red walls and floors and chairs hemorrhaging around me until I felt sick.

That was when I heard his voice. "Liv?"

Fuck, I thought, who is it now, as I steadied myself against a chair, the closest life raft in this hellish sea. Then he called my name again and I turned around.

It was Damon. The familiar voice on the other end of the line. My next-door neighbor before I left New York. As he walked toward me, his presence seemed to part the crowd, the noise around us muting to a murmur. I exhaled sharply, as if he were the brightly lit exit I had been seeking all along.

"If it isn't a ruby in the New York rough," Damon said.

"I thought rubies were too conventional for you," I said.

"True, but fire opal sounded a little too heavy-handed," he said. "Even for me."

He was more handsome than I remembered. There was still a broody intensity beneath his charm, yet the years had softened his rougher edges. His hair was longer, a dust of silver-streaked scruff on his angular jaw, and a crease between his eyes that gave him an almost bruised masculinity.

"You know, from a distance I was convinced you were a mirage," Damon said.

"Maybe I am. Maybe I'm just a projection of years of subliminal longing," I said.

He lifted a hand from his glass and touched my collarbone. My eyelids fluttered closed, an electric current running through his calloused fingers.

"Oh no," he said, "I'm afraid you're very much real."

He studied me, his eyes like pools of glacial ice. I felt my skin turn liquid, limpid, as if he could reach below the surface and dredge up my former self from the murky bottom. I shivered a little and he removed his hand.

"So why didn't you tell me you were back in New York?" Damon said.

"I didn't exactly send out a mass telegraph," I said.

"If only you had, I would've tracked you down sooner," he said. "And honestly, I was surprised you picked up the phone."

"Then why did you bother to call?"

"I've always been a man of uncalculated risks," he said with a relaxed smile.

There was usually a dreaded pause in conversation when I was expected to fill in plot holes, answer invasive questions thinly cloaked by condolences. I could tell that Damon's curiosity was not about the past, but some unformed present he could shape and mold in his hands like soft, malleable gold.

Still, I hardly knew anything about him. Except that he was a renowned jewelry designer—at once vastly different from most other men, and as irrelevant to my own lusterless life as one could get.

"So, are you here with someone?" he said. "A paramour, a plus-one, a plus-two?"

I looked into my empty glass, embarrassed by how obvious the answer must be.

"Unfortunately, you'll have to settle for just me," I said.

"Good, because you're the only person I wanted to see."

I flushed. "Who did you come with?"

Before he could answer, I heard, "Damon, come back!" We turned to find a table staring at us as if we had just performed an intimate scene from an Inge play. As we walked over, I felt something turn in my chest like a key, cracking open a door to a hidden room. At the center of the booth was a beguiling older woman, swathed in a marigold silk dress that seemed to irradiate her face with sunlight. She had a halo of strawberry-blond hair, partly swooped up in a clip to frame her sculpturally crescent cheekbones. She looked ageless, as elegant women often do, though she could have been anywhere in her sixties.

"Damon, you must introduce us to this lovely young woman," she said in a soft, smoky voice.

"She looks like Ann-Margret," said a man beside her. "Before her accident."

I reddened a little, reminded how I would be defined for

posterity: before and after the accident, those weighted bookends of identity. Or maybe I was being overly sensitive. Not everyone reads a scar as a headline.

"Are you an actress?" said a younger woman at the table in a plummy British accent.

"Oh no, I'm a retired playwright," I said. "But without the Social Security benefits."

"Liv is a brilliant writer," Damon said. "We lived next door to each other a lifetime ago."

"She doesn't look old enough to have more than one," said the man.

"Believe me, I've had a hundred," I said.

The older woman smiled, unfurling her hand across the table in a graceful, feline motion.

"And this is the infamous Isabel," Damon said, gesturing to her. "The other brilliant writer in the room."

"Yet, like you, also retired," Isabel said.

It took me a moment to realize who she was. Isabel had been a notable New York figure, known for a collection of cultural essays about the grit and glitter of the city in the '70s and a cultish novella about a torturous affair, both now out of print. I had read her work in an obscure feminist lit class in college, with texts that centered around psychically disintegrating, stylishly detached women—which, at the time, we aspired to become.

"Was that frozen-faced cunt—sorry, *vulture*—attacking you earlier?" Isabel asked me.

I nodded, reporting what the publicist had said without the context of my personal backstory. Isabel listened with incisive slate-gray eyes that didn't miss a beat, at once validating the venom of her words while allaying their emotional damage.

"Listen, last year there was a doc for a famous violinist, and that vile harridan threw one of her parties in his honor at Lincoln Center," Isabel said. "So the violinist enters in his wheelchair—the poor man had polio, for fuck's sake—and as the room erupts in applause, she grabs the handles away from the young man helping to roll him in and screams: 'This party is for invited guests only.' The man looks absolutely petrified and says: 'But I'm his son!'"

As everyone laughed, I felt a swell of gratitude, as if Isabel was granting me a gift of amnesty without having asked for it. She went on to introduce the other woman as Gemma, a regal British Nigerian theater actress in her late forties, whose recent role in a West End production of *Phaedra* had been outshined by her fling with the film star playing her son; and the man, a decorator dressed like a bouncer at a leather bar, whose name I immediately forgot. Then Isabel swiveled her shoulders toward Damon, her face alight with a sibylline smile.

That was when it dawned on me: Damon and Isabel had come to the party together.

"How do you two know each other?" I asked.

"Myanmar, last summer," Isabel said. "I had been in mourning for my late husband, and my friends convinced me to go on one of those archeological trips for bereavement."

"The horror," said Gemma. "That would've made me want to join the bloody dead."

"Trust me, it did," said Isabel. "But I'm glad I went, because that's how I met Damon."

"You were on the trip?" I gave him a skeptical look.

"Can you imagine?" Gemma said. "The man wouldn't have escaped alive."

It was almost absurd to imagine Damon amid a flock of depressed widows, desperate to stave off the terminal disease of loneliness. But wasn't that why I was here, too?

"No, I was on the hunt for this rare gem, a Burmese ruby," Damon explained. "They call it a pigeon's blood ruby because, according to ancient legend, the color is as red as the first two drops of blood from a freshly killed pigeon."

As he spoke, I couldn't take my eyes off Isabel. A refined air of mystery coursed around her, yet beneath it I caught a glimpse of something else. Isabel seemed enraptured by Damon, as if they were connected by some imperceptible thread.

"That's the thing about stones," Damon was saying, his eyes landing on me. "Their beauty often hides the bloodshed."

Gemma squinted, jousting her martini spear at me. "Is *she* coming tomorrow night?"

"What's tomorrow night?" I asked.

"Damon is the man of honor," Isabel said, twisting the gold cuff on her wrist. "So naturally we're all going to honor him."

"You know, one of those wretched charity things," Gemma added. "Where everyone pretends to go for the cause when it's really an excuse to get plastered and flirt with terribly married men."

"Isn't that the only purpose of parties?" Isabel laughed. "So, you should come."

Everyone looked at me, then back at Isabel. Only then, in this slight caesura, did I notice the unequivocal power she wielded, as if every decision was granted or denied by her discerning permission alone.

"I don't know if I can." I shrugged, not wanting to seem overeager. I could barely afford a cab, let alone a ticket to a gala.

"I'll work on him, though he's not easy." Isabel winked, as if we were in on some joke. "I've already filled my table with all men, can you believe it?"

"Isabel and her many men," said Gemma.

"I think that's what people say about Liv," Damon said.

At this, Isabel lit up with a keen alertness, a rapid flash of calculation behind her eyes. I couldn't unravel what the nature of their relationship was—it was an oblique, magnetic tether, like the tidal force of the moon. But looking back, that was what I found myself riveted by. There was a perverse ambiguity to it, a tightrope of things at play that could land in one direction or another, and I wanted to see which way they fell.

It had stopped raining when I resurfaced at street level, the pavement crawling with low fog. I was about to walk home when Damon emerged from the doorway. I looked at him warily, uncertain what was meant to happen next. "Come on," he said, and before I could protest, we were walking uptown, close but not touching, a stillness stretching over the city, over ourselves, as if no time had passed between us at all.

Damon had lived next door to me on the fourth floor of a dilapidated brownstone on the East Side. I was subletting a cheap rent-controlled studio in the corner while in graduate school for playwriting, and tutoring private school girls to help offset my massive student loans. A large apartment occupied the rest of the floor, but it always appeared uninhabited. Once, while hauling my laundry to the basement, I ran into a man sporting a tennis racquet whom I assumed was my neighbor; he invited me to play tennis in Harlem, so I put him in my phone as Hot Harlem Tennis Neighbor, but it turned out he was only crashing next door in exchange for watching my neighbor's dogs.

A few months later, I came home drunk at 2:00 a.m., and when I climbed the three flights to my apartment, I found a stranger waiting on my landing. He had a destabilizing presence, the kind of man who could dissolve the most guarded layers like a coat of paint thinner. This was my real neighbor: Damon.

"So you're the girl who almost got me evicted," he said, leaning against the doorframe.

He must have been referring to the email I sent to management, complaining about his howling dogs.

"That's my side job," I said. "Evicting mysteriously absent neighbors."

"If I had known you were my neighbor, I would have been home more often," he said.

"Then it's a good thing we only met now."

He looked at me with surprise, as if something dormant had been roused within him—a look specific to men past the age of forty, who had left behind a long enough contrail of aggrieved women and heedless mistakes to seek a course correction. I was seeking the same thing, in a way, yet from a different slant.

After that night, we didn't see each other again until the day before I left New York. That year, my grad school play—a provocative thriller about the teenage girls I was tutoring—had been produced downtown to moderate buzz; a producer optioned it for film, so I took it as my cue, as one does, to move to Los Angeles. It was March. The city had barely emerged from a polar vortex, a winter so brutal it merited its own name, when a blizzard struck overnight. I put on a coat and headed outside in a cinematic gesture, like the scene in *The World of Henry Orient* when the troubled girl traverses the park alone after a snowstorm. When I stepped onto the street, there was Damon.

"I've been waiting for you," he said.

"Downstairs, or forever?" I said.

"Perhaps somewhere in between," he said. "Shall we take a walk?"

I hesitated. "This was meant to be my solo swan song, bidding New York goodbye."

"You know if you say goodbye to New York, it will give you a reason to stay. It's a scientific principle, like Bernoulli's law."

"What do you know about fluid dynamics?"

"More than you might think," he said.

We walked for hours through the park. The snow refracted the stray sunlight like a polarized lens, and we shielded our eyes from its icy iridescence. I told him why I was leaving, and he told me where he had been that year: the mines in Kashmir, the gem show in Hong Kong, sailing with pearl fishermen in Indonesia. At the top of Belvedere Castle, we paused to catch our breath. We looked at the field below, hushed by the heaviness it carried, then looked at each other.

"If you leave, you can always come back," Damon said in a low voice.

"That sounds like defeat," I said. "Surrendering to some misquoted line about New Yorkers not being able to live anywhere else."

"That's not what I mean." He touched my cheeks, his hands furnacing my frozen skin.

When we got back to our building, the strange intimacy that had swelled between us in the snowdrifts now felt too real, the proximity too close. We climbed the stairs, lingering on the landing before our adjacent doors.

"Will you come in for a drink?" Damon said. "If only to compare our apartments."

"I'm not *not* tempted," I said.

"It's just a glass of wine."

"Who said it was anything else?" I don't know if I was deterred by our unnerving attraction, or a brewing sense that he was offering an alternative to a predetermined choice—but since I didn't know, and my puffy jacket was suffocating me, I didn't go through with it. We said good night, and in doing so said goodbye. Later that night, I put my ear to the wall, listening to the low hum of music in his apartment. Chet Baker's somnolent tenor, singing *I get along without you very well, of course I do . . .* I imagined what would happen if I were there now, drinking wine, moving through the space uncertainly. Maybe nothing, or maybe something.

The next morning, I left for Los Angeles. I hardly thought of him; I became consumed with other things, and soon another man.

Now over two years had passed, and we were walking again on the same street beneath an unfamiliar night. A beam of red light strobed across the wet pavement like an alarm. Finally, I asked him where we were going.

"Don't you trust me by now?" Damon replied. "Have I ever led you astray?"

"The last time I followed you blindly, we almost froze to death," I said.

"I can imagine much worse outcomes," he said. "For example, I could've kidnapped you that night so you'd have never left the city."

"If only you had." I smirked. "It would have saved me a lot of misery."

Our arms slid against each other as we passed the Arsenal on 64th, standing vigil over the park, fluorescent green lights frosting its perimeter like icing.

"You know, Buck Sausage asks about you sometimes," he said.

"I'm sorry, do I know who that is?"

"The tennis pro who was dog-sitting in my apartment," he said.

I laughed. "Wait, he was an actual tennis pro?"

"Oh yeah, and he was fucking the wife of a hedge fund guy who'd let him stay at their house in Sagaponack all summer to teach their kids tennis."

"So he's the stereotype of a tennis pro," I said. "Why do you call him Buck Sausage?"

He smiled. "I'll tell you when I can show you."

As we passed the Frick, he placed a hand between my shoulder blades and steered me to the side gate. Through the iron bars, purple crocuses blanketed the damp grass, and I wanted to slip their velvety petals between my fingers. I thought of Isabel, how she gazed at Damon as if he might possess the missing piece of herself. I wanted to feel that way: the undiluted hope that someone else could collect all the splinters, glue them back together. My life, too, had been cracked open like a geode, and I was left staring into the raw hollow of two irreparable halves.

"So, are you and Isabel . . . you know, together?" I asked awkwardly.

"Of course not," Damon said. "She's obviously just a friend."

"It wasn't so obvious by the way she was looking at you."

"Listen, I think she's a fascinating woman, but it's a delicate situation." He sighed, running a hand over his scruff. "Not to mention she must be at least two decades older than I am."

"So?" I shot back. "If the genders were reversed, that wouldn't impede you."

"Are you really going to make that argument?" Damon said with a side glance.

I knew he was referring to my fifteen-year age gap with Graham—indicating he'd tracked the story more closely than he let on. My neck prickled with heat, wondering what else he had read or heard, his subjective perception of public events. I glanced at him, trying to decode a change in his demeanor, but he kept walking as if he had already moved on.

When we turned the corner, I realized where we were. He had taken me to our former address, but the brownstone was no longer there. In its place was a cavernous gap, like a missing tooth in the jaw of the skyline.

"Where did it all go?" I gasped.

"Where it always goes," he said. "A Russian oligarch bought the block. Half for his ex-wife, and half for him."

"She should've hired a better divorce lawyer."

The adjacent building was also demolished, yet its facade remained intact. A brick wall with nothing behind it, the night rushing in to fill the vacant shapes with thin blue air. The empty windows glowed in the pale moonlight, staring down upon us like portraits of dead ancestors. I thought I'd feel more rueful for this burial ground of our shared past, the bricks scattered across an empty lot, but when I looked back over at Damon, I felt a strange sense of rebirth. A large rat scampered across the sidewalk, darting under the construction.

"Walk me the rest of the way?" I said. And he did.

When I got home, Sam had dozed off on the couch with an old collection of Czesław Miłosz poems rising and falling on his stomach. His living room resembled a cloistered library, with crowded shelves of books and dusty records, and eerie still-life paintings of serene vessels by a now deceased friend. His modest apartment had barely changed since the '60s when he bought it from the wife of a renowned pop artist who used it as her *pied-affaire*. Sam stirred when I came over, his full head of hair a rumpled shock of white.

"You got out, Slash," he said, raising an eyebrow.

He had affectionately called me Slash since I was nineteen because he said I was always pulled in between things, lingering in the liminal spaces. It was almost a self-fulfilling nickname now, for I did not know who I was supposed to be, or what I was meant to become.

"I made a valiant attempt," I said.

"Not valiant enough if you're already home."

"I remember when parties used to be thrown for celebration," I said, helping him up. "Now they're only thrown for distraction."

"Don't delude yourself, my dear, that has never changed,"

he said, chuckling. "But as I always say: A party is never thrown for someone. They're thrown *against* someone."

Sam kissed my forehead, then slowly shuffled down the hall to his room. I washed my face in the kitchen sink and dried it with a paper towel, then dabbed some thick silicone ointment onto my scar. I looked in the fridge for something to eat, but there was only a filmy jar of capers and the papery carcass of an onion.

When I got into bed in the maid's room, I checked my phone. There was a text waiting from Damon, and I quickly opened it.

It was a photo of me at the top of Belvedere Castle—not of my face but the back of my hair, a red flame against the snow. In the distance, the trees looked skeletal, brittle hands scratching at the sky. I wasn't aware Damon had taken it, that it existed as proof of what nearly transpired between us. I wondered what I was thinking then, looking out over the field like the white space of a poem, and if I would have left the next day knowing what was to come.

I stared up at the ceiling, black veins of mold branching through the center as if my own body. The party felt faraway, part of a distant story that had nothing to do with me or my life without Graham. He arrived now as he did each night, prowling through the dark like an ashen shadow. I shut my eyes and tried to stop him, but I could already feel the grip of his arms, his elbow locking around my neck, as if we were back in our old bed. *You're never allowed to leave me, you know that, right?* he whispered, his voice garbled with alcohol. *Because I'll find you wherever you are, that's how much I love you.* I held my body still then, a corpse, as he stroked the vein in my neck, thumbing my windpipe until I couldn't breathe.

I sat up, choked with useless tears, the shadows fleeing like pigeons. I pressed my palm into the cold wall, telling myself that I was safe here, back on the floor of the maid's room. Still, my lungs were burning, compressed by an invisible weight. Or was it something else: a fear he had switched on inside of me, searing like a hot iron.

It would always be this way. It was stupid to think I could escape into another life, that the memory of him would disintegrate and crumble like burnt paper in my hands.

I threw my phone into the bathtub and didn't respond.

2

The next day, there was another invitation.

I was circling the reservoir in Central Park when my phone rang from No Caller ID. My route, shared by many, was the same each morning, the worn path of gravel, the tired loop of strangers. But the water, like the weather, was one of shifting moods. Some days, the surface was a gloomy shroud of fog; and others, it reflected the skyline like a concave mirror, an inverted city of sun and steel.

I debated taking the call, assuming it was my agent, whom I was actively and inactively avoiding. The problem with writing was that I couldn't; I had been rendered wordless, worthless, vacant of any vehicle of meaning. Since my return, I'd been offered a job to write a film adaptation for a beloved action star—who wanted to play a polygamist, for some reason, to prove he wasn't wooden. But feeling wooden myself, I had turned it down. Now I really needed money—my savings were nearly depleted—so I grudgingly answered on the last ring.

"Tell me what you're doing right now," Damon said, and my heart lurched.

"Something unspeakable," I said. "I couldn't possibly tell you."

"So that means you must be thinking of me," he said.

I smiled a little to myself. "You called me, not the other way around."

I didn't want to tell him that I was walking. As if my routine would somehow reveal my circuitous state of grief, the same relentless spiral. I depended on dissolving into this carnival of strangers, faceless and adrift, their unguarded misery a consolation to my own.

"Meet me on the corner of 86th and 5th," Damon said.

"I can't just stop everything to meet you."

"Sure you can," he said, and hung up.

I wanted to see him again, of course I did, but not like this—wearing sweaty workout clothes extracted from the floor, my face bare and my scar unconcealed. Still, as I passed the runner with a severe neck tic, the saxophonist beneath Trefoil Arch morosely playing *Spring Is Here*, and turned down the hill past the elderly tai chi class encircling a budding saucer magnolia tree, an unfamiliar anticipation surged in my chest. I took down my dirty ponytail, raking out the side bangs to cover the right side of my face.

As I approached the 84th Street exit, my phone rang again: No Caller ID.

"I'm almost there," I answered with a nervous laugh.

The call ended abruptly. I checked for bars of service in case there was a dead zone, but a text popped up from an unknown number—sent via an encrypted messaging app. I hadn't opened that app since my final months with Graham; he'd insisted we use it to communicate, paranoid his phone might be hacked by the press. Strange, I thought, my finger hovering over the text as I sidestepped birdwatchers craning to view a hawk mutilate the thrashing body of a rat.

When I looked back at the screen, I stopped moving.

It was a grainy photo of a night scene, slightly out of focus: a dark parking lot, a white car, the smeared outline of a man and woman. The sharp throb of memory returned before the image cohered, like pressing on a bruise without recalling the injury. I studied the photo for a moment before realizing the woman, at the center, was me.

I paused by a bench, the reflux of dread burning my throat. The photo was taken the night of The Blaze: a secret corporate retreat held at a resort in Half Moon Bay, hosted by Graham's company. A welcome reception set above the sandstone cliffs, dropping precipitously into the ocean below. The air thick with a nearby wildfire, a black pillar of smoke coiling in the distance. A burnt orange moon. We were in the middle of cocktail hour when the breaking news hit, a vibrating wave of alerts. Guest after guest checked their phones, then looked in silent horror in our direction. Graham was fired effective immediately, the report said. He had fueled a toxic work culture, a male-dominated ecosystem of intimidation. According to allegations, he had a disturbing history of bullying. My hands shook so hard my wineglass slipped and shattered on the ground. Security arrived within minutes, instructing us to leave the premises, then escorted us out before a burning sea of eyes.

No one knew it would be our death march. No one saw the fight in the parking lot, my arm slammed against the car door.

Except maybe someone had.

It didn't make sense. The Blaze was a classified event, each eminent guest required to sign an NDA: no recordings, no photos, no press. Still, here it was, the image emitting a guilty sheen of evidence. I zoomed in on my face, as if my expression could reveal a clue I had missed, a gap in my own ruptured memory of that night. But only the grip of fear returned to me, the crippling nausea of it, and I braced myself against the bench, the trees curdling into a sickly smear of green.

When I looked at the screen again, the photo had vanished. Only a spectral white rectangle stared back.

I glanced around in a panic, like the lens of a hidden camera was fixed on me now, tracking my response. But around me, life carried on. Schoolgirls in rolled-up plaid skirts were vaping on a rock, a homeless woman was cleaning her feet with Lysol wipes in a slant of sun, an old man in a bucket hat was walking six identical brown standard poodles.

As if the photo was an optical illusion, a trick of my scarred mind. Or never existed at all.

When I finally pulled myself together, I exited the park. I crossed the street and found Damon waiting on the corner in a sharp blue suit, brightening when he spotted me. I was overcome with a rush of relief, his handsome, familiar face detached from the startling intrusion of the past. Then I remembered how awful I must have looked—my ugly scar, my spooked expression—but he offered an inviting smile as if he didn't see that at all.

"I was meeting a client nearby and figured you might be around here," Damon said.

"Was she interested in jewelry, or was it more of a full-service commission?" I said.

He tipped his head with an amused glance. "Her husband is away on business with his mistress, so she needed a viridian ring, as green as chlorophyll, to console her."

"How does the husband feel about her chosen form of consolation?"

"I suspect he's very indebted to me," Damon said. "He's the one who asked me to throw a massive tourmaline at the problem."

"Not what I would have chosen."

"No? What would you have asked for instead?"

"The massive amount of cash," I said, and he laughed.

I didn't know why Damon wanted to see me. He didn't offer an explanation, and I didn't dare ask for fear of disrupting something tacit between us—though I couldn't identify what it was. I followed him into the Neue Galerie, and he gave a friendly wave to the guard.

"You're taking me here?" I asked warily.

"Why, do you have somewhere better to be?"

I didn't, of course, but seeing art together midday was an act of intimate exposure. I had grown accustomed to going to museums alone, like everywhere else, walking through still rooms in numbed contemplation. I would now have to account for someone else's viewpoint when it had become safer to protect my own.

Damon walked behind me as we climbed the marble staircase. I moved unsteadily on wobbly legs, imagining his eyes on my tight green bike shorts. On the second floor, past Schiele's spread-legged girls, he led me to a display of Wiener Werkstätte jewelry, tiny tobacco cases, and sculptural brooches I would have skipped otherwise. And he talked to me about stones: *malachite*, *carnelian*, *bloodstone*, *leopardite*. I repeated them aloud, turning their names over in my mouth like sour candy. As I listened, all that had happened outside this space—the jarring photograph; my protracted months of grief—receded into the background. His words were transporting, the way he dimmed my darkness and replaced it with shades and shapes, the refuge of bright stones. I didn't know it then, but this was the beginning of my education; so that later, I would think back to this hour in a quiet room, and realize that our beginning, like so many others, had crept up on me unrecognizably, almost treacherously, until it was too late.

"See how they barely used diamonds?" Damon said. "They valued meticulous craftsmanship over precious gemstones."

"Whereas you value both?" I said.

I had looked at his jewelry online. They were admittedly

exquisite pieces, an unexpected mix of organic materials and vibrant gems, derived from unlikely sources of inspiration: a ring of banded agate twisted into a diamond-spiked tail, after a scorpion he killed in the Wahiba Desert; earrings of sliced abalone shell and peach sapphire, like the scales of a tigerfish caught in the Congo; golden roots sprouting from a pink spinel brooch, resembling a radish planted on the North Fork.

"What I value is feminine shapes, sensuous color, and strange bedfellows," Damon said into my ear as he walked past me. "There are no fire codes in jewelry."

I rolled my eyes. Normally, I avoided men whose "art" entitled them to speak in dramatic turns of phrase; yet Damon didn't sound performative but playful, almost teasing, his language an extension of something serious and unserious at the same time. He led me to a bench in the next room, a chapel of Klimt paintings, and we sat down in the sliver of silence above the city.

"So is this one of your tricks?" I said. "Taking girls to museums in the middle of the day?"

"I like to think my tricks are less cultured, more uncouth," he said, leaning back on his hands. "And no, I took you here as a reminder of why you came back."

"Yeah, the Vienna Secession was all it took. What are you, my cultural ambassador?"

"Consider me your border agent of entrances and exits."

"I think that's more like a customs officer," I said.

"Baby, I'll stamp your passport anytime," he said.

I thought back to that night in the snow, on the cusp of leaving; now I had returned, but to the hull of my old life. I chewed my lower lip and stared straight ahead at a painting, not ready to expose my scar beneath the harsh overhead lights. It was a standing portrait of a sensuous female figure. The plaque read "Ria Munk III (1917)."

"Do you know what happened to her?" Damon asked.

I shook my head, studying her rosy face enveloped in a lush sea of ornamental blooms. It took me a moment to notice the painting was unfinished, her body left partly bare, a phantom space of charcoal swirls and faded lines.

"Her fiancé got cold feet and sent her a letter ending their engagement," said Damon. "She was so heartbroken that she took his gun and shot herself in the chest."

I looked at her again, at the vacant vessel of her body, her arms, her breasts, her flesh dissolving into the canvas, into death. How could Damon have known this was exactly how I felt? Hollow, waiting to be colored in. I thought about the bullet entering her heart and became irrationally defensive—I didn't want to be seen by him, by a man who cited art as a reference point for trauma.

"Did you bring me here just to tell me that story?" I said.

"No, of course not." Damon frowned. "I brought you here to see some art."

"In the middle of the day?"

"Why does the time of day matter?"

I didn't know. I looked down at my bare legs, splattered with thick black mud from the reservoir, remnants of the morning rain, and crossed them self-consciously.

"Give them to me," he said. "Give me your legs."

"What?" I said. Before I could stop him, he lifted my legs onto his thigh. I glanced around, but the room was empty, folding us in the thrill of a secluded space. Damon licked his thumb and worked his way around my ankles in a circular motion, washing away the crusted splatters of dirt. His hands were large, his fingernails lined with solder and silt, traces of the earth. I closed my eyes, his touch loosening the gnarled knot in my chest, or was it my heart, as it had when he held his hand to my neck at the party.

"Look at me," he said. I shook my head, but he lifted my chin toward him. I held my breath as he examined my scar, studying it with the care of a rare jewel, as if its flaws contained a radiance only visible to him. I don't know why, but I trusted him then—though part of me knew it was a mistake. I wanted a new disaster, glimmering and doomed, one that could obliterate the memory of all others.

"My fiancé wasn't trying to kill us," I said suddenly. "I know what everyone says, but it really was an accident."

"Liv," he said softly. "I didn't ask."

I knew the front-page stories had read like the gruesome end of a golden dream: Graham at the wheel, disgraced and drunk, speeding around the jagged cliffs of Devil's Slide. The night sky smothered by smoke and fog. Our wedding two weeks away. The car mangled by the treacherous coastline, by the treachery of a fallen man.

Still, no one knew about the gun.

How I had begged Graham for months to get rid of it. Yet there it was: its sleek metal body in the glove compartment, waiting like an unwrapped gift. The cold blink of the barrel, coaxing his trembling hand as he reached across my lap and drew it toward his head. *If you leave me now, life isn't fucking worth living*, he cried. But as I grabbed his arm, the wheel turned at a sharp right angle, and then: the swerve, the cliff, the fall.

I shuddered, thinking of the encrypted photograph. An abrupt warning that someone was still out in the world digging for a different story, trying to wrench open a dead-bolted lock.

The gun had never been found.

I kneaded my palms, clammy with sweat, but then Damon calmly took my hand, and together we stood up.

We left the museum and walked toward Madison. The air was thick with a gold dust of pollen, and I decided to stop questioning the purpose of the hour. Damon pulled me into a French chocolate shop on 84th Street.

"I think someone needs a little treat," he said.

"What did I do to deserve it?" I said.

"I wasn't referring to you."

We scanned the case, and he let me select ganaches veiled with mint and pistachio and cinnamon. Then he paid, and we returned to the street.

"Open your hand," Damon said, and poured a few into my palm. "Now open your mouth."

I gave him a look that he didn't indulge, then slowly I parted my lips.

"Wider," he said.

I opened them wider, then wider still, and he placed a square of chocolate on my tongue like an illicit pill. It was then that I realized Damon was asking for my complicity in a game only we could play, and though the rules were still being negotiated, I had agreed.

The chocolate was dark and bitter, and left a thirst for salt in my mouth.

"I almost forgot," he said. He removed a white envelope from inside his blazer and handed it to me. "Your invitation for tonight."

Before I could respond, he took off down the street. I stood on the sidewalk, watching him dissolve into the rush of the distant crowd. When I opened my hand again, the chocolate had melted into the cracks of my palm.

3

As soon as I arrived at the party that night, I regretted going at all. Couples were flowing into the cavernous marble hall, crowding at the base of a double staircase that ascended toward opalescent stained-glass windows. The women were dressed in bright frilly plumage, an onslaught of florals, and I felt anemic in comparison. I grabbed a flute of champagne, then skulked over to a giant floral topiary for temporary cover. Up close, the topiary was not made of flowers but tiny pastel macarons, sitting atop a candy cane trunk planted in a pot of pink cotton candy. Some kind of art installation for the event, though unclear how it was thematically related. Then a woman in a pink feathered gown who resembled a hostile flamingo squawked, "Can you please move?" so she could pose with the topiary as if it were her date.

I saw Damon then, across the crowded room. He was dressed for the part, in a deep blue tuxedo with a black satin shawl collar, his hair groomed back, entertaining a swarm of adoring women. It was intimidating to observe him from a distance, the object of female desire, sought-after in a world I neither belonged to nor wanted any part of. At least I would never be like them, I thought. These women who substituted jewelry for love, who had a daily Pilates practice, who glided through parties without knowing the pleasure of despair. I took a mouthful of champagne, imagining my trauma set me apart, that I was haloed by a lustrous sheen of melancholy. But I knew that wasn't true.

When Damon looked over at me, my breath caught in my chest. His gaze seemed privately charged, as if to remind me that he had studied my scar earlier, his hands encircling my muddy ankles in his lap. Then he looked back at the other women, and I was left standing alone again.

"They're like a vicious hive of bees, aren't they, hungrily buzzing away."

I turned to find Isabel. She looked like an actress from an Antonioni film, an enigmatic star who could burn both bright and cold. Her presence seemed to flood the night with purpose, a field of magnetic energy pulsing around her that pulled all eyes in her direction.

"You look like the one who should be honored tonight," I said, kissing her cheek.

Isabel shimmied a little, her shoulders exposed in a figure-hugging red-and-white floral gown.

"Don't be fooled. We both know he would never let me steal his thunder." She held my hand at arm's length, appraising me in one definitive gesture. "But you, on the other hand, didn't need my help scoring an invitation, I see."

"I almost didn't make it tonight," I admitted. "I didn't even have a dress, so I had to borrow this one last minute."

The dress was a jade-green liquid satin, with a knee-high slit and black straps draped down a low open back. It was borrowed from a friend, since my one carry-on suitcase—packed for me while I was recovering in the hospital—contained mostly ratty leggings and useless summer clothes, erasing any remnants of my once spotlit life.

"Why didn't you call me?" Isabel trilled. "I would have come to the rescue, or rather the dress-cue."

I laughed, relieved by her warmth. I felt an inexplicable instinct to please her, to prove I was worthy of standing in her circle of light. Then a toweringly beautiful man with a burst of dreadlocks bounded toward us and draped his arm around Isabel.

"Isabella, how many men does it take to make you happy, huh?" he said. "Am I not enough to sate your insatiable appetite anymore?"

"And this is Pierce, our modern-day Mercutio." Isabel beamed, palming his oxblood velvet sport coat. "Bad boy art star responsible for—what the fuck is that thing exactly?"

"Come on, you don't love my tumescent topiary?" Pierce said, nodding to the art installation. "My garden of earthly delights?"

"Seems appropriately inappropriate for the occasion," Isabel quipped.

"It's a comment on how we live in a world of excess," Pierce said theatrically. "Where desires are indulged without guilt or consequence."

He flashed a mischievous grin. I had read he'd created a Frieze sensation when a famous rapper bought a suite of his Thiebaud-inspired pornographic paintings of nude young women posed with baked goods.

"And you must be the notorious next-door neighbor," Pierce said.

"Guilty as charged," I said.

"Unfortunately, Pierce is the man who got away," Isabel said. "I didn't have room for him at my table, so you and Liv have one all to yourselves."

"There are worse things, I suppose," Pierce said. "But hopefully someday we'll be lucky enough to make her ruthless cut."

"Oh, don't make me out to be such a shark, Pierce," Isabel cooed. "I have yet to kill anyone who didn't *deserve* to be killed."

It took me a moment to realize that my seating placement had been strategically devised in advance—before I was even aware of my invitation. My presence was not so much a threat as an imbalance to a controlled ecosystem, an indistinct shift of dynamics already in motion. What I hadn't yet grasped, and would continue to overlook, was the reason Isabel could masterfully puppeteer the many strings.

I saw Damon walking over and reflexively pivoted my shoulders toward Isabel to avoid looking directly at him.

"It's the man of the hour!" Pierce announced with a royal bow. "Are all of these women here for you, or are they here for the tax write-off?"

"The profound question I find myself asking," Damon said.

According to the invitation, the event was a fundraiser for a nonprofit whose mission was conserving the city's parks and gardens in underserved communities. How this cause related to Damon's opulent jewels was questionable. Still, it added another layer of intrigue to his image. That was always the danger of charming men: doubts about their character didn't act as a deterrent but intensified the force of their appeal.

"Damon, you have yet to notice," Isabel said, sweeping her hair back to expose her long neck. "My Lightning Ridge black opals are in top form tonight, aren't they?"

"Only overshadowed by the woman wearing them," Damon said without a trace of sarcasm.

I tried not to gape at her earrings. The opals floated against her skin like celestial bodies, swirling with an inner nebula of light. It hadn't occurred to me that Isabel might also be a collector of his jewelry, and it subtly recast their relationship in my mind.

"Why isn't Liv wearing any of you? Even I am." Pierce turned his head to show off a large baroque pearl dangling from his ear. "Don't you want to mark your territory?"

"I wasn't offered the option," I said.

As their eyes fell on me, I blushed. I thought it was from mild embarrassment—my small stud earrings were pathetic in comparison—but beneath it, I felt a jolt of something else. For a brief moment, Damon and Isabel were looking at me as though I were the unknown variable in their complex equation—one that I might hold the power to solve.

"Well, we can easily fix that," Damon said, his tone turning professional. "My assistant can help you find something suitable to wear for the evening."

Damon gestured to a girl with false eyelashes and trout lips. She blinked at me, assessing what kind of treatment I merited, then led the way to a high-top table, where jewelry pouches were carelessly scattered like cocktail napkins.

"So, do you own any of Damon's pieces already?" the girl asked, knowing the answer. I said that I didn't, and she pouted. "But you're *so* pretty."

I didn't ask what the correlation was. As I removed my studs, I wondered why Damon had been so quick to outsource the task to her, masking his faint discomfort. As if he didn't want to be caught attending to me in a roomful of women who craved the clasping and unclasping of his singular attention. The girl leaned in close to secure the selected earrings.

"Wow, these colors are *stunn*-ing on you," she said, holding a small mirror to my face.

The stones held me in a trance: sea-blue aquamarine, acidic drops of peridot, like an algae-laced pond lit with sun. Until tonight, I had never seen his work in person, never felt the rush of physical contact. Now, looking in the mirror, I glimpsed a fleeting shift of self: my ruined face could be transformed into a bright and burnished thing. It became clear why women like Isabel cross-wired their wanting. The jewelry was an extension of Damon himself, their metamorphic power, and it was easy to confuse the two. I almost felt ridiculous wearing them, unworthy of their splendor, when I could barely afford a manicure at a dive place on 1st Avenue for this event.

Still, I wanted him to see me. I wanted him to stare at my neck, my clavicle, the curve of my shoulder, before all these women who could afford what I couldn't but lacked what I had: the history of our unmet desire.

But in the mirror, it wasn't Damon's reflection that I caught. A tall brunette woman was staring at me from a distance. She looked a decade older than I was, her body hidden by a shapeless navy dress. I noticed her earrings were identical to mine, except the stones were swapped with hot magenta and deep violet. When I met her eyes, she quickly looked away, but it was clear she had clocked me.

"Someone else is wearing the same pair," I said. "That woman in the navy dress?"

"Oh, you mean Caroline?" said the girl. "Well, I guess she can wear whatever she wants."

"Why is that?"

"Why?" she repeated with a derisive little laugh. "Because she's Damon's *wife*."

I lowered the mirror, a sharp heat crawling over my ears. I pried an earring out so quickly that my lobe tore, leaving a smudge of blood on my fingertip.

"Do you want to try on another pair?" the girl said.

I shook my head, fumbling to pick up my studs from the table. A dinner bell chimed, and guests were herded in the direction of the ballroom. I stood back and watched the woman glide across the room with ease as if this were her party, her friends, and wondered why Damon had invited me at all.

Table 14 was positioned at the back of the candlelit ballroom, a barrage of gold, set beneath a Renaissance-style ceiling mural of cumulus clouds and cherubic angels. I was seated next to

Pierce, whose leggy date named Cadence arrived late wearing a cut-out lurex dress that exposed a large percentage of her torso.

"I need more *wiiiine*," Cadence groaned, draining the rest of her glass. "How can anyone be expected to endure the torture of these things without their own personal bottle."

"It's a charity gala, babe, not a Siberian labor camp," Pierce said.

Cadence moved the breadbasket toward her plate, waved her hand above it like a magic wand, then pushed it away and declared she was heading to the bar.

"Never date a performance artist," Pierce exhaled, buttering an olive roll. "They can't survive without some element of dramatic tension at all times."

"I'm familiar with the type," I said. "It's Aristotelian, really."

"Except it doesn't arouse fear or pity, but the urge to ship her back to Bed-Stuy."

I looked over at Damon greeting an eager line of guests close to the stage. At his table, a white-haired man who closely resembled him chatted with two women on the host committee. And sitting in silence was his wife. I tried not to stare at her but couldn't help myself.

"Look at our boy," said Pierce. "He claims he hates these things, but he's so smooth at being the belle of the bullshit ball."

"How do you two know each other?" I asked.

"Oh man, we both ended up on this wild trip to Northern Kenya one winter. While the other guys were complaining about their wives, we were tripping out of our fucking minds and comparing the shades of sunrise as it cracked through the horizon."

Out of the corner of my eye, I watched Damon approach Caroline and give her a quiet, authoritative directive, and she nodded without any romantic affectation.

"And what about his own?" I asked, trying to sound casual. "Wife, that is."

Pierce squinted slightly, then said, "Oh, you mean Caro? What about her?"

"I mean, how long have they been married?"

"Well, I don't think they're, like, *married* married. Caro's been sort of lurking in the background forever, but she didn't fully come back into the picture until he went through a pretty dark, fucked-up time a few years ago."

I wanted to ask what he meant by this, if it was a wave of darkness that vibrated at the same frequency as my own. But I knew the damage of secondhand sources and vowed to wait and hear from Damon himself.

"But they live together?" I pressed.

"I guess, but he's never home," Pierce said. "You should know that, neighbor."

Still, it didn't explain why Damon had made this glaring omission—by inviting me tonight, he knew I was bound to find out about his wife. It occurred to me, with queasy certainty, there was only one explanation: I had misread our connection. It had not meant the same thing to him as it did to me. He had probably invited me tonight as a charity case, a gesture of sympathy, which I foolishly misconstrued for deeper feelings. How pitiful did I seem? Or worse, even. I had let him believe my vulnerability was accessible to him, as if he alone could lift the blade of sorrow that pressed against my heart. I took a roll from the breadbasket and rabidly skinned off the crust, eating it dry.

Cadence returned to the table, not with a glass but with an entire bottle of white wine, which she stamped down triumphantly in front of Pierce's plate.

"Look what we women are capable of all on our own," Cadence announced.

"Who'd you blow to get that?" Pierce asked, half kidding.

"The source is not important," she said. "Only the desired outcome is."

Cadence refilled my wineglass to the brim, and I swallowed it down as fast as I could until my chest radiated with a satisfying burn.

After the main course was served, Damon took the stage to deliver an impassioned speech about how his work was heavily influenced by elements of urban nature. But I barely heard a word of it. When it was over, I got up to find the bathroom, and make a stealthy exit. I had seen enough.

I passed Isabel on the way out, rummaging through her clutch, and she implored me to sit with her.

"Shit, I don't have my glasses on. I thought this was my lipstick!" Isabel laughed, pulling out a vape pen. "Damon grows this stuff on his farm, along with his beloved apples and tomatoes."

"He has a farm?" I blinked.

She took a quick hit. "On the North Fork, right near my little beach shack in Orient."

I wondered if that was a geographic coincidence. There was so much I didn't know about them, about their private lives, though in fairness, they could say the same of me. Isabel swiped on her lipstick, a satiny nude, then smiled at me plaintively.

"These parties can be hard sometimes, can't they?" she said.

I wondered if she had intuited something on my face that I thought was safely concealed.

I nodded. "That's why I stopped going to them."

"The only reason I force myself out is so I'm not sitting at home depressed, eating chocolate and thinking about my husband," she said. "How did you meet your late fiancé?"

I tensed, caught off guard by her question. How did she know who I was? Had Damon told her? Yet there was something about her, an intrinsic perceptiveness, that easily coaxed disclosure.

"We were introduced at a party in LA," I said. "He used to say it was love at second sight because we had briefly met once before. So when we saw each other again . . ."

"It was written in the stars, as they say," Isabel said.

I could still picture Graham, smoking a cigarette alone on the balcony outside his own party. His maverick charisma, at the height of his power. How he looked at me, against the smoggy lights of the Sunset Strip, as if this could be the inflection point of his life, a night that would curve into days, into years. How could I tell her the stars that once shined on us had darkened, leaving behind nothing but a void?

"You know, sometimes you'll walk into a room just like this one, dancing and drinking," Isabel said wistfully, "and you'll be hit with a gust of him, like a ghost, as if he's really there."

"Will it ever not feel that way?" I said.

"I'm not sure, but you're still young," she said, squeezing my hand. "There will be plenty more parties and plenty more men—they'll just never be him."

Isabel sighed, gazing across the room as if tracing the arc of the sun. But as I followed her eyeline, expecting to find Damon, my stomach clenched. A suave older man with a swoop of silver-white hair was strutting toward us, his mouth curling into a roguish smile.

It was the same man who had been staring at me across the bar last night.

"Well, if it isn't the last viper of Fleet Street," Isabel announced. "What in the world are you doing here?"

"I'm on the lam, as always," said the man in a robust British accent. "Hiding in plain sight amongst the power brokers, as it were, so I can excoriate them later in the press."

"Rex Wright, you charming fucking rascal," she said.

Rex gallantly kissed her on both cheeks. He looked like

a cross between a rakish member of the House of Lords and an aging rocker, his gray wool suit tailored to his slight cabernet belly.

"I don't know how it's possible, but you seem to reverse age," Rex said. "You look exactly the same as you did when Bowie retired Ziggy Stardust at the Hammersmith Odeon."

"Oh, fuck off, that line just dated me a hundred years." Isabel laughed, the thrill of possibility alight on her face. "This man remains one of the last of a dying breed of print journalism, a real whistleblower back in the day."

"I haven't put my pen down yet," he said, waggling his eyebrows. "As much as you would like me to."

"And have you met our Liv?" Isabel said.

Rex squeezed my hand, his eyes slowly vaulting over me as if there was no mistaking we'd previously met.

"In fact, I believe we have auspiciously crossed paths before," said Rex.

"Perhaps in a past life," I said.

"Oh no, you would be impossible to forget," Rex said. "Though I have a sneaking suspicion it wasn't in New York, is that correct?"

I shrugged. "Sadly, I can't be held accountable for other cities."

"Well, it's a good thing you escaped LA when you did," said Rex, his voice fraught with hidden knowledge. "Everyone loves to gloat about the weather, but last time I was there, the city nearly burned to the bloody ground!"

I shuddered, extricating my hand from his sweaty grip. I wiped it on my dress as if it had been soiled.

"Didn't you start that new publication?" Isabel inquired.

As they continued to talk, I tried to focus on my glass, something real, but my fingers were turning translucent, melting into the stem. I excused myself to use the bathroom and hurried through the overheated room toward the open doors. I glanced back, but no one was paying attention to me. Still, a hot wire of dread coiled within me that Rex had come to find me, and he knew more than he should.

The bathroom was nicer and larger than any New York apartment I had ever lived in. I sat down in the pink powder room, relieved to have a moment alone, and glanced in the mirror. My face looked pale, a thin line of sweat pilling around my scar. I winced, digging up a half-dry tube of concealer from the bottom of my bag. I dabbed on a peachy glob, muting the redness, layering a thick coat like a second skin. Though you could still see an elevated line running down my forehead like a barbed wire, a zipper, a rope.

I took a sip of champagne, trying to ignore a dull throb behind my eyes. There was no reason for alarm, I told myself. Rex was just another journalist, like so many others, and most of them had dropped the story since the accident, out of respect for the dead. What I didn't tell Isabel was that the ghost was not Graham, the secrets between us were. And I carried them with me like my own scar: the invisible sutures dissolved beneath my skin, absorbed into my bloodstream. But still living inside me. I shuddered, slipping the concealer back into my bag.

A woman entered the bathroom, fanning herself with her hand. She was wearing a sapphire stingray brooch, its bejeweled tail curling around her breast as if under attack.

"These old gentlemen's clubs never have proper air-conditioning," she exclaimed.

"Maybe it was meant to keep the women out," I responded, but she had already entered a stall.

When I exited, Damon was standing there, waiting in the

secluded hallway between the bathrooms. He feigned mild surprise when he saw me, but I knew, with a little stab of vindication, that he had come to find me.

"Do you always take your drink to the bathroom?" Damon said.

"Only when I can't take a man," I said, before adding, "I'm kidding."

His eyes flickered. "No, you're not."

I swallowed a mouthful of champagne, licking a drop that had spilled onto my lip.

"I thought you might have fled the party already," he said.

"You caught me in the act," I said. "I was about to abscond into the night."

"No surprise, really. If I recall, you fled from me the last time we found ourselves in a hallway alone."

"I have a slightly different recollection of past events."

"Oh yeah? I'd like to hear it," he said. "I've been going over it in my head ever since."

We let the memory pass between us as stealthily as a cigarette between our fingertips. I leaned back against the wall, letting him soak in my dress. His gaze seemed different from that of other men, who only saw the sum total of parts. Damon saw color before anything else; skin shifting from shadow to light, the soft curve of things. A ripple of green satin in silent images: palm leaves, peridot, the wing of a grasshopper, the flesh of a pear.

"I am very glad you came," he said genuinely. "I didn't know if you would."

"How could I miss seeing you honored and extolled by the women of New York?"

"Come on, you know I can't stand all of this. And that's not the reason I invited you."

"Then why did you?" I said. "It remains a mystery to me."

"Because you're not meant to hide away, Liv," he said.

"You're meant to step into the light again, even if you pretend I'm the only one who sees you."

I reddened, thinking back to my catatonic months of drab isolation. Only two nights, two parties, had passed since that state, yet already Damon was coaxing me to look out at life again. As if he were holding up a lens to a solar eclipse, revealing the first crescent of light after the sun had gone dark.

Then I remembered his wife. I crossed my arms, ashamed.

"Isabel certainly seems to be enjoying her table of suitors," I said.

"Is that what they are?" Damon smirked. "Like gentleman callers?"

"Well, at least the available ones."

"Trust me, none of those men are right for you," he said. "You deserve an original, a visionary, a rarified gem."

"Oh, like you?" I said. "Unfortunately I didn't realize you were married."

He flinched at the word, the air pulling taut.

"I'm not married," he said under his breath. "It's a . . . complicated situation."

"Does she think of it that way, too?"

Damon ran a hand over his jaw as if this subject was physically depleting.

"I'll explain it to you when I see you next," he said.

"Why not explain it right now?"

"I think you know why."

We locked eyes, a flicker of challenge rising between us. But then the lady with the stingray emerged from the bathroom and thrust her chest forward: "Damon! Did you see my brooch?"

"It looks like it was made just for you, Mrs. Whitaker," he said.

Without waiting, I wandered back into the ballroom and sat down at my table. A couple was chewing slabs of steak in silence, while Pierce was on the dance floor with his very drunk date, propping her up as she flung her head back and laughed at nothing as a jazz quartet played. I popped a roasted potato into my mouth, now rubbery and cold, and saw Damon re-enter the room. He looked in my direction, but when I turned, it wasn't his eyes that I found.

Rex was standing in the doorway, his gaze fixed on me as if he had somehow passed from my former life into this new one. And suddenly I feared that, by stepping into the glare again after months of invisible darkness, I was courting the threat of exposure that could not be undone.

4

Somehow I ended up staying till the night was over. As the party died down, Isabel asked if I would join her for a nightcap and I eagerly agreed. I was flattered that she'd want to spend time with me alone, but mostly relieved to delay my depressing return to the maid's room. As we stood in the grand hall, gathering our coats, a young man from her table approached to say goodbye. He was unremarkable yet had a nice enough face, with soft brown eyes and thick dark hair.

"Peter's father is a great oncologist and took excellent care of my husband before he died," Isabel said as she introduced him. "And now he is on the path to becoming a great doctor himself."

"I don't know about that," Peter said with a shrug. "What are you two doing now?"

"We're off to hunt for a second dessert. I can't go to bed without some form of chocolate," Isabel said, elbowing me in the ribs. "Maybe you want to join us?"

"Um, I'd love to, but I have an early shift in the morning," Peter said.

Damon emerged into the hall, followed by Caroline a few feet behind. She wore a curated look of unreadable restraint, as if it were a fixed feature. I couldn't figure her out; she didn't seem like an embittered wife, hardened by years of disappointment caused by a mercurial man. But if she was in the camp of women who averted their gaze, then I envied her. Her life was not dictated by the volatile climates of love, like my own, but by a series of calculated choices that led her to inhabit a distinct role.

"Thank you so much for coming," Caroline said, directly addressing Isabel. "I don't think we've met before, but I've heard so much about you."

"I can say the same," Isabel said smoothly.

"And is this your daughter?" Caroline asked.

Isabel blinked, the corners of her mouth tightening. I realized she was referring to me.

"Uh, no, Liv was my neighbor years ago," Damon quickly clarified, taking a step forward. "You know, when I lived uptown?"

"What a coincidence," said Caroline. "You just randomly ran into each other tonight?"

"Last night, actually," I said. "We were all at the same party."

Caroline opened her mouth, revealing large, glossy teeth. Up close, she was taller and broader-boned than I was, and carried herself with a stern maturity that made me feel insubstantial. She looked like a woman who had grown up competing in horse shows, the antithesis of my modest upbringing in New Haven. I couldn't imagine Damon relating to her on any emotionally complex level, or sleeping with her, for that matter—but maybe something else bound them together.

"And you both were in the same building?" Caroline asked.

"Our apartments were next door to each other," I said. "But you know Damon. He was never home."

She paused, lifting her chin. "No, I suppose that's the only consistent thing about him."

By admitting this, I had accidentally positioned myself as someone familiar with his specific incongruities. I glanced at Damon, positioned between Caroline and Isabel in a strange triptych: as if one were his wife and the other his mistress. But neither appeared to play those parts. I wondered, if ever, these lines would cross, or if they would remain on parallel tracks until something, or someone, forced a convergence.

"And where do you live now, Liv?" Caroline asked.

"Oh, nowhere, really," I said. "I'm practically homeless."

"So you live on the street?" she said.

"She's not homeless, she's just in between things," Isabel cut in with authority. "Cities, apartments, men—you remember how it is to be young and enviably unattached."

"Vaguely," Caroline replied with a stiff laugh.

"She can go anywhere and be with anyone she wants," Isabel added.

"So can you," I said to her.

Isabel gave me an approving smile, as if I had passed a private test of allegiance.

"So, how do I get in touch with you?" Peter awkwardly interjected.

"Give me your phone," I commanded, holding out my hand.

Fumbling, Peter handed over his phone. As I entered my number, I could feel Damon's eyes piercing my flesh like a dart.

"Perhaps we could go for a drink another time?" Peter added.

"Sure," I said, looking at Damon. "I'd love that."

Afterward, Isabel took me to Jacques Bar nearby. We sat at a corner table sipping French 75's, picking at an order of truffle fries and chocolate soufflés, conversing with ease about the night. I wanted to ask about the details of her relationship with Damon but tried to suspend my burning curiosity. When my phone buzzed with a text from Peter, I showed her the screen with a sarcastic groan.

"Go out with him," Isabel said, shaking a spoon at me. "What you need, more than anything else, is a bridge. Doesn't matter if it's a drawbridge, a suspension bridge, the fucking Verrazano Bridge. You need someone to get you over and through."

"What kind of bridge is Peter, then?" I said.

"I don't know, a small one," she said. "Maybe a pedestrian bridge."

I laughed. "And what about Damon?"

"Damon isn't a bridge." Isabel closed her eyes as if making a wish. "He's what's waiting on the other side."

The fervid abandon in her voice made me question whether something had transpired between them, or if the prospect wasn't closer to truth than to speculation. I wondered if Damon had been honest with me; Isabel struck me as a woman grounded in lucid reality, not easily swept up in romantic reverie without tangible signs.

"How did you become so close with him?" I asked delicately.

"It was after the death of my late husband," she began. Isabel opened up then, weaving a panoramic overview of her life. How she quit college to marry a boy from the Bronx, who was killed in a mob hit when she was only twenty-two. Unmoored, she ran off to Cambodia to cover the rise of the Khmer Rouge, then embarked on a spiritual sojourn, and upon her return attended an early Pride March in Central Park—which was where she met Jack, an older, radical reporter, and fell in love. By then Isabel was known for her trenchant essays about the city, invoking the entropy of an era. But eventually, she gave up her personal writing to help Jack build one of the leading private intelligence agencies, conducting classified investigations around the world.

I didn't know what that meant, exactly, but also didn't want to pry.

"We were an unmatched team. Jack was a bulldog, but no one saw me coming," Isabel said with a suggestive smile. Then she sharply snapped her fingers. "I could smell blood in the water from a mile away. Betrayal has always been my sixth sense."

My eyes widened. If there was a hint of real danger in her voice, a shadow girding the mythic version, then I missed it—I was too mesmerized by her dark allure.

Her marriage was one of passion and purpose, she went on, until Jack was diagnosed with cancer and rapidly died two years ago.

"My husband came from a Northern Italian family, and as is tradition, you are supposed to mourn for exactly one year and a day, when the soul of the dead passes on to the next world." Isabel paused, pressing her palms together. "I know this sounds crazy, but on day three hundred sixty-seven I met Damon. And he brought me back to life again."

I shook my head in awe as these narrative fragments coalesced. It seemed Damon was not merely a crush but a conviction, a symbol she'd assigned meaning to. Maybe this was her chance to relive those stolen years of girlhood before her life, like mine, had been reversed by death.

"I've lived a very full life. I don't need a husband—two was plenty," Isabel continued, swirling her spoon into the chocolate center. "What I need is a companion, a travel partner, and maybe even . . ."

"A lover?" I offered.

She smiled, licking her spoon. "Yes, maybe even that."

Then she leaned in close, the opal earrings bathing her skin in a lunar glow.

"Have you and Damon ever . . . ?"

My breath caught in my chest, though there was no reason to lie. But I could sense Isabel reading my face like a polygraph examiner, measuring the physiological indicators of reaction without so much as a word.

"Oh god, no," I said quickly. "I barely know him."

"Good, that's what I thought," she said firmly. She leaned back again, the creases around her eyes softening. "But you, angel, had the worst kind of loss—because it was not only the death of him, it was also the death of an unlived dream. He was your great love, wasn't he."

"Yes, but he was also . . ." I swallowed. "He could be very difficult."

"Unfortunately, powerful men often are, and trust me, I've known many," she said, unfazed. "But that doesn't mean you didn't love him."

A sharp sting rose in my throat. Beneath her words, there was an intimation that Isabel understood the ravages of love, the toxic wreckage of it, in a way no other woman had grasped.

"We all have three lives, to paraphrase Márquez—a public, private, and secret life. And perhaps writers most of all," she went on. "In your case, the public drama eclipsed the other two—in part the fault of the high-profile company he ran. But with time, you can preserve his private memory however you choose."

Isabel squeezed my hand, and before I could stop them, tears were falling into the dish.

"Oh god, I'm so sorry," I said. "See, this is why I don't go out."

"Don't apologize, darling," she said. "A soufflé is meant to be cried on."

I wasn't ashamed to cry in front of her, but surprised by the ease with which my tears fell. Isabel had surgically unstitched a hidden seam within me, one I barely had access to, even though I hadn't shared my story at all.

"Wait, what about his company?" I said, wiping my chin with the back of my hand.

She paused slightly, as if weighing her answer, but then her phone lit up on the table: No Caller ID. Of course I knew who it was.

"Speak of the devil," Isabel said, jumping in her seat. She accepted the call on speaker, then said in a low, throaty purr, "Are your ears burning? And no, I'm not alone."

"I'd be shocked if you were," Damon said. "Which of your many suitors are you with?"

"Even better, I'm with the hottest babe in Manhattan."

She nudged me, and I said, "Hey."

There was a slight pause before he said, "Uh-oh, double trouble. What kind of mischief are you two getting into?"

It struck me as strange that Damon was calling Isabel at nearly midnight, after his event—and that he reached out, not the other way around. It revealed a reciprocal closeness I hadn't foreseen and, despite his denial, confirmed her hope was not as false, or unfounded, as I had initially thought.

"It was a wildly successful night," Isabel said. "You should be very pleased."

"Couldn't be more," he said. "And now I'm just out walking the dogs."

Isabel said she would call him when she got home, and hung up. I imagined the scene of their conversation later; she would talk quietly to him from her kitchen, or maybe from her bedroom as she lay atop the covers, turned away from the empty side of the bed. They would review the details of the party, exchange confidences, and say good night.

I was the interloper here. I was the trespasser, crossing a barrier into treacherous terrain—but how could I step away now?

"You see how he's out with the dogs?" she said. "The man escapes every moment he can."

"From the wife?" I dared.

"If that's what you would call her." Isabel raised an eyebrow, methodically spooning ice cubes into her coupe. "My instinct tells me they have some sort of arrangement, though I'm not quite sure."

"So, what does he get out of that?" I asked. "And what does she?"

Isabel looked at me, her lips twisting into a collusive smile. As if she detected, in this moment, a potential value in my loneliness—that I would be willing and adept at playing both sides of this game.

"I have my theories, of course, but that's a very good question," Isabel said. "Why don't you find out for us?"

Later, after Isabel paid the bill, I snuck downstairs, stealing a few fancy pencils inscribed with "The Lowell" on the way. Each bathroom was private and large, with marble sinks and oversize mirrors. My head was blurry as if underwater, after drinking for six hours straight, and I remembered giving head here months ago, how my kneecaps cracked against the cold tile floor while I forced myself to do it, to swallow it all down as a way of forgetting. Somehow it made me remember more—and remember worse.

I took out my phone and snapped a photo in the mirror. My body turned sideways, the long black strap draped down my bare back, the white curve of my breast exposed. I was looking just above the lens, my chin tilted upward, lips parted and smudged with red. I knew what I was doing, every girl does; still, a pang of guilt gnawed away at me. It would be a small act of betrayal, my first. Not that the photo was so lurid, but it posed an invitation, another move in the game he initiated earlier when he asked me to open my mouth, and I did. My fingers hovered over the button, and then I pressed Send.

5

A few mornings later, I accompanied Sam to his cardiology appointment. We sat in the dreary waiting room, Sam calmly scanning *The Sewanee Review* while I read the same sentence in an old *New Yorker* over and over again. I considered all the patients who had flipped through the puckered pages of this edition, and wondered what percentage were now dead.

I opened my phone and idly searched the internet for images of Isabel and Damon together. The screen instantly filled with tiles of photos featuring the pair at various glamorous events—his arm wrapped around her back, her hand grasping his lapel. I scrolled until I hit the bottom, shocked by how unmistakably they presented as a public couple, without a single photo of Caroline to offset this image. I had begun to grasp the infatuation through Isabel's eyes—her distorted lens of grief—but it was Damon I didn't understand, Damon I couldn't figure out.

"Do you know this writer?" I said to Sam, holding up a photo of Isabel on my phone.

Sam folded the magazine over, squinting at the screen. "I don't know if you can call her much of a writer these days," he said. "She hasn't written anything in forty-some-odd years."

"That doesn't mean they revoke your title."

He chuckled. "If only it did, I woulda knocked out a lot of competition."

Across from me, a teenage girl in baggy jeans was scraping off her black nail polish. Until her father grabbed her wrist and she stopped.

"I used to run into her at literary parties, ages ago, before I got tired of that whole scene," Sam said, as if trying to see far into a clouded past. "But then she married some guy, a private investigator type, a high-end spy if you will, and rumor has it that she became his fixer."

"His *what*?" I scoffed. "What do you mean by fixer?"

"He ran one of those shadowy firms, working undercover for a lot of notorious people," Sam said, taking a slow breath. "I heard she was involved in his bigger cases—you know, arms dealers, the mob, corporate scandal, that sort of thing."

My jaw opened. "You mean, like she killed people for him?"

"I don't know about that," Sam said. "This isn't *Thunderball*."

"Did you sleep with that Bond Girl, too?" I said.

Sam let out a raspy laugh. "Only in my dreams."

It seemed absurd, comical even, to envision the self-possessed Isabel entrenched in a nefarious underworld of criminals. But I recalled the other night—the way she fluidly elicited information. Her eyes homing in on me with laser-sharp intensity.

"Either way, she certainly had a reputation of being a killer," Sam went on, glancing at me. "Whether she was or wasn't, she's a supremely cunning woman. I wouldn't mess with her, Slash, that's for sure."

I paused. "And she never had any children?"

"She did, I think, a daughter, but there was some horrible accident." Sam exhaled, his mouth slightly agape. "Maybe that's around the time she stopped writing."

Before I could ask him more, a nurse appeared in the doorway and called his name.

"I'm up," Sam said, wincing as he stood. "Time to go to bat."

While Sam was in the exam room, I waited in Dr. Murphy's office. It resembled a generic film set: degrees from Yale framed on the wall, medical textbooks aligned on a mahogany shelf, a photo of his happy family of five on the Cape. The signposts of a linear life, dictated by the calendar of normalcy, unmarred by sudden reversals of fate.

I opened my phone and googled Isabel, clicking on the *New York Times* obit of her late husband. I scrolled until I found the line: ". . . their four-year-old daughter, Lucy, died of injuries when a propane stove exploded in their Laurel Canyon rental home." My heart tilted. Isabel had disclosed her bereavement over both husbands but left this gaping omission in her narrative arc of loss. When she said that Graham's death was the worst kind, an ending before a beginning, she was thinking of her daughter, and now I understood why she had stopped writing. Isabel had survived the rupture of her own life, a guillotine cleaving it into before and after—halves that could never again be conjoined. There was life with her daughter, and life without.

The air-conditioning was on full blast, a cold sweat pooling beneath my arms. I picked up a plastic model of a sliced-open heart from the desk, tracing the four chambers carved out like rooms in a doll's house. How strange, I thought, the terrifying and mysterious aberrations of the body, all these vessels and valves poised to fail.

The door opened, and I quickly put the heart down. Sam entered, his lavender linen shirt now creased, followed by Dr. Murphy, an avuncular man with round horn-rimmed glasses and a plaid bow tie. I wondered if he had any fetishes.

"I see you brought your partner in crime," Dr. Murphy said, taking a seat at his desk.

"I can't keep up with this one," I said.

"She keeps me young," Sam said. "One foot in the club, one foot in the grave."

These painful exchanges with doctors usually acted as a warm-up to bad news. Dr. Murphy went on to talk about the surgery; it had caused a certain arrhythmia in Sam's heart that might necessitate a pacemaker. I took diligent notes about the potential risks and complications, while Sam wanly glanced out the window like a schoolboy stuck in a seminar. Finally, Dr. Murphy gave me instructions for a follow-up with the cardiothoracic surgeon. Sam stood up and smoothed out his jeans, towering over the doctor as they shook hands.

"By the way, where'd you get that shirt?" Dr. Murphy said.

"My favorite shop in Roma," Sam said with a wink. "A man should always dress appropriately for the occasion, even if that occasion is his own demise."

Dr. Murphy was about to close the door behind us when I abruptly stopped him.

"Can I ask you something quickly?" I said.

Assuming it was a question about the pacemaker, he gestured for me to re-enter his office while Sam shuffled off toward the waiting room. As Dr. Murphy closed the door behind us, the cold sweat spread down my spine.

"What can I answer for you?" Dr. Murphy said, leaning against his desk.

"It's not about Sam, actually," I said, nervously parting my side bangs. "I think there might be something wrong with my eye."

That morning, staring into the cracked bathroom mirror, I thought that I was still caught in an anxious dream. My right eye below my scar looked grotesque, like a prosthetic in a horror film: the pupil was massively enlarged, only a sliver of green iris around the perimeter. I stared hard into the flickering bulb above it, then the mirror again—but the pupil didn't constrict. My eye blinked back, vacant and glassy, a black marble rejecting light, reflecting nothing.

Dr. Murphy took out a small flashlight from his pocket and shined it into my eye. At least I could still see, I thought, focusing on the plastic heart, but it seemed to be dissolving into a faint, fuzzy orb.

"Can you tell me what your forehead incision is from?" he asked.

I reported the accident with clinical detail, as if it were a secondhand story. The car plummeting two hundred feet off a cliff. The deep facial laceration caused by the shattered windshield. The emergency surgery to remove the hyperdense foreign bodies of glass, lodged near the inferolateral orbital rim.

"Oh dear," Dr. Murphy said. "And what happened to the person driving?"

"He didn't survive," I said.

Dr. Murphy lowered the flashlight, his face melting to sympathy. I thought about adding "my fiancé" for dramatic effect, but since I was asking a cardiologist to do an ophthalmologist's job, there was no need to burden him with the subspecialty of psychiatry.

"It seems like you have mydriasis, known as a fixed pupil," Dr. Murphy said, not masking his grave concern. "It can be a serious indication of a brain injury, a cranial nerve neuropathy, a trauma to the—"

As he continued, his words began to form a roar of white noise, the metallic glare of his stethoscope ricocheting off my head like a bullet.

"—to the emergency room," he concluded.

"What?" I blinked.

"I implore you to go to the ER, immediately," he repeated sternly. "They can do a CT scan and assess what might be going on."

I thanked him and promised to follow up with the results. I found Sam in the waiting room, and we took the elevator down to street level and stepped out into the cloudless morning.

"Everything okay, Slash?" he asked.

I nodded but shielded my eyes. The city seemed wrapped in a film of gauze, gray sunlight seeping through narrow cracks, until all I could see was a halo of buildings, a green smudge of trees, the bare ring finger on my left hand.

6

Instead of going to the emergency room, I went to another party with Isabel.

It was the first warm evening of the year, so I walked west through the Ramble toward the 1 train. All around me, spring was blooming over the crimes winter had committed, forcing the trees to relinquish their ravaged selves. The cherry blossoms burst as if overnight; they seemed surprised to be there, their soft pink flesh indecently exposed, pried open with refusal. Maybe it was their arrival, the petals unclenching like a fist, or the strange coincidences of the past few weeks—but something else, besides the season, seemed to be turning.

Near Cedar Hill, I passed an old woman painting in a beach chair, bundled in a ratty raccoon fur coat and hat like the ghost of Edie Beale. Before her, a large canvas was propped up on an easel, a palette of acrylics covering her lap. She was painting the trees with globs of candied fuchsia and clotted reds, the petals clinging to their limbs like swollen tentacles.

"I love your cherry blossoms," I said over her shoulder.

She looked up, jerking the canvas away. "Get out of my light, you *cunt*!" she screeched.

I apologized, then ran down the hill until I reached the lake, bordered by a flock of hostile geese. I took out my phone and called Graham, knowing he would laugh and say, *She's a perfect character for your next short story, darling.* But our bodies retain the memory of pain more than the mind. It rang twice before I remembered no one would answer on the other line.

I met Isabel on the corner of Charles and Morton so we could walk into the party together. I was surprised that she had asked me to go with her alone—to an event unconnected to Damon—and eagerly accepted the invite. After a glimpse of her diverting world beyond the bleak borders of the maid's room, how could I look back? Isabel did not treat me as a marred widow but as someone worthy of inclusion, worthy of acceptance. Maybe part of me did question why, exactly, she had chosen me, but feared where probing further might lead.

Isabel waved when she saw me, raising her large black sunglasses. Without the formality of the past few nights, she looked even younger, in a sexy sheer black top and jeans, her hair haphazardly wavy. I was wearing a short black dress and gold sandals badly scuffed at the heels that I hoped no one would notice.

"You look like a teenager," I said, kissing her powdery cheek.

"Good, because I feel like one," Isabel said. We linked arms, navigating the cracks in the cobblestone. "I've lived down here since the '70s, which was a chaotic fucking time. Back then, no one shaved or gave a shit about money. The Weather Underground townhouse blew up, Yoko and John were our neighbors on Bank Street. My code name was Elena. We were all fighting the good fight."

"Why did you need a code name?" I asked.

"All sorts of covert operations," she said flippantly. "Depending on whose side we were on."

We arrived at the address, a brick walk-up, and were buzzed into a nondescript entrance. Isabel slipped off her white sandals, going barefoot, and we began to climb the stiflingly hot staircase to the sixth floor.

"Are we sure he's an ambassador?" I groaned, already sweating.

Isabel had mentioned the party was hosted by a former French ambassador to an unspecified country, who owed her an unspecified favor.

"Oh, don't be such a snob. Parisians think it's poetic to schlep up the stairs!" We stopped on a landing to catch our breaths. "Once, Damon and Pierce took me to a preview of the Lucian Freud show, and we were discussing his endless affairs that swung both ways. I admitted I'd never had one—I was always loyal to Jack—and Damon called me a prude! That prick," Isabel said with a defiant smile. "So Pierce said: 'Don't listen to him. The best part of an affair is not the affair itself—it's walking up the steps and seeing the door waiting ajar at the top.' And I thought that was so romantic."

"Not if you're drenched in sweat when you arrive," I quipped.

On the top landing, Isabel slipped her sandals back on, and I complimented her anklet—a delicate gold-and-leather chain with dangling coral beads.

"I told Damon he could come to Italy this summer if he made me this," Isabel said, kicking out her leg provocatively. "Men are Pavlovian. They respond best to a system of rewards and punishments."

Before I could ask further questions—Italy, summer, Damon—we were ushered into the party. The crowd was mostly French, willowy wives in shift dresses and slick buns, while a chef passed around shot glasses of yellow gazpacho, barking *amuse-bouche!* with faint hostility. We grabbed glasses of rosé and headed outside onto a terrace overlooking a ramshackle interior garden. Isabel waved to a woman in a low-cut black jumpsuit whom I recognized as the British Nigerian actress from the first party.

"You told me to dress up, you little turncoat," Gemma exclaimed. She gave Isabel a double kiss, since we were French now, then blinked at me with delayed recognition. "That's right, I saw you weaseled your way into that party after all."

"She didn't have to weasel," Isabel said, "she was properly invited."

"By the weasel himself," I said.

Gemma smiled at this. "Speaking of, is *he* going to grace us with his presence tonight?"

"We won't know until he walks in the door." Isabel sighed.

My phone dinged loudly in my bag, and I knew it was Damon. After I sent him that photo from the bathroom, a text exchange had erupted between us, hovering on a heated edge. When my phone dinged again, Isabel's eyes bounced to me.

"You haven't heard from him, Liv, have you?" Isabel pressed.

I shook my head. "No, not for a while."

"Because I told him you were coming tonight," she stated.

Her gaze lingered on me, her eyes turning the color of mottled silver in the late sun. I shoveled a cheese puff into my mouth as a server passed by.

"Oh god," Gemma moaned spitefully. "I need to go back on my divorce diet of bone broth and despair before summer begins."

Isabel went off to talk to the host, a little man who resembled Pepé Le Pew, leaving us behind. I grabbed a fresh glass of wine, dying to check my phone. But then Gemma intercepted, cornering me with dramatic urgency.

"It's insane, isn't it?" Gemma hissed under her breath. "Tell me you think it's gone off the bloody rails, like *Sweet Bird of Youth* levels of delusion. And I know because I starred in that play."

"What do you mean?" I said, innocently leaning toward her.

"The Damon debacle! Surely you see what's going on?"

"No," I denied. "I barely know him."

Gemma shot me a disapproving look to say she knew I was playing dumb. And I was, yet I was curious to know if their entangled dynamic was not as discreet as I thought. Or was I becoming as morbidly obsessed with them—with the ambiguity of their attachment—as they were with each other? I took a gulp of wine, trying to cool myself down.

"Look, we both know she's in a delicate place. And yes, he's gorgeous, *I get it*, I'm not fucking blind." Gemma threw up her hand, her arm of bracelets jangling. "But he's toying with her, enabling her even, calling her late at night and gifting her jewelry? Of course I can't say a word, no no, because she would *literally* slaughter me in cold blood. So my lips are sealed. In fact, they are wired shut until Italy," she declared, stuffing two cheese puffs into her mouth.

I glanced over at Isabel, hoping she couldn't overhear us. She was still engaged in a conversation with the host, but I could see her eyes sliding over to the door. Her face stretched with longing, as if waiting for an oracle to deliver the prophecy of a new life.

I excused myself and slipped down a narrow hallway in search of the bathroom, finding the master bedroom instead. I closed the door behind me and sat down on the bed. The last dregs of sunset leaked through the window, staining the crumpled duvet with resinous light. On the nightstand was a photo of the host with a little girl in Saint-Tropez, probably his daughter, and I recalled the photo on Dr. Murphy's desk this morning, which now seemed like weeks ago. I pressed my fingertips against my right eyelid, releasing a small amount of pressure. Then I opened my phone:

D: Where are you right now?
L: In the host's bedroom . . .
D: Is he there with you or behind you or beneath you . . . ?
L: Why don't you come find out for yourself . . .
D: I fully intend to
D: But I don't know if I'd want to watch or participate
L: Thankfully we'll never find out
D: Or will we?

I chewed my lower lip, trying not to admit a smile. I should stop, I told myself, put an end to it now. There was Isabel to consider; and, evidently, a wife. But his words were a lasso, reeling me in, tightening with every tug.

Down the hall, I could hear Isabel's voice rising in excitement over the arrival of a guest—it must be Damon.

I scanned a pile of books on the nightstand and pulled out a tattered copy of Sartre's *Les Jeux Sont Faits*, which I had loved as a girl in French class. I vaguely recalled the plot: a man and woman meet and fall in love in the afterlife, and they are granted a day on earth to change their fate. I couldn't remember the ending, except that it was tragic. I artfully arranged the book, propped up by my thighs spread ever so slightly, and sent Damon a photo.

L: The die is cast
D: So he's an existentialist? Doesn't seem like your type . . .
L: Oh what is, pray tell
D: English as a first language
L: I prefer when they don't talk . . .

A pale shadow stretched beneath the doorway, just out of reach as he was years ago when I placed my ear to his wall and heard the sigh of sad music.

D: You know what French men love . . . ?

I knew what I could say—filthy responses flashed through my head—but we'd never explicitly crossed that threshold, slippery and perilous, and once we did, there was no undoing it. As long as I withheld, relying on the decoy of words, we weren't doing anything wrong.

But I had become good at hiding things, and most of all from myself.

I selected a baguette emoji, thought it was stupid, deleted it, and wrote: ennui? An ellipsis bubble appeared, then vanished. The door began to open, the knob slowly turning as if inside my own skin, and I sat up on the edge of the bed, adrenalized, waiting.

But when the door opened, it wasn't Damon.

"You scared me," I said with a jump.

"That's what all the girls say."

Rex stood in the doorway, his face cut with twitchy shadows. My disappointment quickly drained into a shiver of unease, and I didn't know why.

"Looks like I caught someone red-handed," Rex said. "Or rather, red-haired."

"Except I haven't done anything unlawful yet," I said.

He gave a crooked smile, stepping into the room and closing the distance between us. I tried to stand up, but my body felt weighted down to the bed.

"The Santa Anas," Rex said. "Ring a bell?"

I frowned. "Do you throw random Didion references at all the girls you meet at parties?"

"Imagine if I did," he said with an indulgent chuckle. "And no, I was referring to the party we met at in LA, thrown for some film, when the winds were going bloody crazy."

Fragments of the night resurfaced. The hot winds blowing through the canyons, gusting across the party. Graham's face hardening with cold fury when he saw the place cards set before each plate: my name next to another man. A man who wasn't him. I watched helplessly as Graham picked up the place cards and rearranged them, fuming as if it were my fault. It was just a jealous episode, I had told myself. He was drunk. It would pass. But I knew, when we got home, that would not be the end.

"Don't you remember?" Rex said.

"Vaguely," I said, pushing the scene away. "You must have an excellent memory."

"Hawkish, really," said Rex, tapping his wrinkled forehead. "Which is miraculous, given all those louche, lascivious London years."

"Have you retired from them?"

"I think they've retired from me," he pouted. "Sadly, no one appreciates the fine arts of depravity and debauchery anymore."

Rex approached the bed, rattling the ice in his glass like loose teeth. I could smell the tannin of cigar smoke on his blazer, and my muscles churned with sense memory.

"What else do you remember about that night?" I said.

"Oh, lots of things," Rex said. "But what would be the fun if I gave it all away at once?"

"I'm sure we can find more productive ways to have fun," I said.

"Is that so? Well, I will say this much. Your fiancé . . ." He let the word ripple through the air like tear gas. "My deepest condolences, by the way—your *late* fiancé, rather."

I tried to swallow, but my throat was parched. "What about him?"

"Complicated old chap, wasn't he?" Rex paused. "That

night, he made it perfectly clear that I was never to talk to you again."

"Maybe he had a good reason," I said dismissively.

I could hear Isabel calling my name. I stood up too quickly, a flare of white sparks in my field of vision. I needed to get out of this room, but Rex was blocking my path to the door.

"Even if he did," Rex said, "he's no longer here to prevent that from happening."

Later in bed, back in the maid's room, I opened the Sartre book stolen from the nightstand, slipped stealthily into my bag. I skimmed the French dialogue in the dark, trying to translate the fate of the two lovers, the black-and-white film version merging with my dreams of falling, my dreams of death. The female character was poisoned, I remembered—poisoned by her husband.

Then, drifting into sleep, the end of the party in the canyons floated back to me. Graham had disappeared for a cigarette and I wandered alone to the pool. The wind shrieked through the trees, palm-fringed shadows slinking across the water like snakes. A dark stencil of a body stretched across the surface, and I whipped around. A man was standing behind me, as if he had followed me there. He smiled, ashing his cigar in the pool. *Why are you marrying that man when you could be with someone like me?* he whispered, his belt buckle grazing my waist. *At least I'm not a monster like he is.*

The name on the other place card was Rex Wright.

When I finally fell asleep, I dreamt that Graham returned to the party, and he kissed me and said he was sorry, it wasn't true. *That man is the monster, not me.*

But it was too late. My eye, the bad one, had been gouged out of my face.

7

The next morning, I decided it might be time for the ER after all. I walked to Lenox Hill Hospital on East 77th, next to the subway entrance, and stepped into the admission holding pen as if I were a criminal turning myself in.

I was given an ID bracelet, then escorted to a bed next to a man who had been knifed in the stomach during a parade—though I never asked which one. A nurse took vials of blood, and a procession of male doctors put me through a series of tests, blinding lights and infrared pupillary devices. A resident in a Grateful Dead surgical cap pressed a probe against the surface of my eye, asking if I had done shrooms. I said no, I wish, and he joked, "Don't worry, it's cool. You just look like Bowie now." Finally, a nurse helped me into a wheelchair and pushed me down a long hallway toward an empty holding area to wait for a CT scan.

"Well, there is some good news," the nurse said cheerily. "At least you're not pregnant."

Somehow that depressed me more than the prognosis of fatal brain trauma.

As I waited alone in the cold, sterile room, I checked my phone. A text from Damon: 7pm sharp, Red. I smiled to myself, relieved to have something to look forward to. Isabel had offered me two theater tickets tonight—she had decided to spend the weekend at her beach house instead—with the sanction to invite Damon as my date. A covert operation, she had enticingly framed it—an opportunity to gather more intel about his private life. And I had gladly accepted the assignment.

As I formulated a reply, I felt an intense urge to tell Damon where I was, to share as a form of emotional documentation, so I took a series of selfies with my hospital bracelet. But when I reviewed the images, it was scary how bad I looked: my grotesque eye, my cheeks tinted with the purplish-white pallor of death. For the first time, it occurred to me that something might actually be wrong. If I stayed still, I could almost feel blood sloshing and seeping into the ventricles of my brain, like a bathtub filling to the edge with water. I shut off my phone and closed my eyes, taking breaths through my nose. Just as the door opened and a young doctor rushed past.

"Hey!" the doctor said with a confused smile. "What are you doing here?"

I looked at him blankly before registering that it was Peter—the doctor from the charity event. The one I'd given my number to as a cheap ploy to make Damon jealous. Oh god, I thought, I'd be better off in the waiting room for my execution.

"I guess you can check my chart to find out," I replied.

"You know, I texted you." He awkwardly thumbed his stethoscope. "A few times, actually? After the night we met, but alas . . . no reply."

"Sorry, it's been a particularly crazy time," I said, shrugging. "So crazy, I ended up here."

Peter smiled sheepishly. "Well, hopefully the next time I see you won't be in an ER."

His pager went off, and thankfully he left to attend to an emergency. As the door swung closed, a splitting ring began to pulsate behind my eye sockets. I'm alone in a hospital, I thought. If something happens to me, I have no one to call. My new life with Damon and Isabel was a flimsy curtain, one that could be torn down at any moment. My hands were trembling, and I dug my dirty nails into my thighs as hard as I could until the skin broke. Finally, a nurse emerged and wheeled me into the scan room.

On the table, another nurse hooked me up to an IV to inject contrast dye into my veins and warned that I might feel a strange urinating sensation. "Think of your happy place, like the beach," she said, inserting the catheter into my arm. Then I lay motionless as the scanner bed pulled me into a claustrophobic tunnel.

The room went dark. I shut my eyes as the machine whirred around me, shooting thin beams of light into my skull. I tried not to think of the ocean, only the warm rush of dye flushing through my veins, rinsing out my organs, my body floating away. But slowly the waves returned to me, crashing against the rocks below. Out the car window, I could hear their unbroken rhythm through the smoke and fog, pulling my gaze over the cliff. *I would do anything not to lose you*, Graham was crying. *You have to believe me, you have to believe me.* Maybe if the horizon hadn't bled into the sea, maybe if I hadn't said that I was calling off the wedding and leaving him when we got home, then he would still be alive.

But I didn't know what to believe anymore. I had no belief system left. How could I find my bearings when the moon was an orb of oxidized blood, like a virus had spread through air and water, infecting everything it touched?

In that second, as he reached for the gun, I saw a flash of truth in his manic eyes: he wanted us both to die. I grabbed his arm to stop him, but it was too late: the swerve, the cliff, the waves I could never love again.

The lights came back on. The scan was over. A caustic fluid

bled through my mouth, like battery acid or rusted metal. The nurse helped me sit up slowly, a trickle of nausea in my throat. She told me to take a few deep breaths through my nose. "I'm okay," I repeated, "I'm okay," but she smiled as if I had said something sad. She dabbed my face with a tissue, and for a moment I thought it was soaked with blood. But this time it was only tears.

That evening, I walked forty-five blocks to the theater. I was in need of air after the hospital, though my chest was sweat-laced by the time I reached Times Square, my feet blistered from the sandals I hadn't worn since LA, when there was no need to walk but merely stand in place and smile. Before I approached the theater, I responded to Isabel's text—promising to call her as soon as the play was over. I was nervous about the night ahead, nervous to see Damon. We hadn't been on a date like this before, even if it had been orchestrated by the shrewd hand of Isabel. Elbowing through the inert tourists on 8th Avenue, I couldn't tell if the cause of my anticipation was Damon himself, or the twisted angle of this proposition, but still—it was a feeling I had missed.

Damon was waiting on the street beneath the marquee, his hands idly in his pockets. He was wearing a white button-down with jeans and brown boots, his hair tousled like he had stepped off a ranch. He nodded approvingly when he saw me, taking in my short red dress with a line of black buttons down the front.

"Are you all gussied up just for me?" Damon said.

"No, for five acts of Norwegian tragedy," I said. "You're just an incidental recipient."

"Way to crush a man's soul."

"It is Ibsen, after all," I said. "And I invited you, remember? Not the other way around."

He leaned so close I could taste his aftershave in my mouth, smoke and cinnamon, but he didn't kiss me.

"I don't think you had much autonomy in that decision," he said.

"So if I felt obligated to invite you, did you feel obligated to come?"

"Of course," he said. "I can't think of a more punishing task than sitting beside you in a dark theater on a perfect spring night."

I looked up at him, his eyes like cool chips of ice. Then a cab blasted its horn, veering within an inch of my body, and as Damon pulled me toward him, the hordes of tourists and scalpers and bums seemed to dissolve into the sidewalk, so I was only aware of his hands on my bare shoulders, steadying me in the street.

"I was also given strict orders that you're not allowed to touch me," I said.

"Oh yeah?" he said. "And who issued that mandate, I wonder."

We shared a look as he let go and I wobbled backward, destabilized again.

The play was a modern adaptation of *The Wild Duck*. The seats were positioned in a three-fourths thrust around a bare stage, set beneath a blaze of house lights. I sat down first, tucking my knees into my chest, as a large Midwestern tourist wearing a *chicks & ducks & geese* T-shirt squeezed past. Damon stood in front of me, tightening his blazer against his chest to showcase a protruding shape beneath it.

"I won't say I'm happy to see you, but . . ." he said.

"You know, if that's a gun, it has to go off in the third act," I said.

"This ain't the kind of gun you're looking for, baby," he said with a cowboy twang.

Damon flashed a mini champagne, then sat down beside me. He slipped the bottle between my bare thighs, and I shivered a little from the cold shock of condensation.

"Have you ever shot one?" I asked.

"I've been shot at," he said. "You may not realize, but jewelry is a pirate's business."

I laughed. "Protecting yourself from all the oil tycoons after you fuck their wives?"

"I don't fuck anyone's wives," he said with a reproachful look.

Even your own, I thought. But I didn't say it.

"Listen, in Africa, diamonds have fueled wars and financed revolutions, drug cartels smuggle Colombian emeralds, Russians barter weapons for gold," Damon said. "Once, I knew this Tanzanian marathon runner who was like a movie star there, and he took me on a tour of a local mine. As the miners were chipping away, we saw this huge chunk of tanzanite fall to the ground, like a blue asteroid. So I swiped it, thinking no one would notice—but it almost got us killed."

Damon reached over and gripped the neck of the bottle, which was still between my thighs, and pushed out the cork with a loud pop.

"You're going to get us killed now," I said, glancing at an unsmiling usher.

As he handed me a straw, his eyes gently passed over my face.

"I just thought you could use a dose of effervescence after your rough day," he said.

Before I could react, the play began. But the house lights stayed on, as bright as the ER, harshly exposing the faces of the audience. What I loved about theater was the moment of surrender, of submersion into its soft body of darkness; a suspended release from life beyond the fourth wall. Here, though, there was nowhere to hide. I kept nervously taking sips of champagne, imagining the conversation between Damon and Isabel earlier. I had told her, in confidence, about my hospital visit, when she called before the play. I couldn't believe Isabel would breach my trust, divulging the ugliest part of myself: the internal damage of my body.

Meanwhile, Damon's eyes stayed focused on the stage, his large boots mindlessly flexing. I crossed my legs, wanting him to look at me, to notice my goose-bumped thighs, the faded freckles on my knees despite the pale hairs I missed shaving. He seemed so unbothered by the proximity of our bodies, while it was all I could think about, but I couldn't even tell what I wanted. Aside from a different lighting designer.

Finally, the theater dropped into darkness like a swift nightfall, absorbing me into the play. The little girl Hedvig was losing her eyesight from a hereditary disease, and she retreated into a solitary dream world of her own, escaping to the attic, where she kept a wounded duck. My bad eye had started to pulse, and I squeezed it shut, pressing my wrist into my lid, when I felt his calloused fingers. Brushing the damp underside of my knee, the concave curve of skin beneath my thigh. I held my breath, flooded with heat like a burner switched on in my center.

"I thought you weren't allowed to touch me," I whispered in the dark.

"Is that what I'm doing?" he said.

Slowly, his hand moved downward, tracing the half-moon of my calf, kneading the muscle until it eased into his thumbs. You can know everything about a man from how they touch you; if they understand the edge of pleasure, the slow fire of it, how it was wanting and hating something at the same time. My breath quickened, my body sank deeper into the seat. I turned to him, but his attention remained steadily fixed on the stage while his hand encircled my ankle, tightening like a handcuff.

How I wanted him and I hated him.

Meanwhile the scene carried on, the little girl retreating to the attic with a gun. I shut my eyes, trying to black out the glove compartment. The gleam of the barrel. Graham had reached for it, hadn't he, the jolt of his arm, his finger on the trigger. The flicker of death in his eyes. A gunshot split the air in a deafening crack, and I jumped in my seat, or was it the car, trapped as we fell and fell through the sky. I felt the cut of a seat belt across my sternum, but when I opened my eyes, it was Damon, his arm securely holding me down.

On stage, the wild duck was dead and so was the little girl, her white dress soaked in a pool of blood. She had shot herself in the chest. I wiped my eyes, watering from the burn of gun smoke, or was it my own terror. The stage lights came up then, glaring as day, and for once I was grateful to be released from the dark.

8

After the play, we walked to the bar at the New York Athletic Club. The room was dusky, bathed in mahogany and cigar smoke, and empty aside from a table of old men drinking scotch and playing chess. While Damon ordered us drinks, I sat down by the window with a view of the park. I checked my phone and texted Isabel, dutifully reporting that I would call soon. Outside, a row of horse-drawn carriages lined the street, awaiting the nocturnal rush of tourists. One auburn horse, spooked and thin, seemed to stare straight at me, though his eyes were covered by black blinders. I wondered if he could see me, or if the night was playing tricks, riddled with signs of my disintegrating vision like the girl going blind in the play. I cupped my hand over my bad eye, but through the slits in my fingers, the horse was still staring.

Damon's phone lit up on the table, and I glanced at it while he chatted with the bartender. A text from Isabel, then another. I felt a small jab of shock—how quickly she'd sent him a separate message, knowing we were together. I was reminded that Isabel may have enticed me on this furtive assignment tonight, but she also had a stake in the game. As Damon returned to the table, balancing two drinks and a bowl of Chex Mix, his phone lit up again.

"I think someone just sent you a nude," I said.

Damon sat down, his back against the window, and quickly picked up his phone.

"It's from Isabel." He frowned but opened it and responded immediately.

"But who did you *think* it was from?" I said. "Or rather, who did you *want* it to be from?"

"If it was a nude, not from her," he said. "Though recently, a former neighbor of mine sent me a rather tantalizing photo from a bathroom, unsolicited . . ."

"She did? What in the world was she thinking?"

Beneath the table, he clamped my knee between his thighs, and I inhaled audibly.

"Now that I'd love to know," he said.

He released me, and I touched my leg, hot and prickly like a sunburn. I held my Negroni to the candlelight, then took a long sip. The redness flushed through me with bitter heat, like the chemical dye injected into my veins this morning. I had barely eaten since then, but all I wanted was something weightless in my stomach, liquid and lethal. Damon was drinking a Coke, and didn't have any champagne earlier, and I wondered if it was connected to the dark period that Pierce had alluded to.

From his jacket pocket, Damon removed a parcel of white tissue paper and placed it on the table between us.

"Is this a gift?" I asked.

"You haven't done anything to deserve one yet," he said. "Open it."

I unwrapped the paper and softly gasped when I saw the pearl. A vivid orange-red, large and lustrous, the shade of a solar flare, or a ripe tangerine.

"It's a melo melo pearl, produced by the elusive melo melo snail, fresh from the Andaman Sea," Damon said casually. "I once lived with a bunch of fishermen off the coast of Vietnam, and these guys had to sail out fifteen hours from the shoreline and dig up several thousand shells just to find one pearl. I picked this one up right before I met you at the theater."

"And you just carried it in your pocket?" I asked, baffled.

"Where else would I put it?" He smiled.

Damon held the pearl to the candlelight. Its color caught fire, a billowing saffron-gold that burned from within.

"You see how it contains chatoyant striations?" He pointed out thin lines on its porcelaneous skin, like ribbons of watery silk. "It's referred to as their 'flame structure,' as if a fire was dancing on its surface. But they are just thin bands of lamellae, or tissue."

"Chatoyant," I repeated to myself.

"These little flames run parallel to each other, but when they lie perpendicular to the axis, it creates this penumbra, a transfixing trick of light like a cat's-eye."

I cupped the pearl in my palm like a crystal ball, a portent of some future stolen from me. I was transfixed, not by the pearl but by him; the way he saw beauty as an act of passage, into glimmering spheres of another life. It was terrifying how much I wanted to be transported by him, far from the ugliness of the hospital and the maid's room, from my misshapen past, and here he was offering it like a rare, precious gift.

Damon laid out another parcel before me. This time, I unwrapped a pair of earrings in the shape of an anchor. Spiked with inverted diamonds, a row of pearls dangling from its crown like a mobile of pastel moons.

"These are rare natural conch pearls, which the Incas believed were the mouthpiece of the gods," he explained. "I have to return some of them to my pearl dealer tomorrow."

"Excuse me, your pearl dealer?" I said.

"Oh yeah, he's a total nutcase. I'll take you to meet him one day, if you're lucky."

One earring remained unfinished, and I watched Damon arrange a few loose pearls beneath it. Swapping cream for copper, lilac for rose, with the intensity of a color field painter.

"In life, as with stones, demand and scarcity are correlated. The rarer and more unobtainable something is, the more coveted it becomes, even when it has no inherent value. I love how precious stones are an expression of that, a tangible symbol for the invisible force of lust within it." Damon held the one finished earring up to my ear. "Try this one on for me."

"What makes you think I won't abscond with it?" I said.

"If you want to learn how to become a little cat burglar, I'll teach you," he said.

I stood up, my head swimming with alcohol, and walked over to a tarnished mirror by the bar. My cheeks were flushed, the earring glinting like the blade of a knife. The last time I had tried on his earrings, the reflection of Caroline glared back; now, as I looked at my own, with Damon watching from afar, something sharpened within me. I never liked pearls—in fact, pearls reminded me of cold wives. I walked back over, tilting my head to expose my neck.

"How do I look?" I said.

Damon reached up and raked back my hair. Gently at first, but then his fingers tightened until he was pulling a fistful, hard. I closed my eyes, imagining what else he could do to me.

"Why do you think I couldn't forget you all these years?" he said.

"You barely even knew me," I said.

"You were unattainable, elusory, a fiery gem in a dark sea."

"Are you making me a metaphor for your fucking pearls?"

"That would be too easy, wouldn't it," he said.

He gripped my hair even tighter. I thought of Isabel's

mandate then, and though I didn't want to do it, preferring to linger in this suspended space, I needed to deliver on my promise.

"And how would your wife feel about that?" I said.

Damon released his hand. His eyes dimmed, as if all these varnished surfaces were no more than a smokescreen for something beneath it.

"I told you already, we're not married," he said. "It's a complicated sort of arrangement."

"An arrangement? How traditional." I smirked, sitting back down. "Tell me what that's like."

"Look, historically women have used jewelry as a proxy to make them feel adored and adorned, often when they've been neglected by men in their lives," Damon stated factually, refolding the tissue paper. "So I'm not only creating a desirable object but also offering the intimate attention it awards them, like having their portrait painted or something. And some women can become . . . *attached*."

"You mean, like Isabel?" I said.

"Well, right, she's a perfect example."

"I don't understand," I said, skeptical. "What does this theory have to do with your *wife*?"

"Because it's helpful for these women to know that I'm not available to them in the way they might romanticize."

I finished my drink, while a waiter brought over a fresh round. I could tell Damon was using a rehearsed narrative, crafted to avoid uncomfortable questions about his life. Still, it inverted my perception of who he was, what he wanted. It was less confounding to reckon with marriage because an arrangement was, by its very nature, an artifice, a front—a lie.

"Good to know you're not available to me, then," I said.

"You're not one of those women," said Damon. "And you know that."

He touched the inside of my wrist, indenting his thumb

into my veins. A wildness spread through me, knowing I had touched a hidden nerve. I wanted to slip off the restraints of outside life, and push him right against the edge, without consequence, without penalty.

"So then, tell me," I said. "What are the rules between you?"

"We don't have any rules," he said. "I mean, it's never been explicitly discussed."

"So she's allowed to fuck other men, you're saying."

His eyes flickered like power in a windstorm.

"If she wants to, I guess," he said. "But if she does, I'm not aware of it."

"And how often do you sleep together?"

He shifted in his chair. "We don't."

"Oh, come on, Damon, you *live* together. You don't have to lie about it."

"That was never the nature of our relationship," he said tensely.

His face darkened, as if the shadow of some unseen loss was passing through him. I perceived that Caroline was linked to a deeper emotional dependency, one that filled him with shame. Perhaps he was telling the truth, or at least a version of it; not as a ploy to seduce me, but to share a disjointed part of himself.

"That sounds like you're engaged in a healthy relationship," I said.

"Can you honestly tell me *yours* was so healthy?" Damon shot back. "That's not what I heard from—"

He stopped himself, but I knew who he meant.

I put down my glass, blood rushing to my ears. What had Isabel told him? And how did she know anything about my relationship? It seemed she had a deft ability to harbor dangerous secrets, and I didn't fear her as much as my self-destructive impulse to do the same thing.

"We were about to get married," I said, my throat tight. "It was never an arrangement. There's a difference."

"I'm sorry," he said gently. "I shouldn't have said that."

He held my wrist to his mouth, pressing his lips to my veins. At least I'm not like her, I wanted to say. But I no longer knew which woman I meant.

It was late, the club already shutting down, when we snuck upstairs to the top floor. Damon said he wanted to show me the view, and I said *yes, show me.* He led me into a dark, musty billiards room, crowded with pool tables and rusted plaques of members long-dead. I walked toward the blue windows, murky like an aquarium. On the sill sat a chessboard, and beyond the park fanned out, a roiling black sea, the skyline guarding its edges. From up here, the park was not my own; it was a topographic construction, a contained wilderness belonging to everyone and to no one.

Damon came up behind me, every muscle in my body a tensed spring.

"Did you know that the Dutch bought this entire island for glass beads?" he said.

His hand slid up the back of my leg, and I braced myself against the window, my knees bending and buckling to his touch, the park fogging through the glass.

"Why would they trade something valuable for nothing?" I said, but my voice was full of air. He teased the hem of my dress, gently parting my inner thighs. I tried to turn around, but my limbs felt warm and shapeless like wax. He was hovering at the edge of my thong, his lips grazing my neck, and though I heard myself saying *we can't we can't*, my own body willfully defied me, thrusting backward to meet his hand. I inhaled loudly, the contact radiating up my spine as he slipped a finger inside me.

"We can't do this," I said.

"We're not doing anything," he said.

Finally, I turned around. Our eyes locked as he jammed his fingers into my mouth, pearled and salty like the inside of a shell. In one swift motion, he lifted me up and placed me on the chessboard, the pieces falling to the ground. I closed my eyes as he unbuttoned my dress, kissing my neck, my breasts, everywhere but my mouth, and then my scar, its corners and folds, the hidden places that stored my pain. His fingers were inside me again, and I pressed my back into the cold glass and imagined falling backward into the vast swath of darkness below, the trees catching me like a parachute, landing safely on the other side of my life.

When he pulled away, the room slowly floated back as if I had passed through a cloud. He was crouched between my legs now, his tongue sealing the seam of my thong. He gazed up at me with the complicit thrill of a criminal, uncaught.

"This can never happen again," I said hoarsely.

"It never happened to begin with," he said.

I dug my heel into his chest, and he grabbed my leg, hooking it over his shoulder. He sank his teeth into my thigh, my flesh electric but my body numb. Then we heard the hum of a vacuum cleaner in the hallway. He took my hand, and we scrambled downstairs and out onto the street, tumbling into the misty vertex of midnight. I looked for the auburn horse, but he was no longer there.

I awoke in the maid's room, foggy and cotton-mouthed, dressed in all my clothes. In the dark, I fumbled in my bag and found my phone nearly dead: 2:14 a.m. There was a text from Isabel, time-stamped two hours ago: Are u home yet? "Fuck," I said aloud as bleary splices of the night rushed back. I groaned, regret sinking in the pit of my stomach. As soon as

I responded to her text, my phone rang. I told her I was sorry, that I had fallen asleep.

"Of course, angel, I know you had a long day," Isabel said.

"What are you still doing up?" I asked.

"I never sleep, and if I do, it's with one eye open."

The ER now seemed like a bad, distant dream. I could barely swallow and staggered into the kitchen for some water. Over the sink, I looked out into the dirty brick interior, window after window framing kitchens just like this. In one, a gray-haired woman in a bathrobe was watching a baking show, a black cat curled at her feet. In another, a bald man was brandishing a phone like a weapon while a distressed woman in a chemise tried to grab it, begging him to give it back.

"So, is it what we suspected?" Isabel ventured. "An arrangement after all?"

I paused, considering how to reframe Damon's answer—I couldn't say the function of his wife was to deter the advances of older women, such as Isabel.

"It certainly seems that way," I said, clearing my throat. "He claims that the impression of being married makes his clients' *husbands* feel more secure."

"Sounds like she's more of a beard to me!" Isabel quipped, and I laughed. "Did he say they ever had a romantic history?"

"No, he didn't," I said. "Maybe I would've gotten more out of him if he drank, but weirdly he didn't all night."

"You know why, don't you?" she said with a solemn pause. "His little brother died of an overdose the year before we met. A terrible death, the boy was so young. Apparently, addiction runs in his family—his mother died of alcoholism when he was a teenager. So now he rarely drinks."

My chest tightened, realizing the undercoat of loss on his face was not a pretense. How uncanny this timeline was between us: Damon and Isabel had met during their year of grief, as I met them during my own.

"But then why live together? Why not live separate lives like every other couple on Park Avenue?" Isabel mused. "Given how much he prizes his creative and personal autonomy."

"That's what's strange," I said. "Maybe that's a condition of their arrangement, or maybe he feels trapped by her."

"Or maybe—" she sighed heavily "—maybe she's really in love with him."

The alcohol rose in my throat, the acidic residue of deceit. My phone vibrated hotly against my ear, and I knew it was him.

"Anyway, he's leaving town tomorrow, so we won't see him for a while," Isabel said.

"What do you mean?"

"Didn't he tell you? He's heading to Monterey for a jewelry show."

My head pounded, a blunt kick of shock. How could Damon have failed to mention he was leaving? I was reminded of their enmeshment, a boundary I could not breach. I thanked Isabel for the tickets and said good night. Before I hung up, a silence crept over the line, not filled with strain but with sadness.

"Do you ever have dreams about him?" she said.

When she spoke of our dead, I always knew their pronouns.

"Sometimes," I said. "Sometimes I dream about the night it happened, but in the end . . ." I took a shaky breath. "I'm the one who dies. Not him."

"I've had that dream before," Isabel said, and I knew she was referring to her daughter. "You're feeling the guilt of being left alive. But, my angel, aren't we lucky that you are."

The word *guilt* rang in my ears, like the blare of sirens from a distant avenue.

"Love you," she said. "Sweeter dreams tonight."

"Love you, too," I replied.

I steadied myself against the sink, counting my breaths. Out the window, the woman had taken her phone back and clutched it to her chest like a stuffed animal. I wondered what text he had read, what private part of herself he had violated. How many midnights had I been forcibly awoken like that? Quavering in bed as Graham maniacally waved my hacked phone, spewing jealous accusations. I had locked myself in a hotel bathroom once, terrified to emerge for hours until he passed out. *It's just our crazy love,* he'd said in the morning with an apology. *Love in an epic, operatic form. You're not meant for anything ordinary.* And I had believed him.

I swallowed an Ativan from Sam's prescriptions atop the microwave, two Advils, a handful of shredded cheese followed by another of cardboard fiber cereal, and climbed back into bed. I pulled off my damp thong and tried not to look at my phone. But it was a futile exercise.

D: Check your purse . . .
L: . . . ?
D: Sunken treasure . . .

I emptied the contents of my purse onto the bed. Between the gum wrappers and perfume samples and rolled-up playbill, I found the parcel—the one that contained the melo melo pearl. In the dark, I cupped it gingerly in my palm. The same color as the moon on our final drive home, a burning coal, an infected scab in the virulent sky. I didn't understand why Damon had planted it there. As though it were collateral, or contraband, smuggled across the illicit borders of ourselves.

Then something else caught my eye: the theater ticket. Strangely, Isabel's name was not on it—the ticket was under Damon's name. Why would Isabel entice me to go with Damon if the tickets were his to begin with? I lay down on top of the flimsy quilt, staring at the ceiling. Then I realized: Isabel was supposed to be *his* date tonight. When she couldn't go, my invitation was her way of moderating the night, exerting her presence even in absence. She was always, unnervingly, one step ahead, but now the game had changed.

I touched the inside of my thigh where a purple bruise had blossomed, an inkblot of evidence. How guilt, I thought, was no more than an irritant trapped in the soft shell of our bodies. How we, too, wrap it in layer upon layer to soothe the wound, until it hardens into something unrecognizable, not a pearl, but an aberrant shape, a tumor.

When I finally fell asleep, the orange pearl burning beneath my pillow, I could hear my own voice saying *love you, too*, but it was drowned out by the heavy drone of garbage trucks, awakening the city to the vacant break of dawn.

9

I spent nearly every night with Isabel while Damon was away. While we were together, diverted by the parade of night, the clamorous crowds and the coming of spring, my attachment to her deepened and our closeness grew. It wasn't that I couldn't call up my life before meeting her, that cadaverous state of living, the thick paste of despair that grimed my days. But with Damon miles away, it was easier to convince myself that nothing could endanger or complicate our bond. Not even that brief slip after the theater that had amounted, almost, to nothing.

Or at least, I wanted to pretend it was nothing.

Until afterward, when the parties were over. And somewhere on my lonely walks home, between the somber scrim of trees on the west of the avenue and the cold marble lobbies on the east, when the albatross of depression would claw its way back into my bones, my phone would vibrate with a text from Damon. Always after Isabel had spoken with him, so he knew I would be alone.

Sometimes, he would send a photo from his trip. An amethyst poised on a purple thistle, a blue chalcedony pebble set on a dune above the Pacific, accompanied by an elliptical caption: *blue rider . . . moonstone jellyfish . . . mandarin garnet sky . . . the curve of purple noon.* I loved his palette of lapidary phrases, mixing images and textures like paint. And it formed a visual vocabulary, a secret code we were writing together, while resisting the subtext beneath it.

Occasionally, he would tip the balance ever so slightly, and I would engage, tentatively, if only to be reminded that desire existed somewhere, even if contained to a screen:

D: I dreamt about the rhythm of your breath
L: Fast or slow . . .
D: Uneven . . . anticipatory . . .
D: My hand cupping your mouth
D: The low vibration . . .
D: . . . of your moan

His texts were like talons, sinking through each layer of my skin. We weren't being outright deceitful, I told myself. Our exchanges were limited to the parameter of words, and words no longer held any weight. They did once, when I knew how to compose a line on a blank page. They did when a man asked me to marry him, and four simple words meant the promise of a shared lifetime. I had said yes, not knowing those words would turn into an elegy, a dirge howled over a shallow grave.

Words, I had come to understand, were like the weather, like your life: you could map their meaning and forecast their patterns, but ultimately they were subject to shift, to reverse, to bear disaster.

And then, one night, I didn't hear from Damon. I didn't hear from him for a full week.

Isabel continued to speak with him nightly. But as I walked home alone, passing the rattling hot dog carts, the workers catcalling from their milling trucks while they excoriated the asphalt like burnt skin, the homeless man who slept outside the Church of the Heavenly Rest, his sketches pinned to the sidewalk by water bottles filled with dirt, I forced myself not to check my phone.

When I got home, still no new messages. Words didn't carry any weight until you felt the absence of them, their vacancy flickering like a neon sign.

By then it was approaching the end of May. One evening, Isabel invited me over to pick her up before a book party. It was startlingly hot, an augury of summer, and I walked toward the subway in a sullen mood. In the street, sulfurous eddies of steam rose up through orange-and-white-striped funnels, bleaching the sidewalk air. I weaved around a group of crop-topped girls on Park, engaged in a photoshoot with a bed of crimson tulips. All around me, life seemed to be erupting above the surface, while my own remained unthawed below the ground.

I didn't know Isabel lived in a townhouse until I arrived at her address. A nineteenth-century Greek Revival–style brick home on Bank Street, close to the water. She had mentioned once that her husband was gifted the property in a quid pro quo deal in the late '70s—though she never said by whom. I walked up the stoop and through an open red door into a vestige of a fabled bohemia. In the front parlor, a wood-burning marble fireplace sat beneath a Vivian Springford painting, with a Buddha statue tucked below it. I heard Isabel call my name and followed her voice down a long foyer adorned with iconic photographs of her life: partying with Lou Reed; sitting for a black-and-white portrait by Avedon; holding a baby in a christening gown. I realized this must be her daughter.

I found Isabel in a book-lined library painted in malachite tones, with French doors opening to a tranquil back garden.

She was sitting on the floor, smoking a cigarette in a silk kimono, surrounded by lit candles and a mess of scattered papers.

"I have so much shit all over the place. Notes, journals, articles—the paper trail of my life," Isabel said, waving the flaps of her sleeve. "Some of it at the beach, some of it here, scattered as ashes in the wind."

"Are you looking for anything specific?" I asked, stepping over a pile.

"I wrote this slim little autobiographical book, which has been out of print for centuries, and now a publisher wants to reissue it for some crazy reason." She exhaled a thin rill of smoke. "I'm only telling you this, and you have to swear to secrecy, because I was asked to write a memoir in addition."

"You absolutely must do it," I said. "It's not even a question."

"I have enough material to fill several volumes. The scandals, the undercover missions, the love affairs—though most secrets will be taken to the grave." Isabel lifted a file box and dropped it onto the desk with a thump. "But it would be such an undertaking, and I can't write if it's all a mess. What I need is someone I trust to help me sift through it, to organize it all." She paused. "You wouldn't want to do it, Liv, would you?"

I hesitated, not expecting this. "You mean, as an assistant?"

"Only for the next few weeks while I'm away. I know it's below your pay grade, but you might find it a welcome diversion," she said. "And you'll still have plenty of time to focus on your own writing."

"If only I could write again," I muttered.

"Listen, there are times you can write *through* something, in a volcanic purge. But mostly, distance is required to shape experience into meaning. The writing of aftermath, I call it."

I told Isabel that I would consider it while she went upstairs to change. The fact was I desperately needed money, a problem that could only be avoided for so long. The endless medical bills piling up from the accident, the cost of movers to pack and ship my belongings before the sale of Graham's house—but to what address would the boxes even be sent? Panic rose up that I tried to push down. Maybe Isabel intuitively sensed that I needed a job adjacent to writing, without having to write.

"Oh, Liv, I forgot to tell you," Isabel said, pausing in the doorframe. "Damon took me out to dinner last night, and my god, was he gorgeously tan from all that California sun."

I tried to swallow my shock. "I didn't know he was back in town."

"He should be at the party, but you know he's such a wild card," she said.

For the first time, I realized, I was jealous. Damon actively continued to nurture their private relationship; but he had gone dark on me, switching off the lights while I was still in the room.

"Which is why I also invited a new worthy rival—a contender, if you will," Isabel said.

"Really?" I said. "Who's the lucky suitor?"

A streak of sun hit her face, lighting up a mischievous smile.

"Rex Wright."

I inwardly shuddered. "How do you know him, again?"

"Oh, he's been on the scene for years. Sometimes he'd work for us, sometimes against us, depending on the case," Isabel said. "Like any cutthroat journalist, Rex could either help you or destroy you, but he intends to do one or the other as long as it serves his story."

While Isabel went upstairs, I wandered into the ivy-draped garden. A table sat beneath a magnolia tree, its yellow buds cupped to the sky. I tried to distract myself from the spiral of anxiety in my head, but I couldn't shake it off. For some reason, I had the gnawing suspicion that Rex was not a convenient foil, that his pervasive presence was not random. But he had deliberately invaded the sphere of our lives, tilting the axis on which we were all precariously poised.

A hot gust of wind rushed through the doors, scattering the piles of papers across the library. I went back inside to collect them. Kneeling on the floor, I sifted through the jumble of articles, transcripts, and notes—a riveting glimpse into Isabel's covert life. Each page a cryptic clue, constructing an archive of her shadowy past: files from the Girgenti Report on the Crown Heights riot; the Central Park jogger; the Beatles' lawsuit against Capitol Records.

Then a folded page, tucked into a folder, caught my eye.

It was a recent *New York Times* article, dating back to last fall. I felt my palms go damp as I picked up the paper and scanned the text:

> . . . the incident occurred when the car swerved off Devil's Slide, hurtling over the cliff and plummeting two hundred feet into the rocky beach below . . . preliminary investigation determined that the disgraced chief executive was under the heavy influence of alcohol . . . reportedly driving off in an emotionally unstable state after he was publicly fired . . . young fiancée managed to extricate herself from the passenger side and swim to shore . . . she was airlifted to the hospital . . . rough weather hampered rescuers' attempt to retrieve his ejected body until daybreak . . .

My hands were quivering, the print smearing into a black clot of ink. I closed my eyes, but there it was—the past at hand. The salt-sting of water seeping into my lungs. The burn of rope as it hauled my broken body above the shore, suspended in the air between life and death.

I didn't understand. Why had Isabel saved this article? What personal interest did she have in the story at the time? I noticed a faint pencil mark on the page, underlining a single word:

unstable. As if she were noting a discrepancy, a chink in the details that didn't track.

I heard footsteps coming down the staircase and quickly stood up, dropping the paper on the floor as if it were a bomb.

I made my way back into the foyer, but my vision was woolly as though a swatch of cloth had been pulled over my eyes. Isabel slowly descended the spiral staircase in a low-cut powder-blue dress, gold shimmer swept over her slender clavicles.

But my eyes fell on her left hand.

"Your ring," I heard myself say.

Isabel regally waved her long fingers through the air. The gem caught the stray sun, speckling the wall with a galaxy of green light.

"It was a present from Jack, on our last anniversary before he died," she said with an elegiac smile. "A rare mint tourmaline."

Isabel extended her hand over mine so I could examine it up close. The absence of my own ring sliced through my finger like a serrated blade.

"My engagement ring was that color," I said.

"Oh, angel, I'm sorry," she said, touching my cheek. "I hope you're keeping it somewhere safe."

How could I tell her the emerald ring was gone? Lost in the wreckage of the accident. Here I was surrounded by all these gems, all these unearthed stones, yet the only one that mattered to me was thousands of miles away, decaying at the bottom of the ocean or entombed in a ravine, like the bones of a missing girl.

If ever recovered, it wouldn't be a sign of life: it would be proof of death.

At first, the party was like every other, a variation on a theme. It turned out to be a packed celebration for a book on jewelry that included Damon's work, held in a Tribeca loft. Maybe the novelty of parties had worn off, or a persistent unrest had seized my nervous system, but everything tonight struck me as meaningless. Jewelry: who actually cared except the few women who could afford it? I was waiting at the bar on the terrace, beside a phallic sculpture of a gourd, overhearing two women with unnaturally toned triceps comparing their spoils. "And this was from my ex-husband," one said, jangling a bracelet, "after I found him on top of the dryer with our housekeeper."

It depressed me, these women who considered jewelry to be part of a severance package, a form of contingent compensation. Or maybe they were smarter than I was—they had heirlooms and assets, they understood the word *provenance*. I never asked Graham for anything, and all he left me with, aside from destitution, was the crippling inability to trust anyone again.

I saw Damon then, walking into the party with Pierce. I ordered a white wine spritzer, and the bartender asked if I was an old lady in the body of Rita Hayworth, and I said no, I'm just an old lady, and *fuck off* I thought, then switched my order to a spicy margarita. When I turned around, Rex had somehow crawled his way into the circle. Isabel placed her left hand on his chest in an unsubtle gesture, alerting Damon to this new oppositional element. I took a sip of my drink as I headed over, spilling a drop down my teal silk slip dress, which left a dark water stain.

"Look who it is, our stray," Pierce announced. "Did we decide to adopt her yet?"

"Nope, we're still inspecting her papers," Damon said.

"Isabel was showing us her ring from the Godfather," Rex said jovially. "But won't tell us what she had to do for the Godfather to get the ring."

"Oh, I'll never kill and tell," Isabel said. "Whoops, did I say kill? I meant *kiss*."

Damon coolly glanced at me. He was tan, like Isabel had

said, and ruggedly unkempt in a gray T-shirt and black jeans, a leather bracelet on his wrist. I hated how it made him look more attractive, like a hot actor roughed up to play a tormented role that might shamelessly win him an award.

"Don't they say your mistakes reveal your secrets?" Rex said, looking straight at me.

"Freud's *Psychopathology of Everyday Life*," I retorted.

Rex raised his glass. "Slips of the tongue like slips of the pen."

"Like slips of the—" Pierce thrust his hip into Isabel's side, spilling her wine.

"Naughty boys." Isabel elbowed him. "Everyone seems to have caught a little spring fever tonight."

The air was oppressive, dense with sweating bodies. Damon leaned toward me, pressing his weight into my hip. I crushed a cube of ice between my teeth, trying not to think of his mouth on my inner thigh, his anguished week of silence.

"So, is Liv coming out east with us for the long weekend?" Rex asked.

I looked at Isabel. "I wasn't aware there was one?"

"Memorial Day weekend," she said. "Can you believe it's already here?"

"Doesn't Damon have room for you on that big old farm of his?" Pierce said. "You can throw her in the stalls with your beloved horses."

Damon shifted away so we were no longer touching, as if the idea of me in his domestic sphere posed a threat. I spitefully bit into a jalapeño slice, and my tongue started to burn.

"I don't know." Damon shrugged. "My horses are always telling me they need more space."

"Yeah, I hear non-monogamous horses are all the rage these days," Pierce said. "They love being ethically slutty."

"What will you do all alone in an empty city?" Rex said.

Their eyes fell on me. The low sun pierced my bad eye like the hot tip of a needle.

"I guess I'll have to suffer," I said.

Isabel gave me a sympathetic smile. "I'll have you out there soon enough."

They went on to discuss their plans, some concert on the beach they'd been invited to, and I slipped away to get another drink. In the stagnant line for the bar, I couldn't help but fixate on their holiday weekend ahead. Isabel and Damon strolling on the beach together, her hand slipped into his arm, beneath the spangle of fireworks that signaled the inception of summer. I would be left behind in a desolate city, back to muted nights drained of their color. How could I have fooled myself into believing they'd include me? Or even want me there? I was no more than a minor card in their continually shuffled deck. I wiped my forehead, lightheaded from the heat, my own sickening despair. A sweaty hand clamped my shoulder, and I turned around.

"Come on, darling, shall we sneak away for a smoke?" Rex said.

"What's in it for me?" I replied.

He thrust a glass of white wine into my hand. "Aside from the pleasure of my company?"

Fine, I thought, you win. I followed him to a less populated corner of the terrace, the push-pull of fear and curiosity tugging at my center. Rex was either toying with me or baiting some valuable knowledge, but I felt a sick compulsion to find out. He rolled an herbal cigarette, lighting it with a gold Zippo engraved with a skull.

"You know, I shared a smoke with your fiancé once," he began, inhaling through his teeth. "And I asked him how I could get so lucky as to ensnare a fiery little fox of my own."

"And what did he respond?"

"That you were inimitable, incomparable, a rare mélange of brains and beauty," Rex said. "Essentially, I was shit out of luck. Though I suppose you're back on the market now."

"But sadly off the market to you," I said.

"Surely you don't mean that," he said, clutching his heart like he'd been stabbed. "I always thought you and I would make a rather winning duo, don't you?"

"I guess a man can dream," I said.

I plucked his cigarette and took a shallow drag, looking out at the view. The river was a silvery wire of steel, snaring the sun as it fell.

"Why not?" he pressed on. "Historically, the record shows you have a weakness—or fondness, rather—for men of a certain generation. So why not have a go?"

Despite his jaunty tone, I could see in his stare, flinty and filthy, that he was serious. I recognized this distinct look in narcissistic men, at risk of losing their primacy, their virility, intent on proving it was not yet dead. They seek validation in the eyes of younger women—not from sex itself even, but the tepid illusion of its promise—to restore the balance of their fragile egos, to stroke their perverted fantasies. As if this was our job.

"Unfortunately, I'm not in a state to think about men of any age," I said, dismissively handing back the cigarette.

"Oh, is that so?" Rex sulked. "That hasn't been my personal observation."

His eyes hardened like mud, as if my rejection had coagulated there. I glanced back at the party, wanting to return to the protection of Isabel. But she was whispering something in Damon's ear, with a seductive laugh, as if I wasn't even there.

"You know, something else occurred to me," Rex said, squinting into the distance. "Another memory from that party in LA."

I swallowed a mouthful of wine. "And what might that be?"

"I remember the end of the night. Your fiancé stormed off so abruptly, in quite a nasty rage," Rex said. "He almost left you behind, poor thing."

I shook my head, the reflex of denial like flipping a switch.

"I don't remember that," I said.

"No? I found the whole episode quite . . . *disturbing*, really. The way he treated you," he continued. "But I suppose we expect men like that to have a legendary temper—or at least, we used to overlook it. The fairy tale often hides its own ugly shadow."

Rex tapped his cigarette over the edge, sending a comet of ashes into the wind. As I watched them drop, the skyline began to tilt. The rooftops slanting toward the street, a dark blot of clouds dripping into the river like wet paint. I edged back, trying to steady my teetering vision. I wanted to return to the party, to the refuge of Damon and Isabel, but I didn't belong there anymore. I belonged nowhere. One by one, Rex was peeling off the bandages of my mummified self, exposing the raw, unsightly skin beneath.

"Impressive how much you seem to recall from meeting me that one time," I said.

"Did I say once?" He cocked his head. "I think you may have forgotten the other time."

I swallowed. "It couldn't have been that memorable, then."

Rex licked his lips, dropping the cigarette and crushing it beneath his loafer like a roach. He took a step closer, the treble of threat on his sour breath.

"Or perhaps, my dear," he said, "it's possible that you don't *want* to remember it."

10

When I got back uptown, Sam was in his favorite chair, watching an old black-and-white film on TCM. I kicked off my heels and lay down on the threadbare red couch, depleted and distressed from the party. He passed me a Carr's cracker with a smear of blue cheese on it.

"You know I hate this cheese," I complained, but I hungrily ate it anyway.

"Watch this close-up of her face," Sam said, handing me another. "She cycles through horror, hurt, and humiliation in one fell swoop."

"Sounds like me on any given night," I said.

The film was *Sudden Fear.* In the scene, a matronly playwright played by Joan Crawford was listening to a recording on her dictation machine and discovered that her much younger husband and his young lover were plotting her murder.

"You know, I ran into Joan once in the elevator of the Waldorf."

"And did you go back to her room?" I said.

"That was one ride where I got off on my own floor," Sam chuckled. "Just like you, she couldn't give a man her hand without taking off his arm."

I tried to watch the film, but my mind was contorted by the illogical tangle of events. The article about the accident in Isabel's library. The pervasion of Rex. The way that Rex was teasing and withholding information, details he possessed that I did not—to assert some kind of sadistic hold over me. Why couldn't I recall the end of that party? Or were all of Graham's scary episodes blocked out in my head? And when had I met Rex for a second time—or was he lying? Now that I hadn't reciprocated his advances, I feared what he might do to me. I sensed Rex was a man who took pleasure in terrible things, propelled by some bestial drive for retribution. I searched my broken memory for a clue, some repressed encounter, but it felt like I was blindly moving through a pitch-black room, bracing myself for the door. Gloria Grahame's voice was skipping—*I know a way I know a way*—and Sam shut off the TV.

"So, did they feed you at this party of yours?" Sam said.

"Tequila with a side of PTSD," I said.

"Come on, Slash, I'll make you a little pasta." I helped Sam to his feet, and he towered over me like a tired tree. "Or else I'll have to change your name to Slim."

I followed him into the kitchen and slumped down at the table, heaped with galleys, unread copies of *The New York Review of Books*, and fresh reams of vibrant handmade paper that he used to collage. Each week, Sam took the subway to a small printing press in the Brooklyn Navy Yard, where he would add pigment to pulp, then paint swirls and swoops with a thin brush onto the wet sheets. I once asked why he had traded words for color late in life. It was an escape from constructing meaning, he said, and now I understood.

I watched him while he cooked, stirring a bowl of cherry tomatoes in a pan until they wrinkled and burst.

"Can I ask you something?" I said.

"You can certainly try," Sam said, throwing a dash of salt into a pot of water.

"Why would an older woman become obsessed with a much younger man?"

"Well, in the moving pictures, isn't the older woman trying to stave off the cruel realities of aging?" He glanced at me, throwing a pink dish towel over his shoulder. "But you're asking the uninteresting version of that question—try again."

I frowned, then said, "You mean, why would an attractive young man become entranced with an older woman?"

"Getting closer." Sam poured me a glass of Sancerre from an open bottle, testing out a small sip. "You know, I fell madly in love with an older woman once, when I was on a Fulbright in Florence, back in my youth. The ravishing wife of a famous Italian writer whom I was studying under. And to this day, it remains one of the most rapturous affairs of my life." He paused. "Not to mention, some of the best sex."

"Thanks, Sam, that's helpful," I said.

Sam chuckled. "And the younger man is that cad your neighbor, I presume?"

"Why do you presume he's a cad?"

"Because that's the way these stories always go, isn't it?"

A Billie Holiday song came on the scratchy public radio station. I watched Sam drain the boiling pot into a colander, then spoon the pasta into a simmering sauce.

"So you're saying you were also a cad, then," I said.

"Most likely." He nodded.

"And how did your affair end?"

He paused. "Catastrophically."

Sam looked up, wincing as if the memory still pained him. Then he planted a steaming bowl before me and grated a veil of parmesan over the top.

"Now *mangia*, Slash, eat. I should've been a short-order cook, but instead I was a long-suffering poet."

I ate large forkfuls of the warm pasta, listening to Billie morosely croon *blue moon, you saw me standing alone*. Sam watched me eat for a moment, his soft hazel eyes clouding as if the melody carried him off to some distant night.

"The question, my dear, isn't what he sees in her," he said gently. "But why are you searching for answers in their lives, instead of in your own?"

I sat up defensively. "I don't think that's fair."

My phone buzzed loudly on the table, and I picked it up.

D: Be outside your building in 10 minutes . . .

"Oh god," I said, and typed back: NO. I put the phone down, looking helplessly at Sam. He slowly shook his head, the deep lines sagging around his square jaw.

"Slash, you're plunging from one disaster headfirst into another," he said.

"That's not true," I protested. "This isn't a rebound."

"That's not what I mean." Sam sighed, putting down his fork. "I was like you once, I trafficked in turbulence. I was drawn to the same flame. You're trying to fill the space of your real loss with some shiny emulation, but it will only leave you with a deeper absence in the end."

I could tell myself it wasn't true. I could tell myself I wasn't going downstairs, that the loss I felt had nothing to do with them, but I was already heading for the door.

Damon was waiting on the corner when I stepped onto the sidewalk. The night had cooled, the leaves overhead rippling like wet scales. I wanted my distrust to take hold, to dissuade me from any jolt of attraction. But as I warily approached him, I could feel my inner resolve slipping out of me.

"I thought we could take a little walk," Damon said with an airy smile. "I wanted to show you the rocks."

"Just your nightly geological tour?" I said, crossing my arms against my chest.

"Exactly. Did you have something better in mind?"

I followed him into the park. It was empty, nearing midnight. A welter of silver clouds scudded across the sky from the west side. As we walked along East Drive, Damon really did talk about rocks. At first, I was only partially listening, consumed by the litany of uncertainties in my head. I needed to grant myself permission to be absorbed by him, by his telluric world of life underfoot.

"The thing about stones is they contain secrets of our earth's evolution, billions of years of volcanic eruptions and plate tectonics, trapped within these little fiery prisms," Damon was saying, his voice unrushed. "And trace elements in the ground, and natural chemicals in the earth, can alter the saturation of the stone. In South Africa, for example, there's a lot of nitrogen in the ground, so Cape diamonds have a yellowish tint. In Golconda, they found boron in the stone, derived from ancient oceanic crust, and the diamonds are as blue as the bottom of the sea."

His words coursed with mystery, his voice hushed against the shrill chorus of cicadas, the distant thrum of traffic. We stopped by a looming outcrop of rock, beneath a bronze sculpture of a panther. It had begun to drizzle, pooling in the striations like dark blue veins.

"You see these grooves and scars? They formed as glaciers slid and scraped over the city," Damon said. "Most people have no idea that buried beneath the skyscrapers, the city's bedrock carries a trove of gems. If we cracked open this rock, you know what we could find?"

"A nest of rats?" I said. "A buried body?"

He smiled, taking my hand and running it over the slippery contours.

"We could uncover aquamarines, chunks of smoky quartz, golden beryl, black tourmalines, and wine-red garnets."

"You're insane," I said. He traced my collarbone with his cool, wet fingers, and I shivered, wanting him to touch me more.

"Don't tell me you don't like it a little bit," he said.

I pushed him away, and we walked farther, turning past the Boathouse toward Bethesda Fountain, its bronzed angel wings carrying the weight of night. Someone had filled the water with lotus leaves and papyrus sedges, a sign that summer would soon resurface again.

"See, all stones have stories to tell, but some can be elusive, taciturn, like you," Damon said, touching my arm. "You have to study their inclusions, the imperfections hidden within their radiant depths—whether crystals, needles, or feathers—to understand their history. And these flaws can be the most beautiful thing about it."

Everything he said seemed absurd, yet I was rapt. He was aware of an entire subdural layer that I wasn't, and it drew me out of myself, out of my own dark tunnel, to imagine that once the oceanic crust crashed into the continental shelf with such force that something miraculous was created and crystallized, waiting to be uncovered.

"What I love about this park is that it's all soft bends and curves and folds," he said. "There's only one straight line in the entire park."

"Where is it?"

"You're looking right at it, Red," he said.

We had arrived at Literary Walk, enclosed in a leafy cathedral of trees. The branches seemed to part like lips, thin shadows slipping through their openings. Damon led me over to a bench and pointed out the silver plaque at the top:

In memory of Spencer
"The stars moved through you"
1978–2016

"This is my brother's bench," he said. "We would come to the park all the time as kids, for sledding and baseball. I remember our mom took us to see Blondie one night."

I touched the plaque, my wrist heavy. I had walked through the park with Graham right after he proposed, too wired to sleep. Was that the last time I had been here at this late hour? Now, thinking back, the tremor in my body was not elation, but the aftershock of fear for what my future held.

"I wish I knew you'd gone through that," I said.

"Well, I guess we found each other again when we were meant to," Damon said.

He touched the damp spot between my shoulder blades and guided me to a lamppost nearby. The glimmer of closeness between us startled me, so unfamiliar I almost couldn't name it. I pressed my back into the cold cast iron and looked up at him, the moonlight spilling over us like milk. My heart was beating fast, charged by the sliver of night between our bodies, the empty park, the rain.

"So, is this where you're planning on killing me?" I said.

"It wasn't premeditated, but now that you mention it," Damon replied.

He traced the indents of my collarbone, wrapping his hand around the base of my throat.

"How would you do it?" I asked. "If you wanted to kill someone."

His grip tightened. I parted my lips, drowsy, defenseless, drugged.

"Hmm," he said. "Well, I might crush up a diamond and sprinkle it into their drink. So when swallowed, it would slice up their internal organs."

A police car drove past, soaking us in a lurid glow. He raked his fingers through my hair, cradling the back of my neck as if he might snap it.

"Or I could grind up cinnabar into a brilliant vermillion powder," he continued. "And then heat it up to release its deadly mercury vapor, which has killed many painters."

"How else?" I said. "Keep going . . ."

"I might bludgeon them with a bar of gold. And then melt it down afterward so it left no trace."

He softly thumbed the veins in my neck. I tilted my head back, inhaling loudly.

"And how would you kill me?" I asked.

"For you, just for you . . ." he said. "I would break off a branch of oxblood coral, the color of your hair, and puncture your jugular vein right here."

Oh, I moaned, my breath straining against the pressure of his palm.

"But I couldn't cause you pain without some pleasure first," he said.

"So what would you do . . . ?"

He traced a rivulet of rain down my chest. He stopped below my breasts, cradling the cage of my bones as if he could lift them out and set me free.

"Well, first I would kneel before you right here and kiss you gently, the back of your knees, the crease of your hip," he said. "And then I'd press my mouth between your thighs and lick you slowly until you were close . . . but I wouldn't let you come."

"No?"

"No. I'd bring you right to the edge, and just when you couldn't bear it anymore, just when you were begging and begging me to fuck you, that's the moment I would kill you."

It was all senseless words, but I was wrapping my leg around him, pulling him into me against my will. I pushed my spine hard into the lamppost, wanting to feel the cold crack of metal, anything other than the betrayal of my body.

"But that's never going to happen," he said.

"Why not?" I said.

"I solemnly gave you my word."

He abruptly pulled away, holding my gaze with restrained composure. I was breathing hard, his assertion of control unleashing a feral animal in me, and I grabbed his throat, his pulse beating against my hand. I wanted my nails to leave marks for other women to decode like hieroglyphics.

"Then what are we doing?" I said.

"I told you, I was just showing you the rocks."

This time, I kissed him.

I thought about what Sam said, how absence was protean, expanding or contracting with time, but I knew it wasn't true. Absence is fixed; it stays in the shape it arrived in. What ruins you is desire, how boundless it feels, how violently it waits.

11

It was a windy Thursday before Memorial Day weekend, and the city was emptying out. The blare of cabs crawling toward train stations and jitney stops, doormen dragging trolleys of beach bags to open trunks, a mass exodus that invaded the sidewalks and clogged the streets, like the swarms of gnats sieging the air. Even Sam was leaving, heading upstate to the house of a crime novelist friend. And I would be left alone.

I couldn't sleep and went to the park in the early morning. An agitated wind shook the trees, flinging petals into the air like confetti for a deserted party. Tulips were slumped as drunks, their heads lolling on the ground. I avoided the route I had taken with Damon, trying not to think about him, the grasping collusion of our bodies. I mindlessly circled the Bridle Path, passing a pink Post-it on a fence that said, "sleeping bat do not disturb," a cluster of lost keys dangling on a branch, a graveyard of flowers heaped beneath a tree paying tribute to a killed owl, until I reached the north side near the 97th Street transverse.

A line of NYPD cars was blocking the entrance. I paused, stopping before a barricade of yellow caution tape that warned DO NOT CROSS. The park had recently been put on high alert, following an uptick in brutal assaults: the rape of a female runner near Swan Lake, an actress bashed in the head with a rock and held at knifepoint. I wondered what violence another man had committed. Ducking beneath the tape, I scaled the wooded incline to the upper path of the reservoir and stopped at the iron railing.

A scuba team was descending a ladder into the sludgy water below, ringed in a yolky-brown film. They dove below the surface, one by one, through weeds and beer bottles and condom wrappers and tennis balls, while a family of ducks swam by in an unhurried procession. Confused, I turned to a nearby maintenance worker, sawing a venomous porcelain vine, and asked him what had happened.

"We got another floater," he said, clucking his tongue. "Happens like clockwork every springtime. Third one in the park this week."

"What's a floater?" I asked.

"Warm weather brings all the bodies to the surface. Speeds the decomposition, makes it more buoyant, and they rise right to the top."

I peered into the turbid depths and covered my mouth. I looked over my shoulder, but the city savagely pressed on. A clown with smeared makeup blew bubbles from a bench, two girls in tie-dye sports bras jogged past, a man mumbled to a large cockatoo perched on his shoulder.

No one noticed the scuba divers cradling a dead body in their arms. His face bloated and waterlogged, his eyelids peeled back in the cold morning light.

That afternoon, I met Isabel before her weekly bereavement support group at Mount Sinai so she could give me a copy of her keys. She had finally convinced me to work for her while she was out of town. It would be good for me, I concluded: the money, of course, and the immersion in her dynamic life. I didn't want to admit that guilt was a subliminal factor, a muffled voice in the back of my head. That I agreed as an act of contrition, a way to nullify any incremental breaches with Damon—and erase that they'd happened at all.

Isabel was waiting under the awning of the hospital in a long cream-colored dress, taking a drag from her vape pen.

"I hate being at the beach all alone." Isabel sighed, referring to the weekend ahead. "I'll be busy, of course, but when I come home to an empty house . . . sometimes I want to fill my pockets with rocks and walk right into the sea."

"You can always call me," I said. "Or better yet, call Damon and invite him over for a little late-night comfort."

"He's my date to a party on Saturday night," she said with an impish smile. "Even though I assume the fake wife will be out there, too."

Isabel offered me the vape. I shook my head, but she insisted, and I took a deep hit. As I handed it back to her, she said, "Do you think they sleep together?"

I exhaled with a loud cough. "He said they don't."

"When did he tell you that?" Isabel lowered her black sunglasses, studying my face with forensic intensity. "Do not lie to me, *Livia*. I'll be able to tell."

My lungs were burning. It was the first time she had used my full name—had I ever told her what it was? I couldn't remember now.

"I think the night we went to the play?" I hesitated. "Though I don't know if it's true."

By the time Isabel pulled me into the hospital, a glaucous haze had settled over my senses. We passed a march of white coats and wheeled gurneys, the stench of sickness souring the air, until we arrived at a harshly lit corridor. I paused before a faded print of Joan Mitchell's *Before, Again I*, a frenetic cyclone of color that seemed to burst from the antiseptic walls. I wondered how strong Damon's weed was.

"Here we are," Isabel announced, as if we had rolled up to a party.

In an adjacent doorway, a professional-looking woman in a thin scarf emerged and introduced herself as Dr. Meller. She gave Isabel a warm hug, then turned to me.

"I am so delighted you could join us," Dr. Meller said brightly. "I assure you, this is a safe, confidential space."

I hesitated. "Oh no, no, I'm sorry. I was just dropping her off—"

"Why not?" Isabel said. "You're already here. You might as well stay."

Isabel took my arm and guided me into the room. As I entered the clinical space, softened by a candle and a dying orchid, my throat closed. Four women of all ages were sitting in a circle, informally chatting as if this were a book club and not therapeutic purgatory. Isabel must have orchestrated my attendance, I realized; otherwise, she knew I'd never have agreed to come. It was meant as a compassionate gesture, but I felt undeserving to be here with her, an unworthy source of anyone's sympathy.

"We have a special guest with us today," Dr. Meller said. "A dear friend of Isabel's."

The women collectively smiled and nodded. Dr. Meller opened with a grounding meditation, guiding us to root our feet and center our breath. Then she asked each woman to give the logline of their widow status. There was a painter whose husband died of a pulmonary embolism. A professor whose wife died by suicide. A pediatrician whose partner died of an overdose. A yoga teacher whose husband died in a helicopter crash. Then they turned to me.

"Hi, I'm Liv," I said, kneading my palms.

You're not one of them, I told myself. *You're not a widow.* These women were in a universal class of grief that did not belong to me, one with a delineated path of stages and rituals and burial plots. I had no path, no point of longitude or latitude, for I did not know who I was meant to mourn: fiancé or ex-fiancé, lover or monster.

Isabel gently squeezed my arm. "Liv also lost her beloved this year."

"Yes, but he wasn't my husband yet," I said, though my voice sounded faraway. "He died two weeks before our wedding."

Their faces drooped in unison, as if they were wearing kabuki masks, performing the bereavement on my behalf.

"Would you like to share your grief journey with us?" Dr. Meller said.

I took a breath, but my throat was locked. How could I begin to chart the map of grief, an impassable maze that I could not find my way out of? Our final moments in the car, the bloodless resolve in his eyes as he lifted the gun to his head. It was not grief that ran through me, but a guilt I could not admit, a rage I could not name.

I shook my head. "No, that's okay."

The group went on to share their week. The painter, a wiry woman with a long silver braid, told a story about a man she met on a dating app. "So we finally get to his bedroom, and he unzips his pants and whips it out . . . and I just *stare*, in total shock. He starts to go limp, and I blurt out: 'I thought you were Jewish?' And he says: 'Only from the waist up!'"

The women laughed until they cried, and I pretended to do the same. Then Dr. Meller asked if any "memories or milestones" had come up recently. The room grew somber as each woman shared a private moment of pain. Isabel volunteered that next week would have been her forty-fifth wedding anniversary with Jack.

"And tell us, how will you commemorate this milestone?" Dr. Meller asked.

"I will sit on Jack's bench, the one he planted in the garden for me," she said, closing her eyes as if calling him in. "And I will be there with him, and with our daughter."

Isabel dabbed her eyes with a tissue as the women hummed in a chorus of empathy. And for the first time, beneath the unsparing hospital lights, I saw her real, unvarnished age.

"And, Liv, how about you?" Dr. Meller said. "It can be anything, even something small."

I took a shaky breath, looking down at my dirty sandals.

"Well, I guess this Sunday would be the one-year anniversary of our engagement," I said.

Dr. Meller paused. "Why don't you share that romantic story with us."

The room grew still. I hadn't realized the date until I said it aloud. I thought back to that surprise trip to New York, when Graham proposed at midnight in the empty foyer of the Carlyle. *I would do anything not to lose you*, he said on his knees. But if I told this story aloud, if I gave voice to it, then I feared it would become real again, and he would materialize in some molecular form. The reactivation of a curse. So I shook my head.

"That milestone must be very difficult for you," said Dr. Meller. "We all collect those 'firsts' like beads of grief—first birthday, first anniversary. Allow yourself to commemorate it gently, remember the joy it brought you, and then let it go."

I felt tears stick in my chest. Isabel took my hand in hers, her skin papery and smooth. How could I admit that I didn't want to remember, but to obliterate it completely? I had asked my heart to hold disparate truths, flame and shadow, and even if you can't know one without the other, they are irreconcilable. His love had seeped and spread like black mold, and even now, after his death, it poisoned my vessels and damaged my nerve endings. It warped the light through one eye so I could not fully see.

12

The rain began on Saturday, a cold, punishing rain. I wasted the entire day in Sam's apartment, too listless to get dressed, shopping online for things I would never buy, and finally forced myself out for a walk in the late evening.

The park was abandoned, a discarded mess of spring. The temperature dropped to forty-six degrees, a raw wind stripping the branches of any last blossoms. White petals plastered the benches and garbage cans, flecking the mud-encrusted paths like dead stars. When it got too dark, I walked back home. The fountains had been turned on in front of the Met, an operatic light show for no one, while a group of wasted teens half-ironically blasted Portishead's "Glory Box" on the steps.

Back at Sam's apartment, I changed into Graham's Led Zeppelin T-shirt, made myself come a few times, and drank half a bottle of red wine. Then I masochistically checked my phone. Already, Isabel had posted a photo of her and Damon at a beach party, geotagged at Orient Point. She looked goddess-like in a flowy yellow dress, her hand positioned on his lapel, their conjoined bodies outlined in a neon band of sunset. My stomach churned with envy, wishing I was with them. Or maybe not—I zoomed in on another face in the background. Rex was there, too, martini in hand, grinning at someone behind the camera as if directly at me. I shuddered and closed my phone.

I drank the other half of the bottle, my depression sinking heavier into my bones, into the marrow, until I felt as waterlogged and windbeaten as the weather. Near midnight, while I ate a handful of stale pistachios over the sink, my phone buzzed:

D: I'm coming back to the city tomorrow . . .
D: Shall I collect my orange pearl?

I dragged myself into bed in the maid's room. After waiting exactly thirty-eight minutes—the longest I could bear to withhold the gratification of an immediate response—I texted back:

L: Sorry I sold it on eBay

My phone rang, but I didn't pick up. I didn't want to imagine where Damon was calling from; I didn't want to hear the distant laughter of party guests, or the rush of salty air through his windows on the drive back to his farm. I turned off my phone and threw it into the bathtub.

I recalled what Dr. Meller had said, but saw no purpose in commemorating what had turned on me, like the cherry trees that waited all year to blossom, their beauty bursting only to fall and shrivel, a ring of rotted petals at their feet.

That night, I dreamt I was back in the park with Graham the night he proposed. We were circling the Bridle Path, pausing to kiss beneath the trees, when we came upon streamers of caution tape. I let go of his hand and dropped to my knees, crawling uphill through the tangled yellow maze in the mud. When I made it to the reservoir, Rex was waiting by the iron gate. *I know*, he said. *I know what you've done.* I looked into the brown water below. The scuba divers were dredging up a dead body, his face distorted, but his eyes blinked open and stared directly at me.

It was Graham. I screamed, but no one heard me. I crawled back through the yellow tape, but he was gone.

I woke up shivering badly, my chest drenched in cold sweat. "It's okay," I said aloud to no one. "You're okay."

But it was the Sunday of Memorial Day weekend. One year after I had said yes to a wedding, not knowing it would become a funeral.

I was still in the hospital when they buried him. I didn't see the shovel passed between hands, dirt falling from its concave edges, the crack of rock hitting the casket. I didn't see him returned to the earth. His once-warm body, the one that held me every night, turning to stone.

It was pouring when I got up, a grayness smeared over the city like wet ashes. I forced myself to put on jeans and head to Isabel's. The subway was a flood of putrid water and the trains were delayed. I waited on the empty platform, watching drowned rats bob and float down the tracks. I tried not to give this day any special weight, but it felt unbearably heavy, dread clinging to my skin like a leech.

After an hour, I finally made it downtown. I spent the day in the insulated fortress of Isabel's townhouse, wandering from floor to floor. I buried myself in her archives, organizing large boxes of letters and notes and articles. I drank a stream of Nespressos and ate a sleeve of fig crackers with some nice cheese. I slathered on an expensive face mask from her bathroom vanity that smelled of rotting pumpkins and reread most of her out-of-print novella. I briefly looked for the article on the accident, but it was nowhere to be found.

By the end of the day, the rain had stopped. I poured a glass of Vermentino from an open bottle in the fridge and roamed into the garden, sitting down on a soaked cushion. The sky looked drained, and the ground was strewn with little branches like broken fingers. After a second glass of wine, I decided my anxiety had been silly, unfounded even. My eye was still cloudy, Graham was still gone—but the worst already happened to me, hadn't it? I had made it through the abyss of day and emerged unharmed into night. There was no reason to be frightened anymore.

So I left. I walked across 11th Street to the East Side and took the train back uptown to Sam's apartment.

But as soon as I entered the lobby, I knew that I had been horribly wrong.

A small white package was sitting on the rickety console table, as if awaiting my return. Wasn't it a federal holiday? There were no mail deliveries today. I heard a slow creaking noise on the staircase and clutched my throat, fearing the horror that lurked on the dark landing, or behind the basement door. Like I was being watched. I took a small step closer.

The box was addressed to me—with no postmark and no return address.

I climbed the five flights to the apartment, my pulse hammering in my ears. I placed the package on the kitchen table and stepped back, staring at it. Maybe I was being ridiculous—it was probably some stupid insomnia-related purchase, a lip balm or a bra. But the box seemed to tick with the terrible silence of an unmarked bomb.

Finally, I retrieved a large bread knife from the counter and sliced it open. I unwound layer after layer of bubble wrap until I found the object at the center: a black velvet jewelry box. No, it was impossible, illogical even, I told myself, but my hands were trembling badly as I pried it open and gasped.

It was the ring. My lost engagement ring, glowing with mutant, alien light. An emerald vow of eternity, an emerald omen of death.

The room began to waver, my bad eye wobbling against my skull. I fumbled to the bathroom and cradled the toilet, vomiting again and again until I was heaving sour air. I slid down onto the moldy tile floor, winded and sweating, leaning against the tub. Everything around me seemed to hover and float in my field of vision, even my own hands. Maybe I was hallucinating? Maybe the ring was a trick of my damaged mind? Some psychic punishment for failing to assign meaning to this day? I was not meant to have any relic, no radiant symbol, no vestige of love. I clenched my fist around the ring until my knuckles turned white, until the veins popped, but still I could feel the faceted edges cutting into my flesh. When I opened my palm, the ring burned brighter, a dark green sea of fathomless depth.

Someone knew the truth. Why else would the ring have arrived on this day, without warning or postage stamp, without any indication it had been found?

I began to shiver, and the shivering dissolved into tears. They sprang from a place so tightly sealed that my throat burned as if I'd been screaming. I had chosen love that would ruin me, an inescapable anathema. Now that the ring had been unearthed, and the bones of the dead rattled, I feared what I was capable of.

I heard ringing in the other room. I hauled myself off the floor, bracing against the sink for support. In the mirror, I could barely look at myself, my scar an inflamed wire, broken blood vessels speckled around my eyes. I made my way to the kitchen and found my phone next to the open package.

For a moment, I couldn't breathe. And when I did, it was the first inhalation I'd taken in a long time.

13

I waited in the doorway for Damon to arrive. As I listened to the creak of the staircase, I thought of the blizzard years ago, the icy footprints we left on the steps before we reached the landing and went our separate ways. Nothing was going to happen this time, I told myself, nothing could happen. But I felt the sting of a second chance swelling in my chest like a hive of bees.

Damon emerged on the landing in a white T-shirt and jeans, holding a brown paper bag.

"Looks like someone had a rough day," Damon said. "Or maybe a rough weekend."

"Unfortunately not the kind I usually like," I said.

He came closer, towering over me in my bare feet. I wanted to touch his soft, full mouth, the silver dust of scruff on his jaw, but instead I flicked the rim of his hat.

"Are you going to let me in, or should we just stand in the hallway?" he said.

I hesitated, realizing the ring was left out on the table. How could I possibly explain its uncanny arrival, like a delivery from the afterlife? I didn't even understand it myself.

"I think I might need some air first," I said.

"Then let's find you some," he said, and dashed up the tattered staircase. I followed him, yelling out that there was no roof, but when he reached the top and pushed through a door marked ALARM WILL SOUND, an ultraviolet night unrolled before us like a map. It was a black tar field of rusted chairs and tangled wires. We walked close to the edge and scanned the skyline: billowing chimneys, wooden water towers, stars spilled like flakes of salt. I wanted all that haunted me to dissolve like day into night, and it was frightening how much I relied on Damon for this sense of transfiguration.

"How's this for a bit of air?" Damon said.

"Better," I said, taking a deep breath. "Much, much better."

I wanted him to take me into his arms, to hold me, but he was already wandering over to the barricade that sectioned off the adjoining roof. He scaled the tall hedge and jumped down, so I could no longer see him.

"You're in for a surprise," he called out. "I'm waiting for you . . ."

Reluctantly, I climbed over, the spindly branches scraping my legs, and came down the other side. My breath caught when I saw it: a swimming pool. A gleaming slice of topaz, rippling beneath a sickle moon. It seemed like a mirage, a surreal image in an oneiric sequence: a body in the reservoir, my ring dug up from a watery grave. How could I make sense of any of this? How could I wring a smooth narrative out of the chaos of the day, of the years?

Damon was sitting at the far end of the pool and called me over to join him.

"Just don't ask me to skinny-dip," I said.

"I would never make you do something so unimaginative," he said.

I sat down on the cool Moroccan tiles beside him.

"What would you make me do, then?" I said.

"I can think of a few imaginative ideas."

I dipped my feet into the water. I wanted to sink below the surface, into the blue cave of light, and emerge pure again, clean and untarnished. From the paper bag, Damon took out a crate of wild strawberries from his farm and a bottle of pét-nat. He filled a plastic cup and handed it to me. The wine fizzed on my tongue and tasted of blood oranges.

"Do you want to tell me what happened tonight?" he said.

I sat back on my hands, watching my legs glide underwater like detached ghosts.

"I keep thinking how memories can turn on you," I said finally.

"How do you mean?"

"How a moment can feel joyous at the time, but then you look back later, through a different lens, and the memory of it seems warped and ruined," I said. "Maybe I'm just in a fatalistic mood, I don't know. But how can you trust your own experience of anything again?"

I pulled my legs out of the pool, goose-bumped and wet, and hugged them to my chest.

"I'll tell you a little story," Damon began. "Once, when I was young and needed cash quickly, I bought a massive Paraíba tourmaline from this criminal in Brazil. Have you ever seen one?"

I shook my head. He traced the beads of water on my knees, and my legs unfurled into his lap.

"The rarest ones are electric blue, Windex blue, the color of blue fire—they get their color from copper, formed by volcanic heat. But I bought this stone rough, a chalky white. In order to resell it, I needed to transform the stone into the desired color by treating it with heat. But each one is mysterious—you can never predict its secret color from rock to rock."

He ran his fingers up and down my legs, my muscles softening.

"So I put the stone over an open flame, and it doesn't turn blue. I turned up the heat a little more—still not blue. If I turned it up any higher, there was a risk that its invisible fractures would cause the stone to crack and shatter. And then I would be really fucked."

"So what did you do?" I said.

"I blasted the heat as far as it would go, and finally the stone turned the most otherworldly blue I've ever seen."

I lay back on the cool tile, the night enfolding me like a net. Damon rested on his elbow, his face so close to mine I could feel his warm breath on my neck.

"What am I supposed to make of this analogy?" I asked.

"Well, my point is that love can leave you shattered, or it can transform into the most luminous thing. But you don't know until you've taken the risk."

"Would you do it again?"

"Fuck no, I've never cooked a stone since." He laughed. "But I'll tell you a little secret." I said *yes, tell me*, as his hand trailed up my inner thighs, lingering at the frayed edge of my denim shorts.

"It's the second color you miss when it's heated, the one that sits right below the surface. That you only notice after it's gone," he said. "The color that carries the flame forward."

I looked up at him, the half-lit buildings bowing over us like branches, my hips rising to meet his hand. He lifted my shirt and kissed my breasts, my stomach, unzipping my shorts with his teeth. He slid them off and threw them into the pool. His mouth hovered over me, dampening the inside of my thighs, until finally he pulled my thong aside, his tongue a match, striking. I covered my eyes, afraid to see, as the night poured through my veins like a dark river.

"I thought you told me we would never do this," I said, gripping his hand.

"Then we'll pretend it doesn't count."

I drew him up, and he slid himself inside me, slowly at first, wanting me to know the punishing edge, to make me beg for more, until there was nothing left to give. My body felt as weightless and submerged as the bottom of the pool, my eyes leaking not from sadness but an overflowing that could not be contained. He held my wrists above my head, pinning me to the tile, and when he said into my mouth *come for me, now,* I was pulled down by an undertow, a tidal wave cresting through me, and I did.

When it was over, he lay down beside me, his arm stretched over my chest. We stared up at the sky spread thinly above us, catching our breath. Then we turned to each other. The stars were watching us coldly, unblinking, as if they had tried to prevent this from happening, and now there was nothing left to be done.

After he left, I sat dazed at the kitchen table with a blanket around me. I had no proof of what had happened except the empty aftermath of my body.

I took out the ring and held it there, cradling it in my palm like a vengeful talisman, like a broken wing, until the pale light of morning seeped in through the cracked window.

14

We slept together through the first weeks of June.

I continued to work at Isabel's during the day, but my nights were spent with Damon. Sam stayed in Rhinebeck, so I had the apartment to myself. Damon would drop by earlier than expected, bearing cartons of stone fruit like plums and peaches and cherries, and though my hair was still damp from the shower, he'd hastily unwrap my towel and press me against the foyer wall or the kitchen table, our irrepressible urgency leaving no room for pause. It was sweltering that week; we couldn't get the mildewed air conditioner to blow anything but swampy air, and afterward we'd emerge beneath the dome of evening, salt-slicked and gorged with heat. He would never let me wear underwear. We'd share spaghetti alle vongole outside at a little Italian place, or we'd sit on an old beach towel near the Greywacke Arch, and I would listen to him muse about the lore and lure of stones.

One night, as we lay behind the Met Museum at sundown, dipping tart apple slices into cinnamon honey from his farm while I drank chilled cups of Montrachet, Damon told me a story about illegally diving for coral.

"This coral hunter took me on an expedition once, to an

underwater cave off the coast of Corsica," Damon was saying. "It was like diving into a lush red forest, coral branching from the walls and the ceilings."

"So did you end up smuggling any?" I asked, half joking.

"Oh yeah, of course," Damon replied seriously. "The black market for coral is like cocaine there."

"Oh, come on." I laughed. "How would you even do it?"

"Lots of ways. You can paint it black with lacquer to conceal its color, or you can sew it into the hem of your blazer or jeans." He traced my collarbone with a blade of grass. "When I go to Italy this summer, I'll smuggle some just for you."

I looked away. The sun struck the sloped wall of the Met, torching the glass with molten light. I tried to dismiss the stark intrusion of the future, but a wave of anguish rolled through me. I knew Damon was traveling to Isabel's rented villa in August, and I would be left behind in the city. Again.

"Maybe you'll even be invited," he added.

"Right, you and me in Italy with Isabel?" I said, giving him a disbelieving look. "One of us would surely not make it out of the trip alive."

"I'd say that sacrifice would definitely be you."

He kissed my shoulder, biting my neck with vampiric hunger. These were the languid nights I came to long for, two forbidden lovers on the cusp of summer. The city flipping our fate like a tarot card, the razor's edge between desire and doom. I lay my head on his chest and touched the small tattoo etched above his heart. It resembled a jeweled brooch of a beetle.

"When did you get this?" I asked.

"The year my brother died," Damon said, stroking my hair. "It's a winged scarab."

I traced its curved mythical body, its elongated, feathered bird wings.

"It was inspired by the amulet found in King Tut's tomb,"

he said. "When they opened it up, he was wearing this mysterious scarab on his breastplate, carved from a celestial green-gold gem. They discovered it was made of glass, created by a meteor collision in the Libyan Desert."

"What was it meant to symbolize?" I asked.

He cupped my hand over his own beating heart, as if it belonged to me.

"It was part of their burial process, a symbol of rebirth. They'd place the scarab right here above the heart, facing upward, as protection during the afterlife," he said. "A way of eternally linking the earth to the sky, and the living to the dead."

After those evenings, we'd stumble back to the apartment and have sex for hours, until one or two in the morning. I was in a trance, a somnambulist possessed by some ungovernable force. I would do whatever he wanted. I would crawl across the floor, I would come as many times as he granted permission, I would let him loop his belt around my wrists, my ankles, until I was bloodless and boneless, begging for more. I would tell him that he owned me because I wanted it to be true.

He never stayed. When we were finished, I would drag myself to the bathroom in a sedative haze, and by the time I emerged, he'd be holding his shoes in his hand. I didn't want to know what this meant, if he was leaving to slip into another woman's bed.

One night, while we were naked before an open window, my hands braced against the glass, my phone rang. I glanced at the screen on the side table: it was Isabel, on FaceTime.

"Fuck!" I said, panicking. "Do you think she can see us?"

"Through the phone, or through the window?"

I elbowed him, and he slipped out of me from behind.

"You can't get it," he said. "Are you out of your fucking mind?"

"I can't *not* get it. She'll know!" I grabbed a ratty leopard blanket and wrapped it around my flushed chest, gesturing for him to get out of the frame as I picked up.

"Oh, Liv, I thought you might be out on a date," Isabel purred into the screen.

"No, alone as always," I said, sitting down on the couch.

"You should have been out here with me tonight. I took Rex as my plus-one to this fabulous party."

"Rex is still out there?" I asked skeptically.

"Yes, and surprisingly quite the gentleman—he picked me up and brought me sunflowers, my favorite," she said dreamily. "My friends were in shock I wasn't with Damon."

"And what did you tell them?"

"Let them think I have dueling suitors, why not?" She paused. "Speaking of, have you seen *him* yet?"

She squinted at me as if climbing through the screen. I tried not to look at Damon against the windowsill, smugly flipping through a Hopper book, his aroused silhouette limned by the streetlights.

I coughed a little. "I assumed he was out east with you?"

"No, Damon is back in New York. I just spoke with him earlier this evening."

Finally, I glared at him. The book slipped from his hands and landed with a thud.

"Livia, is someone there?" she asked.

"No, sorry, I just left the window open," I said.

"I'll call him and tell him to take you out," she said. "He knows how lonely you are."

After I hung up, Damon sat down on the arm of the couch. I felt irrationally incensed at him for putting me in this position, even if I was an active and willing participant.

"I don't trust that Rex guy," Damon said. "I think he's using Isabel for something."

"Isn't that what people say about you?"

I dug my heel hard into his thigh, and he kneaded the arch of my foot.

"Come on, do you trust him? He just seems so opportunistic, in a shady sort of way."

But I didn't want to think about Rex, not now, not during our time together. The only nights when my encroaching past seemed to retreat into the distance, the only hours I felt impaled not by fear but by desire.

"Or maybe you're just jealous," I said.

"Does that turn you on?" He slipped his hand beneath the blanket. I was so wet it was almost distressing. "I know how *loooonely* you are," he mimicked.

"It's not funny," I said. "She could have easily found out you were here."

"Do you want to stop? Just say the word and we will."

"Yes, I think we should stop," I said, dropping the blanket and crawling over to him.

"No one is forcing you to do anything you don't want to do," he said.

"You force me to do things all the time."

I straddled his hips and slid him inside me, pulled by some higher gravitational force. He hooked his fingers around my teeth and covered my mouth, my breath straining, and as I rocked against the sharp plane of his hips, my vision went dark as if dragged beneath the tide, swallowed so deep below the surface that my body was wrung of air. When he released his hand, it felt like a resurfacing, a brief gasp of air and light, and then he made me come again.

I smacked his chest, and he clasped my wrist, twisting my arm behind my back so I couldn't smack him again.

"I hate you," I said.

"Don't be mad, or I'll have to punish you," he said.

"Fucking you is punishment enough."

He stood up and pulled on his boxers from the floor. I stayed on the couch, my head heavy against the arm, drowsily watching him as he got dressed.

"Tomorrow morning," he said. "Be ready, and bring the orange pearl."

He kissed my shoulder and carried his shoes to the door. I wondered why he never put them on in the apartment. By slipping out without a sound, it was as if he was never here at all.

The next morning, Damon was waiting in front of my building in a beat-up vintage Mustang. It was scorching out, the sun burning without any cover, and I was wearing hot orange shorts and a white tank. He opened the door and said, "Jump in, Red."

"Where are you taking me?" I said, putting my feet up on the dashboard.

"On a little adventure, of course," he said, and we sped off. A warm cross-breeze flooded in as we sped down the FDR and "Tangled Up in Blue" played on an old cassette. Damon sang the line *wondering if she'd changed at all or if her hair was still red* over the drone of traffic, twisting a lock of my hair. As we soared across the Brooklyn Bridge, an unfamiliar freedom spread through my chest, that fugitive flush of summer I had lost long ago. Damon found a parking spot, and we walked down to the waterfront, the steel web of bridge cables glinting in the sun. Waiting by a bench was a boisterous man in Hawaiian shorts and white crocs, his mass of curly hair tied back in a bun. He pulled Damon into a hug with a raspy laugh.

"Yo yo yo, my brother!" he said. "You hang me out to dry, motherfucker. I'm on the line for fifty fuckin' grand, and I got these Honduran guys banging down my door!"

"This is my pearl dealer, Dimitri," Damon said cooly. "And his partner in crime."

A little girl in a sequined crop top and winged eyeliner shot me a dubious look as she sipped a juice box.

"I've got all *au naturel* right here. Conch, clams, sea snails, oysters—you name it," Dimitri announced. "I get to deal with the fuckin' loco fishermen so this schmuck doesn't have to."

Dimitri unzipped a pink backpack and removed a few plastic tackle boxes. Inside were hundreds of wild pearls, creamy and candy-colored, shaped like gumballs and icicles, teardrops and moons. He dropped a cratered purple pearl into my hand, the size of a black plum.

"This guy FedExed me this thing, fifty-five carats," Dimitri said, "and then next day I learn he's dead!"

I held the pearl between my fingers like a key, unlocking a world amplified by color, encoded with symbols. I was grateful for access to this passage, like the transit of a planet passing between a star and earth. Yet it petrified me, too, how this sphere did not feel real; and soon, I could be violently shaken awake to find that it was not even a dream, but on the other side of the door lay a nightmare.

"You want to keep yours or this one?" Dimitri said. "Don't play three-card monte with me."

I took the melo melo pearl out of my bag and handed it to Damon. As he arranged it beside the smaller pearls, studying the composition, he mindlessly ran his fingers up and down the back of my arm.

"So this your girlfriend?" the little girl asked, crumpling her juice box. "What's the fucking deal?"

"Yeah, what's up with you two lovebirds?" Dimitri chimed in.

"I fell in love with her years ago when she was my neighbor." Damon passed me an affectionate smile. "But alas, she made a huge mistake."

I shook my head, but I was smiling, too, as though I had forgotten all the shadows hiding beneath it.

That night was our last together in the city. Isabel had finally invited me to the North Fork for the weekend, so my time with Damon had come to an end. We were standing in the dim kitchen after dinner; I was pouring glasses of chilled sparkling water while Damon admired Sam's unfinished collages spread out on the table.

"Whose ring is this?" he asked, and I turned around.

Damon was holding my engagement ring, and my chest tightened. I had stashed the velvet box next to Sam's medications, hoping to forget it was there.

I told him what it was, how I had lost it the night of the accident.

"It was never properly sized," I said. "So I assumed it slipped off my finger."

He held the ring up to the light, studying its clarity and cut with spectroscopic precision. A numb shock spread through my center as he examined it like a precious artifact, cradling my past in his hands.

"And someone found it?" he said. "But how did they know it was yours?"

I shook my head, unable to speak. I had never shared any details of the accident with him, preferring to remain in our narcotic haze of pleasure, as if this would deter any external disturbance. How could I explain the trajectory of the ring? The hidden malice that its mystifying presence now posed? That it wasn't just a ring, but a presage of danger.

Damon came over, enfolding me in his arms. I buried my face in his neck, breathing in his comforting scent of sweat and smoke.

"Talk to me," he said into my hair. "Tell me what's wrong."

But I didn't want to talk. I wanted to mute my resounding fear. I kissed him hungrily, undoing his belt as I pushed him into the maid's room. We had never fucked in there before. In bed, he knelt upright on the thin mattress, my legs wrapped around his shoulders, his back, the open shape between us creating a foreign distance. He was moving inside me slower than usual, more cautiously, as if I was a delicate object he could easily crack. But that was what I wanted him to do, to dissolve my edges, to split me open from the inside. *I want you to break me,* I heard myself say. His thumbs dug sharply into the grooves of my pelvis, lifting me upward. I felt more exposed than I'd ever been; not my body itself, my pale breasts splayed in the blue shadows, but my relation to the room we were in. The rusted box spring squeaking shrilly, the cracked yellow walls of my nights spent trapped by grief. Damon could come and go anytime, he existed outside of its confines: there was a woman, a farm somewhere, days made of shimmering stones. But I was still here, months after I'd first arrived, and it no longer felt like a cocoon but a prison of my own making.

I tried to turn over, but he stopped me, firmly pressing down on my breastbone.

"Liv, look at me," he said.

I turned my cheek toward the wall, ashamed. He leaned down on my chest so I could feel him beating wildly inside me.

Then he said into my ear, "Let me feel close to you."

"Don't." I shook my head. "Everyone who feels close to me dies."

Tears were slipping sideways from my eyes. I didn't know what was happening to me; I was dissolving but in the wrong direction.

"I'll take my chances, then."

He flipped me onto my stomach, threading his arm around my neck. He was so deep inside me, breaking down a hidden wall, and I kept saying harder and harder, pushing my face into the pillow, leaving a wet bloom of pain. My throat was making guttural sounds, my eyes leaking tears, and when he pulled my hips back and asked if he could come inside me, I was saying *yes, yes, I want you to*, while all the fear seemed to exit my body, lift away from my center, leaving me brimming, breathless, full.

We lay there for a long time, unmoving. I felt a perverse satisfaction, like I had won something I didn't know I wanted. He had always pulled out in the past.

"I could stay like this forever," Damon murmured into my neck.

Eventually, I turned back over. He rested his head on my chest, his lashes fluttering against my breast. But as our breathing slowed, an ache crept in between the spaces of my ribs. I felt close to him in a way I had not foreseen, our accrued hours together threading me like a needle. To him, I was merely a passing diversion, but to me, he had become something else: I was counting on him, not for love, but to carve out an opening for light to pass through.

I tried to get up from the bed, wanting to break the feeling, but he wrapped his arms around me, and I closed my eyes.

When we awoke, I was disoriented. We had never fallen asleep together, and for a minute I dreamt we were somewhere else, somewhere beautiful. But then the yellow walls came back into view, my eyes slowly reacclimating to the grim textures of my life. Damon buried his scratchy chin under my arm before forcing himself to sit up.

"When do you go back to the farm?" I said.

"I'll probably head out tomorrow," Damon said. "June is strawberry season. I'll make jams and tarts and pies, and lick the ripe red juice off your ripe red body."

"Right, with everyone else out there, too?"

He turned his back to me. "We'll find a way. I'm not worried."

He slipped on his boxers from the floor, and I knew acutely this wasn't true. My throat felt dry, a dull pounding between my ears.

"So, what time are you picking me up tomorrow?" I asked.

"I don't know yet." He distractedly searched for his pants. "I have to drive to the workshop to pick up some pieces first, so you're better off not relying on me for a ride."

I pulled on a T-shirt from the floor, not wanting to be naked. I knew that I should act indifferent, leave our last few weeks alone; let it exist as a thing unto itself, an interlude, a brief encounter. But then he would walk out of here into another life, while I would be left staring at the mold-stained ceiling.

"You're not driving up alone," I said flatly.

I saw the muscles tense in his back. He was still turned away, buckling his belt.

"Let's not get into this now," he said.

"It's a simple question," I pressed him. "Why can't you just admit it?"

"Liv, don't do this," he said, whipping around. "It's three in the fucking morning, okay?"

I flinched. Something about his tone sent me reeling back to those manic nights with Graham. His voice pitched to an unnatural register, jealous rage undercut with a hint of violence. For the first time, I looked at Damon as if he were a man capable of cruelty, as most men are, and once this thought slipped in, it colored everything.

Damon must have read it on my face, and he immediately softened.

"Look, she wasn't supposed to come out with me this weekend." He sighed, his shoulders drooping with defeat. "She was set to visit her sister on Nantucket but then changed her mind for some reason."

I wondered if Caroline had adjusted her plans in response to Damon's nightly absence. I couldn't wait to report this discovery to Isabel—but then realized I couldn't, and felt a little sick.

"Then it sounds like you have a romantic weekend ahead, harvesting all your strawberries together," I said.

"Oh, come on, you know there's nothing romantic about it."

I flashed a vicious smile. "I wouldn't know, actually. I've never slept in the same bed with a man who didn't want to fuck me."

His face hardened, this time calcified with hurt. And beneath it, a primal flicker of defense—defensive of her. He abruptly left the room to collect the rest of his clothes. The throbbing in my head had traveled to my eyes, and I pressed my fists into my temples. I was being ridiculous, acting out like a child, goading him to feel something for me after all these months when I had felt nothing. The problem was that now I genuinely did.

Damon returned, pausing in the doorway for an agonized moment. He looked as if he wanted to share something that might make it all better.

"My T-shirt," he said finally.

"What?"

He gestured to the shirt I had pulled on from the floor. As I took it off, everything he had filled me with came flooding out, until the only thing left was my own drenching shame. I handed it back and covered my chest with my arms, sitting on the edge of the bed.

"You know how I feel about you," he said softly.

Then, holding his shoes in his hand, he left. The worst part of an affair, I thought, is hearing the same door shut on the way out.

15

That morning, I took the Jitney to the farthest end of the North Fork. I spent the three-hour ride trying to a read a slim Shirley Hazzard novel about a girl in Italy, but as I moved from one dense sentence to another, my mind kept drifting back to last night. I snapped my legs together, sore and depleted, pressing my forehead against the tinted window until the city gave way to an unclouded stretch of sea and sky.

I was nervous to see Isabel. While these past few weeks existed in a cloistered space, I was anxious she would read the evidence on my face like a map. I thought about preparing a set of answers—if I had seen Damon, and when specifically—but it seemed more dishonest to devise a false narrative in advance. And meanwhile, as I sat on an overcrowded bus, Damon was probably driving with the windows down, talking about gems and bulbs to his wife in the passenger seat. I wondered if they listened to the same Dylan cassette, or if she asked him what he did last night.

When I got off at the Orient stop, Isabel was waiting beside an old red Jeep convertible. She was in white shorts and a white T-shirt, her skin balmy with sun and hair rippling in strawberry waves beneath a straw hat. As soon as I inhaled her beachy scent, something shifted within me, the needle of a compass realigning north, pulling my loyalty toward her and away from Damon. She threw my duffel into the back seat and we sped off.

"This is my first time out of the city since I came back," I said, realizing it had been seven months since I'd left LA. "I forgot anywhere else existed."

I breathed in the clean marine air as we turned onto a road that paralleled the bay.

"Now, I want you to lower your expectations, Liv. This isn't wild on the Hamptons, thank god," she said. "We got our beach shack back when this place was still a bunch of writers and farmers and fishermen. Even though these yuppie crypto bros are trying to ruin it, like everything else."

"I'm just grateful for a scene change," I said. "And a sea change."

I adjusted my eyes as we drove past stretches of farms and vineyards, giving way to rocky inlets and lobster shacks, faded signs with names like Potato Beach, Plum Island, Bug Lighthouse. We turned into a tiny hamlet and drove down a long pebbly road that ended in a cloudburst of white hydrangeas, and above it, an elevated wood-shingled house looming over the waveless bay. Inside, the living room was airy and awash in sea-salted light, piles of sun-bleached books and ceramic jars of sunflowers tipping their heads toward the water. In the open kitchen, we found her energetic housekeeper Julio stirring bowls of melted dark chocolate while *Astral Weeks* played over the speakers.

"We're making a torta caprese," Julio exclaimed. "It's Señor Damon's favorite."

"Except this time, we're sprinkling *un poquito* of arsenic in it," Isabel said.

I swallowed hard. "I didn't know he was coming over?"

"Liv, are you insane?" she said, taking out her phone. "He is *ghosting* me, the fucker."

Isabel showed me the text in question: a photo of Damon's tan hand holding a crate of plump strawberries in the sun. Below it, the caption: *ripe to bursting.*

"It began when he promised to bring me strawberries," Isabel said. "So I wrote back: '*ripeness wants to be ravished.*' Which is from a line from the same poem he referenced."

"That sounds flirtatious to me," I said—because it did.

"But here's where it takes a turn. He was supposed to come over for dinner on Memorial Day, but then he bailed at the last minute and went to the city instead. I haven't seen him since."

That was after we had slept together, my body pressed against the edge of the pool, the edge of the skyline. Maybe I was a horrible person.

"So when I didn't hear back, I texted him: 'When can I collect my spoils?' And you know what he responded?" She paused dramatically, working up her fury. "He wrote back: 'Maybe you should grow your own.' Can you believe that? I wanted to tell him to grow his own fucking pair!"

Julio snapped his fingers, and I joined in. While I pretended to be outraged on Isabel's behalf, I was rattled for a different reason. The suggestive tenor of their text banter closely resembled my exchanges with him; and while it lacked our direct erotic charge, it revealed that his intimate shorthand, his poetic tease of inflection, was not exclusive to me.

"But, Livia, usually he calls or texts every day," Isabel said, forlornly holding her phone to her chest. "And this week something was off. What did he say when you saw him?"

I blanched, surprised that Damon had disclosed we met—unless, of course, Isabel was testing me.

"He didn't mention anything," I said quickly. "But I only saw him briefly."

Her eyes narrowed into stainless slits, performing a silent computation. It wasn't about the strawberries, of course. Isabel had sensed an energetic imbalance, a drift in the flickering beam of Damon's attention. Perhaps, too, she had intuited a minor shift in our own dynamic. Aside from that one FaceTime, we had barely spoken at night like we used to. I realized, with a start, that this was the reason Isabel had summoned me to the North Fork: to use me as bait, as a lure, to test the vagaries of his behavior. I existed only as a conduit to him, like the Sound stretching beyond the window, a small tidal estuary carrying water into a more important ocean.

But then there was Damon, prodding her, promising her another sort of seed, the tempting fruits of his labor. In bed with him, I stupidly believed we had created a sanctified bond; yet I had again underestimated that their relationship, bound by some indeterminate force, existed not only outside of me but also without me.

"You know, I ran into her last week. The fake wife," Isabel said, raising one thin eyebrow. "And she invited me over for dinner at the farm tomorrow night."

"This is why we are baking a cake!" Julio clapped.

"Does Damon know that she invited you?" I asked.

"No, but he's about to find out," Isabel said. "He called to tell me he was driving back up, with *her*, this morning."

I gritted my teeth, suppressing a surge of jealousy with no place to land. In a way, I was no different than Isabel, hanging on by a thread of longing, one that had frayed overnight.

"Technically he's not ghosting you if he called this morning," I commented.

Isabel glanced up, registering the slight edge in my voice. "I mean *psychically*, he's slipped from my grasp," she said, her eyes flashing. "Which is why I've devised a brilliant plan for tonight. Now I need you to do your part."

That night, we went to an art opening in Mattituck. The party was housed in a restored barn on the edge of a rambling vineyard. The sky was a pale sepia, soaking the vines in rusted light beyond the open doors. We cut through the room, accepting cold glasses of blush-tinted wine. It was a laid-back crowd; women were wearing slouchy pants, and men flaunted a sleeve of tattoos, or a baby, or both. Isabel elbowed me in the ribs, pointing her chin in the direction of the bar. Rex was standing beside a display of wine, talking to the featured painter—known for her sapphic portraits of nude women in the wilderness—who had collaborated on the wine label.

"He does look rather dashing from afar, doesn't he, in a silver fox sort of way?" Isabel said approvingly. "He has a bit of Jeremy Irons in *Damage* vibe."

"I'm not sure that's a positive comp," I said. "But I can see the appeal."

Isabel had informed me that Rex would be here—his new publication was cosponsoring the party—which was part of her master plan. I had tried to surgically excise him from my consciousness these past few weeks, write him off as a minor character. But as Rex waved to us now, gesturing he'd be over soon, the back of my neck prickled. Even from afar, his air of malice seemed to percolate like nerve gas through the room.

"Text Damon *now*," Isabel said, pinching my arm. "We can't wait until the party is over."

"Are we sure it's not more effective if you send it?" I pleaded.

"Livia, do *not* renege on your part of the plan—I thought I could rely on you."

I nodded, swallowing my faint humiliation. Isabel had contrived a plan for Damon to see her in the company of Rex and tasked me with playing the indirect messenger. It felt degrading to initiate contact, to relinquish my last shred of dignity—I hadn't heard from Damon at all today, not since he slipped out of my bed. But my hands were tied.

I snapped a photo of Isabel—her waist alluringly angled, her leg bent beneath her citrine dress—and begrudgingly texted it to him.

"Let me see exactly what you sent him," she said.

As she reached for my phone, I glanced at Damon's last text above the photo—it was unspeakably dirty. Oh god, I thought, praying she wouldn't scroll up, but then we heard:

"Isabella, Duchessa of the North Fork!" Rex came bounding over, kissing Isabel on the cheek. "What did we do to deserve your royal appearance?"

"Nothing that you won't pay for later," Isabel flirted back.

"This place is a little too Walden Pond, a little wrong Egg of Gatsby, if you ask me," said Rex out of the side of his mouth. "But when on Long Island, as they say . . ."

"Then why aren't you in the Cotswolds?" I said. "Too Evelyn Waugh for you?"

Rex waggled his eyebrows. He was wearing salmon-colored pants with a seersucker blazer, as if he had just stepped off a yacht in Antibes after robbing everyone on it.

"And how is our young houseguest?" Rex said. "Is she misbehaving herself already?"

"No grievances yet," Isabel said. "But I'll send her over to you if she does."

"Oh, please do. We can put her to work on the farm—lots of manual labor, lots of filthy emus running amok," he said. "Though I must say the wine cellar is quite nice."

"And whose house are you taking advantage of?" I asked.

"An old pal, this character actor, you'd know him—the son of that famous crime writer," Rex said, and we both nodded.

"So when he's off shooting, he lets me crash if I'm in need of a little R&R with a side of Lyme disease."

I was the first to see Damon walking into the party. We met eyes, his mouth parting in a way that made my face overheat. He looked aggravatingly handsome, in a faded denim shirt and worn boat shoes, soil streaked on his shorts from the farm. It didn't seem possible that only last night I had cried in his arms, that his come had trickled down my thighs. I took a large mouthful of wine. It tasted like sour strawberries.

"I didn't know you'd be here," Isabel said, her voice high with feigned surprise.

"You know me," Damon said as he approached. "I'm full of twists and turns."

"Did you see who I finally dragged up from the city?" she said.

Damon nodded mutely in my direction. But his attention abruptly shifted as Isabel unsubtly rested her hand on Rex's arm.

"I see you decided to stay on our side of the Sound," Damon said.

"You didn't know my new publication is cosponsoring this party?" Rex said.

"I'm sorry, what does that mean?" said Damon, his voice cut with derision.

"We're breaking the parochial rules, as it were. Like a civilized jet-setting rag in your inbox, but with investigative stories that will blow the whistle on uncomfortable modern truths," Rex said. "About tech, media, corporate malfeasance, bad men, that sort of thing."

Isabel flicked her eyes at me, and I could tell she was eager to fuel the tension.

"Maybe you should write a piece on Damon's work," Isabel offered.

"Yeah, he fits the subgenre of bad men," I said.

Rex grinned at me pointedly. "You know a thing or two about them, Liv, don't you?"

There was a slight pause, and I felt the wine rushing to my head.

"But isn't that what makes her so interesting?" Damon said.

I finally glanced at him, and he passed me a coded smile. I tried to keep my face still but it was feverish, a thermostat turned up inside my body. It wasn't until this moment of recognition, our secret contained within open air, that I saw my own unmooring. I didn't feel guilt or regret then. Instead, I felt the weather of desire erupt like lightning, the silent crack of heat and light, and not till later, from a distance, would the thunder come.

Then Damon gave someone a half-hearted wave. My throat closed as I saw Caroline walking toward us, dressed in linen pants and a striped cardigan, her hair tied back.

"I didn't know you were coming, too." Isabel smiled with forced politeness.

"I used to work with the artist when I was still in the gallery world," Caroline said. "I'm thrilled she's having her due after being overshadowed by her husband's work for years."

"Not to mention, his indiscreet affairs with young models," Rex added.

"Which is probably why she's happily partnered with a woman now," Caroline said.

"That'll do it," Isabel said. "We'd all be so much happier, wouldn't we?"

Caroline laughed and introduced herself to Rex. Then her eyes carefully landed on me.

"That's such a cute . . ." She paused, waving her hand. "What do you call that? A jumper?"

I self-consciously looked down at my white one-piece with its low neckline and tie around my waist. "I think it's a romper," I said.

"Or a playsuit back in my day," Isabel chimed in.

"Whatever the proper nomenclature, the girl wears it quite ravishingly," Rex said.

Caroline touched Damon's arm and took a sip from his water glass as if they naturally shared everything. I tried not to stare at them, instead focusing on a painting depicting two voluptuous naked women pointing rifles at an erect python. I suddenly hated Damon, with an almost pleasurable spite that throbbed between my sore hips.

"Can I bring anything tomorrow night?" Isabel asked.

"What's tomorrow night?" Damon gave her a confused look.

"Didn't I tell you? I invited Isabel over for dinner," Caroline said, glancing at her. "You're welcome to bring your assistant as well."

Is that what he calls me, I thought. I glared at Damon, but he was staring into his glass. I wondered if he had described me like that—or did it come from Isabel? I gulped my wine, stoking my spite like a cut rinsed with salt water.

"Don't look so crestfallen, Damon. I'm making your favorite dessert," Isabel said.

"I'm already seething with jealousy," Rex said. "You've never made *my* favorite dessert."

"Then you can be my date, if only to taste how good it is," Isabel said with a kittenish smile. "And besides, we can't let Damon be the only fragile male ego at the table."

Everyone wandered off to see the paintings. I opted to get another drink, not wanting to subject myself further to this torturous triangulation. The barn was stifling now, dense with brackish air and fermenting grapes. As I waited at the bar, trying to flag down a flannel-shirted bartender, I could feel a sweaty body slide up beside me.

"Have we cracked the mystery yet?" Rex said with a slanted grin.

"Which one?" I recoiled. "How a Brit found himself summering on the wrong side of the pond?"

"I'm asking myself that very question, darling," he said. "But I was curious if you figured out when we met for the second time."

"Perhaps it's destined to remain a mystery."

I started to sweat. I wiped my upper lip with my hand, but my palms were already damp.

"I'm surprised you haven't asked Isabel by now," Rex said.

"Why would she know?" I said.

"That woman is the definition of omniscient, or haven't you noticed." His eyes slid over to me. "She seems to know *everything.*"

"How do you know each other so well?" I asked.

"Ah, well, we both started out as young, hungry reporters, waging the 'speak truth to power' fight as it were, trying to make a buck on a story," Rex said. "Before her husband sold out to start a private intel firm, digging up dirt no matter the means."

"I thought that's what you do," I said.

"Close." Rex smiled. "I kept my lousy byline, whereas he dove into a shadowy underworld, employing much more underhanded tactics—using Isabel as his deadliest weapon."

"She doesn't seem to scare you," I said.

"I'm not easily scared, but trust me, Isabel has made my blood run cold on more than one occasion." He tipped his glass in her direction. "And very hot, too."

I looked over at Isabel, standing in her light. She was the focal point of Damon and Caroline's attention, her cheeks contoured by a ray of sun. Isabel said something that made Damon laugh, and I saw Caroline rest her hand on the small of his back in a proprietary gesture. I felt a roil of resentment in my acid-filled stomach and turned back to Rex.

"And now you're still trying to make a buck on a story, it seems," I said.

"I follow the scent of blood in the water," Rex said with an exaggerated sniff. "Especially when it leads to quite . . . succulent subjects, such as yourself."

"I don't know what you mean by that," I said.

"Oh, I think you have quite the story to tell, but you have yet to tell it." He cocked his head with a glance at my scar. "Or at least, the honest version."

"Maybe you're mistaking me for someone else," I said faintly.

"You really don't remember, do you? Perhaps I should give you a hint." He poked my arm with his sharp fingernail. "What about The Blaze?"

I shook my head obtusely, but a stabbing pressure began to build behind my eyes.

"What about it?"

"I was there that night, with you—and Graham," he said.

As Rex wandered off to rejoin the group, a cavity of fear opened in my chest. For all these months, I could not access the truth within me; it was a dark vault without a door. Graham had left me no vessel to hold it, no container to give it shape. But now, like a gun, it was pointed at my own head.

When we got home, Isabel made a pot of lemon tea with fresh pressed ginger. We ate thick slices of cold chocolate cake with our hands while standing at the kitchen counter, gossiping with Julio. Then we went to bed.

I stared awake in the dark, watching aquatic shadows swim across the wall. I tried to calm my spinning mind, listen to the lilt of waves below my window, but the image of the encrypted photo kept creeping in. The parking lot, the burning sky. The unseen lurker in the dark. Could Rex have really been there that night? Was he the pair of eyes behind the hidden camera lens? I sat up in bed in a cold sweat. No, I told myself, it wasn't possible. Rex must be bluffing—he was a shrewd journalist, a sly manipulator of susceptible sources. It was unlikely he would be invited to an event with such a prominent guest list.

I grabbed my phone from the nightstand and searched my email history. An email came up dated last summer, sent by the head of communications at Graham's company:

> Please find attached the full guest list for The Blaze. Keep this confidential and do not forward under any circumstances.

I scrolled down through the list of attendees, name by name, dread coursing through my veins like lighter fluid until, at the bottom of the list, I stopped: Rex Wright.

That final scene had replayed on an incessant loop in my head, over and over, disjointed and murky like a night terror upon waking. But if Rex had really trailed us after the party, his camera clicking away in the dark, he would have witnessed what the others had missed.

I got up and opened the window. The marshy drift of air swelled like a wet sponge, the backs of my thighs erupting in a heat rash. I tiptoed downstairs to get some water in the kitchen. The house was dark and hummed with insects, though I saw a slit of light at the end of the hallway. I crept over and peered through a partly open door.

Isabel was sitting on the floor in a billowy nightgown, her eyes hollow and milky like opals. Without any makeup, she looked at once older and younger, her forehead etched with faint lines, her body sagging with fatigue. She was riffling through an archival box, photographs piled on the floor. When she looked up, there was a lost, frantic look on her face, as if I might be an intruder, or an apparition from a wrenching dream.

"I'm sorry," I whispered, "I didn't mean to scare you."

"Oh, it's you." Isabel blinked as if snapping out of a trance. "I'm not used to having anyone else here."

She gestured for me to come over, and I sat down beside her on the floor. In her thin hands, she held a faded photograph of a family: a little girl with pigtails skipping on the beach, holding hands with a young Isabel in a peasant dress. Her face awash in the joy of motherly love, her strawberry-blond hair floating in the wind. A familiar sorrow flowed through my arteries like blood.

"Sometimes absence can almost become a presence," Isabel said, a thin wire of grief in her voice. "We never stop trying, in our own way, to bring back the dead. So we seek signs and symbols of them in everyday life. We look for patterns to cling to in order to delude ourselves that they are not really gone."

I looked at the photo again. The faded wash of sunlight on her daughter's face, as if beaming her into the afterlife. How could I tell her that Graham had come back, like the emerald ring, but in his darkest form? A numinous presence that threatened my days, blackened my nights.

"I was pregnant once," I said suddenly. "But I lost the baby in the accident."

My voice sounded faraway. Isabel touched my hand, a shadow passing behind her eyes.

"Oh, I'm so sorry, angel," she said. "Did your fiancé know?"

I paused, then shook my head. She held my hand, and we stared out at the blue-black sea. I had planned to tell him that night when we got back to the hotel room. The test sealed in an envelope and packed in my suitcase. A letter unopened, arriving too late.

16

The next day, we took a beach walk at sunrise, and later Isabel took me to the farm stand for flowers and the marina for overpriced lobster rolls at lunch. Julio massaged my forehead scar with a pungent oil from an energy healer in Cuixmala while he said a little healing prayer: *Please clear her third eye of any fears, energies, entities, or other intrusions so that she can see again.* Then it was time to get ready for dinner.

I left my hair in beachy waves and put on a lime-green dress with scalloped straps that showed enough cleavage without setting off wifely alarms. Rex picked us up in a borrowed old Porsche, and we drove off to Damon's farm. Isabel laughed and sang along to a Neil Young song in the front seat, the sleeves of her blouse ballooning in the wind. Out the window, the thicket of trees seemed to trickle with bilious light—or was it my own mounting unease? I tried to redirect my swirling thoughts away from Rex, now singing along with Isabel, and toward the night ahead. I would soon see how trapped Damon was in his domestic situation, like a Chekhov character bemoaning his dashed dreams in a stifling country house. His dull marriage no more than a sham.

I had started to take a perverse comfort in this narrative when we arrived at the house. We drove up a gravel path between two faded red barns, and beyond sprawling acres of fertile fields. Damon came out to greet us, a bandanna around his head, holding a dusty bottle of Bourgogne Blanc from his cellar. He kissed Isabel's cheek and nodded a vague "hey" to me. Here we go, I thought. But as soon as I stepped inside the renovated farmhouse, my self-delusion wore off. I took in the honey pine beams with copper-rimmed skylights, the wall of windows framing an algae-green pond sequined with lily pads. Dogs were running inside and out while a scratchy Sam Cooke record played. And then Caroline was standing at the kitchen island, her hands wet with pulpy juice as she sliced a bounty of tomatoes. She was on the phone and apologetically gestured for us to go outside. It was such an idyllic vignette, in stark contrast to my vision of agrarian misery, that I immediately felt like the imposter.

In the garden, a table was set with green tapers and jugs of sunflowers, their heads drooping lazily toward the waning light. A strapping man in small tennis shorts rose from a lawn chair, his muscular thighs flexing as he came over. A joint loosely dangling from his fingers.

"The man, the myth, the Buck Sausage!" Damon announced.

"Oh shit, look who it is." Buck smiled, shaking his floppy hair beneath a sweatband.

"You're the tennis pro who I mistook for my neighbor," I said.

"Like the man who mistook his wife for a hat," Rex said.

"Except there were no wives involved yet," I said.

Damon ignored my unsubtle comment, pouring wine for everyone but himself.

"You look the same," Buck said sheepishly. "Maybe even better than I recall."

"That's not saying much," I said, "since we met while I was doing laundry in the basement in the middle of the night."

"Ooh, that sounds like the opening of an erotic thriller," Rex exclaimed.

"It could've turned into one, knowing these two," Damon said. "You thought my dogs were loud? One night, Buck reported that my neighbor here was even louder—so loud she shook the walls like an earthquake."

Buck held up his hands innocently. "Don't shoot the messenger."

I opened my mouth in shock. Damon grinned at me, his eyes catching and releasing the light. I couldn't believe he would say something that provocative in front of Isabel. Was he trying to embarrass me? Or encode the anecdote with our private history? I couldn't figure it out. Isabel snatched the joint from Buck's fingers, directing the energy back to her.

"Have you boys been cheating on us already?" she said.

"Just a little head start," Damon said. "An *aperitivo*, if you will."

"Then you better let me catch up," Isabel said.

Damon lit the joint while she held it in her mouth, touching her hand as he did.

"It's my new strain, in bloom for summer. Farm to table at its finest," he said. "I smuggled these seeds in my socks from Marbella, Buck's hometown, and they grew like a charm."

Isabel inhaled, closing her eyes and tipping her head back. She pursed her lips as she exhaled, as if blowing through a bubble wand. She wanted the men to see it on her: the possibility of sex. And, as I scanned their faces, they did. I wondered how much of her performance was triggered by Damon's comment, or her own insecurities about his domestic life. Isabel offered the joint to Rex, but he waved it away.

"Only cigarettes and other sins of moral turpitude for me, love," Rex said.

Caroline came out of the house then, carrying a large platter. She was wearing a white caftan with blue embroidery that covered her wide hips, her hair in a messy bun.

"I'm so sorry about that," Caroline said. "The auction house wants to change the dates of his showcase, but we'll still be in Telluride then, so it's all sorts of scheduling chaos."

Caroline placed the platter on the table. Thick shingles of yellow and orange tomatoes were wedged between mozzarella disks, lashed with olive oil and basil leaves.

"You're still doing your trip out West?" Isabel asked.

"We go every summer without fail," Caroline said. "We'll drive out in a few weeks."

I swallowed more wine, aggravated by her usage of the plural, the unavoidable intimacy of this yearly ritual. Hours spent on the road together, stopping overnight in small roadside hotels. I watched Damon slicing a loaf of olive bread, his biceps tensing as he put his weight into the knife. The same arms that pinned my wrists and covered my mouth, that lifted me flat against the kitchen wall.

"At this point, I can't really afford not to do it," Damon added. "I have a surprisingly loyal following in the mountains, all those lonely cowboy wives."

"One of them even threatened to leave her husband for him," Caroline said teasingly.

"I think I felt more threatened than her husband," Damon said.

"Was this the much older lady?" Buck asked.

Isabel bristled, a muscle aside her mouth twitching slightly.

"Oh yeah, she lost her fucking mind," Damon said. "She told her husband that she was leaving him because we were having a torrid affair! I mean, at most we exchanged a few Miles Davis songs, maybe a book, while I was in the process of making her a pair of earrings."

"Oh, don't lie. I bet you loved it," Buck said.

Caroline let out an odd laugh, as if to prove how unbothered she was. Isabel caught my eye to share a judgmental glance, and I was relieved to know we were still aligned.

"The best part was that the husband tried to stage an actual duel!" Damon stood, picking up the wine bottle. "He sent me a long text that began: 'As Churchill once said: "Up with this I will not put."' And then offered to provide the pistol and location."

"I've had many men offer to provide me with both," Isabel declared.

"And did you accept?" Rex asked.

"Take the pistol, leave the cannoli," she said with a wink.

Damon reached over to fill Caroline's empty wineglass, but she discreetly patted his arm, and he stopped. It was their only form of physical touch, I noticed, a nonverbal cue devoid of erotic love. With Graham, we held hands at every table, we kissed madly on twilit streets around the world. But what did that prove? The high voltage of passion often had a lethal threshold—within seconds, a kiss could turn into a bruising fight. Still, watching them now, Damon and Caroline were unmistakably together: planning trips and baking bread, making a home where tomatoes rubied their vines, ripening beneath the dusk of summer. So maybe it wasn't marriage, but it was a full, real life. And now I had no one's hand to hold, not even the man who was using me for sex. I didn't entirely think that was true, but I gave myself a moment to seethe about it.

"You know, you must have done *something* to provoke the use of weaponry," I said. "No one threatens to leave their husband without probable cause."

Caroline opened her mouth but didn't say anything. Damon didn't look at me, shifting with an edge of agitation.

"Because the obsession with coveted objects, like jewelry, has historically been part of dramatic events," Damon said, placing the bottle down. "Think about Marie Antoinette's necklace sparking the French Revolution, or the Romanovs sewing diamonds into their underwear as they fled Russia, or the Dutch buying Manhattan with a bunch of beads."

I tried not to roll my eyes, thinking of how he had cited this same anecdote to me—and I'd foolishly fallen for it. I looked at Isabel, who gave me a little nod of encouragement.

"And what does that have to do with you?" I asked.

"Reigns of terror?" Rex said. "Brutal massacres?"

"They're about the complex economics of desire," Damon asserted. "I mean, Buck has the same problem, don't you, Buckman?"

Buck shrugged, twisting the gold chain around his neck. "Uh, not on that level, no. The only thing I'm ever challenged to is a tennis match."

"I should write a piece on duels, like the nineteenth-century version of cancel culture," Rex mused, lighting a cigarette. "You know how Pushkin died, don't you? He received a Certificate of the Cuckold in the mail because his wife was suspected of shagging the tsar."

"That's one way to end up shot in the stomach," I said.

"Oh god, we're only on our first bottle. Isn't it too early for Pushkin?" Isabel groaned.

"But never too early for cuckolds," Rex said, slapping the table.

For dinner, Damon made everything from his farm. Freshly caught striped bass drizzled in green olives and herbs, bright purple Japanese eggplants and corn with black truffle salt, dollars of watermelon radishes with whipped goat cheese and mint. Rex was boasting how his publication broke a viral story—about the recent suicide of a revered tech founder after he was levied with a false accusation. Everyone began to heatedly debate: Had media become the new public square trial, or had it forced a needed moral reckoning? Isabel said, "As men gain power these days, it's increasingly unclear whether they are stepping up to a pedestal or to the gallows." And Damon added something like, "Sure, and it's unethical for shitty journalism to circumvent the legal system if it results in irreparable damage."

I stayed quiet and drank my third glass of wine, the same green-gold shade as the field in the melting sun. I was trying to dislodge a piece of corn stuck in my teeth, while cursing corn on the cob in general, when I heard my name mentioned.

"I'm sure Liv must have a firsthand opinion," Rex said pointedly. "Since she was on the front lines of such a bloody cultural shift, caught in the cross fire, so to speak."

Everyone looked at me, and my cheeks grew blisteringly hot.

I shrugged. "Honestly, I was just lucky to escape alive."

My response was meant to be light, but no one laughed. Damon looked at me with such solicitude that I considered retracting my previously bitter thoughts.

"You know, Liv broke young Buck's heart back in the day," Damon said, clasping his hands behind his head. "She shattered his romantic dreams."

"It's true," Buck said with a sigh. "She didn't respond to my many desperate texts."

I laughed. "Everyone knows you can't get involved with your neighbor."

"Well, at least not until after you've moved out," Buck said.

I stole a glance at Damon, an inconspicuous smile at the corner of his mouth. I smiled back into my wineglass, I couldn't help it—which I hoped no one caught.

"If I were Damon, I would have built a secret door between the wall of your apartments," Rex said goadingly. "Like the trapdoor in *The Seven Year Itch*."

"Oh yeah, so he could try to sneak in day or night," Buck added.

"Who said he didn't?" I quipped.

At this, Caroline put down her water glass, pinching her lips together.

"Sorry to disappoint, but there was no such fantasy portal," said Caroline. "Because it was actually *my* apartment. Damon was only living there while I was abroad for a few years."

I looked at Damon again, but he was no longer looking at me. It was as if Caroline had taken our private history and abruptly shaken it like a snow globe.

"You know what Liv's problem is?" Isabel said, sweeping her hair over her shoulder. "I introduce her to all these men, and she isn't interested in any of them. At least not the viable ones—like you, poor Buck."

"Well, maybe she's not ready yet after the trauma she went through," Caroline said. "There's no requisite timeline when it comes to moving on."

Under the table, my ankles itched with mosquito bites, and I pinched them with my nails until I drew a trickle of blood. It made me queasy to imagine Damon sharing details of my past with Caroline. Did he exploit my story to deter her suspicion? He probably portrayed me as an object of pity so she wouldn't consider me a threat.

"Actually, I set dates with two men next week," I lied.

"Just hopefully not both at once!" Rex said.

Damon's eyes flitted over to me, which Rex astutely clocked. I glanced at Caroline, but she was already gathering the dirty plates and standing up.

Before dessert, Damon took us on a tour of his farm. By then twilight had fallen over the fields. I was starting to feel drunk, and a little high from the chocolate edible Damon had convinced us to try after dinner. As he led us around, I dazedly listened to him weave a travelogue of the land: yellow watermelons from seeds spit into his palm on a beach in Panarea; a Victorian greenhouse imported from a ramshackle garden in Sussex; strains of cannabis, *northern lights, blue sunset,* from his trips to the mines in Zimbabwe and Kazakhstan. There were apples and beets, pears and plums, waiting to be sliced open to reveal their inner color. His harvest no different than his gems, lush and oversaturated, an orchard of temptation.

So bountiful, it almost made me sick.

We ended the tour in a bright red coop, home to his new chickens. Damon admiringly held a large egg to the light, milky blue, with the luster of his wild pearls.

"Name another shape imbued with so much meaning: life, birth, fertility, womanhood," Damon said. "It's traditional, like a Fabergé or a religious symbol, but at the same time it's fluid and ovular, all smooth feminine curves."

"What do chickens have to do with your jewelry?" Rex said snidely.

"Because I breed these little ladies for the strength of their shells," Damon replied.

He reached over and grasped Isabel's arm to showcase her bracelet. As he held her wrist to the light, I watched her lips parting slightly, her face soaked in the pleasure of his touch. I could see Damon watching her, too, entranced by the image of her delicate wrist cuffed by his creation. The bracelet was a glossy white crescent, webbed with thin cracks of black mosaic, pebbled with sapphires and moonstones.

"It's called *coquille d'oeuf,* which means crushed eggshell. An old Vietnamese technique, later adopted by the French," Damon explained. "I collect the eggs, soak them, peel off the membrane, crack them and assemble them, and embed them in lacquer."

I wondered if he had given Isabel the bracelet as a gift—or as part of a transactional exchange, intentionally concealed from me. I felt a ripple of nausea, the pungent reek of chickens with all the wine and weed. As they continued the tour, I excused myself to get some water and walked back to the barn alone. The pond hummed with mosquitoes, lily pads drifting like clumps of green clouds. A navy bathing suit was drying on an Adirondack chair. I touched the damp fabric and imagined Caroline sunbathing here, dipping her toes into the cool water, uninhibited in her own home.

Inside, the house was empty, the lights low and dishes drying on a rack. I picked up a warm bottle of Pellegrino and drank it down in large gulps, skimming the perimeter of the open kitchen. Mason jars of seeded jams and flower-laced honey, tins of dried green buds packed like dead caterpillars. I stopped in front of the fridge. There was a photo of Damon and Caroline hiking out West, maybe in Maroon Bells, and I flipped it over. It was dated two years ago; the same summer that I had met Graham. At least I would never be stuck in something fake like this, I thought. Some ersatz portrait of love, a curated pose of happiness. But then I remembered my own engagement photo, the two of us beaming in Central Park after he had proposed. The silver frame abandoned on our mantel, now coated in dust.

"Everything okay?" Caroline said, entering the kitchen.

I jumped a little, clumsily putting the photo back on the fridge.

"Oh sorry, just dehydrated," I said. "A little too much wine."

I was hoping she would leave, but she leaned back against the countertop with strained exhaustion. She had a small but prominent mole beside her nose that I hadn't noticed before.

"Now that we're alone, I want you to know I'm aware of the situation," Caroline said, crossing her arms. "And to be honest, it's becoming a real problem for me."

I could feel the tendons in my neck stiffening. I had no idea what to say.

"I'm sorry, what do you mean?" I said faintly.

She frowned at me, then said, "I mean with Isabel."

I exhaled a little too loudly, bobbing my head. "Oh right, of course."

Caroline turned toward the counter. I watched her uncover a rhubarb crostata and transfer it onto a serving plate, the seamless motions of a practiced host.

"At first, I thought she was just acting like a maternal figure. Historically, he's sought out these widowed patron types before," she said. "But then she started pretending he was her *boyfriend*—staging all these photos at public events so they looked like a couple."

"I'm sure it's totally innocuous," I reassured her. "Like a crush or something."

"I know, but people do talk," Caroline said. "Even my friends have mentioned it to me."

She glanced at me as she sliced the crostata into thin wedges, and I shook my head in shared exasperation. She was trying to confide in me, I realized, by revealing a private glimpse into her marital insecurities. Maybe she thought it would bond us as women. My stomach churned with guilt, the foul smell of their chicken coop sticking in my throat.

"Really, I wouldn't worry about it," I said. "Especially now with Rex in the picture."

"I'm being crazy, right?" she said. "It's not like I think they're actually sleeping together."

I gave an awkward laugh. "No, I guarantee they're not."

"I just don't want to feel embarrassed," she said, then corrected herself, "I mean, I don't want *her* to feel embarrassed in the end."

Caroline sighed, picking at stray crumbs with the pad of her index finger. I almost felt sorry for her then. She wouldn't feel threatened by an older woman if her relationship with

Damon was secure. But hadn't that very insecurity provoked a similar reaction in me?

"Do you mind getting the bowl of crème fraîche for me?" Caroline said then.

I opened the fridge, relieved to busy myself with a task. I absently scanned the shelves, crammed with vegetables in various stages of decay, until my eyes landed on the top shelf. Next to the cream, there was a box of syringes and a row of clear glass vials labeled Menopur.

I knew what it was: fertility medication.

I felt faint, as if someone had slapped me between the eyes. I quickly grabbed the cream and closed the fridge door. Caroline was standing there, watching me with a distant look.

"Unsolicited advice," she said with a grim smile. "Don't wait till you're ancient like me to have a baby. It's so much harder than anyone tells you it will be."

"I'm sorry," I said, swallowing hard. "It's a good thing I don't want kids, then."

Caroline frowned sympathetically as if she might offer more advice. I quickly asked to use the bathroom, and she said something about a hallway. I opened the first door on my left and shut it behind me. As my vision adjusted to the dark, I realized it was their primary bedroom. The bed was unmade, a pile of art deco furniture books opened on the floor, clothes draped on a dusty exercise bike. Damon said they didn't sleep together, but I hadn't imagined they might sleep beside each other. With manic desperation, I opened all the drawers in the nightstands, rummaging like a drug-crazed thief to find signifiers of sex—lube, a vibrator, whatever. But I found nothing. What did it matter anyway? It didn't matter they weren't married, because he was still a married man. This was their farm, their tomatoes, their fucking chickens.

And now they were planning to raise a child together, to become a real family.

In their bathroom, I could barely look at myself. A smudge of mascara on my cheek, my bad eye cartoonishly dilated. I considered splashing cold water on my face like girls did in movies, but that seemed unnecessarily dramatic and would make me look worse. I scanned their medicine cabinet and found more fertility medication prescribed to Caroline, and an antidepressant prescribed to Damon. He's probably depressed because of you, I thought. Then hated myself for even thinking something so petty. I smudged on her lipstick in a matte burgundy, not my color, then pocketed it for the perverse satisfaction of taking something that belonged to her.

I needed to tell Damon that it was over between us. He had deceived me, and I had deceived Isabel. I felt irrationally hurt, though I knew it was partly my fault: I had deliberately chosen a man unavailable to me, as if that was what I wanted. As if that was all I deserved.

When I exited the bedroom, I felt the presence of someone behind me in the dark hallway. My heart jolted, though I had no reason to be scared. I turned around, hoping it was Damon so I could get the conversation over with. But by the slightly protruding bowl of his stomach, I knew it was Rex. He staggered out of the shadows, red wine sloshing in his glass.

"What do you think that eggshell bracelet cost her?" Rex asked, his words slurry.

"I don't know," I said. "Probably the GDP of a small African country."

"Or other sorts of quid pro quo, I suppose," Rex said.

I tried to move past him, but he held out his arm. An old fear twisted in my chest, as though someone was gripping my ribs with pliers and prying them apart, one by one.

"I imagine this all must be rather difficult for you," he said.

"I don't know what you're talking about," I said.

"Of course you do, darling." He leaned in close. "To carry

around such a terrible secret all the time must be a tremendous burden on you."

At first, I thought he meant my affair with Damon. But then, with a surge of horror, I read a different story on his face. I had become so absorbed in my new narrative of betrayal that I forgot it was merely a grotesque mask, a pentimento obscuring the more malignant layer underneath.

"Listen, no one wants to rattle skeletons. It's a dirty business for a journalist," he went on. "But in this case, the skeletons have more or less rattled themselves."

The hot acid fermenting his breath turned my stomach. I tried to move around him again, with more force this time, but he blocked me with his entire body.

"Why does it matter?" I said shakily.

"It matters if you think the past holds valuable evidence," he said.

"If you're trying to get information from me, I have nothing new to tell you."

"We both know that's not true," he said. "Because even though the forensic investigation was closed, it seems there may be reason to reopen it—considering there was a glaring error in the accident report."

Rex dug his phone out of his pocket, scrolling through a gallery of images. My knees were wobbling, knocking together like bowling pins.

"Ah, I found it," Rex said, clicking on a video. "See, the thing I'm trying to unpack, the missing piece I want to solve, is why you lied."

He pressed Play. At first, I didn't know what I was watching. A grainy night, an orange smear of moon. Then a parking lot came into focus. A man was pacing in front of a car, clutching a pair of keys, while a girl tried to pry them out of his hand. *Please*, she was begging, *don't do this*. He grabbed her arm and slammed it against the door until she stopped. He was crying now, rubbing his eyes, punching the trunk with his fist. *I'm sorry*, he was saying over and over, *I'm sorry.* Then he threw the keys at her and got into the passenger seat. The door slammed shut. For a moment, the girl stood there, frozen. She looked up at the sky in silent prayer before doubling over and vomiting on the ground. Finally, she got into the driver's seat. Headlights pierced the dark as the car drove into the night. The screen went black.

I knew the scene like a dream returning to my body. Like a film of my own autopsy.

I had been the one driving. Not Graham.

"The truth must dazzle gradually, or every man be blind," Rex whispered.

A hot pain thrashed behind my eye and crawled down my spine. In the distance, I heard footsteps coming toward us. Damon appeared and stepped in front of me, causing Rex to drop his arm.

"Everything cool here?" Damon said.

"Couldn't be cooler," Rex said. "I was just finding my way to the little boy's room."

Rex smiled with one side of his mouth, slipping the phone back into his pocket. We watched him in silence as he disappeared down the hall. When he was out of sight, Damon pulled me back into his bedroom and closed the door behind us.

"What the fuck was that about?" Damon said. "Are you okay?"

I shook my head, my teeth pressing hard against my tongue. I wanted so badly to tell him, to unburden myself of the snarled black nest in my chest. Then I saw his rumpled sheets, the ones he shared with his wife. I had once shared a bed with someone, too; I had known the holy intimacy of each night turning into a new day.

And now, because of me, he was dead.

Damon wrapped me in his arms, holding the back of my neck. My shoulders were shaking against his chest, and I let myself be soothed, surrendering all my strength. Finally, he pulled away and looked at me with a vexed expression.

"Liv, tell me," he said. "Did he suspect anything about us?"

I reeled back. Of course he thought it was about our stupid affair. Of course he only cared if we were found out. My eyes were burning, but I couldn't let him see me cry.

"Don't worry," I said. "It has nothing to do with you and your wife."

I pushed past him and ran out of the house into the open field, gasping for air. Across the orchard, fireflies flared like wild embers in the dark. I could hear the faint laughter of others, sharing dessert at the table. I closed my eyes, but the scene didn't fade into the night. It stuck beneath my eyelids, it made a home like termites in the walls of my body.

Rex knew what I had hidden all along. But who could I tell? Who could I tell that he was threatening to unearth the truth like a landmine? That he alone could detonate my life with one small click.

PART II

17

July broke like a fever, soaking through the sheets of night. It was the season of rooftops and emergencies, acidic trees and sidewalk garbage, a city in search of the fallacy of outdoor space. Black pavement stuck to my sandals like gum. *Tarry tarry nights* a friend called it, and we laughed though our soles were ruined. The weeks were spent discussing the weekends, but there was never anywhere to go. As long as I kept moving, as long as I rode the centrifugal force of summer, spinning away from an invisible center, I convinced myself I could evade everything: the weight of gravity, the incursion of my past.

I had rescheduled my appointment with the neuro-ophthalmologist so many times that I finally forced myself to keep it. The Eye Institute was on 168th and Broadway, so I took the train to Washington Heights and got trapped in a car without air-conditioning. Across from me, a teenage girl was curling her eyelashes with a metal spoon while Marley's "Concrete Jungle" blasted on an old-school boom box to accompany the mood of our collective heat stroke.

In the institute's drab waiting room, I tried not to look at my phone. An elderly woman adjusted a yellowed bandage over her eye, and a young man in a Knicks T-shirt, clutching a white cane in his lap, stared at a dead plant with filmy cataracts. Everyone was waiting alone, as if they had no one to accompany them. Just when this setting had thoroughly depressed me, a nurse called my name. She led me into a dark room and projected a pattern of lights onto the wall, like constellations at a planetarium. Then she squeezed cold stinging drops into my eyes and sent me back to wait again.

Finally, I caved in to my own deplorable weakness and checked my phone. The screen pulsed with a text from Damon, and my stomach flipped. Two weeks had passed since that night on the farm, and now he was leaving for his trip out West.

D: I need to see you tonight before I leave
L: Do you deserve that?
D: I can prove that I do . . .
L: Too late

I wanted to see him, desperately, though I knew how terrible it would be if I did. It wasn't even about self-respect, or my lack thereof, but my own startling dependency. He had become an inexorable addiction, like a drug rush, the chromatic overflow of heat and light. And without him, I was dropped back into the dreary procession of days—another subway, another waiting room—staring up at a stained ceiling. A cruel comedown, a chemical withdrawal. The quiet hours of night left to spiral, to crawl back into the darkest zones of my own memory.

The places that Rex was threatening to expose.

As I texted Damon back, the letters began to bleed into the screen like runny ink. My hands were melting into white globs of wax, the chairs levitating off the ground. This is it, I panicked, I'm going blind. When the nurse called my name again, I told her what was happening. "It's just the dilating drops," she said, before escorting me into the doctor's office. She could have mentioned that.

Dr. Mehta was a patient Indian woman with red glasses and a soothing voice. I clinically reported the details of the accident: the shattered windshield, the surgery. Then she displayed the images from my CT scan on a monitor, sent over from my recent emergency room visit. Using her pen, she traced a faint white line in my skull, like an eraser mark, obscured by my luminescent bones.

"You see that sliver right there?" Dr. Mehta said. "That's a splinter of glass they missed during your surgery. It seems to be putting pressure on the optical nerve, causing your fixed pupil."

"And the glass has been under my skin this entire time?" I asked, numb with shock.

"Inert foreign objects can live inside the body for years," Dr. Mehta explained. "Sometimes the body will form scar tissue around it, often embedding it more permanently."

She went on to perform a cursory examination of my eye. I heard her mention something about optic trauma, about a future surgery that would involve re-excising the scar and removing the piece of glass, but a tinny ring had erupted in my head.

"It's not impossible it could resolve itself on its own," she continued. "But you're very lucky. If the windshield had shattered at a different angle, you could have lost your eye."

How fortuitous, I thought, the near miss of calamity. Dr. Mehta turned off the lights and asked me to place my head inside a metal contraption. I stared into a ring of fluorescent light while she looked through the other end, a needle inching directly toward my eye.

"Think of something relaxing, like the ocean," she said.

The waves, the waves again, the crest and break of those beckoning tides. On the road, hugging the foggy curve of night,

I told Graham that we couldn't get married, not like this, not now. I was leaving him, flying back to New York on the next flight. I took off the ring, tears blurring the road, thinking of the baby growing inside of me, my future as scorched as the burning horizon. How much easier it would be: the other side of the cliff.

Then the glove compartment opened, the barrel winking in the dark. *If you leave me, life isn't fucking worth living,* he sobbed. *I'll have nothing left.*

Do it, I thought, *so my baby doesn't have a father like you.*

His eyes changed, a light gone out. Only then did I realize I'd said those words aloud. They had come out of my mouth.

He lifted the barrel to meet his temple. I reached out to stop him, lifting my hand from the wheel to pull the gun away, but the road bent at a sharp angle, and then: the inversion of sea and sky, of smoke and water.

The endless plunge.

I awoke in the hospital. My life ravaged to a carcass, my memory as mangled as my own bandaged face. In that nightmarish slur of time, in and out of consciousness, I wished for death. That I would wake and discover I was the one who'd died, not him. But I was left alive, nursing his exit wounds of love. The metastatic cells of guilt occupying a home in my womb where the baby had been. I had miscarried from the impact, a doctor informed me. For days, I howled in barbaric pain, spongy shreds of fetal tissue hemorrhaging out of me, congealing into gelatinous black clots. Until there was nothing left to bleed.

I don't remember the precise moment when I lied. At some point, the police came to question me. They assumed Graham was driving, the alcohol in his system above the legal limit—a plausible explanation. And how could I correct them? The merciless public inquisition of our life, our love, the horrors of a criminal trial waiting for me after the hospital: it would be my own death sentence. Our final moments in the car, an unbearable violence that would ceaselessly haunt me, of which I could tell no one, was enough of a sentence to endure.

I confirmed to the police that Graham was driving. And the record was sealed.

"Okay, you can breathe now," said Dr. Mehta, turning on the lights.

I heaved and pulled away, my eyes burning like stones held over an open flame.

When I got home, I lay in the maid's room for what felt like hours, waiting for evening to come. At some point, I forced myself up and stripped off all my soiled clothes, leaving them in a pile on the floor. I took a long shower in Sam's bathroom, shampooing my hair twice, trying to scrub away the unrest adhering to my tendons like burrs. Then I wrapped myself in a ratty towel and collapsed on the living room couch. I wanted to call Isabel, knowing she'd try to cheer me up with some fanciful anecdote, but she was at a party tonight. She'd texted me earlier, asking how the doctor visit went, but now my depression made it impossible to respond. Instead, I stared at the wall, my vision still bleary, as a wash of light bleached the spines of old books. When my phone buzzed, I prayed it was Damon.

But it was an email from Delta Air Lines. I threw my phone down, rubbing my irritated eyes. How I hated that it wasn't him, and hated myself for wanting it to be. But as my anger cooled, I picked the phone back up. Because it wasn't just an email—it was a notification to check into an international flight. JFK to FCO in Rome at 8:10 p.m.

I blinked at the screen, confused. Clearly, it must be a mistake, I thought, some glitch in the system. Or a trick of my dilated vision. But when I opened it and saw my own name on the ticket, my chest clenched so hard I couldn't breathe.

It was the flight to our honeymoon.

Days before the accident, Graham had tucked a first edition of *Twilight in Italy* under my pillow, with a handwritten note of our itinerary. He couldn't take a personal vacation until this summer, due to work, so he had arranged the romantic surprise in advance.

Now it was a cruel prank played by the universe, and I let out a crazed laugh. In a sudden, bewildering rage, I dialed the number of the airline and waited for an eternity to the beat of techno music. Finally, a woman's voice came on the other line, muffled by a time lag and a heavy accent. I told her that my honeymoon had been canceled, and requested a refund.

"Unfortunately, it is a nonrefundable ticket," she stated robotically. "The only way we allow an exception is for an unforeseen death."

"Well, that's perfect, because my fiancé died *unforeseen*," I said.

After a static pause, she offered me an airline credit in the amount of the ticket, which I could apply to a future trip. Before we hung up, she said, "I will say a prayer on your behalf, wishing peace for his departed soul so that he can continue on his journey."

I sat there paralyzed for a long time, listening to the arrhythmic beats of summer outside. The hydraulic hiss of a crosstown bus, a cyclist blasting a tragic opera aria on speakers, a party raging on a fire escape down the block. Eventually, I got up and went over to the living room window. Below, the treetops were glazed in a sticky film of sunlight.

And Damon was sitting on the stoop.

We wish peace for the dead, but no one bothers with those left behind in the realm of the living. What peace could I hope for if the dead never fully departed but continued again and again to beckon, to arrive?

18

Damon was waiting on the corner when I got downstairs. I wanted to kiss him, to fold myself into the familiar envelope of his body, but I sullenly crossed my arms, keeping them tight against my chest.

"What do you want?" I said wearily. "Why are you here?"

"I thought we could take a little walk," he said.

"Can't you take someone else on one of your dumb geological tours?"

Damon unwrapped my arms and clasped my hand, pulling me down 5th Avenue. We could hear a concert vibrating in the park, some indie cover of a Velvet Underground song, and beams of neon light flashed across the sky. At 82nd Street, he ran through the chartreuse allée of linden trees and up the stairs of the Met.

"Oh no, not again," I said. "Haven't you retired your old museum trick yet?"

"Come on, how many men would take you to watch the blood moon eclipse? The longest eclipse of the century."

"Only the worst ones," I said. "And you forget I can barely see."

"Then it will be like the blind leading the blind," he said.

The museum was closing, but Damon charmed a college-aged ticket girl into admitting us anyway. I followed him through Roman and Greek galleries, racing through Africa, and we breathlessly rode the empty elevator, staring at each other but not touching, until the doors opened onto the roof garden.

A celestial sculpture installation floated high above the city. Bright planetary spheres carved of precious marble, weightlessly suspended in the air by steel frames and intersecting at oblique angles. We walked beneath their orbits to the edge of the roof. I looked at the park below, my vision still clouded. Damon came up behind me, threading his arms around my waist.

"What can you see?" Damon asked. "Or rather, what can't you see?"

"I'm tired of seeing," I said. "I'm tired of everything."

Tilting backward into his chest, I could feel the warmth of his skin, the wings of his scarab tattoo beating through his T-shirt. I was wedged between him and the skyline, like the night we had first trespassed, the park complicitly watching us from below. How long ago that seemed now, a distant season. Damon kissed my shoulder, then cupped his palms over my eyes.

"How about now?" he said. "Is this better?"

"Are you trying to blindfold me?" I asked.

"I figured that was something you might be into."

He pivoted me around to face the planetary sculptures, his fingers loosening over my eyes like slats of a window blind.

"Tell me what you see," I said. "Describe it to me through your eyes."

"Okay." He paused thoughtfully. "Well, there's a milky blue-white planet carved from quarried marble in Carrara, like a topaz cabochon. And a red sphere made of Portuguese marble, ringed like Jupiter, veined with blood. And a deep green one, filled with cloudy malachite whorls, from Masi quartzite in Finland," he said. "Can you see all those?"

"Vaguely," I said, my lashes fluttering against his hands. "Only the shadow of color."

"And the thing is, all of these ancient rocks mined beneath the ground are a visual measurement of time, the earth mirroring the sky, stones carved from quarries but standing in for planets light-years away." He turned me around so I was facing the city again, his mouth touching the rim of my ear. "But then you look out, and there's the El Dorado to the west, and the pencil-dick towers spiking up from the south, and the park spread below. And you realize that you and I, standing up here, we're just like everyone else, we're minuscule, we're specks of dust. Except the difference is that our orbits collided in this filthy fucking city, and it makes you wonder if there's some star-crossed cosmic design after all."

Damon released his hands. I blinked a few times, disoriented by the sun, the city glowing sharper and brighter as though held under a floodlight. And I realized, suddenly, that the danger did not reside in our duplicity. Damon had slid into an unseen crack, and in some terrible way I had come to love him, the worst kind of love, carved out of pain like these marble orbs, something curved and beautiful born from a violent outcrop of stone.

And meanwhile, to him it was a game. I knew it was my fault; I had allowed him to show up whenever he wanted, to seduce me with color, to fuck me and leave me again and again. And now he would go out West with his wife, and I wouldn't hear a word from him for torturous days and nights. I could no longer let him have it both ways.

"What are you thinking?" Damon said. "I can never tell what you're thinking."

"I think," I said slowly, "that you're full of shit."

He gave a confused smile. "What?"

"You pretend to be this maverick artist with some profound vision to see the deeper geology or gemology in everything," I said. "But really, it's just masking the painful reality that your own life is based on a lie."

"Wow, okay." He rubbed his jaw, taken aback. "I'm sorry, where is this coming from?"

"I don't know," I said. "Maybe the fact that you're married to one woman, leading on another, and sleeping with me?"

"You knew about my situation," he said carefully. "I was transparent with you about that."

"Well, congratulations, you've successfully set a new bar for transparency, then."

I was acting overly dramatic, even unfairly, but I didn't care. I had guarded myself for so long that now, like a rubber band poised to snap, the release of control made me vibrate with a heady and unhinged power.

"Liv, you know how I feel about you," he said, sighing a little impatiently.

"How would I possibly know that?" I said.

"We've always had something between us that we don't share with anyone else."

"What?" I smiled cruelly. "Because I let you fuck me and your wife doesn't?"

He nervously glanced around, as if worried I was making a scene. And maybe I was—but I hated him for turning me into some pathetic archetype of the hysterical other woman.

"Jesus, would you stop it?" he said in a lower voice. "You know that's not what I mean."

"Okay, fine, then tell me what you mean. Since that's the only objective difference."

"You've never asked me for anything more," he said, turning up his palms.

"I'm sorry, what should I have asked for?" I said. "Pearl earrings, maybe? A chicken coop?"

A hot rage ached in my throat. I thought of the little IVF bottles lined up in their refrigerator, all those cold hormones waiting to be injected into his wife's stomach, multiplying her follicles, stimulating her ovaries, swelling her eggs. All of his beloved fucking eggs.

"Or maybe I should ask for a baby," I said. "But I guess you already have that covered."

He tensed, his jaw tightening. "Who told you that?"

I didn't feel like responding. He took a small step away from me, rubbing the back of his neck. I stared furiously at the planets, as if their vast cosmic indifference could provide an answer to anything within myself.

"Look, it's been a stressful situation, okay?" Damon said in a pained voice. "And I don't really feel like getting into the emotional nuances of it right now."

"I never asked for nuance, but you could have at least told me the truth," I said.

"Right, Liv, like you're so forthcoming?" he said. "You won't even talk about what happened to you—you've never once told me the story."

I felt my ribs constricting, squeezing the air out of my lungs. "What does that have to do with anything?"

"Because you're acting like I'm the bad guy here when you're not so honest yourself," he said. "In fact, I think you're even more fucked-up than I am."

I shoved him then. Damon looked stunned, and then I shoved him again, harder this time, a hollow thwack of skin on bone. He grabbed my wrists and pinned them together, so tightly I could feel my pulse beating wildly in his hands like a captured bird. I felt out of control, provoking him only to humiliate myself. I realized, too late, that even though I never asked for anything, I wanted him to reassure me he had something to offer, something real. Now I knew this would never be true.

Our eyes met and he let go. I staggered backward, rubbing my wrists. Wishing he had hurt me more.

"You know, maybe we should cool things off for a while," Damon said, not looking at me. "At least while I'm gone."

My eyes were pounding. It was not meant to go this way. I was supposed to be the one to end things—not the other way around.

"Fuck you," I said. "Enjoy the trip with your wife."

I took off toward the exit, not looking back. I ran down five flights of stairs, knowing he wouldn't come after me though still lamely wishing that he would. By the time I emerged onto the street, the moon was rising rapidly in the sky, bracketed between two buildings. It was vermillion, volcanic, like the red diamond that Damon had once shown me, cut to refract its inner fire. Who was he to call out my damage when he was part of it now, an active accomplice, after I had offered him my private sorrow and he took possession of it, consumed it, swallowed it whole? Now he would return to the other women who loved him, while I was left to walk uptown alone, red hands blinking across empty crosswalks, only the inflamed gash of the blood moon to guide me home.

Sam was collaging when I got back. Torn fragments of paper were scattered across the dining room table. I collapsed onto a chair and rested my head in my hands, my muscles heavy with exhaustion. He guided each piece like a planchette over a ouija board, the fated accident of color and signs. Until, layer upon layer, they came together to form new versions of themselves, some translucent and others opaque, the shape of a submerged memory.

"What's got you down, Slash?" Sam said, glancing over at me.

"You were right," I said, exhaling loudly. "Maybe I am running from one disaster headfirst into another."

He tore a mottled slice of fuchsia into a crescent shape, its deckled edges creasing like the skin around his eyes. I took a sip of water, feeling the press of tears in my throat.

"I don't know, Slash. He sounds like a real schmekel to me."

"I think you mean schmuck," I said.

"No, schmekel. Have you learned nothing from me? It means small dick."

"Well, unfortunately, that's one thing he doesn't have," I said.

"No wonder. You'd be better off if he did."

I heard myself laugh, but I was crying now, tears spilling down my cheeks and staining the paper in dark radial blooms. Sam came over to me, smoothing my hair as if I were an injured child.

"Oh, don't cry, Slash. You're ruining my fancy paper," Sam said. "Broken hearts are what writers are made of. The pieces are ground up and become the basis for ink."

"I'm not even a writer anymore. I'm not even a widow. I'm nothing," I said. "I'm just some sad story people talked about once."

"Better than if they never talked about you at all," he said, wiping my tears.

Sam poured me a glass of Sancerre, and I followed him into the living room. He sat in his favorite chair, working quietly on an anthology of Russian poetry he had agreed to edit, while I tried not to check my phone. I had a bad headache, my eyes sore from the day. On TV, Rita Hayworth was in a shoot-out in a maze of mirrors, clutching a gun on a floor of shattered glass. I mindlessly rubbed a small bump next to my scar, as if the trapped sliver was trying to break free. What if the love I felt for Damon was false, psychosomatic, a symptom created by my distorted senses? How could I even trust my own feelings for him? I had been about to marry a man who had once, in the dead of the night, hurled my suitcase at a hotel wall, barely missing my head.

Deep inside me, somehow, the bare wires of love and pain had become tortuously crossed, so I could not feel the charge of one without the other. That was the suitcase now living in Sam's bathtub.

"I'm aiming at you, lover," Rita said, and I repeated it aloud, then shut off the TV.

I turned my cheek toward Sam. "Do you think we can ever know another person?" I asked. "Truly understand who they are, or what they're capable of?"

"I don't know, Slash. Can we ever really know ourselves?" Sam took off his reading glasses, staring distantly into space. "As writers, we live two concurrent lives. We live in multiple autobiographies. We are driven by the tension between our desire to reveal and to hide, by the push and pull between our exterior life and our interior one."

"But what happens if they intersect?" I said. "What if you're afraid that your inner life is at risk of bleeding into the other one?"

"Then you must write about your deepest fear, what scares you the most," he said. "And perhaps, when you do, you'll discover that what constrains you is also what can free you."

I thought about this as Sam held a sheet of paper to the lamplight in his tremoring hands.

"Now listen to Akhmatova, will you," he said, "though my Russian is not what it used to be." Then he read:

You will hear thunder and remember me,
And think: she wanted storms. The rim
Of the sky will be the color of hard crimson,
And your heart, as it was then, will be on fire.

Sam stared at the poem after he finished, before slipping it back into his book. His sonorous voice resounded like a requiem, words the dead would never hear. He kissed the top of my head, then covered me with the leopard blanket and turned off the lamp. I finished the entire bottle of wine, watching the lights across the city turn on and off, a checkerboard of windows framing life after dark.

I knew what I had to do. I had to start living as though death were nowhere in the background. I had to unclasp myself from the lives of others. I had to write. I had to stop using my body like a concealed weapon. Maybe I had to stop drinking, or go into therapy. Well, maybe.

My phone vibrated. For a split second, my heart jumped, hoping it was Damon, texting to say that he was sorry, that he missed me. But when I fished out my phone from the threadbare cushions, it radiated with a text from an unknown sender:

> If you're curious about my article,
> darling, meet me for a drink.

I closed my eyes, but even in darkness, in my own dreams, the sky was fated to be the same color as the night he died. So bloodshot, so inflammable, it was like staring into my own combustion.

19

I slept three hours and awoke with a bad hangover, the worst kind, where your body is a bottomless pit of hunger and despair, yet nothing can allay either symptom. I ate a tub of cold leftover pasta with my bare hands, then ordered a bagel with a huge iced coffee and hauled myself around the reservoir. I was avoiding the text from Rex, ignoring the voicemail from Dr. Mehta's office to set a follow-up appointment, half-listening to a Mazzy Star song and to a *New Yorker* podcast of the short story "Day-Old Baby Rats," which seemed disturbingly relatable, and wondering if it was necessary to hold trombone practice beneath Bridge No. 28 at seven in the morning. The fur coat lady was painting the mauve smoke tree beyond Engineers Gate, a family was setting up a picnic with a sign that read SHE SAID MAYBE, an elderly man was pushing four fluffy white dogs in a Victorian baby carriage. The city provided a constant reminder that even at sunrise, after restless hours plagued by fears and failures, a new day was ready to assemble with or without you.

I retreated into Sam's book-filled office with my laptop and third iced coffee. He had left that morning to visit a friend in

Martha's Vineyard, a figurative painter dying of cancer. I sat on the floor and, for the first time since my return to New York, tried to write.

I began to write a short story about the secret retreat in Half Moon Bay, yet with an alternate fate. I imagined if Graham had never been fired that night, if death was not the incontrovertible end. Would I have put on the white dress and walked down the aisle in two weeks as planned? Or would I have finally gathered the strength to leave him, heeding the chronic gnaw of doubt that afflicted me like a disease? In this version, there was no dramatic deus ex machina to make the choice for me. I was left to decide, of my own volition, whether to stay or to go, to marry or to escape, to endure the turbulent life I knew or to risk an uncertain future.

The truth was, I did not know. I could be living in Los Angeles now, strolling on the beach with my newborn baby. Or I could have found myself living in the same maid's room, dislocated by a different kind of grief. You can narrowly dodge a bullet and still walk away with a gaping wound.

I wrote every night until two or three in the morning, though I would still work at Isabel's during the day. Maybe I was trying to deconstruct the narrative until it became a dissociative form of fiction. Or I urgently wanted to distill my own emotional truth before Rex threatened to distort it and expose a more damaging one. When the story was finished, I felt exhausted and excavated like a burial ground. I titled it *The Blaze*, printed it out, and left it on Sam's desk to read when he returned. Then I let it go.

The next week, Isabel called to say she was coming into town, and asked me to meet her at the bereavement group. The city had issued a heatwave advisory, the sun scalding every surface it could reach. I dragged myself to the hospital, a mess after my sleep-deprived weeks of no human contact. As soon as I saw Isabel waiting in the lobby, I took a deep breath of relief. She looked like she was about to check into a wellness center in a taupe yoga set, her shoulders dusted with freckles from the beach. I hugged her tightly, almost embarrassed by the gratitude I felt to be back in her effulgent orbit.

"The only thing worse than grieving in winter is grieving in summer," Isabel said.

"Now I know why everyone skips town," I moaned, wiping the sweat from my chest.

"But on the bright side," she said, "New York in summer is the only place where you can actually escape New Yorkers."

We walked down the sterile corridor, weaving around beds of sick patients and tables lined with stainless steel instruments, ready to cut. The initial blast of air-conditioning overpowered by chemical fumes of disinfectant, masking a putrid base note of death.

"Can't they hold this group somewhere less, I don't know, clinically depressing?" I said.

"Like where, Bemelmans?" She lifted her large black sunglasses with a sideways glance at me. "Though it looks like you could certainly use a night out."

She wasn't wrong. We turned the corner past the faded Joan Mitchell poster and arrived at the same room, with the same women sitting in a circle. It seemed not much had changed since I was last here. Dr. Meller sat at the center, perplexingly wearing a white turtleneck, and commenced with the same guided ritual of closing our eyes and rooting our feet on the floor.

"Anyone want to share any news on the summer romance front?" Dr. Meller inquired.

The women glanced around, seeking disheartened expressions that mirrored their own. The painter was no longer seeing the uncircumcised man. The professor had mistakenly signed up for a fetish dating app instead of a lesbian one and got flooded with messages from doms making demands. Gradually, the focus landed on Isabel, beaming with a surreptitious smile as she adjusted the tortoiseshell clip in her hair.

"Isabel, out with it," Dr. Meller said. "What are you keeping from us?"

"Damon has been in touch nearly every day from the road," Isabel began in a dreamy voice. "Sometimes he'll share a photo of the mountains, or a country song he heard on the radio. This morning, he sent me a selfie with this ridiculous mustache—I told him he looked like a '70s porn star! But of course, it made me melt."

As she spoke, I glanced around the room. The women were leaning forward in their chairs, a flare of desperate hope on their sagging faces, as though they, too, were the recipient of such flirtations from a younger man. I couldn't believe these adult widows, inured by the vicissitudes of life, would subscribe to this absurd fantasy. But part of me understood. It allowed them to nurse their own private illusions and tenuous self-delusions, with which they carved out more bearable lives. And why was I exempt from that? In truth, I wasn't, and this was simply jealousy. I hadn't heard from Damon at all; not one word since the night I lashed out and stormed off the Met Roof. Maybe I had become the delusional one.

"And why do you think he feels the need to stay in close touch with you, Isabel?" Dr. Meller asked. "What are his intentions, do you think?"

"I don't know. My husband and I were rarely separated, except for the months I was pregnant when it was too dangerous to travel with him. But oh, the love letters he sent, the phone calls every night," said Isabel, her hand over her heart. "So perhaps Damon is holding me close. He is keeping me near."

The women nodded encouragingly, and I dumbly mimicked their gesture. In my early courtship with Graham, he had flooded me with lyrical letters and rare editions of poetry books, whirlwind trips, and visions of our future. Rendering all younger men inferior. His phone calls on our nights apart soon morphed into check-ins: *Where are you? Who are you with?* It was intoxicating at first, the power differential, for a man of his stature to take an intense interest in me. Then one night, he asked to track my location on his phone. Indefinitely. *Trust but verify*, he said. They were just little tests, I told myself, until tracking wasn't enough. A losing game of confirmation bias. Proof of my loyalty could only exist by ceding the elements of my meager life: my tiny apartment, my single friends. And why would I need them now? I could occupy his influential sphere, live in his place by the ocean, reap the grandiosity of his love.

And I loved him, I did. But by then, it didn't matter: I had no life other than the one he controlled.

"And what about you, Liv?" Dr. Meller asked. "Anything spicy on the horizon?"

I cleared my throat. "No romantic interests to speak of. Only romantic disinterests."

Dr. Meller smiled. "Perhaps something about your late fiancé that's been on your mind?"

I glanced around at the expectant faces of the group. Isabel was still lost in dreamy absorption, though she offered a melancholic smile. My throat locked up, my palms limp in my lap.

"No," I said finally. "I have nothing to share."

After the meeting, Isabel and I walked to Sant Ambroeus to pick up iced coffees before she headed downtown.

"You know, I'm not sure *she* went out West with him," Isabel said as she stirred a splash of almond milk into her coffee. "The fake wife."

"How do you know?" I said.

"My intuition tells me that she stayed behind." She shrugged suggestively. "Otherwise, why would he be texting me every day?"

I stabbed a straw into the plastic lid, spilling coffee on the counter. If it was true his wife hadn't come on the trip, then Damon's cold silence couldn't even be excused as a precaution, but worse: a choice. I thought of the startled look in his eyes when I shoved him, my wrists like branches snapping in his hands, and felt my humiliation doubling.

"Does he really have a mustache?" I asked.

Isabel pursed her lips, then pulled up the photo on her phone. My jaw dropped. Damon was standing before a mirror, shirtless and wearing only a cowboy hat, so he appeared to be naked. His chest tan and muscular, his torso cropped right above the pelvic bone. I barely registered the mustache.

"Jesus," I said, "it's like he woke up and thought he was Sam Shepard."

"Talk about a thirst trap." She laughed. "Don't worry, I didn't reciprocate the gesture."

But now I was worried. We walked back outside, weaving through a mob of screaming camp kids in front of an ice cream truck. My outrage felt as searing and torpid as the heat, burning without any reprieve.

"Don't be upset you haven't heard from him, love," Isabel said. "You know how fickle he can be."

"I'm not." I crushed a cube of ice with my teeth and met her eyes. "Did I tell you that I have a date with that doctor this week?"

"Peter?" She poked my arm. "You didn't tell me, you little vixen."

So maybe I hadn't texted Peter back yet, confirming a date, but I couldn't resist the impulse to use it as a test. If Isabel was in frequent touch with Damon, as she claimed, then I could track the dissemination of information, determine if she was still using me as bait. It was a little stab of retaliation, too—to see if I still had a distant effect on him. I wanted to prod him through the tangled wires our game of telephone had become.

When we got to 5th Avenue, Isabel hailed a cab as it lurched toward a yellow light.

"Have fun on your hot date," she said with a wink. "Don't do anything I wouldn't do."

"I wouldn't dare," I said as I helped her into the back seat.

"Oh, and, Livia? I forgot to mention." Isabel paused before slamming the door. "You're invited to Italy in August."

The next night, I met Peter at Balthazar at 8:00 p.m. I was hoping he would show up in scrubs for theatrical effect, but instead he was wearing a gingham shirt and jeans, standing outside the restaurant like an awkward tourist. He said how funny it was that we'd run into each other at the ER, and I laughed uncomfortably as if he'd said an orgy. I was already on my second glass of wine when he mentioned his recent breakup. For no reason other than to make conversation, I asked what had caused it.

"Well, she had this irregular mole that concerned me," Peter said.

"Didn't think the story would begin there," I said into my glass.

"Yeah, right? So I sent her to my superior, a top melanoma specialist, to evaluate it. Then a few weeks later I see a text from him on her phone, which I assumed was the biopsy report. But turns out it was a photo of his, you know—" He made a clumsy hand gesture.

"His dick?" I said, and he nodded painfully.

Thankfully, the waiter sensed my desperation and refilled my wine. I forgot how much men loved discussing their exes in alarming detail—their dietary restrictions, their sexual pathologies. As if this disclosure proved their own saintliness, exculpating them from any personal wrongdoing. I had an almost fond recollection of the divorced novelist whose ex-wife revealed, in couples therapy, her anal sex fantasy with their kid's algebra tutor. Turned out it wasn't merely a fantasy. I wondered what happened to that guy who confided his worst trauma was going bald—he never once mentioned an ex. Was he so bad? I considered texting him but then couldn't remember his name.

"What about you?" Peter asked. "When was your last serious relationship?"

I dunked a handful of fries into a pot of ketchup and shoveled them into my mouth.

"None worthy of discussing right now," I said.

"Oh shit, I totally forgot," he said, setting down his glass. "I googled you. I'm sorry."

After dinner, I was drunk enough to go back to his apartment on Grand and Orchard, which resembled a dorm room. He made me a watery vodka soda and asked if he could turn on "the game." I couldn't tell if I was more offended that he wanted to watch baseball or that he was a Red Sox fan. At some point during the seventh inning, he reached over and attempted to finger me, jabbing and prodding with the subtlety of a gynecological exam. This was normal, I told myself, he was a nice, single doctor, we had mutual friends. But my body had already taken a sabbatical, to return at some unannounced time. His eyes were still on the game when he took off his jeans and started to knead his thin, veiny dick. I repeatedly told him to put it back, in an appeasing voice, but when he climbed on top of me and tried to jam it inside, it was eventually easier to give in. He kept pumping so repetitively it felt like a dry rug burn, and while I was trying not to think about Damon, all I could think about was Damon—how it was his fault I was even here to begin with. Finally, to get it over with, I said, "Where do you want to come?" and he did, immediately, all over my dress with a whiny sputter, clutching his slimy tip in his hand. I left shortly after that.

In a car heading up the West Side Highway, the river smeared with the sallow lights of New Jersey, the same emptiness from the morning crept back in, except this time more violently, as if I had been gouged. I cracked open the window and let in a torrent of rancid air, roaring so loudly I almost didn't hear my phone ringing.

The screen radiated: No Caller ID.

The test worked after all, I knew it—Isabel must have informed Damon of my date tonight. I felt a singe of vindication that just as quickly burned off into self-loathing. I hated who I had become, hated that only Damon could jolt me out of my anesthetized state, like an electrode inserted under my skin. What was wrong with me that my body could only feel the voltage of betrayal, its electrifying shocks of pleasure and pain? I would never be normal again. On the last ring, I picked up.

"So, darling, will you have a martini with me tomorrow night?" Rex said. "Or do I have to get on my knees and beg?"

A sour reflux seeped into my mouth as I heard myself reply, "Tell me where to meet you."

Outside, the sky was boarded up with clouds, rain pouring through their leaden darkness. The driver asked me to raise the windows, but I rolled them down as far as they could go, coaxing in the flood of night, submerging me until I drowned.

20

The next night, I walked to Polo Bar on the hottest night of the year. The air simmered with oily streams of heat, like water about to boil. I was sick with nerves, with spiraling nights of insomnia, and my armpits slick with sweat by the time I reached midtown.

Rex was already sitting in the private parlor by the fireplace, dressed in a dandyish khaki linen suit. I tried to coolly slip into the banquette beneath a framed gallery of horses, but the backs of my thighs stuck to the leather. He kissed me on both cheeks as a server delivered two martinis with small bowls of fried olives and potato chips.

"I didn't know if you'd like my trusty old vesper," Rex said. "So I took the liberty of ordering you something a little less dry and a little more dirty."

"No surprise," I said.

"Cheers to that," he said, jovially clinking my glass.

I took a sip, the briny vodka soaking my empty stomach. I tried to maintain a mask of inscrutability, but my hands were shaking slightly. Now that I knew Rex wasn't bluffing, that his evidence held incriminating weight, I feared how he planned to torment and extort me with it. The only way to protect myself was to play this like a round of poker. The problem was that he held all the cards.

"It must be kismet, really, how our paths have crossed in LA and now New York, without even intending to," Rex said. "We could be an international power couple, you and I."

"Seems like you're angling for that status with Isabel."

"Sadly, she seems to have her sights set on younger pastures, though I suppose an old boy like me can dream."

"I would offer to put in a good word for you, but you haven't exactly earned one yet."

"Oh, but haven't I?" Rex pouted. "Even so, I'm not entirely keen on being with someone who could dispose of me in my sleep."

"Maybe that's exactly the kind of woman you need," I said.

"Then perhaps I've come to the right place," he said.

His thin lips curled into a raptorial grin as he popped a fried olive into his mouth. I took a long sip of my drink, my head already spinning.

"Listen, I'll let you in on a little secret," he said, leaning forward. "Do you know what the most valuable currency in the world is right now?"

"I don't know, a swimming pool?" I said. "Or jewelry, perhaps."

"Good one," Rex sneered. "The answer, my dear, is intel. Intel is the oil of our digital era. *Muckraking* used to be a dirty word, but now investigative journalism is king. And those who traffic in it, who leverage and distribute it, have the most power: because we can determine who may rise and who must fall, with the click of a button."

"Nice monologue," I said. "Is that like your *Richard III* version of a TED Talk?"

He chuckled. "I practice on occasion—naked in front of the mirror."

"An image I now can't erase from my mind," I said.

Across from us, a table of young married couples was debating how to get their toddlers into private school. Mandarin lessons and a diverse last name, they agreed. At least I'll never be some insufferable elitist parent at happy hour, I thought. But I would probably never be part of a young married couple, or even a mother, and I felt the depth of my inadequacy, my own abject failure.

"What's going on behind those enigmatic eyes of yours?" Rex said.

"I don't know," I said. "Maybe that your perspective perpetuates the same corrupt sense of power that you are purporting to expose and hold accountable?"

He raised one bushy gray eyebrow. "Oh, is that so?"

"Or maybe you just like saying it because it makes you feel like a man."

"What else would I be?"

"The devil," I said.

"If I'm the devil, baby," he said, "then perhaps you'd be willing to make a deal with me."

A hostess informed the couples that their table for dinner was ready downstairs, and they got up and left. Now that we were alone, the room seemed to contract around me. The fire crackling with visible heat, the rabid eyes of the horses boring into my flesh.

"Right on cue! Now I don't have to use my stage whisper." Rex loosened his scarf, the white hair on his chest exposed. "See, in the weeks before your wedding, the pillars of protection that allowed men in power to operate with impunity had been demolished. Boom! Suddenly, it's a search and destroy mission, everyone out for blood. And your fiancé finds himself a target."

"I know. I lived through it," I said, trying to keep my voice steady.

"Reports start to simmer, rumors swirl. He's a bit of a toxic bully, inebriated at one too many events, some off-color remarks. Nothing . . . *criminal.* But Icarus not only flew too close to the sun, he also made one too many enemies—the kind that can destroy you. And finally they did. Graham was fired, his reputation ruined. His life came crashing down in a flash. But most importantly: his future with you in it."

"Why are you recapping what I already know?" I said.

"Because you, lovely Liv, blushing bride-to-be, found yourself in an intractable dilemma. You thought you were marrying a master of the universe! But now were hitched to a burning ship."

Rex subtly inched his phone closer to me. Was he taping our conversation? I could feel my thighs erupting in a patch of hives beneath the table.

"This is all old news," I said. "And he's not even alive."

"Ah, well, we both know how that happened. But the fact is, you *lied* about it."

"It was an accident," I said futilely.

His eyes flashed. "I didn't say it wasn't, did I?"

A server entered and delivered another round of martinis. I drained my first glass, stamping it onto the hammered brass table with a clink.

"Look, I don't give a damn why Graham was fired—he was a tyrant, big deal," Rex said. "What I'm trying to figure out is just how much of a tyrant he was to *you.*"

"Why do you care so much?" I said.

"Because I happen to care about you, darling, I do," Rex said. "And I can imagine when you sped off that night, you were blinded by rage. Rightly so—it was a no-win situation. If you were to marry him, you'd be publicly shamed for standing by a disgraced man. But if you were to call it off, you'd still be marked as his collateral damage. So there was only one remaining option."

"What do you want?" I said. "Or are you just trying to terrorize me?"

"I'll admit, I've terrorized far less alluring subjects."

"You mean all the women who've rejected you?" I said.

"Now she's cooking with gas!" he exclaimed, knocking back his drink. "What I want is your story. A personal account of what unfolded on that fatal night, to clarify the many burning questions I have."

"Well, you're out of luck," I said. "I don't have the answers you're looking for."

Rex slid his finger around the rim of his glass, then licked it.

"That's too bad. Because if I were to, say, write an article about you—and what a juicy read that would be—I think the police might have many more questions. And the media, too, if the investigation were to be reopened. Such as, how did she get away with it? Who was responsible for burying the evidence? Did she hire someone to cover it up?"

"What?" I shook my head. "What are you talking about?"

"Oh, my dear, you can't be that naive," he said, clucking his tongue. "Surely you don't think the police took your word at face value that you weren't driving because of your . . . feminine wiles?"

I felt a ripple of confusion, alcohol scrambling my brain. *They never found the gun.* I reached for a glass of water, but my bare left hand seemed to detach from my wrist, like in a dream of amputation.

"But *you* were the one who sent me the ring," I blurted suddenly.

"What ring?" Rex said.

"My engagement ring, you know, the emerald?" I stuttered. "In the mail?"

"Are you okay?" He frowned with concern. "You're looking a bit unwell."

I could see he didn't know what I was talking about, and fear twisted around my intestines. If Rex hadn't sent me the ring, then who did? Who else could have been involved? I couldn't think, my eyes pulsing against my skull.

"Trust me, I wouldn't want you to be charged for wrongful death either. Even if intent *can* be proven," Rex said. "I'm just granting you an opportunity to save yourself. To empower your own female voice, as it were, to share your own side of a traumatic story—which I'm sure many women will find sympathetic."

"That's something I'll never give you," I said.

Rex lowered his gaze to my rashy thighs, letting it linger there. I could see his eyes pinwheeling with deranged pleasure, getting off on the control he held over me. I wanted to scream or throw my drink in his face, but I was paralyzed, my legs glued to the seat.

"No? Surely you want to show me just how . . . *compliant* you can be," he said.

A server entered, asking if we wanted another round, but I abruptly stood up, bumping into the table, and stumbled back through the bar.

Outside, the city was a quivering pool of steel, and the streetlights seemed to bob and glare overhead like vitriolic globes. I hauled the dense heat into my lungs, wanting to collapse and surrender to this scorching bed of concrete.

But I knew there was one thing left to do.

I had to call Isabel and ask her for help. Isabel would understand the reason I had lied, and know how to expertly fix this. She could protect me from the imminent damage, put a stop to Rex's insidious battery of threats. I frantically dug through my bag, my hand shaking. But when I opened my phone to call her, it wasn't her number that I dialed.

21

I took a cab straight down to Damon's apartment. He lived in a prewar building on West 11th, a tree-lined block that was strangely a five-minute walk from Isabel's townhouse. When I buzzed up, a garbled voice on the intercom said, "Come on up, Red," and I could almost hear the weakened beat of my own lacerated heart.

In the lobby, I tried to fix my makeup in the mirror, my smudged eyeliner, my faded lip tint, but my skin appeared to be melting off like a special effect. I was drunk, so drunk that I sensed an immense infusion of possibility, the alcohol flexing inside me with a strange omnipotence. I was doing the exact opposite of what I should have done, yet it seemed like a good idea, a correct decision to let my self-sabotage win out.

I took a small elevator to the fifth floor and walked down a dimly lit hallway. Isabel was the only reason I knew Damon was back in town—apparently, he'd arrived this morning. He hadn't reached out on his own, which felt demeaning earlier; now, after the havoc of Rex, it was a minor concern. I approached a partly opened door and anxiously knocked.

Damon appeared in the doorway, tan and unshaven in a white T-shirt, his hair fairer from the West. We stared at each other with a sort of existential angst, as if we were creating a tableau of all the thresholds we had nearly crossed.

"Looks like you got rid of your mustache," I said finally.

"So it seems," Damon said. He touched his mouth, processing how I would know that. "Apparently, they don't let you re-enter the city with one."

"Really? I thought you were in charge of border control."

He smirked. "Should I allow you entry now?"

"Not if you don't want to," I said.

I took a small step back, as if to assert some visible free will that I could, in fact, leave.

"You were the one who called me, remember?" he said.

"Then I'm happy to go back where I came from."

"Liv, stop," he said. "I want to see you."

He pulled me inside but didn't immediately close the door. He kept his hands nervously by his sides, glancing behind him as though Caroline might make a surprise appearance. The apartment was smaller than I'd imagined, a dark green foyer opening into one main living space. How different this seemed from his sprawling farm, open to a steady stream of summer guests; for some reason, stepping inside his apartment felt even more voyeuristic with its compression of private space. Finally, I shut the door behind me.

"Are you okay?" Damon said. "You sounded pretty badly shaken up on the phone."

"Oh, you know, just another sadistic man trying to ruin my life," I said.

I shrugged like it was nothing, but my jaw felt painfully tight.

"Not another one. You want me to take care of him for you?"

"Yes, please," I said. "Maybe you can bludgeon him with a bar of gold."

"Anything for you," he said. "Come here."

Damon pulled me toward his chest, and I released into him.

He held me for a long time, stroking my back with unfamiliar affection. His skin was warm, scented like cedar and vanilla. I thought of the closeness we shared only weeks ago, and wondered where it had gone, evaporated into molecules of air.

"You know, I worry about you sometimes," he said. "I worry about how you are, and what you're doing, and if you're taking care of yourself."

"You don't seem like the type," I said.

"Well, I'm here to surprise you with my occasional sensitivity," he said.

Damon kissed my forehead and my eyelids, his mouth soft, and I wiped my face on his T-shirt. Then he disappeared into a small galley kitchen to get me a glass of water. I floated around the periphery of the living room, taking slow breaths. The walls were studded with a haphazard composition of travel photographs and color field paintings—a Jules Olitski, a small Kenneth Noland—and art books piled up on the hearth of their fireplace. I stopped before the mantel. On display was a framed photo of Caroline and Damon in a lavender field, her hand on his chest, caftan billowing in the breeze. Another snapshot of marital bliss, reminiscent of the photo at their farm—displayed on the fridge that held the precious vials of their future family life.

A hot bloom of shame spread beneath my skin. In the depth of my despair, I had pathetically believed that I could find a sense of comfort here—in the apartment he shared with his wife. A grave misjudgment, like revisiting the source of a wound. Now, staring at the photo, I was reminded that his marriage was not a front, not a transactional exchange. His only fraudulent relationship, in fact, was with me. I felt a floodgate lifting inside of me and a torrent of resentment sweep in.

Damon returned to the living room and handed me a glass of lukewarm water.

"Show me your bedroom," I commanded. "I want to see it."

"Hmm." He frowned. "Maybe we should go outside, get you some fresh air. We can take a walk along the river."

"Most men try to lure me to their apartments, not get rid of me the moment I'm there."

I touched his belt, but he quickly pulled my hand away, as if it would leave incriminating fingerprints.

"Liv, come on. I feel like we should talk," Damon said. "The last time we saw each other, we left things sort of dangling, and you stormed off upset—"

"Why do you think that is?" I said.

"Well, right, and I understand that. But now you seem, I don't know . . ."

"I seem what?"

"Just not like yourself," he said delicately. "I can never really tell what's going on with you beneath the surface, and I'm trying to make sure you're okay."

I wanted to say: Don't pretend you care. But I could see on his face that he did care, in a shockingly sincere way. Who was he to suddenly demonstrate restraint, to act invested in my well-being? He didn't get to decide when to sleep with me or when to express tender concern so that he could selfishly pretend to be a better man. I could feel the alcohol pulling tautly inside me, like a wild animal straining against a rope. I grabbed his belt with a forceful tug.

"If you don't show me your bedroom, I'll assume someone's chained up in there," I said.

Damon let out a tense laugh. "I can assure you that you won't find anything nearly as interesting as that."

"Then why don't you prove it to me."

Holding his belt, I pulled him in the direction of the hallway. The bedroom wasn't large; the bed sloppily made, two half-open suitcases, a clutter of his leather jewelry cases. There was nothing particularly personal about it, with one glaring exception near the door: a painting. A nude, wide-hipped brunette straddled a pink cloud of cotton candy, seductively gazing over her shoulder with glossy pink lips.

"Is that your *wife*?" I scoffed.

Damon looked stricken for a second, then said uncomfortably, "Uh, well, Pierce painted it a while back, before he blew up."

"You asked him to paint her or, like, he voluntarily offered?"

"I don't know. They were friends before we were," he said, his voice tight with agitation. "Why does it matter?"

I took in the profile of her protruding brown nipple, different from my small pale pink ones, then turned back toward him with an insolent smile.

"Maybe Pierce should paint me," I said. "It would be a more persuasive portrait."

I was being obnoxious, but I wanted him to agree. Otherwise, her nudity on brazen display, at the entrance of their bedroom, cast everything in a garish light. Caroline wanted to be seen as a desirable woman through the male gaze, even after years of marital neglect. The painting was a plea, a provocation. And though I refused to see myself in this desperate position, begging him to want me, begging him to love me, I had more or less come here for the same thing.

A prickly contempt shot down my spine, landing between my thighs. I dropped down to my knees below the painting, unbuckling his belt and unzipping his jeans.

"What are you doing?" Damon asked, as if he didn't know.

I pressed my mouth against his briefs, rapidly bulging beneath the fabric.

"Liv, come on, stop—" he said, making a weak attempt to pull me up.

I peeled back the fabric and took him in my mouth. He

groaned, hitting the base of my throat. I wanted to behave savagely, barbarically, to stain every surface so he could never see his bed or Oriental rug in the same way again.

"Are you sure you want me to stop?" I asked.

I looked up at him from the ground while he surged in my mouth. He locked my gaze, gripping the back of my head in a tight fistful of hair.

"No hands," he demanded. "Just your mouth."

I knew I had him then because he relinquished all control. After a while, he took off my dress and forcefully pushed me down onto the splintered wood floor, kneeling over my face.

"Is this what you want?" Damon said, and I nodded. "Say it to me."

"Yes, I want it," I said.

And I did, but something was different this time. He stroked the strained muscle of my throat, a flare of brutality in his eyes that said I had pushed him too far.

"Did you fuck anyone while I was gone?" he asked.

"No," I said.

"Don't lie to me. Did you?"

He slipped his fingers deep inside me, and I moaned.

"Yes," I said, serious now.

He gripped my jaw, jamming his wet fingers into my mouth. I wrapped my teeth around them, biting down hard, and he lightly slapped me. I felt myself smile, a cold burn spreading across my cheeks where his hand had made contact. I wanted him to leave a mark, a scar that could erase all my others.

"Did he make you come?" he said.

"Yes," I lied.

The veins in his neck swelled. He pressed his knee into my chest, pinning me down like the weight of a knife. He could break me, I thought, sever my body cleanly into two parts: the one who was the betrayer, and the other who was betrayed.

"Did you think about me when he was inside you?" he said.

"Not at all," I said.

He shoved himself so deep in my throat that my eyes watered, my breath trapped inside my lungs, and I shut my eyes and imagined it was Graham, choking me, strangling me, cutting me off from the world. This is what I deserve, I thought, nothing more than this.

He asked where he should come. I didn't want to give him the satisfaction of anywhere inside me, so I commanded, "Stand up. Do it."

Damon hesitated briefly, then stood and straddled my body between his legs. I stayed still and supine, looking up at him in surrender from the floor, harnessing a force so powerful that I could make him do whatever I wanted, even this. He came with a loud cry, showering my neck and chest, until I was saturated and glistening. Then it was over.

We were silent for a moment. I propped myself up on my elbows, and he used his boxers to wipe me down. Then he balled them up and said he'd be right back.

As soon as he left the room, every ounce of power drained out of me, vacating my muscles and organs, a fatigue so physical it left me winded, numb. I don't know what had possessed me, a depraved need for abasement even I couldn't understand. I put my dress back on and ran my fingers through my sticky, knotted hair. I picked up my soiled red thong, then impulsively pushed it beneath a laundry basket for his wife to find. I knew it was a cruel gesture, but I had no kindness left. I had begged a man to degrade me, who offered me nothing yet pushed me to the verge of obsession, of love, and not even this could save me from my own ruin.

Damon returned with another glass of water, and I took a slow slip. He watched me for a moment, his forehead creasing with worry, but beneath it I saw the aftershock of regret for what we had done.

"Are you sure you're okay?" he said.

"I've never been better," I said.

I handed him the glass and quickly turned to leave.

"Liv, wait," he said. When I turned back, he touched my cheek so tenderly that I stopped breathing. I knew if I stayed a second longer, I would shatter in his hands, a girl of broken glass, and I couldn't let him see me like that, not now.

So I left. The moon was hanging high above Greenwich Street, overripe as the flesh of a rotting white peach. My bones ached as I walked uptown, the back of my throat coated with his bitter aftertaste. A bum was peeing next to a heap of trash, a group of drunk girls were raucously eating slices of pizza on a stoop, and above them on a fire escape, an old man in a stained undershirt was waving a cigar, yelling at them to shut the fuck up.

I had to escape this city, its filthy sidewalks and bituminous nights, my febrile search for something I would never find.

So I called the airline and rebooked my ticket to Italy.

PART III

22

Three weeks later, I took an overnight flight to Milan that arrived late in the morning.

Isabel arranged for a driver named Fabrizio to pick me up and transport me to her villa, on the southwest branch of Lake Como. Above the dashboard of his car was a small glass ladybug glued to the leather.

"*Fortuna?*" I said, pointing to it, dredging up my high school Italian.

"Ah, *sì*, *una coccinella porta fortuna*." He smiled. "From my daughter."

After an hour, we ascended the foothills of the Alps, the water revealing itself languidly until below us and beyond us stretched an unbounded release of blue. The hairpin turns didn't alleviate my residual anxiety from the flight, nor did the crumbly Seroquel I'd taken from a bottle found in my duffel bag, nearly expired, prescribed to Graham with two refills left.

Finally, we passed a sign announcing the sleepy village, with a population of nine hundred thirty.

"In this town, you have *buco dell'orso*, a cave where the bones of a prehistoric bear were found," Fabrizio said. "And also nearby, they found a grave of decapitated Romans."

"That's a lot of skeletons," I said.

"*Sì*, we have a lot of ghosts here." He nodded. "But we also have a big movie star."

My ears popped. I turned on my phone, despite potential roaming fees, and waited impatiently to connect to the foreign network. I was still nursing a demented modicum of hope there'd be a text from Damon—even after our wrenching weeks apart. I'd only heard from him once since our last night together; he'd sent a cryptic photo of a coral branch styled atop a bowl of persimmons. Of course I had fallen for it, and now cringed thinking of my idiotic response. Sitting there, unanswered.

All at once, a flurry of messages came in—but they weren't from Damon.

Six unread texts from Rex.

The driver put the car in reverse, jerking down a steep incline so a bus could squeeze past. I swallowed a hot shudder of nausea. Why wasn't it ever the ruinous man you actually *wanted* to hear from? Since our last encounter, Rex would not leave me alone. A crazed barrage of texts, trying to break me down and provoke a response. I had mostly ignored them, willing them to stop. But they kept coming. I stuck my face out the window, sucking in the clean alpine air, but over the railing, the road dropped vertically into the water miles below. I shut off my phone and threw it into my bag.

We arrived at a cast-iron gate that creaked open onto a palatial buttercream palazzo, its neoclassical colonnades and curved archways framing a verdant haze of pines and palms and slender cypress trees. A gravel pathway snaked toward a forested grove, where we parked between a rusted red boat and a frescoed shrine. Lugging my suitcase, I wended my way around the oval swimming pool toward the distant voices. Watchful faces of terracotta saints sprouted between blue hydrangeas, and above, ledges of lemons and grapes climbed the terraced gardens like tangled ladders into the sky.

At the end of the path, I found Isabel. She was sitting at a green table beneath a wisteria-laced pergola, her wavy hair tinted nearly platinum in the sunlight. She lowered her white sunglasses, squinting at me as if this were an unbelievable coincidence.

"Look who's arrived, and shockingly in one piece," Isabel announced.

"Barely," I said, kissing her cheek. "I can't believe I'm actually here."

Seated beside her, Gemma raised one eyebrow at me above the rim of her espresso cup.

"So the little one came after all," Gemma said wryly. "Quite the classic unexpected houseguest."

"Gemma is also staying for a couple of nights," Isabel said. "Before she heads down to Ischia to meet her Italian lover."

"Well, technically I'm still in the trenches of a divorce from a man who would use that as incriminating evidence to fuck me over even harder than he's attempting to right now, so don't go spreading that about," Gemma said, lighting up a cigarette. "But yes, it's true."

"And he's younger," Isabel said. "*Molto, molto.*"

"And most importantly, he has a cock the size of his Fiat fortune," said Gemma.

"A massive fortune, to be clear," Isabel said, smiling. "He's her sizzle, just like mine."

Gemma flicked her ash into a cup. "Eat something, or do you not do that sort of thing?"

An extensive spread lay across the table: a hand-pressed oval white pizza with shaved truffles, bresaola from Valchiavenna, bruschetta drizzled in olive oil, and a bowl of fusilli with fresh tomatoes and stracciatella. I felt bloated from the flight but piled my plate with food.

"Is your sizzle still coming?" I asked, trying to sound disinterested.

"Of course he is, though god knows when," Isabel said. "He's supposed to arrive in the next few days while you're here, but hasn't confirmed when yet."

"The girl barely takes a carb while I'm ballooning into a *bombolone*," Gemma muttered.

Isabel released a small sigh. "You know Damon, never not unpredictable and impulsive."

"He thinks he's Alain fucking Delon, the playboy of the Mediterranean," said Gemma. "And, to be clear, he is *not*."

I took a large bite of bruschetta, the chopped tomatoes sliding off onto my plate.

"Did you tell him you were coming?" Isabel asked, eyeing me intently.

"Um, no, I haven't spoken to him at all," I said, my mouth full.

Isabel absently lifted her teacup, performing a quick recalibration in her mind.

"I haven't told him yet either," Isabel said.

I picked at an oily tomato with my fingers. It occurred to me, suddenly, that Damon was the underlying reason Isabel had invited me to Italy. I'd naively assumed she was offering me an escape from the city, carefully staggering my dates to avoid any overlap with him. Now I saw it differently. She couldn't rely on Damon's erratic vacillations of behavior, so she had embedded me here as a lodestone, to draw him in if necessary.

She wasn't aware that my presence had since turned into a repelling force.

"Hasn't he been stuck on his farm?" I asked.

"The farm?" Isabel scoffed. "He's been zipping around the Tuscan countryside on a motorcycle, working on his sculptures in Carrara and god knows what else."

I stared at a wasp circling a vase of white lilies. Damon had texted me that photo of coral from Italy? When he sent it, I had insanely tried to scrutinize the metadata for a geotag, but couldn't identify a location. I thought of the last night I saw him, how I had slavishly dropped to my knees below the nude portrait of his wife. All these weeks, I'd been suffering alone in that infernal city while he'd been here—and I didn't even know.

A cherubic-faced housekeeper named Cosima appeared, depositing a plate of freshly sliced peaches and a bowl of cream. She asked if I wanted a coffee, which I desperately did.

"*Bellisima!*" Cosima exclaimed, clapping her hands. "Signora, this is your daughter?"

"My sister, *mia sorella*," Isabel corrected her with a polite grimace.

I excused myself to wash up, and Cosima directed me inside the villa. The ornate bathroom was encased in terrazzo marble, flecked with rose and rust and malachite, and a large zodiac dial was carved into the floor. I touched the stinger of the Scorpio with my toe, which of course was Damon's sign. It was better he wasn't here, I told myself, stripping off my dirty sweatshirt from the plane. After the past few months, this trip offered a necessary respite, a chance to recharge without the disturbances of men. I needed a break from my torment over Damon, a break from using Damon to distract me from my tormenting fear of Rex. Now, at least, I was protected by miles of distance; both men were in another realm, one I could pretend didn't exist.

I changed into white shorts and knotted a sheer gauze button-down at my waist. In the mirror, my face was puffy from lack of sleep, my bad eye a little bloodshot. Still, I sat down on the edge of the copper tub and snapped a photo in the mirror. My bare legs crossed, a hint of my black bra, my face demurely hidden by the phone. And a turquoise flash of water out the window—so it was indisputable where I was.

As I turned down the long, arched hallway, I fought the urge to send the photo to Damon. A crazy move, maybe—but who else had I taken it for? Part of me wanted to arouse him, assail him with my existence, make him agonize over whether to come. I was so distracted by my indecision that I made a wrong turn and ended up in a library on the far side of the villa. Dusty bookshelves were stippled with sunlight from a high window. I scanned the shelves—mostly in Italian except for Ferrante, randomly in French—and pulled out *È stato così* by Natalia Ginzburg, reading the first line: *I shot him between the eyes.*

When I turned back around, I gasped and dropped the book on the floor with a thud.

"Well, well, if it isn't the little red spy."

It was Rex—he was here. An ill panic flooded my system. He walked toward me in his half-open polka-dot shirt and straw fedora, a hand-rolled cigarette dangling from his silver-white beard. How could Isabel not have told me she'd invited him? I would never have come to Italy had I known, and now it was too late.

"What are you doing here?" I managed to say.

"I could ask you the same question," Rex said. "If I didn't know better, I'd think you were the ghost of Mussolini's last lover, haunting the halls of the palazzo."

"Maybe I am," I said. "Though hopefully I won't end up hanging upside down."

"Or at least, not against your will," he snickered.

We studied each other as if deciding how to play the scene. If I had just met him here, the classic English houseguest, I might've been amused by his rakish advances, his sinister charm, even oddly enticed by it. But that was a dangerous delusion, a misappropriation of his character that could, with one false misstep, cost me my life.

"Oh, don't pretend you aren't happy to see me, darling," Rex said, plucking the cigarette from his mouth. "I promise I won't tell."

"Don't I seem thrilled?" I said.

"As thrilled as when the Germans occupied Paris," he said with a raspy chuckle.

I bent over to pick up the fallen book, his eyes crawling down my bare legs.

"How did you worm your way into this invitation?" I asked.

"I happen to be en route to Venice to write a piece on the brouhaha around the festival, that old dinosaur. You know, the tired debate of separating the art from the artist—must we judge the work based on their conduct or misconduct, blah blah."

"And what has the old dinosaur concluded so far?"

"Well, if it were the latter, every museum would have bare walls."

Rex extended backward over the sofa, flicking his cigarette into an ashtray shaped like a minotaur. I anxiously inched toward the door, a spear of light piercing my eyes.

"You don't think I'd let you slip away, would you?" said Rex. "It's been crickets since I last saw you. Very impolite to ghost me, you know. I feel like a scorned lover."

"A feeling you must be familiar with," I said.

As Rex came closer, my muscles cramped with dread. Now that I'd been ignoring his texts, refusing to engage in his psychotic mind games, I was scared of what he might do next.

"Listen, I'd prefer to be a corporate whistleblower. It's more lauded these days," Rex said, coming up behind me. "You can win a Pulitzer, or at least a hefty book deal."

"Then why don't you aspire to such noble pursuits?"

"Nobility, my dear, doesn't rent you a villa in Italy," he said. "And it certainly doesn't uncover the dark, delicious truth."

"And you're here to tell me they're not mutually exclusive."

"Indeed. In fact, it's indisputable that nothing quite sells like a sordid tale of ill-fated love." He exhaled a hot stream of smoke into my ear. "A vengeful bride at the wheel, a fatal act of perjury. The story practically writes itself."

"Too bad I haven't changed my mind," I said.

"Ah, unfortunate indeed," he said. "Though I did have a thought that perhaps you'd be open to consider an alternative solution—an equitable compromise, if you will."

Rex brushed the hair off my shoulder, the nerves twitching in my neck. I thought of the party in the canyons, how his belt buckle had pressed into my waist, wanting me to feel the hardware of his body, and I shuddered.

"You know I've always carried a little torch for you," Rex said. "And found it quite insufferable, really, that you were engaged to that man instead of me."

"Please tell me you're not trying to proposition me," I said with a derisive laugh.

"Me? Gosh, no, who do you think I am?" Rex smiled with diabolical pleasure. "Though I can think of many worse ideas, now that you mention it."

"Signora?" Cosima interrupted from the doorway. "Your caffè is getting cold."

I hurriedly followed her through the villa, though I could hear Rex's footsteps a few feet behind us. Outside, the cypress trees were backlit by sun, flickering like wild green flames. I realized, with a shiver of horror, that not even this lush scene change, this flight of escape, could prevent the past from tracking me here. Rex would never let this go, not really. He would continue to play this like a sadistic blood sport until, eventually, I was gored.

Gemma looked up as she poured a glass of rosé, her eyes pinballing between us.

"Conspiring to hop the border to Lugano, are we?" she said.

"I tried very hard to convince her," Rex said. "But she wouldn't agree to hide the contraband diamonds in her *pu*—how do you say in *Italiano*?"

"Purse?" Gemma said.

"Precisely!" Rex said. "What else is Switzerland good for except sinister neutrality?"

"Don't forget money laundering," said Gemma. "And excellent skiing."

Meanwhile, the microclimate of lunch had shifted. Isabel ignored them, glued to her phone with a grim look of dejection. I could sense that everything was pressurized by the absence of Damon, its friction building like a blood blister over the skin of the day.

"Isabella, it looks like you're planning a funeral," Rex said.

"If he doesn't come, someone is going to end up in the ground," Gemma muttered.

Isabel gazed into the distance, thumbing the gold pendant of Artemis around her neck, then said, "He's not coming."

There was a brief silence as she let the gravity of this news sink in.

"What do you mean?" said Gemma. "That's bollocks. Of course he's coming."

"No, he's not." Isabel shook her head despondently. "He texted me to say his plans have changed and he's heading to his mate's villa in Forte dei Marmi instead. With no further explanation."

As they discussed this, my phone burned in my hand. So now I would be stuck here, subjected to Rex's psychological torture, while Damon sunbathed on a Tuscan beach. It didn't matter what I sent him—he didn't care if I was here or not. Beneath the table, I ragefully texted Damon the photo I'd snapped in the bathroom.

"It's for the best, really," Gemma was saying. "We don't need him to have a good time."

"No, we're perfectly capable of pretending to do that all on our own," Rex said.

Isabel looked at them forlornly. "Do you think I should call him?"

"Oh, give me your fucking phone. I'll FaceTime him topless if I have to," Gemma declared, attempting to snatch her phone away. "Maybe that will scare him off forever."

Isabel slapped her hand, then looked at me beseechingly. "What does Liv think?"

"Yes, what does the young one think? She knows the rules of the game," Rex said, draining his wine. "And I'm not referring to the Renoir film."

Isabel looked at me. I couldn't discern if she was accusing or entreating me, but I was too reeling to care. I was sick of playing the pawn, sick that I was even here at all. I slugged down my tepid cup of espresso with a little shrug.

"Call him," I implored her. "You've got nothing to lose."

Isabel exhaled slowly. Then she dialed his number and placed her ear to the phone. We all stayed quiet, waiting.

"Damon?" Isabel said, lighting up like a bulb. "We thought you might have died—"

As Isabel rushed inside, we exchanged loaded glances until she was out of earshot.

"Can someone please explain this obsession with him?" Rex said. "I don't get it. He's what we used to call a 'walker' back in the day."

"Except he doesn't suck cock," Gemma said. "Although nothing would shock me."

Rex reached for the sweating bottle of wine and refilled each of our glasses.

"So if he's a walker, what does that make you?" I said to Rex.

"What do you mean?" Rex said with mock exasperation. "I'm a proper suitor, a veritable old swain baby, with nothing but . . . what do you call them?"

"Pure intentions?" Gemma said.

"Correct, those are the ones!" Rex said.

My phone buzzed in my lap, and I discreetly glanced beneath the table:

D: Lean back . . .
D: How I've missed those legs . . .
D: . . . and those parted lips

My cheeks instantly flushed. I couldn't believe Damon had texted back—and while he was on the phone with Isabel. An idiotic rush of elation flooded my veins. His words were merely a Roman candle, quick and explosive, its dazzle dissolving as quickly as it burst, yet I stood under them, wanting more.

"Be honest with me," Gemma said, pointing her cigarette at my face. "Have you and Damon ever smashed? Even once? I swear on my divorce settlement that I won't tell."

"What? Are you crazy?" I tucked the burning phone beneath my thigh.

"There have been crazier accusations," she said.

"Fine, then have *you* smashed him?" I said.

"Touché!" Rex said, lowering a slice of mortadella into his mouth.

"I just pray he doesn't show up while we're here," Gemma groaned, ashing her cigarette into an empty cup. "Even I can't tolerate the ensuing theatrics, the histrionic farce of it all. I just want to enjoy my fucking wine and fucking pasta and fucking lake view in peace!"

We heard Isabel's voice, floating above the vibrato of cicadas. As the high of his response waned, I realized his words were meaningless. Damon knew he wasn't going to see me on this trip—so he could shoot texts through the air, as errant as arrows, indifferent to the harm of their landing. I took a large gulp of wine, rinsing my mouth with its citrusy sting.

"Trust me, he won't come," I said brusquely.

"How do you know?" Rex said.

"I just know," I said.

They cast suspicious glances at my embittered certainty. Under the table, I furiously texted back: Too bad you'll miss the rest of me. Three dots appeared, wavered, then vanished. I finished the wine, my anger toward him resuming as if I had lifted my finger from a pause button.

Then a text appeared: I wouldn't dare . . .

I looked up, confused, as Isabel came running out of the house, panting with unbridled excitement, waving her phone like a letter that had arrived with auspicious news.

"He's coming!" Isabel exclaimed. "He's coming tonight."

After lunch, Cosima escorted me to my assigned room so that I could settle in and unpack. Naturally, I headed into the villa, but then our house manager, Barbara, yelled after us in Italian, clapping her hands and emphatically gesturing in the direction of the road. She seemed to be saying that I would be sleeping in the lake.

"Ah, you're in the *casa barca*," Cosima said apologetically. "The boathouse."

I followed her around the pool and across the gravel alcove to a hidden pathway of uneven stone steps, ascending into a dense copse of trees. At the top was a long private bridge, suspended high above the road, covered by an arched trellis of ivy. As we crossed, the open metal railing vibrated beneath our feet, swaying slightly as cars and motorcycles hurtled below. I tried not to look down, focusing on the luminous stretch of water beyond, until I heard Cosima screaming, "STOP, SIGNORA, STOP!"

I would have missed the opening in the floor—a gaping hole without a door, descending into the other side.

"Don't cross this bridge when you've had *molto vino.*" Cosima giggled nervously.

I didn't say that was precisely when I would have to cross it. We cautiously climbed down a glass spiral staircase, no railing to grasp onto, no landings to brace a sandaled slip, as if willing the injury of a misstep. Finally, we reached the boathouse, a narrow white room that opened directly onto the dock, the water sloshing below. Cosima pointed out that my suitcase had been delivered, and inquired if I needed anything else.

"How many bedrooms are in the house?" I asked.

"Ah, there are five," she said with an apologetic shrug. "Signora is on the second floor with two empty bedrooms, and the other two guests are on the third floor."

After she left, I slid open the glass door and collapsed onto the bed. The sun had punctured a reef of clouds, sending phosphorescent ripples across the lake. Isabel must have placed me here, isolated from the villa, as a cautionary measure. It was a master stroke, really; her bedroom would be accessible to both Rex and Damon, while mine was unreachable in the unmonitored hours of night. And wasn't it better this way? The boathouse would provide a protective barrier, distanced from the potential escalation of danger under one roof.

The wine from lunch watered me down, the bed rocking beneath me like a boat unmoored. I closed my eyes, trying to anchor myself. I was safe here, wasn't I, sheltered by this fortress of water, by the snowcaps brushing against the sky. But even I knew this was a false consolation; the scenery might as well have been a set piece, painted on. How was I supposed to feel safe when, in another life, I could have been in bed on my honeymoon with Graham? Listening to him read aloud as the sea knocked against these same ancient slabs of stone. I could feel him now, the imprint of his body beside mine, whispering a warning in my ear: *he knows, he knows, he knows.*

I awoke disoriented, having drifted off to sleep. The sun was lower in the sky, an aura of occulting light around the mountains. I checked my phone and found several texts from Isabel, asking me to come to her room before dinner. I quickly unpacked and placed my passport in the safe, then showered without washing my hair—I didn't have a converter, so my blow-dryer was useless. I chose a long tangerine dress and held my fraying espadrilles in my hands to climb the perilous spiral staircase and trek back to the villa.

I entered through the side door by the pool and turned down a black-and-white marble hall that accidentally landed me in the kitchen. A staff of older Italian women were in the middle of cooking dinner, stirring pots and chopping vegetables, and when I entered, they clapped and shouted, "*Bellisima!*" An effusive chef named Maria, with dyed aubergine hair, fed me a hot spoonful of bright yellow risotto, while Cosima handed me a ruby-tinted drink, bittersweet like burnt caramelized oranges, before shooing me upstairs.

On the second floor, I followed the voice of Nina Simone crooning "My Baby Just Cares for Me" down a mirrored side hallway and found Isabel dancing around her room in a floral silk kimono. When she saw me perched in the doorway, she called out, "Livia? Get the fuck in here!" and I entered her bedroom. The suite, regally enrobed in gold, opened onto a wraparound terrace overlooking the lake on one side, and the pool and gardens on the other. I sat down on the edge of her bed, while Isabel surveyed her closet with a glass of prosecco in hand.

"Damon just called to say he's on his way and should be here in time for dinner," Isabel said with jittery excitement.

"Isn't that good news?" I said.

"Yes, but I'll throw myself in the lake if I don't find something to wear," she said. "I just bought this for the trip. What do you think?"

Isabel spun around, untying her kimono to reveal a lacy blue bra with embroidered flowers and underwear to match. For a moment, I was stunned—she had never exposed herself like this before. Her face was anxious with girlish hope, yet her body contained an erotic force, an assured autonomy of self that only came with age. Why wouldn't Damon want her? I tried to detect any inhibition over her mature body, but I found none. I could suddenly picture her entwined with Damon on the bed, straddling him against the ornate headboard, losing herself through lust. As I once did—before he dropped me.

"You look unbelievably sexy," I said. "It's giving Monica Vitti in *L'Eclisse*."

"I've never bought my own lingerie. Isn't that awful to admit? Jack would always surprise me, slipping it under my pillow, before he'd whisk me away on some hot weekend." Isabel glanced at a framed photo of her late husband, propped on her nightstand. "I haven't been with anyone else since we got married . . . But I saw this at Bergdorf's before the trip and said *fuck it*, it's time to feel alive again."

"I couldn't agree more," I said. "So, which man will be the lucky recipient?"

Isabel shot me a look, as if to say we both knew the answer.

"We can't pretend I'm not playing favorites," she said. "Trust me, when you get to be my age, you'll understand the *benefits* of a younger man."

Isabel dropped her kimono onto the bed and walked over to the terrace. I could almost see the anticipatory thrill of the night ahead moving sinuously through her spine—the prospect of Rex and Damon under one roof, producing the theater of rivalry. She threw open the doors, the sheer curtains fluttering like diaphanous wings.

"I'll tell you a little secret," said Isabel, turning back to me. "All men look the same in the dark . . . give or take a few inches."

I laughed. Isabel wrapped herself in the curtain, her figure silhouetted in amber folds of light. As I watched her, the nude portrait of Caroline materialized before me, swathed in impasto layers of cotton candy. I felt the urge to tell Isabel about the painting, to catalyze the same spiral of madness that had consumed me—but then it would beg the question why I had been inside his bedroom in the first place.

"Maybe I should send Damon a photo of you, just like that," I suggested.

"Compared to the ones that girls probably send him, this would seem virginal," she said.

"At least we know they're not coming from his fake wife."

"You're terrible," she said, unwrapping herself from the curtain with a twirl.

As Isabel got dressed, I wandered onto the terrace. Over the lake, the sun was sinking fast, casting a dark lattice across the mountain. I couldn't figure out if her sensual display was in preparation for Damon's arrival, or aimed to subtly intimidate me. Did she suspect that Damon knew I was here? And that was the reason he changed his plans? As Isabel glanced at me through the window, tightening her bra strap, I felt nervous that she would be watching me more closely now. And so, too, would Rex.

When I re-entered the room, Isabel had slipped on a shimmery bronze dress, dipping between her ample breasts. We stood in front of a mirror as I zipped up the back, our faces set beside each other.

"Don't be upset he didn't tell you he was in Italy, angel," Isabel said.

"I'm not upset," I said quickly.

She glanced at my bad eye in the mirror.

"But you should know that I told him you were here."

We went downstairs to the loggia by the pool, beneath a colossal sequence of archways that framed the lake with postcard symmetry. Gemma and Rex were lounging on a green-striped sofa, sipping jewel-toned cocktails and picking at a large spread on the table: bowls of herbed olives and parmesan flakes, crostini with warm ricotta topped by broad beans and mint. The ritual of *aperitivo* hour meant to delay dinner while we waited for the arrival of Damon. As Gemma and Rex discussed Brexit, and Isabel stared fixedly at her phone, I climbed the stairs to the terraced gardens that rose above the villa. Hedges of lavender quavered with bees, and lemons dangled like alarm bells from the branches above. I climbed another level to the grapevines at the top as I heard the gate creaking open and the crush of gravel below. And suddenly it seemed everything that had brought the four of us here, to Italy, was without any logical coherence, yet now terribly real.

When I looked down, Damon was getting out of a red Fiat, stretching his back from the ride. I popped a grape into my mouth, chartreuse and pulpy with bitter seeds, then spit it out. Isabel rushed over to embrace him, whispering something in his ear, then led him by the arm toward the villa. From this aerial view, it was as if I was watching a scene from a '60s European film about two lovers, a moment of coming together that anticipates a tragic parting, a beginning embedded within a closing shot. And I, out of frame, an ancillary observer, the girl always the most disrupted in the end.

I nervously made my way back down to the group. Damon was sitting on the edge of a wicker chair, holding a glass of sparkling water. I stood behind him in his periphery, but he didn't turn around. He was exquisitely tan in a pale blue shirt, his hair pulled back into a small bun.

"We thought you might have drowned in the lake," Gemma said, gesturing to me.

"Not yet," I said. "But that boathouse could be swept under at any second, really."

"Liv has already been deported," Rex said, biting into a crostini, the ricotta sticking to his beard. "She's a woman in exile."

Damon glanced over his shoulder as if just noticing my presence. "Exiled? What punishable crime did she commit?"

"She's like poor Cordelia!" said Rex. "Thrown out of the kingdom for refusing to declare her filial love."

"'I cannot heave my heart into my mouth,'" I said, quoting the play.

"Well done. I played her once in a terrible production," said Gemma. "Which became quite awkward when I started shagging the man who played my father."

"Wasn't he quite famous, at least?" Rex asked.

"Yes, very, and became more famous for heaving his knob into his nanny," Gemma said.

I leaned over the table to pick up a fresh cocktail from a tray. I could feel Damon watching me from behind, his eyes lingering on my dress.

"Don't listen to them," Isabel said. "I gave Livia the boathouse so she can have some solitude to write."

Is that why you put me there, I thought.

"And so she doesn't have to be stuck with us geriatrics," said Gemma.

"Speak for yourself," Isabel retorted.

"That doesn't sound too rough," Damon said.

Isabel innocently took a bite of an orange wedge from her Aperol spritz. "Well, I couldn't have her sharing a bathroom with you, could I?"

"No, I would've definitely requested a room change," Damon said.

I met his eyes then, as placid and clear as the surface of the pool.

"Nice man bun," I said sarcastically.

"You like it?" Damon replied.

"Fuck off, no girl likes a man bun!" Gemma said, reaching over to grab it. "We want our hair pulled, not the other way around."

For dinner, we ate at the table beneath the pergola, lit by orange tapers dripping tributaries of wax onto the tablecloth. There were bowls of buttery saffron risotto; roasted fluke in a soup of capers and tomatoes; pizzas with roasted eggplant, provolone, and smoked anchovies; and many bottles of wine. Everyone was rapt while Damon told stories of his trip to the Apuan Alps, its quarries dating back to Ancient Rome, to Michelangelo, haunted by ruin and marred by severed fingers, the dreams of crushed stonecutters. His weeks were spent working on some sculptures, he said, taking a break from jewelry making.

"When you look at the mountains, you think the peaks are snow-covered, but the snow never melts," Damon mused. "It's marble: a self-contained world of stone and dust."

I felt drunk by the time dessert was served, and overly full, but still devoured the olive oil plum cake with a dollop of vanilla gelato. I had stayed mostly quiet throughout dinner, mentally noting that Damon had barely made eye contact with me. Now, on my fourth glass of wine, I felt a tingly heat in my chest, coagulating my anger over his weeks in Italy without contact.

"And where were you staying?" Isabel asked him. "While you were carving away."

She flicked me a glance, as if the question were asked on

our behalf. And I did want to know, if only to gauge whether Caroline had been with him or not.

"Up in the hills," Damon said with a vague shrug. "A farmhouse of a client who houses artists and writers."

At this, Isabel pulled her shoulders back, her body tense with a rush of envy.

"Oh, I know Beatrice, that old slag—sorry—*contessa*," Gemma said, slurring her words. "Don't tell me she tried to sneak into your room at night, as is her wont. Or do tell me."

"We're just good friends," Damon asserted. "I knew her husband back in the day."

"Conveniently, that husband is now dead," Gemma said, then waved her lighter at Isabel. "Weren't you close with her?"

"I was." Isabel coldly put her spoon down. "Before she wronged me."

I could see Damon looking at her, silently issuing a gesture of remorse while a wisp of candle smoke rose between them. I dipped my finger into a puddle of gelato and announced I was going to bed.

I walked back to the boathouse, guided by the flashlight on my almost-dead phone. The cypress trees were marbled with moonlight, rising like obelisks over the bridge. I imagined what would unfold in the villa tonight without me. If they'd all have a nightcap, then Isabel would invite Damon into her bedroom to show him something. They'd sit on her bed and talk quietly, about the sculptures he had carved, about the sienna-dusted hills that moved him, while Isabel let her kimono fall open, revealing a hint of lace, a fallen strap. She'd softly caress his cheek, leaning in and—

I stopped short. The door in the bridge gaped open before my feet, with the fatal gravity of a black hole. I could have fallen, I thought, cracked all my ribs. And no one would even have known until morning.

I took off my shoes and inched down the spiral staircase, gripping the edge of each step. When I finally made it to the boathouse, I flung open the doors to the lake. The sky was crowded with stars, and sequins of light popped across the dark water. I stripped off my clothes and climbed into bed, placing my phone on my chest.

During my last night in the city with Damon, he had tried to unlatch my barricade of feelings, make room for an honest exchange between us. And instead, I had begged him to saturate me on his bedroom floor. How did I expect him to act now? I covered my bad eye, watching the shadows ripple across the ceiling. If Rex had not been terrorizing me, dangling blackmail to dredge up the dead, then it might have been different. I wouldn't need to debase myself in order to obliterate the memory, stored in my body, of what I had done. Maybe Damon would have invited me to Carrara, or later tonight slipped into my bed. Why was it so hard to admit that I missed him, that I had not stopped thinking of him? And what if he felt the same way? He could—it was possible he did. Why else had he changed his plans when he found out I was here?

Yes, I decided as I closed my eyes, I would tell Damon my feelings tomorrow. Maybe that would solve everything.

The boats were softly knocking against the dock, lulling me to sleep. I was half-awake when my phone vibrated, but the message was not from him.

It was from Isabel: He kissed me, it read. He finally kissed me.

23

I slept fitfully until sunrise. I threw on a T-shirt, in need of coffee, and stumbled across the bridge in bare feet to the villa. The air was heavy with dew, a pewter mist drifting over the lake. I crept through the pool door, relieved no one was awake except an elderly housekeeper drinking an espresso at the kitchen table. I told her not to worry, I would make coffee myself, and she shrugged and mumbled something like, "Fine, if you want it to be terrible." Then I sat on a damp sofa in the loggia and tried to write for a few undisturbed hours while an old Italian man fished a swarm of dead honeybees out of the pool.

The local church bells chimed at 8:30 a.m., when breakfast was set out in the garden: bowls of wild cherries and green plums, apricot tarts and lemon cake sliced thinly like bread, and pots of fig jam. I ate alone and drank three more coffees while the procession trickled downstairs. Gemma, draped in a chaotic Pucci caftan, announcing she'd slept "like a psych patient thanks to an Ambien and these gummies from an actor I banged in LA," then requested a poached egg but proceeded to eat two chocolate croissants. Rex, in a red Breton boat shirt, smoking a cigarette and yelling on the phone to one of his editors in London. And Isabel last, in a white linen dress, a secretive smile on her face as if the kiss had happened moments ago. I didn't ask where Damon was.

After breakfast, Isabel instructed us to meet promptly at the dock for a private boat tour—which, she specified, was not an optional activity. I applied sunscreen and changed into crochet shorts, grabbing my straw visor before heading back to the villa. When Isabel saw me, she asked if I would grab her hat as well; her knee was bothering her, she said, so she didn't want to run back upstairs.

I went up to her bedroom and did a cursory scan. In front of the bed, a hat was perched on a velvet bench, next to a neat pile of clothing. And on the floor: the lacy blue bra. Splayed out like a jellyfish, as if hastily removed. I wondered if Isabel had slept with it on, hoping her kiss with Damon would go further. Or had it actually gone further? His fingers fumbling to unhook it, sliding the straps off her shoulders to kiss her nipples, as he had mine. I quickly grabbed the hat, trying to erase this scene from my mind.

As I headed back, I heard footsteps approaching from the other end of the hallway. Damon walked out of his bedroom, sleepily buttoning a wrinkled shirt over green swimming trunks.

"Oh, hey," he said, stopping when he saw me. "I was hoping it was you . . ."

We stood there, staring at each other. I could feel my stupid heartbeat tripping over itself, my thick curtain of hair sticking to my neck.

"The boat is leaving in five minutes," I said, turning toward the stairs.

"Can we talk for a second?"

"Everyone is waiting downstairs—"

"Please, Liv, just hold on." Damon came toward me, and I stopped moving. I leaned against the wall, twisting my hair over one shoulder. Up close, his face contained a weariness I hadn't noticed yesterday, a soft, almost pretty angst that made me want to touch his full mouth.

"How have you been?" he said. "It's been a while since . . . the last time."

"If you genuinely wanted to know, there are ways you could have found out."

"I know, and I'm sorry. There's a reason I haven't been in touch."

"Because you've been in Italy this whole time?"

Damon let out an exhausted sigh, rubbing his eyes with the back of his hand. "It's been a difficult couple of weeks, trust me. And I didn't want to involve you in my mess."

I nervously rubbed my collarbone. I thought of saying something cute like: Did you miss more than my legs? But the image of him kissing Isabel flooded my vision. I considered mentioning it to see if he would laugh it off, explain in confidence that it had been an embarrassing mistake—he meant to kiss her cheek. But there was the possibility it was intentional, and the joke had always been on me.

"Let's just forget about it," I said. "It doesn't matter now."

I tried to slip by, but Damon pressed his hand to my chest.

"It does matter," he said. "There's something I need to tell you."

My breath was rising and falling against his palm, the space between our bodies vibrating like a slow earthquake. Our eyes met, and I felt my entire body lift toward him as if he was pulling my center of gravity with an invisible string. He leaned so close to my mouth we were breathing the same air, so close I could almost taste him.

Then we heard the banister crack like a spine, and we quickly pulled away.

Rex was standing at the top of the stairs, keenly watching us. A deranged smile spread across his face as if he'd been handed a nuclear code.

"Very sorry to interrupt," Rex said. "But I came to inform you the boat is waiting."

On the water, everyone was generally in a good mood. I sat alone in the back of the boat, while Rex and Gemma were in the middle, and Isabel was at the front with Damon and Lorenzo, our energetic guide. He wore Ray-Ban aviators and would periodically yell at the captain, Ricky, who would yell back, "Okay, then, you drive!" We stopped to tour a few gardens and landed in a small fishing village for lunch, then strolled around with cups of fresh gelato. By early afternoon, we were all tired and ready to head back. We piled into our same seats while Lorenzo explained the many conspiracies behind the murder of Mussolini—he'd been caught hiding with one of his mistresses in a village nearby.

Rex raised his hand. "Wasn't Mussolini known to be a sadomasochistic lover?"

"I've never fucked a fascist dictator myself," Gemma said, "but it wouldn't shock me."

"It's true." Lorenzo nodded. "Apparently, he would schedule up to four women per day."

"Gosh, you'd think he'd be too exhausted to invade Ethiopia after that," Rex said.

As we passed Lezzeno, a tiny hamlet, Lorenzo went on to tell a story about a fifteenth-century coven of witches who had placed a love spell on the local young men. I tried to listen, but Rex kept flashing me unhinged messages with his eyes across the boat, and I was starting to feel a little seasick. Too much sun and gelato and gothic horror. I turned around and leaned out the back, the frothy wind whipping my hair.

The wake-stream sliced cleanly between the mountains, but in the distance, the clouds were swelling into purple-black contusions. Now that Rex had witnessed my charged moment with Damon on the stairs, I feared everything was about to get worse. He would add this to his arsenal of scare tactics, leverage it in some maniacal way. I didn't know what subterfuge he was plotting next, but he now held the power to ruin me in Isabel's eyes.

"So then they burned all the beautiful witches at the stake!" Lorenzo said.

"Should we burn Liv at the stake for not listening?" said Rex.

I felt his eyes on the backs of my bare thighs and turned around to face the group.

"Livia, pay attention!" Isabel clapped from the front. "You don't do this every day."

The boat slowed as we approached a forested island. "We are now approaching Isola Comacina, the only island on the lake," Lorenzo said. "During the Middle Ages, the Bishop of Como cursed it, declaring: 'The bells will not ring anymore. No stone will be put upon stone. No one will ever host anyone again or he will die a violent death!' Nobody came back for centuries. It turned into an uninhabitable island of snakes. Anyone who tried? *Dead*. Then, in 1947, two men said forget this curse, we are going to build a restaurant! Well, one was burned to death when his speedboat caught on fire. And the other, Carlo, was shot in the head by his mistress, Countess Bellentani, a beautiful young poetess, after he had broken off their affair."

"We should take an actual shot every time someone says the word *affair*," Gemma said.

"Or *mistress*," said Isabel.

"Then we'd be wasted the entire trip," Rex said, tossing me a wink.

"It was the scandal of Como," Lorenzo went on. "The

night it happened, Carlo was at a fabulous party at Villa D'Este, where the countess was also in attendance with her husband. When Carlo saw her, he declared: 'An ill wind is blowing for me tonight.' And it was. While everyone was drunk and dancing, the countess took her husband's pistol, and *pow pow*! Shot Carlo right in the head as the orchestra played. A crime of passion!"

A peal of thunder suddenly rolled across the lake. Beneath our feet, the floor began to quiver from its unseen rumblings. We looked out at the sky, a flock of storm clouds sweeping in, hovering above us like birds of prey. Then the sky cracked open, releasing a torrent of rain.

"Don't worry, it is nothing!" Lorenzo shrugged.

But the rain came down harder, pouring through the open windows, drenching our hair and our skin. Damon jumped up to help Lorenzo close the glass panels, but their weight tipped the boat to one side, throwing us against the other, as a branch of lightning came crashing down.

"It's fine, everything's fine!" Lorenzo yelled, but his face had turned white.

"Was this supposed to happen?" Gemma bellowed. "Did we all forget to check our weather apps?"

"I don't know. It's, how do you say, a tempest?" Lorenzo said, befuddled.

"Oh jolly, just a bloody tempest," said Rex.

Another bolt of lightning fissured down into the water nearby, hurling the boat sideways, and we all screamed.

"Don't worry," Lorenzo said, grabbing on to a metal pole. "You can't get struck by lightning on a boat!"

"Isn't that exactly where you *can* get struck by lightning?" Gemma exclaimed.

"Livia, get my purse, please," Isabel commanded. "I think I have some Xanax in there."

The wind was gathering speed and lashed at the windows,

sending a surge of waves beneath the boat. I was shivering, my hair soaked, and through my blurred eye and the blurred glass, I could almost make out a bending funnel of spray between the water and the clouds. Isabel pulled me over so that I was seated beside her, holding her hand, and Damon sat down on the other side of me to balance the weight. Even amid the chaos, I was still aware of his shoulder against mine, the press of his wet skin like a cold secret.

Finally, we approached our dock, but the captain refused to let us off. It was too dangerous, Lorenzo said. We would have to circle around for another forty-five minutes or so. But when another bolt of lightning struck a church nearby, bursting into flames, Gemma shrieked, "LET ME OFF THIS FUCKING BOAT! MY PSYCHIC SAID I'M NOT MEANT TO DIE IN ITALY!"

The rain was torrential now, pummeling the boat on all sides. We were instructed to leave our bags and sandals behind as we evacuated one by one. Damon got off first so he could help the rest of us deboard. The boat was slamming wildly against the dock, the water rising and falling beneath. When it was my turn, he wrapped his hands around my waist, and I slid down his torso until my feet were planted on the ground. Isabel was last to go. She stood on the rim of the boat, paralyzed with fear, gripping both Damon and Lorenzo's hands as they shouted over the ear-splitting rain to come down. But as she took a step, her heel slipped, the boat rocking backward as she flew forward, and she plummeted into the water with a piercing scream.

We all ran to the edge of the dock, shouting her name, the rain pounding down so hard that I could barely make out the image of Damon diving after her and vanishing beneath the black surface. For a terrifying moment, time seemed to slow. The rain stung my eyes, the pull of death so close it thrashed beneath my feet, and I could suddenly taste the salt-sting of a colder sea, drowning me in the car, filling my nostrils and lungs until there was no air left to breathe.

Damon finally resurfaced with Isabel in his arms. We watched him swim toward the rocky shore, cradling her like a child, and together they emerged from the water, her soaked white dress clinging to her skin. Her body was tremulous with shock, but even from the dock I saw her surrender into his arms, burying her face in his neck as he said *don't let go.*

Later that night, after we had taken hot showers, we met in the formal dining room for dinner. Hot bowls of courgette soup drizzled with pesto, creamy cacio e pepe, and paper-thin veal Milanese. The brass candelabra had been lit, a fire burning in the stone fireplace while the rain murmured like a fugue outside the window. Isabel barely touched her plate and retired early, her face bone-pale with exhaustion.

After we finished, I was sent upstairs to deliver a tray of tiramisu and fresh mint tea. When I entered her bedroom, Isabel was lying on the bed in pink silk pajamas, her face drawn in anguish. I placed the tray beside an altar of flickering candles and climbed onto the other side of the bed.

"Oh, Liv, I feel like such a fucking fool," she said, her eyes sagging.

"It could have happened to any of us," I said. "Who could have predicted this freak storm?"

"No, it was so stupid of me. I should have been wearing my knee brace, but I wanted to feel young and hot, and now look at me, like an old invalid." Her jaw trembled as she took a raspy breath. "This whole trip is ruined."

"Nothing is ruined! By the morning, you'll feel back to normal, I promise."

Isabel lifted her pajama top, revealing a vicious bruise on her hip where she'd hit the corner of the boat. She asked me to apply a special cream that Barbara had given her. I didn't tell her the label specified it was for hemorrhoids.

"Bruises can be sexy," I said. "Maybe Damon is into that sort of thing."

Isabel laughed weakly, but a single tear rolled down her cheek before she wiped it away. As I rubbed the ointment into her warm skin, I could feel her humiliation seeping into my bones, clinging like a damp chill.

"I know it sounds silly, but when he dove into the water to save me and carried me to the shore, I felt so secure in his arms." Isabel sighed deeply, glancing at the photo on her nightstand. "I haven't felt that way since my husband, and it reminded me of what I may never have again."

"But you will," I said. "I know you will."

"Did you feel safe with Graham?" she asked.

I hesitated, my throat tightening. The way she posed the question almost implied that she knew the answer. "That's not the first thing that comes to mind," I said.

"No one tells you that feeling unsafe can be the most terrifying feeling of all," she said.

Isabel smiled, a doleful smile, as if she understood the context for which I had no language. How could I say that his love was no safer than seeking shelter in the arms of the enemy? In the end, certain men protected only what they could easily destroy; they built what they could break without accounting for the wreckage left in their wake.

"I want to show you something," she said.

Isabel removed a red pouch from her nightstand. In my palm, she shook out a pair of vintage diamond cufflinks in the shape of a coiled snake, a ruby crowning its head like a drop of blood.

"I gave these to Jack as a wedding present," she explained. "The serpent is an amulet of protection, meant to ward off danger and guard the sanctity of our love."

"They're beautiful," I said.

"I've decided to give them to Damon as a gift, to thank him for saving my life. Today, of course, but in other ways, too."

The emerald eyes of the snake blinked in the candlelight, venomous and alive, like my ring. A sudden chill of clarity ran through me, and I realized what I had to do. Now that Damon had kissed her and rescued her from the storm, Isabel finally had solid proof of his romantic interest. She no longer needed to use Rex as a foil: his role was complete, he had served his purpose. This was my chance to beat him at his own game. I could confide in her that Rex was causing me acute emotional distress; he had been acting inappropriately, trying to pursue me behind her back with coercive force. And wasn't that all true? Isabel would be horrified by his predatory behavior—she would expel him from her villa, from her inner circle. It might not solve the bigger threat, but it was a place to start. I passed the cufflinks back to her, my temples pounding with urgent pressure.

"Isabel, there's something I need to talk to you about," I began.

She looked at me, her eyes churning inscrutably. "I already know what everyone thinks, Liv, that Damon is using me in various ways. You don't have to elaborate—"

"No, not at all. That's not what I wanted to say—"

"But every so often, a relationship comes along that defies taxonomy. A deep, nearly spiritual connection for which there is no classification system," Isabel said. "And when I fell into the lake today, and thought I might not make it, I realized that even if it never turns romantic between us, still, that is enough."

I shook my head, confused. A sharp gale of wind struck the windows, as if someone was banging on the glass.

"But Damon *kissed* you," I said. "What do you call that if not romantic?"

A pained, puzzled look crossed her face. "What are you talking about?"

"You texted me last night, remember?" I said. "That he finally kissed you?"

"It wasn't Damon," Isabel said. "Rex was the one who kissed me."

I walked back to the boathouse in the drizzling dark. The lake had risen from the storm, the waterline inching up to meet the dock. The bridge was slippery, every step of the staircase daring me to yield to its spiraling descent. When I finally made it down, I collapsed onto the bed, too drained to wash my face. I stripped off my damp clothes and curled into a ball over the covers.

So Damon hadn't kissed her after all. My assumption almost seemed silly now. But the fact that it was Rex, a cunning offensive move, felt like a vicious blow of defeat. Now what would I do? Rex had rendered it impossible to seek Isabel's help, leaving no one to confide in, no one to protect me, alone again with my crippling dread.

I closed my eyes, the boats clinking like ice cubes against the rocks. Without warning, my chest heaved with a contraction. I wanted Damon, and he was not here. I didn't know if it was longing, or loneliness, or the incalculable distance in between, but I no longer cared about the consequences. In my head, I heard myself calling him in, praying to the moon in some crazed manifestation, sending a message across the lake.

But as I drifted off to sleep, it was Graham who appeared instead. His arms reaching out across the water, forcing my head beneath the cold surface until my lungs ran out of air.

I awoke gasping to the sound of footsteps. The staircase creaking with the heavy weight of a body. My throat closed up. Maybe it was the wind banging against the glass, or I was still half-submerged in a dream. But the noise was coming closer, a thud on the landing. Oh, I thought, fear writhing inside me—it was Rex. He's come to fuck with me, to force me into some depraved exchange. I couldn't move, a black shadow spreading across the wall as the footsteps approached the bed.

I felt a hand on my back, sliding the hair off my bare shoulders.

But I knew, by the imprint of his palm, who it was. I turned over and looked up at Damon. He stroked my face, tentative and tender, as if my skin were brand-new, my body a chrysalis, and beneath it the unfolding of bright wings.

"I really did miss you," he said.

"How much?" I said.

"Enough that I would risk my life coming down those stairs."

He knelt on the bed and kissed me, a slow, open kiss. His mouth slid over my ears, the basin of my hips, digging his chin into my thong. I could feel myself dissolving, until I was so close that I clamped his jaw between my thighs.

"Fuck, I've missed this so much," he said.

I said that I did, too, but I could barely form words as he turned me over and dragged me to the edge of the bed. When he was inside me, I lost the ability to see. He kept moving steadily as if he was carving stone, smoothing some calcified edge only he could reach, and when he held me down, repeating my name, my body caved open for him.

When it was over, Damon lay on top of me for a long time. The thunder had faded to a low murmur, like a distant conversation in another room.

"I think she put me in the boathouse so this specifically wouldn't happen," I said.

"Little does she know that you can't be trusted anywhere," he said.

"You mean we can't be," I said.

He slid out and pulled me into his chest. We were quiet for a while, staring out at the night. I wanted to ask what he'd been on the brink of confessing this morning but didn't want to break this stillness, wrapped in the end of the storm.

"I am sorry again about the past few weeks," Damon said with a sigh. "It's been a pretty stressful time, in a way that's been hard for me to process. And I needed some time to work through it on my own."

"Well, it's been pretty bleak for me, too," I said.

"I hope not all because of me, but I'll accept a portion of the blame."

"Don't give yourself too much credit," I said.

He pressed his lips to my shoulder blade. My fingers were still sticky from the ointment I'd applied to Isabel's bruise, and I felt a twinge of guilt.

"To be honest, Liv, since you came back into my life, I was reminded of everything I had failed to become over the years," he said. "There's this version of myself I envisioned, and then there's the one I haven't been able to escape."

"We all have unlived lives inside us," I said. "The ones we nearly chose."

"I know, but in my mind, you were the one I kept returning to."

In the air, he measured my small hand against his large one, all the marble and soil and gold etched into his palm. He pressed my hand above my head so I was staring up at him, and then he was kissing me again as if I were someone else, someone he might have loved all along.

24

The next morning at breakfast, the sun was out as if it had never been missing, and everyone was discussing their plans for the day. Gemma was meeting a girlfriend for a spa day, and Damon offered to take her by boat, since it was on his way to a fishing village for a "pickup." Gemma asked if he meant *la cocaina*, and he flashed a roguish smile and said, "Something equally illicit." I offered to stay in the villa with Isabel, who was taking a day to rest and recover, but she encouraged me to go along and get a facial or something. I didn't say that the cost of a facial would literally bankrupt me. Instead, I would arrange to meet up with an old friend, Luca, the manager of one of the new hotels on the lake.

"Sounds like Liv is plotting a naughty little assignation of her own," Rex snickered.

"Good for her," said Gemma, castrating the tip of a flaky croissant. "Why should she be sitting around with us when she could be underneath some hot young man?"

"Oh, she was, quite recently," Isabel said. "You should've seen how fast she gave that doctor a blowjob—on their very first date."

There was a comical pause where everyone glanced up at me, including Damon.

"*Ripetere?*" Rex put a hand to his ear. "I haven't had my second espresso yet."

"Isabel!" I said loudly, setting down my cup.

Isabel spread a glob of fig jam onto a slice of almond cake with a wicked little grin.

"What? You did it, not me," Isabel said, looking at Damon. "We all know what men like, and they don't care who they get it from. A mouth is a mouth."

I turned red. I had never actually disclosed the specific details of that date, but clearly Isabel was in mind to rouse a reaction. I worried she had heard Damon sneak out of the villa last night, or subconsciously intuited his movement in her sleep. The cautiously opened door, the squeak of footsteps on the marble floor that separated their bedrooms. I concentrated on spreading a glob of jam onto my toast, nervous that she could detect him on me, glowing in my veins like radioactive evidence.

"See, this essentially is the problem with dating right now," Gemma bemoaned. "Liv is competing with women like me who no longer have to listen to the crushing chime of their biological clock going *tick-tock tick-tock*, thank god, but I'm dealing with girls like her who think the orgasm gap is a fucking social movement."

I clarified that the hotel manager was *gay* and we had met in *theater school*, but everyone had moved on. After breakfast, Gemma and I piled into the extra boat, a 1968 Riva Ariston with an orange stripe, while Damon drove. The water was glossy and smooth like tinted green glass. After we dropped Gemma off at the Villa d'Este, Damon and I were finally alone. I turned to him uncertainly, almost bashfully, as if we had narrowly fled some sort of confinement and now didn't know what to make of our newfound freedom.

"So what do we do now?" I said.

Damon twisted the strap of my green dress, kissing the freckles on my shoulder.

"Now I take you on another adventure," he said. "A little *l'avventura.*"

As we sped off, I felt a sense of expansion in my chest. In the city, alone together, I had always been wary of our rigid perimeters, hemming us in like the enclosed skyline. Now, on this boat, with Damon at the wheel, saying something that I couldn't quite hear over the wind about the water catching the light like a slab of labradorite, I saw a glimmer of happiness. To feel this way again, on the brink of something, gliding toward another life as unbroken as the ridgeline, these endless blue distances.

We docked in Careno, a sleepy hamlet with rusted roofs embedded like seashells above the shore. Damon held my hand as we walked up the cobblestone steps as if we were runaway lovers living inside a delirious fiction, slipping in and out of the pages of escape.

"Are you going to tell me where you're taking me?" I said.

"Have I ever disappointed you before?" he said.

I rolled my eyes. "Do you really want me to answer that?"

"Fair enough." He smiled. "I'm taking you to meet the coral dealer."

"Naturally," I said. "Is he related to your pearl dealer?"

"Oh no, he's much more nefarious," he said, pulling my hair back as we walked. "In fact, he has a predilection for anything red."

At the top of the hills was a hidden trattoria that hung over the water. We were led through the restaurant and into a dark back room, with dusty cases of wine piled up against a stone wall and a row of salted cod hanging by their tails. A large man named Bruno greeted us, a thick cigar in his mouth. He had leathery brown skin and a large gold signet ring, like a mobster fisherman. Spread out on a table were various species of Mediterranean coral, fiery branches fanning out like flames, forking like arteries, thorny vermillion skeletons. Damon compared the shades of red, mixing pigment by sight: Sardinian scarlet, angel skin pink, crimson, carmine, cadmium orange, rusted ruby, petrified blood.

"Do you know what they call this?" Bruno said, holding a russet branch up to my hair. "*Oro rosso.* Red gold."

"That's what they call her," Damon said.

"Are you going to trade me on the black market, too?" I asked.

"For you, we would get a very good price," Bruno said with a hoarse laugh. "You know how coral was formed?" He plucked out his cigar because it wasn't a question. "After Perseus slayed Medusa, whose glance could turn men into stone, he sliced off her head of snakes. On his journey back, he rested on the shores of the sea, placing her dripping snake head down on the sand. The blood of Medusa seeped into the water, turning the green seaweed into hard, bloodred coral, shaped like its snake-haired mother."

"I definitely did not know that," I said.

"So coral is said to protect against evil," he said, "because it was born out of the blood of a monster."

I didn't ask if his corals were poached or harvested illegally. When the transaction was over, Damon and I were seated at a gingham table on the empty terrace. A waiter announced that there was no menu, no pasta, only locally cured lake fish with big beady eyes. It was disgusting, briny and bony, but I ate it anyway, starved and happy, washing it down with sweet limoncello pressed from their lemon trees. After lunch, Damon asked the waiter for something in Italian, and he returned with a large Gothic iron key.

"It's for the oldest church on the lake, from the twelfth century," the waiter explained, pointing to the steeple that loomed overhead. "Careno is very special. It is shaped like an inverted triangle because of how the Moltrasio stone was formed. We call it a town of vertical emotions."

"I think that's what I have for you," Damon said, squeezing my leg beneath the table.

We walked down the village steps and entered the church through a portico of double lancet windows, curving around the lake. Inside, it was cool and smelled of sandalwood and mossy stones. We sat on a bench before the altar, looking up at a peeling, gold-leafed fresco of the sky. As Damon slipped his hand between my knees, I thought of our first afternoon on a bench months ago, the unfinished Klimt portrait, the bullet in her chest, the tension between us yet uncharted. Now everything was colored by the lines we had crossed.

"That was a little strange with Isabel this morning," Damon said.

"Do you think she heard you sneaking out last night?" I said.

"No, I think she was testing me to see if I would get jealous."

"I guess you can't get jealous about something you already know."

"If I knew it was that doctor, I might have reacted differently the first time."

He slid his hand farther up my leg, and I squeezed it tightly between my thighs.

"Shall I go to confession and atone for my sins?" I said. "You took me to the right place."

"Don't worry, I won't ask you to get down on your knees," he said.

"No, you'll just force me to," I said.

I considered kneeling down right there, between his legs. But his eyes dimmed, swallowing the light. I was almost afraid to ask what was wrong.

"What did you want to tell me?" I said finally. "Or is it going to remain a cliffhanger . . . ?"

"Well, it has to do with Caroline, actually," Damon said grimly.

My body stiffened at her name, though I didn't want him to notice. He rubbed his neck, removing his hand from my leg so that we were no longer touching.

"She's been struggling for a while. All these rounds of IVF have taken a serious physical and emotional toll on her . . . I don't think she realized how grueling the process would be," he said. "She started to resent me for putting her through it in the first place and recently decided she didn't want to continue."

"But why would she resent you?" I said. "I thought she wanted a baby."

"No, I was the one who wanted a baby. Desperately. That's the reason we didn't work out years ago, before I met you—because she never wanted kids."

I swallowed hard, looking up at the mystic face of a sun painted on the ceiling.

"So then what made you get back together?" I said.

"After my brother died, I spiraled into this really dark place. I was drinking all the time, guilty that I had survived while he and my mom had not. I felt like I deserved the same fate, and for a while I really wanted to die." He paused, closing his eyes for a second. "Then I almost did."

I took his hand. "What happened?"

"One night, I was out on the farm in the dead of winter. I was fucked-up, driving around on my motorcycle like a madman, and rammed straight into a tree. Cracked my collarbone, a bunch of ribs. At that point, I hadn't spoken to Caro in over a year, but she randomly called me when I was in the ER, as if she somehow intuited I needed her in that exact moment. She drove up and stayed by my side in the hospital, then while I recovered. And never left . . ."

"I didn't know," I said quietly.

"And even though it wasn't romantic for me anymore, I felt indebted to her for helping me through my darkness to the other side."

My throat ached. I didn't say he had been the beam of light that had permeated my own.

"So then she changed her mind about the baby?" I asked.

"No, not really. But when she was turning forty, I said it was nonnegotiable for me, so she agreed to try. Then, in these past few weeks, she said she couldn't do it anymore. She'd had enough . . . of everything."

"What do you mean?"

"I don't know. I just sort of . . . left. And we haven't spoken in nearly two weeks," he said. "That's why I came to Italy early."

I was silent for a moment. I had never fully let myself imagine a scenario where he didn't have a wife—what freedom that might permit us, or if his availability would diminish my longing for him. But a wave of hope moved through me.

"So is that your confession, then?" I said. "Should I say a prayer of absolution?"

"I'm not sure you're the right person to do that, but you can try."

He kissed my cheek, then my mouth, exhaling as if a heavy weight had been lifted.

"What's yours?" he asked. "Confession, I mean. Don't you ever want to talk about what happened to you?"

"Sometimes I do, but . . ." I shook my head. I imagined how it would feel to empty myself like a downpour, to live in the clean, crisp aftermath of release. To say: This is what it's like to fall in love with darkness. This is how it feels when death is both a salvation and an undoing, a fault line splitting your body in two.

"There's something you're afraid of—I can feel it—and I

wish I knew what it was," Damon said, serious now. "Or that you would trust me with it, somehow."

My scar was pulsing faintly, as if the glass was trying to break free. I was suddenly overtaken with the insane idea that maybe, if I confessed my story, Damon could be the one to help me. He didn't trust Rex, he didn't even like him—he had said as much before. In the end, Damon and I were both complicit in this affair, so he, too, had something costly to lose.

I took a shaky breath, but my phone started to ring—it was Sam.

I quickly stood up. I told Damon I would meet him outside and rushed out of the church into the clear blue afternoon.

"Hiya, Slash," said Sam when I answered the phone. "How's Como?"

"Sam, is everything okay?" I said, worried.

"Oh, swell, holding down the fort over here. Making sure you're staying out of trouble."

"Moderately," I said. "No global disasters yet."

"Just local ones, I'm assuming," he said.

The line sounded staticky. At first, I thought it was a bad connection, but then I realized Sam was having difficulty breathing.

"Is that jewelry cad there with you?" he asked.

"He's here alright. He took me to this little village so he could buy coral."

Damon emerged from the church, and I gestured to him that I would be a minute.

"What did you say? Coral?" Sam took a raspy inhalation. "What's the point of *schtupping* a jewelry designer if you're not even going to get any jewels out of it?"

"Sam, should I call Dr. Murphy for you?" I said. "I don't like the way you sound—"

"Did you ever read the short story about the coral merchant by Joseph Roth?"

"Did you hear me? I can call him when I get back to the villa—"

"In the story, there's this red-haired coral merchant," he began, cutting me off. "He treasures his precious coral more than anything, but he dreams of escaping his poor town to see the ocean. And then one day he finally does."

Sam wheezed heavily, so labored I could feel it rattling inside my own lungs.

"After a glimpse of the colorful world beyond, he returns to his drab home. And what happens? He abandons himself—he decides to cheat. To sell his real coral mixed with fake coral. Well, it's a catastrophe. These imitation corals bring bad luck, and he is forced to burn them all."

"So what happens in the end?" I said.

"He boards a sinking ship and drowns," he said. "But at peace with his real corals, at last."

Sam began to cough, a thin, terrible cough. I wandered down the path toward the water until I could see Damon in the distance.

"Is that meant to be an allegory for me or something?" I said.

"I don't know. You're the one who mentioned coral," he said. "I'm just here in New York City, sweating my balls off."

I laughed, but my throat burned. I could hear an old movie on in the background, a reminder of another life waiting for me, the one I would soon return to, and I was assailed by an aching sorrow.

"I love you, Sam," I croaked. "I'll be home in a few days."

"Just don't confuse what's real and what's false, Slash," said Sam. "Oh, and by the way, I read your short story."

"Really?" I had nearly forgotten about it. "What did you think?"

"You're the real deal, kiddo," he said. Then, before hanging up: "And I love you, too."

I took a few slow breaths, then walked down to the beach, a secluded strip of sand tucked beneath the church. I sat down beside Damon, leaning back on my elbows.

"Who was that on the phone?" Damon asked.

"Oh, just Sam," I said, wiping my cheeks. I hated that I was crying, which always seemed to be about the wrong thing. "Sorry, I just worry about losing him sometimes."

"Maybe he's worried about losing you," he said.

Damon kissed my knees, then pulled me down onto the rocky sand. I closed my eyes, the sun pouring over my skin. When he kissed me, his mouth was hot and salty like seawater, and I wanted to be absorbed and absolved by it. He was kissing my eyelids, murmuring under his breath *it will all be okay, it will all be okay because I love you.*

Everything seemed to recede then. The belltower chiming overhead. The sky. The water's edge like the curve of a knife. Only his words remained. They seemed to catch the heat and shimmer there. If I said it back, I could open my eyes and realize he'd never said it at all, that I only imagined someone could love me again.

But when I looked up, his face was calm and glowing. I blinked, sitting up with wobbly knees. My head was floating high above my body, filled with warm ripples of air.

"What's wrong?" Damon said.

I don't know what possessed me, but I unzipped my dress and let it fall to the sand. I stood there naked, the sun striking my skin. Damon was saying something then, but I was already heading toward the water. I walked straight into the lake and sank deep below the surface, thinking of coral, of rebirth, of him.

25

That night, Isabel booked a reservation at a restaurant at the top of a mountain, high above Cernobbio. We piled into the Fiat and sped up a steep, serpentine road, my ears popping as we dodged the descending cars. Our table was on the covered terrace, overlooking the lake. By the time the first course arrived, the sky was slashed with crimson, the color of coral we had stowed away earlier, those apotropaic branches, our contraband love. Isabel was at the head of the table, while I sat across from Damon, his sun-drenched beauty so destabilizing in the candlelight I had to avert my eyes. Gemma was in the middle of elaborating on her divorce, which had taken a turn for the worse earlier in the day.

"You have to understand, my father had to migrate back to Nigeria because he couldn't practice medicine in the UK, so I was raised by a single mother in Chalkhill," said Gemma. "And now this bastard has the audacity to sue *me* for alimony? Absolutely fucking not."

"What made you decide to divorce him in the first place?" Rex asked.

"We were on holiday at one of those detox spas dressed up as Austrian chalets—because my husband was *fat*, to be clear,"

Gemma said. "He only liked to go to these horrid places where you subsist on linseed oil and Epsom salts, and they give you separate bathrooms because of it."

Isabel cringed. "That sounds erotic."

A waiter refilled our wineglasses, already on our second bottle. I could feel Damon's leg beneath the table lightly grazing my own and tried to keep my face as impassive as possible.

"Oh, trust me, it was. No one's marriage is staying fuckable while you're purging your colon," Gemma said, stabbing a seared scallop. "So I go to borrow his converter to charge my phone, and on his iPad, a text pops up from someone named Sasha. Turns out it was a photo of a sonogram—because he knocked up a Russian hooker!"

We all glanced around the table, not expecting that dramatic plot twist.

"How do you know she was a hooker?" Damon asked.

"She was from Moscow. Need I elaborate?" Gemma said. "And do you know what their trick is?"

Gemma looked directly at me. I innocently shook my head, burning my tongue on a hot spoonful of magenta risotto, which tasted like merlot and black cherries.

"Robitussin," Gemma stated.

"What?" I nearly choked. "Like the cough syrup?"

"The girls swig it like vodka because it thins out their mucus, if you know what I mean," said Gemma bitterly. "If only I knew this at the time, maybe I wouldn't be childless and now probably barren. So, darling, if ever you want to trap a man, head right off to the cold and flu aisle of your local drugstore."

"Oh god, I hope it doesn't come to that," I said.

"Liv won't need to trap anyone," Isabel said.

"If anything, they'll try to entrap her," said Damon.

He passed me a coy smile, which Rex caught in his teeth

like a snare. I took a sip of wine, trying not to react, but I knew Damon had inadvertently said the wrong thing.

"Then why haven't you taken a stab, old chap?" said Rex. "Entrapping Liv, that is . . ."

Damon shifted in his seat. "That's not really my style."

"No? I hardly believe your pseudo-domestic situation is your 'style' either." Rex snickered. "So, what is your secret?"

"Or rather, what's her name?" Gemma said.

Damon sat up so our knees were no longer touching beneath the table. I could see Isabel stiffen, hawkishly observing this exchange.

"I can assure you, there's no such secret," Damon said uncomfortably.

"You can't honestly tell us that you've committed to a monastic existence," Rex said tauntingly. "No booze, no women, no sybaritic pleasures of the carnal variety?"

"What the fuck's your point, mate?" Damon said.

Everyone stopped drinking and eating then. The red sun struck my cheek like a hot hand, and I tipped back in my chair to avoid its unsparing light, but it was too late.

"I mean, Liv is the perfect example. You can't tell me you've never so much as tried," Rex persisted. "Or perhaps you have, and we've all been woefully duped."

"It's never even crossed my mind," Damon said.

"Not even *once*?" Rex said, underlining the lie. "Since her marital status changed? Just look at her sitting there so . . . availably."

Isabel put down her wineglass. "Oh, Rex, leave the girl alone," she commanded.

"Mea culpa," Rex said, raising his hands in a contrite gesture. "My bad."

As the main course arrived, Rex cut me a savage smile. I could tell the scene had played out just as he intended, a targeted forewarning. I glanced at Isabel, afraid that she had caught on. But now that Rex had kissed her, she was too consumed with her own romantic turmoil to notice. I could tell she thought that Rex was aggressively staking a dominant position—in the rivalry she herself had set in motion—and worried that Damon might feel intimidated.

I would have been relieved, but knew Rex would not stop there.

Meanwhile, the bow-tied waiters presented steaming plates of pasta in synchronized fashion: spaghetti with shaved black truffles and sage butter, ravioli with pumpkin and ricotta, orecchiette with heaps of lamb ragù, squid ink bucatini with glistening lobster tails. As Damon reached up to pass a plate, his wrist flashed in the glare of the candlelight.

"Where in the world did you steal those from?" Gemma said loudly. "The Vatican?"

Gemma grabbed his sleeve, forcefully holding it up so we all could see. It wasn't until then that I noticed Damon was wearing the serpent cufflinks.

"They were a gift," Damon said quickly.

"Then why have I seen them before?" Gemma pressed.

Damon hesitated, looking at Isabel for an answer. Her gray eyes caught the light like hand-cut crystal, hard and breakable at the same time.

"Because you probably remember Jack wearing them," Isabel said.

"I'm confused," said Gemma. "Then why is *he* wearing them?"

"Well, I certainly can't wear them," Isabel said. "So I thought I might pass them along to someone who can."

Rex glowered at the cufflinks, his faint hostility evident. He'd assumed that he had successfully captured Isabel's heart, securing his position of primacy. Now he was made aware

of a different possibility: Isabel might be using him, not the other way around.

"I guess we know who Damon's secret is, after all," Rex said.

Damon retracted his arm, his jaw clenching. Isabel smiled somewhat guilelessly, as if she didn't notice that a cold front of tension had swept in.

"You know the curse," Isabel said. "If you stare deep into its emerald eyes, you will be bitten with the venom of love."

Gemma let out a drunken laugh. "Bitten or blinded?"

"Maybe both," Rex said.

"First witches, then that island, now a pair of snakes," Gemma exclaimed. "What's our next fucking curse? Anybody want to add one to the slosh pile?"

"I pray we've reached our curse quota for the week," Rex mumbled.

The sun had vanished and a crescent moon appeared, cutting a thin white incision across the lake. As we began to eat, an invisible disturbance seemed to tremor in the atmosphere, a foreshock felt in my bones. I wondered when Isabel had presented Damon with the cufflinks, what private moment they'd shared together in her bedroom. Had Damon accepted them gratefully, aware of their eerie significance? Did he voluntarily wear them tonight to please her? Or did Isabel ask him to, hoping that we would notice?

I uneasily watched Rex shovel a forkful of black truffle spaghetti into his mouth and exclaim, "Oh god, it's like an angel crying on your tongue."

Then, I swear, the table began to seismically shake. We looked up in panic as wine sloshed in our glasses, dishes and silverware clattering to the floor. A thunder of gunshots erupted outside, and the restaurant guests ran in manic frenzy to the edge of the terrace, thrusting their faces into the night.

But it was hail. Giant chunks of hail, falling through the sky like a meteor shower. Everyone cheered and began to film it on their phones. The waiters broke out into a song that sounded like "Volare." As I leaned over the railing, I could feel the lens of a single camera zooming in on the back of my neck. Rex was recording me, his wine-stained mouth shrewdly puckered in concentration. I shivered and turned back to the night, where stones of ice rained down like missiles. Like a curse I wished upon myself.

That night, Damon came to the boathouse after the villa had gone to sleep. We were sitting in front of the open window, the coral branches from the dealer scattered on the floor. He was showing me how to sew them into his blazer. With a sharp knife, he skillfully sliced open the seam of his silk lining as if through a layer of skin.

"How much trouble can you get into if you're caught?" I asked.

"For smuggling undeclared endangered wildlife across international borders?" Damon said with a cocky shrug. "It's not a light penalty, I'll tell you that much."

"So then why? You just like the thrill of getting away with something?"

"I don't know," he said. "Do you find this thrilling?"

"Illegal trafficking, or us?" I said.

Damon gave me an amused look, wrapping a branch of coral in a swath of cloth.

"You know what's so precious about Mediterranean coral?" He carefully deposited the cloth inside the blazer. "It's the only species that is scarlet both inside and out. So even though it's opaque, not translucent like a ruby, the coral's interior matches its exterior."

"Unlike yours, you mean," I said.

"Careful, Red," he said.

Damon picked up a jagged branch, sharp as a dagger, and gently slid it across my throat.

"Is this the moment when you finally kill me?" I said.

"Hmm, not yet. There would be no element of surprise," he said with a devious look. "Maybe I should use this one to make you something instead."

He held the oxblood branch to my ear, then traced its tip from my clavicle down to my stomach until my skin turned hot.

"Paired with a peridot or a mint garnet, against the color of your hair," he mused. "As my accomplice, you at least deserve a cut of the spoils."

I thought about what Sam had said on the phone earlier—how Damon had never made me anything. How I should be wary of what was false. But how could I know if this wasn't real? So maybe his love for me was no different than for these smuggled stones: the illicit thrill of trespass, over borders, across seas, en route to somewhere else. Still, I wanted to believe his words meant something, that when he said he loved me earlier, it contained proof: I could be whole again.

I watched Damon stitch up the seam of his blazer, leaving one coral branch behind.

"I was thinking we should go away together at the end of this trip," he said, looking up at me. "Drive down south, then take a boat out to the Aeolian Islands."

I nearly laughed. "Sure, a girl can dream . . ."

"No, I'm being completely serious," he said. "We can go to Panarea, this tiny volcanic island where my buddy has an empty place we can stay in for the week."

"I think you've lost your mind," I said.

"Or maybe it's the sanest idea I've ever had."

Damon pulled me onto his lap so we were both facing the

water, and wrapped his arms around my chest. The night had cleared, blacking out its own memory of ice. Over the lake, a cloud of mist seemed to rise like a body.

"Imagine, we can hike the craters, and watch Stromboli from the porch, and swim in the sea at sundown, and wake up next to each other at sunrise," he said into my ear. "Just you and me together in the midst of the Tyrrhenian Sea."

"I don't know if I could handle that much rapture," I said. "I might die from it."

"Maybe it's time we remembered what that felt like," he said.

Damon lifted my hair and kissed the back of my neck. On a remote island, under the shadow of a volcano, I'd be unreachable, inaccessible, outside the blast radius of danger. Far away from Rex. Even Isabel couldn't invade our privacy there. The dream of flight suddenly filled me with an urgent hope.

Except we couldn't stay on an archipelago forever.

"But what happens afterward?" I said. "When we get back to New York?"

"Don't worry, we'll cross that bridge," he said reassuringly. "After the trip."

The rain had started again. Damon turned me around so I was facing him, running his hands over my arms.

"Do you remember that night, during the blizzard, when we walked for hours in the park?" he said. "And when we returned, I invited you in, but you went back to your own apartment."

"How could I forget?" I said.

"You know, I stayed up all night waiting for you, hoping you would change your mind," he said. "And then in the morning, I finally got up the courage to knock on your door."

I shook my head. "No, you didn't . . ."

"I did. But by then, you were already gone."

I could barely call up that girl now, the one who once

pressed her ear to the wall on a snowy night, the future still blank and unmarked.

"Sometimes I think of that night as the turning point of my life," Damon went on, smoothing my hair. "If only you had come in, maybe the last few years would have been different."

He kissed me then, pulling me on top of him. I slowly lowered myself down, my spine arching in the gauzy moonlight, his hands grasping my hips. I wanted to feel the escape inside me, to know it was true, the promise of deliverance from all that haunted me awaiting on the other side. When it was over, he pulled me down to the floor beside him. He rested his head on my stomach, his chest heavy between my legs. He traced the faded scar that ran diagonally across my stomach from the impact of the seat belt, killing everything unborn inside me.

"We'd have a beautiful baby, wouldn't we," he said.

He kissed the scar, and I stopped breathing. I could feel a faint tug in my center, a pull that I never had before.

"Beautiful," I said, "but she'd have a moody, artistic temperament."

He laughed. "Great legs, though. And great hair."

I closed my eyes, listening to the rush of wind through the olive trees. For so long I had been bound to someone who wasn't here, I had worn his invisible noose like a necklace, and for the first time I imagined it was possible to break free.

26

The next day, we were finishing the remains of lunch—fresh pink figs dipped in a fluffy cloud of burrata and drizzled in syrupy balsamic—while discussing the plans for tonight. Pierce and his girlfriend were in town, so Isabel had invited them over for cocktails before dinner. Damon and I were sitting beside each other, and occasionally he would brush my leg beneath the table. I kept trying not to smile, biting into plump red cherries, each containing a secretive sort of bliss. Across the table, Rex was focused on me, more targeted than before. But I was riding the dreamy high of last night, a film of protective energy around me—I had a romantic escape with Damon now. I met Rex's eyes with a flash of defiance, spitting a cherry pit into my palm.

"What in the world?" said Isabel, looking toward the gravel path.

I squinted into the bright afternoon. Barbara was frantically running toward us. Out of breath, she approached the table and plopped down a large shopping bag.

"I have some not good news," Barbara said grimly.

"Don't tell me, it's another curse," Rex said.

"Sadly, yes," Barbara said. "They are predicting that a bad

tempest is coming back in a few hours, but much, much worse than before."

We looked at her as if this were a joke, and Gemma raised her wineglass up to the sky.

"How many tempests can there be in one week?" shouted Gemma. "Is Mercury in some kind of endless fucking retrograde or something?!"

"I don't know. It's been, how do you say, freak weather?" Barbara said apologetically. "It's the rising temperatures. We've never had summer storms like this before, never."

Everyone started arguing about the crisis of climate change, and the recent major news of a superyacht that had sunk off the coast of Sicily, hit by a waterspout during another freak storm, causing the deaths of a fashion mogul and several others. But the conversation dimmed around me as I caught a glimpse of Damon's phone, lit up on the table.

A stream of texts from Caroline filled the screen. I accidentally bit hard into a cherry pit, nearly breaking a tooth. Damon's face tightened as he quickly flipped the phone face down, and I indiscreetly glared at him. By the time I realized Isabel was observing us, trying to translate our unspoken exchange, I was too clouded by emotion to care.

"This villa dates back to the eighteenth century, so just in case the power goes out," Barbara said.

She unloaded the shopping bag filled with candlesticks, instructing us to stay put in the house for the rest of the day.

"Oh great, so now we're in a remake of *The* bloody *Decameron*," Gemma said.

"Except all those characters did was tell stories of having affairs," Rex said, winking at me. "Instead of actually having them."

Damon's phone rang. I could feel the vibration beneath the table. The muscles in his arms tensed as he abruptly stood up, elbowing me hard in the ribs. I said *ouch* and clutched my side dramatically, but without pause he darted off around the side of the house. I sat there reeling, though I didn't even know why I was upset. On the phone, we could hear him answer and say, "Hey, babe, everything okay?" before his voice faded into the distance. I wanted to interpret his tone as forced and falsely conciliatory; but his voice was soft, almost paternal. He had never called me *babe* before.

I felt Isabel shrewdly watching me. She mouthed, *Who was that?* and I just rolled my eyes and mouthed back, *Fake wife.* I looked at my palm, a graveyard of cherry pits, staining my skin like blood.

"Fasten your seat belts," Rex growled. "It's going to be a bumpy night!"

"We better check our emergency wine supply," Gemma said.

After lunch, everyone agreed to meet back at the villa in the early evening. I decided to take an afternoon walk before the storm and went back to the boathouse to change. While putting on a pair of bike shorts, I noticed two petal-shaped bruises on my hips. Purple thumb prints from Damon's hands last night, when he held me down and came inside of me. I felt a strange, vengeful ache to be pregnant then, which confused me because I didn't think I wanted a baby anymore. After the miscarriage, I was probably as infertile as his wife.

I took a photo of my hips and texted it to Damon. But he didn't respond.

I turned left out of the boathouse, staying on the road that hugged the lake. I tried to clear my head, positively reorient this plague of thoughts. Focus on the landscape, the trip with Damon. Don't think of the phone call at lunch. But if I didn't think of the call, my mind glitched and jumped back to Rex, like a terrible tic, which was worse. I kept cycling through reasons Caroline would be calling after their weeks of estrangement. Maybe she'd found clarity in their time apart and called to definitively end things—she wanted a real relationship, not an arrangement, and had decided to move out. Or the opposite could also be true. Caroline could have called Damon in a moment of weakness, exhorting him to come home and give them another shot.

But what if Damon had lied to me, and they never stopped talking at all?

I had walked at least an hour when the weather changed. The clouds were gathering conspiratorially over the mountains, shrouding its serrated edge. Everything here seemed like that, danger cloaked in elliptical beauty: bridges arching over the road, on the brink of collapse; the splendor of August a ruse for deadly freak storms. The sidewalk had ended now, nothing to separate the road from the lake. I checked my phone—still no text back. The service was spotty. Maybe it hadn't come through? I toggled the airplane mode until a new batch of notifications appeared:

One new voicemail from Dr. Mehta's office.

Five unread texts from Rex.

I shuddered and swiped them off the screen, a quick trick of disappearance. I could deal with my bad eye later, put off ocular trauma until I was back in New York. But Rex wasn't going away. The grenade primed in his hands, the pin waiting to be pulled.

I tried to push these horrors aside, but a muscle was twitching in my eye. In the distance, across the road, a towering stone pyramid rose up from the center of a garden, like a strange mirage, its apex puncturing the slate sky. I dragged myself over and collapsed on the nearest bench, thumbing my eyelid until the spasm stopped. When I looked around, I realized I was in a graveyard. The pyramid was not a sculpture but a tomb, a sepulchral monument, like a gray mausoleum in a de Chirico painting. I wondered if I would ever go back to visit Graham's grave.

A rumble of thunder echoed through the cemetery, and it started to rain. I could feel him, even now, a mutinous uprising that could not be suppressed. Over the tombstones, wilted flowers trembled like my own hands. Maybe I was being ridiculous, overly emotional; the tomb was not some portentous omen. Soon I would be safe and far away on a volcanic island with Damon, I reminded myself. The convergence of fire and water. A fortress of sea on all sides. He had said he loved me, hadn't he? Didn't he promise me this trip? I stood up and wiped my eyes, stinging with rain. I needed to get out of this haunted place.

By the time I turned back, the storm had begun.

When I arrived at the villa a few hours later, I was surprised to find *aperitivo* hour in full swing. Pierce and his girlfriend, Cadence, had arrived, and everyone seemed to be on their third drink. I entered the living room like an uninvited guest, shivering a little. There had been no hot water to shower beforehand, and my dress was wet from the walk over. The Italian song "Via Con Me" played above the drumbeat of rain, but beneath the music I sensed a minor chord of tension in the room, vibrating like a violin string about to snap.

"Well, look who decided to join us!" Pierce said, holding up his glass. "It's our stray."

"Liv, we were waiting for you," Isabel chided. "You're just in time for the surprise."

"Nobody thought to tell me you had started?" I said, annoyed.

"We figured you'd snuck off with this mysterious hotel lover of yours," Gemma said.

"Oh, so she finally has a boyfriend?" Pierce said. "Who is the lucky victim?"

Rex raised his eyebrow at me. "Wouldn't we all love to know."

I glanced at Damon, but he didn't look up. He was leaning back against the sofa, his eyes glazed and distant, nursing a Negroni. It was the first drink he'd had on the trip, maybe since I'd met him back in May, and I knew that something must be wrong. I went over to the bar and mixed a Campari with soda, then sat down on the arm of a chair.

"Okay, ready?" Cadence said, holding her hands behind her back. "Surprise!"

She thrust her left hand into the air to display a large diamond ring. Isabel and Gemma clapped and rushed over to see it, while Rex popped a bottle of champagne, which I suspected had nothing to do with the engagement.

"He proposed in our favorite spot in Capri," Cadence said elatedly. "On a boat, of course, just as we were about to enter the Blue Grotto."

"That ring is absolutely gorgeous," Isabel said.

"That's because Damon made it," Pierce said. "Using my grandmother's diamond from Botswana."

Cadence wiggled the ring off her finger and passed it around. When it got to me, I forced a smile, but an engagement ring was not something I could mentally process right now.

"Do you want to try it on?" Cadence said encouragingly. "Oh, try it, Liv!"

Before I could protest, Cadence slipped the ring onto my finger. As the women continued to discuss the proposal details, I stared at my hand like an inert foreign object. The diamond had a foggy gray fluorescence, set in a cloud of inverted spikes. I thought of the night that Damon held my ring in his hands, back in Sam's kitchen. How I believed he had the singular power to see beyond its cracks, into the depths of its green fire. When I looked up, Damon was watching me, and I felt an ache so heavy I could barely breathe. Then I saw Rex watching me, too, and I quickly slipped the ring off my finger.

"Doesn't it feel so weird?" Cadence gushed as I handed it back. "I almost can't imagine my life without it already."

Isabel must have noticed their eyes on me. When "Superstition" began to play, she ran over to the speaker and turned up the volume, purring, "Oh, I *loooove* this song." She began to dance at the center of the room. Closing her eyes and swaying her hips with the syncopated rhythm, sensually caressing her torso with her hands. We all watched her, equally hypnotized. As the song went on, her body became looser, surrendering to some higher force.

"Are you really going to let a girl dance on her own?" Isabel cooed.

Pierce jumped to his feet and took her hands, twirling her around the coffee table, and she threw her head back, laughing with unrestrained joy. Then Rex began to dance with Cadence, and Gemma pulled Damon up from the sofa, and everyone began belting out the lyrics as if this night did not harbor its own dubious plans.

I stayed on the sidelines, watching the scene as if I were the audience of a rotating performance. After a while, Pierce switched partners so that Damon could dance with Isabel. I watched as Damon placed his hands on her lower back, and Isabel opened to him like a flower, their bodies moving together in tandem to the beat. I thought back to that first party, how something within me was drawn to them as a pair, their dazzling pas de deux. I had wanted so badly to believe they could transport me into a dimension beyond my past, beyond the walls of the maid's room, revealing a passage to a brand-new life, which now I realized, all too late, was never within reach.

Pierce changed the song to "Storms" by Fleetwood Mac, and everyone laughed uneasily.

"Liv, come on, dance with us!" Pierce called out.

I waved him off as Rex seized the chance to cut in with Isabel and Damon.

"May I steal the young lady away?" Rex said, tugging Isabel's arm.

Isabel batted her eyes at him. "What took you so long?"

Isabel fluidly slid from the arms of one man into the other. Her face lit up with a victorious smile, as if this precise moment was the apotheosis of the long game she'd been playing. When she saw me watching her, she passed me an almost pitying glance.

"Why don't you dance with Liv," she said to Damon. "You can't leave that poor girl without a partner."

"Maybe she doesn't want one," Damon said.

But Rex had already whisked Isabel away. When Damon turned to me, all the blood drained out of my limbs. I followed him to a corner by the fireplace. We moved for a while without talking, an exquisite dance of torture. I could feel the familiar magnet of our bodies, forcibly drawing us closer, and part of me didn't care who noticed anymore.

Finally, we looked at each other.

"What's wrong?" I said quietly.

"Nothing," Damon said dismissively. "Don't worry about it."

His face held such chilled anguish that it sent a shiver through me. He seemed so detached and faraway compared with last night, lying on the floor and dreaming of a trip, of a promise that seemed to await us, that I wanted to physically shake him and bring him back.

"I can tell something is wrong," I said.

"Look, I can't exactly talk about it right now."

"Well, it must not be good if you're drinking again."

"So what? Do I have to report it to you like you're my fucking—"

He stopped himself, but the word ricocheted in the air between us.

"You're right, I'm not your fucking *wife*," I said.

"Hey, I'm sorry," he said softly. "I didn't mean that, okay? I'm really sorry."

His face crumpled, and he leaned in so close that his lips skimmed the rim of my ear. I closed my eyes, wanting to bury my face in his neck and tell him that nothing else mattered, that I loved him, too. But as I opened my mouth, I felt the eyes of Rex vigilantly bouncing over to me. Then he dropped Isabel's arm and took a step in my direction.

"Shall we switch partners?" Rex announced.

Terrified, I grabbed on to Damon and shielded myself with his body as the lights began to flicker. We all stopped in place, looking up at the ceiling, and then the power went out.

The room was dropped into darkness. After a confused moment, drunken screams mixed with drunken laughter, the maids came running out of the kitchen carrying candlesticks.

"I think it's even more romantic like this," Isabel purred.

"Oh yes, anything can happen in the dark," Rex said.

I looked out the window. The sky was a block of granite, veiny shadows cutting across the grass. Pierce went off to help locate the fuse box, and Rex followed Maria to the kitchen to figure out if there was a gas burner. "The pasta, the pasta!" she was shouting down the hallway. An eerie quiet trickled through the house, aside from the rain bludgeoning the roof, as if we were waiting for something to happen. I went over to the bar and refilled my glass with red wine, while Isabel and Cadence continued to talk about the engagement to kill time.

"You know, I also got engaged in Italy, ages ago," Isabel was saying. "I bought a pair of magical snake charms on that trip that were meant to protect my love, and they did."

"Oh my god, I'm *obsessed* with snakes," Cadence said.

"Do you want to see them?" Isabel asked. "They'll bring good luck to your marriage."

Gemma muttered under her breath, "Oh, fuck me, not those bloody cufflinks again."

Isabel held a pinched grin, though her eyes twitched faintly.

"Damon, why don't you run and get them while we're all waiting," Isabel suggested.

"You mean, right now?" Damon said.

"Can you think of a better time?" Isabel said.

Damon rubbed the back of his neck with visible agitation but then agreed. After he went upstairs, Isabel gestured for me to sit beside her on the couch. Up close, her eyes shone with unhinged elation, withholding a secret she could no longer contain.

She squeezed my arm and leaned in: "I think the fake wife is out the door for good."

"What?" I swallowed my shock. "He said that to you?"

"Not explicitly. But I found out they had a massive fight before he left New York, in part because she was upset that he chose to be here with me instead of staying with her."

"So then how do you know she left him?"

"I overheard him fighting with her on the phone this afternoon, and she ultimatum-ed him," said Isabel, lowering her voice. "And he said: 'If you want to go, I won't stop you.'"

I wondered if Isabel was right. I had assumed, based on his mood, that Caroline wanted to come back and make it work, placing Damon in an intractable position. But maybe I had only been bracing myself for that outcome. I saw, now, I was wrong; his distress was caused by the crushing finality of her decision. I almost felt queasy with renewed promise and wanted to run upstairs, right now, tell Damon to take me away from this villa and its darkening storm.

"You know my intuition is always spot-on," Isabel said,

then sighed. "I know he's upset, but I'm worried about him drinking again. That he could do something rash . . ."

"I'm sure it's just one of his dark moods," I said, trying to sound reassuring.

She placed a hand over mine, and a pinprick of guilt punctured my hope like a balloon.

"Will you find out for me?" Isabel implored. "I trust you, Liv. You know that."

The door was suddenly flung open, and Rex stood there, drenched, flooding the room with a blast of freezing rain. We all shouted at him to close the door.

"I thought you were just in the kitchen?" said Gemma.

"They sent me to the shed to find more flashlights in case this all gets worse," said Rex.

"Oh god, how much worse can it possibly get?" Gemma wailed. "We might as well be back in fucking New York!"

Rex toweled himself off and headed to the bar. I watched as he poured himself a large glass of scotch from a vintage bottle that Pierce had recovered during his unsuccessful search for the fuse box. I knew I should stay quiet, not prod the bull, but I couldn't help myself.

"So then, where are the flashlights?" I asked.

Rex gave me a demonic look, licking a drop of whiskey from his glass.

"Would you believe it, there were none to be found," he replied.

We heard footsteps coming down the staircase, and Damon appeared in the arched doorway. Isabel sat up, alert, about to jump up from the couch, but registered that something was wrong. Damon was lingering in the shadows, his cheeks drained, a haunted vacancy in his eyes.

"What's happened?" Isabel said. "It looks like you've seen a ghost."

"They're not upstairs," Damon said dimly.

"The cufflinks? What do you mean?"

Her face was very still, but her eyes were flickering wildly in the candlelight. A tense silence spread over the room, muted only by the heavy cadence of rain.

"I don't know," Damon said. "I swear I put them in this little dish on my nightstand before bed, but now they're not there."

"Why didn't you put them in the safe?" said Rex.

"It was so late when we got back," Damon said. "And I didn't exactly think I needed to . . ."

I silently panicked. Had he taken them off in the boathouse last night? No, he was wearing a T-shirt, which he'd used to wipe the damp stream trickling down my thighs. I finished my wine, a cold heat coursing through me.

"They couldn't have just vanished out of nowhere, right?" Isabel said. "I'm sure they were just misplaced after we got home a little drunk from the restaurant."

"Maybe we can all do a search?" Cadence offered with a lilt of excitement.

"This isn't fucking Agatha Christie," Gemma groaned.

"Isn't that the ultimate fantasy, though?" Pierce said.

"Not unless someone ends up dead," Rex said.

We agreed to do a cursory sweep of the property, though at this point everyone was going through the motions to assuage Isabel. I walked aimlessly through the crepuscular rooms, shadows slinking across the walls like thieves. I ran my hands over all the tactile surfaces as if I were blind, marble and velvet, wood and silk, though I didn't know what I was searching for anymore.

I found myself in the library at the end of the hall. I was about to turn back when I saw a flicker in the dark. A reptilian flash of green and red emanating from a corner of the room.

The eyes of a snake, I thought. I followed the source of light to a desk, but as I got closer, I realized it was only an iPad. A ghostly rectangle of chemical light. I glanced at the screen, unlocked on an open Word document:

> The investigative report confirms she gave a false statement to the police . . . New video footage, capturing the young bride getting into the driver's seat, is glaringly inconsistent with the filed accident report.

I reeled back, hitting a sharp corner of the desk. The screen slipped out of my hands and fell to the marble floor, cracking like a skull. I felt sick, the sound rattling through my bones. Rex intended to do harm, to expose the moment I drove over the cliff, over the edge of my life, and there was nothing anyone could do, not Damon, not Isabel, to stop him.

I crouched down and touched the black text, slicing open my finger. The screen was a web of shattered glass, like the windshield that nearly blinded me. But how I wished, in that moment, it had killed me instead.

It was dark out by the time I returned to the sitting room, and everyone was back except for Damon. The air pressure had changed, thrumming at a higher frequency. Isabel was sitting on the couch, glumly nursing a drink, and her eyes widened with deluded hope when she saw me.

"Did you find them?" Isabel asked.

I had forgotten about the cufflinks, and mutely shook my head. I headed for the bar as Rex crossed the room, nearly knocking into me as he staggered by.

"What in the world have you done?" Rex said.

He grabbed my wrist before I could react, holding it up to

the candlelight. My finger was smeared with blood, a fresh trail of evidence.

"Nothing," I said quickly.

"Looks like we have our first suspect in this whodunit," he said.

I wanted to elbow him in the eye, but I forcefully retracted my hand. I hoped Isabel could read the distress on my face, my silent plea for help. But she wasn't paying attention to me; she was staring morosely into the distance, tormented by thoughts of Damon. Meanwhile, Gemma was opening another bottle of wine, her black eyeliner smudged beneath unfocused eyes.

"Tell me you think this isn't absurd," Gemma was muttering to the bottle. "Tell me this charade hasn't gone too fucking far." The cork came out with a pop. Gemma pivoted toward Isabel, wielding the wine opener like a sword. "Why don't we just put it all out on the table."

"Oh lord, this should be interesting . . ." Pierce mumbled.

"What do you actually think is going to happen between you and Damon?" she asked.

"I don't know what you're talking about," Isabel said, sitting up stiffly.

"I'm genuinely curious. Do you think that he's going to be with you?" Gemma said. "Do you think you're going to be his lover, or his girlfriend, or his wife?"

"Don't be ridiculous," Isabel dismissed her. "You know we're just friends."

Gemma took an unsteady step closer, the wine sloshing in her glass. Isabel flinched, her pupils constricting with fear.

"Is that so? You spend all this time pining over him and fantasizing about him, spending thousands on his jewelry that you *pretend* he gifted to you—"

"Stop it—" Isabel hissed.

"You give him your beloved dead husband's wedding present, for fuck's sake, because you consider yourself to be his . . . *friend*?"

"Are you jealous, Gemma? Is that what this is about?" Isabel said, her voice rattling.

"Jealous?" Gemma threw her head back with a drunken laugh. "Jealous of what? No, I'll never be made a fool again by any man. Especially if everyone saw it but me."

Damon entered the room, and we all stared at him with visible horror. Gemma sloppily held up her glass as if she was about to make a toast.

"There he is, the man of the hour!" Gemma slurred. "Shall we ask him directly?"

"Sorry, did I miss something?" Damon said slowly.

"We didn't find the cufflinks, that's for fucking sure," Pierce muttered into his drink.

Isabel clutched her glass with shaking hands, the veins in her neck popping.

"Gemma, I'm warning you," Isabel seethed.

"So let's get this straight, pal, once and for all," Gemma said. "What are your intentions here in regard to your relationship with our dear Isabel?"

"What are you talking about?" Damon said.

"Are you going to date her?" Gemma said. "Are you going to marry her?"

"Stop it—" Isabel pleaded as she stood up, clutching the arm of the couch.

"Do you plan on *fucking* this woman?" Gemma spat.

The questions hung in the air like noxious fumes, strangling us all with silence.

"You owe her the truth after egregiously misleading her," Gemma pressed on. "Do you want to fuck her or not?"

"I SAID STOP IT!" Isabel cried. She let out an agonized, visceral scream that echoed across the frescoed ceiling. Then she ran out of the room with a loud sob, her hand covering her mouth. We sat there unmoving in the darkness, until we heard a door upstairs slam shut.

"What the fuck were you thinking?" Damon said. "Are you out of your fucking mind?"

"Oh god oh god oh god." Gemma stumbled backward, holding her cheek as if she had just been slapped out of a trance. "What have I done?"

"It's not your fault," Rex said, then turned deliberately to Damon. "She was just saying what we've all been thinking."

Damon stepped toward him, his eyes icing over. "I'm sorry?"

"Except she's got the wrong girl," Rex sneered. "Because why would you need to fuck Isabel when you've been getting it from someone younger in this house?"

Damon suddenly lunged at him, strangling Rex with his hands. When he let go, Rex went stumbling backward into the console table, a porcelain lamp shattering on the floor. Damon made a move to strike again, but Pierce jumped in and restrained him, holding him back with the full weight of his body.

"Whoa, come on, easy there, buddy," Pierce was saying.

Rex looked shell-shocked, clutching his chest like he'd been shot. I was stunned, too. I looked at Damon, remembering the night I had shoved him on the roof. Only men capable of quiet violence can draw that out of you: a dark, animal rage that pushes you to the brink, rendering the rest of your life, your own self, nearly void.

"Um . . . maybe someone should go upstairs and see if she's okay?" Cadence suggested.

"I'll go," Rex said.

Rex glanced at me before he left the room, with a chilling hint of a smile. Damon was pacing now, rubbing his forehead in acute distress, and though I tried to catch his eye, he wouldn't look at me. I felt the same sinking fear as during the last night with Graham, bracing for a seismic disaster set into motion that I was powerless to stop.

"Hey, I think everyone needs to take a breather and cool off," Pierce said.

"I'm sorry," Damon said. "I can't be here anymore."

Damon bolted for the door, the wind thrashing through the room as he left. I told myself not to go after him—it would be pathetic, humiliating even—but my feet were moving against my will, yelling his name as I ran into the raging storm. The rain was coming down sideways, welting my face like a hail of bullets. When I finally caught up to him, he pulled me into a stone alcove for temporary shelter. I looked up at his face, my eyes stinging with cold water.

"What are you doing?" I said.

"Listen, I can't stay here," Damon said. "I'll kill someone if I do."

"So then let me come with you, wherever you're going," I pleaded like a child.

"I wish I could bring you, Liv, but I don't think you'd want to come with me now."

His eyes filled with agonized shame. I crossed my arms, shivering wildly. I stared at the Madonna statue carved into stone, her pure white face decayed and cracked, then looked back at him.

"Just to be clear," I said, "everything you said last night was a lie?"

"What? No, of course it wasn't."

"You were never going to take me anywhere, not to Panarea, not when we got back to New York," I said. "It was all empty fucking promises. Admit it."

Damon wiped his face with his sleeve, though the rain made it seem like he was crying. Then I realized he really was crying, a stream of tears falling down his cheeks.

"Is that what you really think?" he said.

"I don't know, I don't know what to think anymore."

He cradled my face in his hands, wiping my wet lashes with his thumbs.

"Everything I said last night was true," Damon said. "I want to be with you, Liv. I want to take you away, and wake up with you at sunrise, and do all the things that people in love do."

"Then what's stopping you?" I said. "Is it Isabel?"

"No, it's . . ." He faltered. "If I could do it all over again with you, I would."

He kissed me then, a deep, soft kiss, holding the back of my neck. I felt my chest caving in, as if he had reached inside and clasped shut the same heart he once unfastened. I pulled away and looked at the cypress trees, bending like broken spines in the wind.

"So it's because of her," I said.

He nodded faintly. I should have left it at that, not pushed him any further, yet I wanted something worse than shame, a lasting injury only he could inflict.

"I don't understand," I said. "You're not married, you don't sleep together, you told me that you don't even love her—"

"I know," he said.

"So? What is it, then?"

Damon took a breath and looked outward toward the lake, toward the faint rim of sky, as if staring into some murky future that now would never lead back to me.

"She called me this morning," he said. "And told me that she is pregnant."

27

I walked back to the villa, not feeling the rain or wind or gravel piercing my feet like thorns. I was shivering uncontrollably when I got inside, though no one was in the sitting room anymore. The house was quiet and dark, only the distant clank of dishes in the kitchen. I wrapped myself in a large blanket and retreated to the library, where I curled up by the window and cried.

I didn't try to stop myself. I let the tears fall until my lungs burned. So I had loved him after all, with all of my emptiness, but now it was too late. Our love had only existed in the tenebrous hours, between the end of a storm and the coming of light. How could I have been so blind to imagine that he could offer anything more? I would be stuck here eternally, not quite living and not quite dead.

And meanwhile, Damon was bringing a new life into the world. A child he would teach to love color and shape, his brilliant parure of stones.

I wiped my eyes with my wrist and looked out the window. Someone had turned the pool lights on, and the trees were still buckling as if they would break, like women in mourning. I thought about calling Damon and telling him everything, begging him to come back, but I couldn't. I had not been able to tell the truth, not even to him, and now I was alone again to face my own reckoning. If Rex's story was published, it would be my own obituary.

I stood up, lightheaded, the blanket still wrapped around me, and walked over to the desk. But the outlet was empty. The iPad was gone. Only tiny splinters of glass were left, scattered across the floor like crushed diamonds. Another way, I remembered, Damon once said he would kill someone.

By the time Maria rang the bell for dinner, it was nearly 10:00 p.m. The rain had thinned, and some of the power had come back on. I staggered into the dining room with a terrible headache, followed by Pierce and Cadence and Gemma, all of us tentatively sitting beneath an eighteenth-century portrait of a chilly baroness. The table had been formally set, fresh green candles lit on every surface and lining the stone fireplace carved with birds. Someone said that Rex was resting and would be down later, and I thought *thank god*. Isabel came in last, taking a seat at the head of the table. She had changed into a long, flowing white dress, her lips painted a frosted white and her cheekbones highlighted with balmy iridescence. She had let her hair down, loose and crimped in strawberry-white waves. Though I could tell it was merely a costume; beneath it, her face contained a fragility that mirrored my own.

Cosima served large portions of pasta alla norma, with chunks of fried eggplant and mozzarella, as a first course. When she approached the empty place setting, she glanced nervously at Isabel.

"Signora?" Cosima asked meekly. "Is he . . . coming?"

Isabel stared silently at Damon's chair, absorbing the shape of his absence.

"No, she killed him," Pierce said, sliding his hand across his throat. "*Assassinio*."

"He's kidding!" Cadence said, and then to Pierce more quietly, "You're kidding, right?"

"Ah, well, we all know Isa used to be a fixer, so anything is possible," said Pierce.

"What makes you say it in the past tense?" Isabel blinked. "There's nothing that will ever be more important to me than loyalty."

Gemma, sitting soberly at the other end of the table, her mascara caked and hair matted down, theatrically burst into noisy sobs. "Forgive me, please forgive me!" she wailed.

She dropped to the floor in supplication and crawled over to Isabel, kneeling at her feet.

"Wooow," Pierce muttered, "that's a choice."

He stepped on my foot beneath the table. I bit the inside of my cheek to prevent myself from screaming or laughing, and thought, this is what it must be like to go insane.

"I love you, Isabel. You're my dearest friend, my sister," Gemma blubbered. "And I just couldn't stomach watching him hurt you anymore. I know I was just projecting, because now I'm old and alone, too, but I promise I only did it out of protection and love for you."

"Get up, Gemma," Isabel snapped. "You're not performing at the Royal Court."

"It would certainly be less cringe to watch," Pierce said.

Gemma held on to the corner of the table and hoisted herself into the nearest chair. Isabel took a composed breath, twisting the gold Artemis amulet around her neck.

"It's not me from whom you need to beg forgiveness," said Isabel coldly.

"No?" Gemma said, wiping her dripping nose. "Then who?"

"Damon may be a complex man, but understand that I will forever be indebted to him for bringing me back to life when I had no life in me left," Isabel said, her voice teetering. "And what you did to him tonight was unforgivable. How could you humiliate him like that when he is now the one in an extremely fragile place?"

"I . . . I'm sorry, that wasn't my intention," Gemma stuttered.

"He would never do anything to hurt me, never," said Isabel.

I looked down at my plate. Isabel had convinced herself that the humiliation she felt was not her own, but on behalf of Damon. Her devotion, even now, was akin to the prayer candles she lit at Mass each Sunday, sacred and unfaltering. I would move through the seasons; I would grow older. My grief might not fade, though it would recede. But Isabel felt the narrowing margins of her years in a way I hadn't fully understood until now, and without his light, she stood in the darkness.

"And now he's drinking again, and I'm worried sick about him," Isabel said. "I could never forgive myself if something happened to him."

"What can I do?" Gemma pleaded. "I'll do whatever you want in order to make things right again."

Isabel glared at her with the chill of an ice cap. "You must apologize to him and ask him to come back before the storm gets worse."

"Of course I will," Gemma conceded eagerly.

Isabel picked up her phone and held it suspended in midair. Then she abruptly turned to me and said, "Liv, you call him. On your phone."

My heart thudded. "What?"

"I've been calling, but he won't answer me," Isabel said. "Maybe he'll answer for you."

"I can't," I said, shaking my head.

Her eyes tapered like arrows. "Of course you can. Why not?"

I turned motionless, but my vision swayed. A freight of suspicion crossed her face, as if this were a test she hadn't expected me to fail.

"Please don't make me," I begged.

"Call him *now*," she commanded. "On speakerphone, Liv."

I couldn't feel my own hands as I picked up my phone and pressed his name. The ring echoed through the room, rattling through my chest, while I silently prayed he wouldn't pick up.

But on the last ring, his voice came through.

"Red, baby," said Damon. "What's wrong?"

I answered in a monotone that I was at dinner with everyone and he was on speaker, but I felt stripped naked, my own anesthetized body splayed on an operating table, its vital organs exposed. I could feel Isabel's eyes flashing, jagged as lightning, as if seeing clearly for the first time. As I passed the phone to her, Cosima came running into the room, shouting, "Signora, Signora!" with a burst of excitement.

"What is it?" Isabel said dully.

"I was turning down all the beds while you were eating dinner, and look what I found!"

Cosima opened her palm. The serpent cufflinks sparkled, its emerald eyes darting with poisonous light. Isabel gasped, her face swelling with refreshed hope.

"Mother of god!" Isabel exclaimed. "Where in the world did you find them?"

"They were in the boathouse!" Cosima said proudly. "With Signor Damon's blazer!"

The blood drained from my body, paralysis spreading through my limbs. I looked at Isabel, hoping she would see it was a meaningless error, an accidental misplacement that could be explained. But the irrevocable rupture on her face, distorting her features, told me there was nothing I could say.

Damon disconnected the line, leaving us in a dome of silence.

"I don't know how they got there," I said feebly, but my words fell flat.

"For how long?" Isabel said unblinkingly.

Her strangled voice struck me like a burning wind. How could I explain everything now? That we were the same, that I, too, was a widow driven mad by the inexhaustible cycle of grief, that Damon was a fleeting light in my own mire of darkness, but it was over now. It had counted for nothing in the end. We were both left on our own.

Instead, I whimpered, "I'm sorry, I'm sorry—"

"Get out," Isabel said.

I stood up on shaking legs. When I turned to go, Rex was standing in the doorway. My eyes began to throb, and I wanted to rip them out of my own head. Rex had returned to the villa earlier in the night: drenched, but without flashlights. He must have gone down to the boathouse and planted the cufflinks then—how else would they have gotten there? Rex leered at me now, issuing a fatal warning that he wielded the power to expose the most private part of myself, and there was nothing I could do but submit and submit and submit.

"You did this!" I yelled. "You put them there!"

"I don't know what she's talking about," Rex replied. "I just woke up from a nice nap."

He shot Isabel a virtuous look that suggested I had lost my mind. I lurched toward him, my fury smoldering inside me. Rex lifted his arms in defense, as if I could hurt a man twice my size, but beneath his posturing gesture I caught a simper of satisfaction that said: *You've lost.*

"You're a fucking liar!" I screamed. "Tell them what you did!"

"That's enough!" Isabel yelled, standing up and stabbing the floor with her chair.

I was breathing hard, the room spinning around me. I took a step toward her, but she recoiled, her eyes shining wildly like an injured animal.

"Get out," she cried. "Get out now."

28

I stumbled back to the boathouse in the dark, the rain whipping the face of the lake. The water level had risen above the dock, inches away from spilling onto the land. I clutched the railing as I crossed the bridge, one foot in front of the other, the metal vibrating in the wind. I texted my friend, the hotel manager, and told him I needed a place to stay for the night. He replied that the roads would be closed down soon—there were mudslides on the western shore and flooding causing mass evacuations on the north, houses buried and residents stuck—so he'd send the hotel car to pick me up immediately.

I rapidly threw everything in my suitcase, wet bathing suits and dirty underwear, forgetting what I had left behind in the main villa. You've done this before, I told myself. You've gone through the motions of flight: bring only what you can carry and empty yourself of the remains, the untenable weight of your own life. I thought about jumping into the lake, wondering how many days or weeks it would take to find my body. Or would I have the same fate as my ring, dredged up after an indefinite state of missing.

Of course, there was a difference between these exits. When I fled LA, nearly left for dead, I could not picture the shape of life waiting on the other side. Now I knew: back to the maid's room, back to discolored nights before Damon and Isabel. This exit might have been a repercussion of the other, but in the end it didn't matter: I was still guilty.

The hotel car arrived a half hour later, and the driver helped carry my suitcase up the stairs and over the bridge to the car. There was a little glass ladybug above the dashboard, identical to the one on the drive here, and I touched its red body as if it were alive. *Porta fortuna*, the driver said, and I nodded, though my own portents of luck were unavailable now. We impatiently got on the road, spiraling up and then down through the vertiginous hills, distant headlights barely visible through the sheets of rain. The roller-coaster motion sent me reeling back to the cliffs, a blur of sea and sky, and as I looked out the window, I was going to be sick. I told the driver to pull over, but I couldn't wait. While the car was still moving, I flung open the door and purged all the red wine and red sauce from my stomach, all the revulsion I had for myself.

It was then, in my abject misery, retching while holding my head between my knees, that I remembered my passport in the safe. "Fuck," I said aloud as panic spiraled through me. If the roads were closed tomorrow, I would be stuck here, with no way to get home.

"We have to go back!" I shouted. "I forgot my passport!"

"Are you crazy?" he yelled over the crash of thunder. "We can't, it's too dangerous!"

"We have to, please, otherwise I can't get home!"

The driver agreed on the condition he would only wait a few minutes. He dropped me off near the gate of the villa. I clawed my way back through the storm, blindly tumbling across the road and pool and bridge and staircase, until finally I reached the boathouse. Panting and drenched, I stopped in my tracks.

The door was left ajar. Hadn't I closed it before I left? Maybe the wind knocked it open. Dread rose in my throat like bile, but I didn't have time to hesitate. I pushed the door open and headed directly to the dresser. The walls were convulsing with a spasm of shadows, the rain beating against the glass. As I fumbled to unlock the safe and grab the passport, I felt the tension of a body behind me preparing to attack.

"Did you forget something, darling?"

My heart twisted in my throat. Rex was sitting in a chair, his face distorted by spidery shadows. I could tell he was drunk, stroking Damon's blazer in his lap. *This is not a horror film*, I told myself, *this is real life*. But I was descending into the darkest latitude of a dream.

"You know, it's not very polite to break other people's toys," Rex said.

"What do you want?" I managed to say.

"It seems my initial offer proved too arduous, so I'm here to provide an easier task." Rex hauled himself to his feet unsteadily. "Easier for you, that is."

"You planted those cufflinks. I know you did," I said futilely.

"Whoops! Though, admittedly, even I was quite shocked and awed by the depth of your betrayal," he slurred. "Given the extensive lengths that Isabel went to protect you."

"What are you talking about?" I said faintly.

"Surely you've pieced it together by now. Or did you think this was all a happy coincidence?" He snickered. "That Isabel randomly pulled you into her world, even invited you to Italy, just because of your . . . neighbor?"

I shook my head, leaning against the dresser. I tried to get ahead of his words, string together some logical conclusion, but my head felt waterlogged.

"Isabel knows everything about you. She was outsourced by your ex's company to help fire him, drum up enough probable cause in the press," Rex went on, staggering toward me.

"But then the fatal crash happened, so she was sent to clean that up, too. And for some reason, she decided to fix it in *your* favor. Like the hand of God, redirecting your destiny."

"I don't understand," I said.

"Turns out nothing in life is an accident—even yours, darling."

I felt ill, the storm churning inside my body like a wheel. I didn't know whether to believe him, but I didn't know what else to believe.

"But I suppose exposing the full story is not great for Isabel either," Rex said, his eyes crawling over me. "I'm granting you a remediation of sorts, so it can be your turn to save the day. Redeem yourself after your little dalliance."

I pressed my back into the dresser, my legs shaking against the wood. Rex was so close I could see his wine-cracked lips, the color of bloody meat. He leaned in like he might kiss me, his breath rancid on my neck, but then he plucked my passport from my hand.

"Hey!" I shouted and tried to grab it back, but he slipped it into his back pocket.

"Consider it collateral," he said smugly. "As long as you fulfill your end of the deal."

He pinned me against the dresser, pressing the squishy bulge in his pants into my thigh.

"Please, Rex, you don't want to do this."

"Oh, I do. Come on, you're better than simply being that jewelry boy's slut," he said. "I know you like them old, don't you?"

My revulsion turned liquid, my eyes and nose leaking tears. As I gripped the edge of the dresser, a razor-sharp object dug into my hand. It took me a second to realize what it was: the coral branch. The slice of red that Damon had left behind. Never to be burnished into a jeweled shape, an emblem of love, but to remain as it was found: a sharp, jagged skeleton. I clenched it tightly in my palm, hiding it behind my back.

Rex unzipped his fly and clutched himself, a limp blob, moaning as he did.

"Now take it in your mouth like a good little girl," Rex said.

He pushed me down, thrusting his wiry gray crotch toward my face. The coral pulsed in my fist like something alive. I tried with all my strength to stand back up, but a wave of darkness curled over my eyes and flooded my vision.

When my senses cleared, Rex was staggering backward in shock, clutching his lower abdomen. I looked at the branch of coral in my hand, smeared with bright red blood.

"You little cunt!" Rex cried out.

Then I ran. I ran out of the boathouse and crawled up the stairs on my hands and knees as fast as I could. When I reached the top landing, a clap of thunder crashed over the mountains, so I couldn't hear his footsteps pounding closer and closer. I knew that if I did not escape, then I would die, but I didn't fear death as much as I feared my own surrender to it.

The bridge, slick as ice, was rocking back and forth in the wind, and as I ran, my balance faltered and my ankle twisted. I fell down hard, the wet metal slats sharply gashing my hands and knees. I tried to get up, my breath strangled by shock, but a gale of dizziness staggered me back down. I stared into depthless space below, only a barrier of air separating my body from the road. I had been here before: the reversal of sea and sky, the end of desire and the desire for the end.

When I looked up, I saw Rex hurtling in my direction. I grabbed on to the railing, trying to haul myself to my feet, but it was too late. His bloodied hands were on my shoulders, pushing me down.

"No, I quite like you in that position," he said. "On your knees."

I wanted to scream but I couldn't, the rain flying down like shrapnel. I don't know why but I found myself praying, not to some divine force but to Graham: *Please save me. I loved you, and look what you've done to me. Please don't let me go like this.*

I opened my eyes and blinked. A spectral figure appeared at the end of the bridge, a miracle sent from the raging skies above. She was rushing toward me, her billowy white dress trailing her like a veil, and for a moment I saw a clarion reflection of myself: the ghost of a bride.

It was Isabel.

In one brutal move, she pushed Rex off me with a forceful shove. He wobbled for a second, as if he might steady himself, but then a howl of wind knocked him back and sent him flying. Time seemed to stop as his entire weight hit the railing, splitting the metal like bone, while his arms flailed and grasped at air, but there was nothing to hold on to. His foot slid off the edge and his body followed, plummeting into the gorge of darkness below. We held our breath in the endless seconds before we heard the terrible thud, the crack of skull hitting the road.

I shivered on the ground, waiting for a sign of life, but behind the rain was only hollow silence, the heaving of my own breath. I looked at Isabel, but she was staring over the mountains, as if watching a scene from her memory projected onto the sky. After a long moment, she looked at me, the light returning to her eyes.

"I was coming to tell you that you could stay the night," Isabel said.

I stared at her mutely, the words stuck in my throat.

"Follow me," she instructed. I trailed behind her off the bridge and down the gravel path out of the front gate. I had forgotten about the hotel driver, but his car was no longer there. How much time had passed since I returned to the boathouse? The hours had turned amorphous, unstructured, like the lake now spilling onto the land. The moon was mantled by clouds and the streetlights down, but the flashlights on our phones were too risky. We held on to each other as we wended our way in the dark, following a thin scythe of light from a nearby window.

We stopped abruptly when we saw him: an inert shape, the limp boulder of a body. His cracked skull ringed in a dark pool of blood. I clamped a hand over my mouth so I wouldn't be sick. He had somehow crawled to the precipice of the road and lay at the verge of a rocky incline, sloping sharply into the water below.

"Oh god," I said.

"Don't touch him," Isabel ordered.

She crouched down to examine him, determining if he was breathing. Then she stood up and wiped her hands on her dress.

"What will we do?" I said.

"We'll do nothing because there's nothing to be done," she said firmly. "We're lucky. The storm will work in our favor. He's just another drunk, reckless casualty." She paused, then gave me a penetrating look. "And if there are any questions, the police will know who to ask."

Then we heard a terrible sound, a last gasp of breath, the guttural moan of a dying beast as a hand slithered out from under him. In one swift gesture, Isabel kicked him hard and he tumbled down the slippery rocks and into the lake below.

At first, I didn't feel anything, neither remorse nor regret. But as I stared into the lake, I saw the body of Graham breaking the surface. He was drifting away from me, toward a distant pearl of light. I reached out my hand to bring him back, but only cold water fell through my fingers. My knees buckled to the ground, sinking into the mud.

"I'm sorry, I'm sorry, I'm sorry," I repeated, heaving with uncontrollable sobs.

I rocked back and forth, the words vibrating through me

like an incantation. Isabel crouched down and took me in her arms, holding me firmly until I was lifeless and quiet, all that had been buried within me exhumed.

"Now there are no secrets left between us," Isabel said pointedly. "Except the ones we will take to our graves."

I didn't ask any questions then. There were no more left to ask. We joined hands and walked back the way we came, following a light in the belltower like a pale star. I didn't look back then, but in my dreams for years afterward, I saw the silhouette of a body, riven, sinking into the rimless dark.

29

I awoke to the sound of a harrowing scream. It was early morning, a blade of sunlight prying open my eyes. At first, I was disoriented, the sheets matted to my skin, then I realized I had fallen asleep in Isabel's bed. I got up, my temples pounding like a terrible hangover, and followed the sound out to the terrace. From up here, the day was clear, the water as blue as a heated sapphire. Still, marks of destruction: a thick brown ring of debris clogged the circumference of the lake, staining the surface like sewage, and roads were blocked by mudslides and fallen trees. I squinted against the sun, trying to see. Then I remembered.

Someone must have found Rex.

I checked my phone, on three percent battery, and saw a message from Isabel instructing me to come downstairs. I reached for a bottle of water on the nightstand, nauseous and parched, and gulped it down. The storm would work in our favor, Isabel had said. Yet I was no stranger to *force majeure*, my marriage contract canceled by death, the death a result of smoke and fog and the weather of intimate violence. And wasn't it all an act of God in the end? I wanted to believe that Rex's death would dim my fear of exposure, but in the light of daybreak, I realized a more painful truth: I was still left with myself.

An hour later, the *carabinieri* were downstairs, drinking cups of espresso. One officer was tall and swarthy, while the other was stout and sweating, like we were in a casting session for an Italian crime drama. Everyone had been gathered in the drawing room: a severely hungover Gemma in feathered pajamas, a hysterical Cadence in a skimpy Missoni cover-up, Pierce on the phone trying to book a private flight to Sardinia, and Isabel dressed as if she were meeting a head of state in a crisp blue dress. Isabel was speaking to the police, while Barbara—more in shock than anyone at the potential liability on her hands—translated in a mix of English and Italian.

"The bridge was built in the late 1800s," Barbara explained. "So you see, our infrastructures were not meant to handle weather like this."

"It is true," the tall officer agreed. "We have had, how do you say, much devastation. The storm caused the tributaries to swell, and now brown water and mud are rushing down the mountains like a landslide, destroying the towns and houses, and turning the roads into rivers."

"Sixty people have been rescued, but this so far is the only reported death," the stout officer chimed in, suspiciously scanning the group.

"But what was he doing on the bridge?" Cadence said. "Wasn't it, like, in the middle of the night?"

"Maybe he wanted to take a dip in the lake," Pierce joked.

"He was very drunk," Isabel stated firmly. "Unfortunately, he had an unsavory history of this sort of rash alcohol-induced behavior."

"As protocol, I need a copy of your passports, please," the tall officer said. "So I can bring them down to the station."

A shiver of panic rose from my tailbone as I realized that Rex had never returned my passport—it was still in his pocket when he fell. It could be in the lake now, sunk to the bottom or caught beneath the dense crust of debris. Or worse: it could be on his body.

"I'm sorry, but why is that necessary?" Pierce said. "It's clear as fucking day it was just an accident."

"It's not so clear." The officer squinted at each of us, milking the suspense. "There was a superficial laceration on the man's stomach that indicates a weapon may have been present at the scene of the crime. Though it is likely he died from the fall itself."

As he let this information settle, our faces shifted from shock to outright alarm.

"You mean it was intentional?" Cadence cried, clinging to Pierce. "Like homicide?"

"Babe, relax, this isn't one of your true crime docs," Pierce said.

The officer cleared his throat. "We need to document everyone who was present last night," the officer continued. "No one is allowed to leave the house yet."

As everyone dispersed to retrieve their passports, Isabel silently ushered me upstairs to her bedroom and shut the door behind us. In a state of hysteria, I told her that Rex had taken my passport, that it was still in his pocket when he fell from the bridge.

"Here's what you're going to do," Isabel said, her face deathly calm. "You're going to tell the police that you left your passport in the safe. The bridge is inaccessible now, so it will take time to find an alternative route."

"But then what?" I said, sick with panic. "What if they find it on his body?"

"If they do, then we'll know who needs to be culpable," she said.

I was afraid to ask who she meant. I had never seen her in fixer mode before, withholding any shred of emotion in order to gain a calculated edge. Still, after my unforgivable act of betrayal, it wasn't impossible to imagine she was shrewdly plotting to exact a form of revenge. I shuddered at the thought, but I had to trust her: I had no other option.

"Do you remember seeing Damon's blazer in the boathouse last night?" Isabel said.

I shrugged, the memory of last night a murky void. "I don't know. Why?"

"You need to think back very carefully now. It's a critical piece of evidence."

Then an image emerged: Rex in the shadows, stroking the blazer in his lap like a cat.

"Yes, I think so," I said.

"Good. Do you understand what I'm asking you to do?" she said sharply.

I shook my head, confused. What did Damon have to do with any of it? He'd left us both. He wasn't even here. Slowly, the pieces began to coalesce, which Isabel had already arranged into an airtight chronology.

She wanted me to implicate Damon. To place him at the crime scene.

Isabel was asking for my collusion in a triangulated plan—as she had when we first met, back at the beginning. Still, I was baffled as to why she wanted him to take the fall. Not me.

I swallowed. "You want me to tell the police that Damon came to the boathouse?"

"I know you've lied to the police before," Isabel said piercingly. "You shouldn't have any trouble a second time."

She looked at me with the intensity of an X-ray. I shuddered, the ring of Rex's final words in my ears: *Isabel knew all along.* Even now, it was too illogical and harrowing to grasp—that she had been the invisible hand, rearranging the aftermath of evidence. And it would take me years to fathom this: Isabel had recut the shape of my life, burnishing the raw edges into smoother facets, and without her I would have been felled by a more tragic fate.

I followed Isabel back into the library, where the officers had been joined by a more official sergeant in a black uniform and beret, a gold military badge on his lapel. Isabel handed over her passport to one of the officers, while the sergeant looked at me expectantly.

"Signorina, your passport, *per favore*," the sergeant commanded, holding out his hand.

"Unfortunately, I left it in the safe in the boathouse," I said, as rehearsed.

"Ah, no, really." The sergeant crossed his arms. "You didn't take it out at any point?"

"Yes, I'm positive." I nodded, glancing at Isabel, but her expression was statuary.

"But you must need it, *non*? When is your flight back to America?"

"It's scheduled for tonight," I said.

"Ah, I see." The sergeant ran his tongue over his teeth. "Then explain, how were you planning on getting back into your country?"

The sergeant's eyes followed the line of sweat trickling down my clavicle to my chest.

"I was planning on packing this morning but didn't realize the storm would prevent that," I said, my voice cracking. "So, if you'll just let me grab it—"

As I started for the door, the sergeant blocked me from passing. The stout officer flashed an accusatory grin, waving a waterlogged passport in a sealed plastic bag like a smoking gun.

"That won't be necessary," he said, "because we already found it for you."

The *stazione di polizia* was located in a pastel-pink building, with flower beds spilling out over mint-green windows. Inside, the atmosphere was charged with chaos. The mass evacuations and structural damage had wreaked havoc on the community, reports of missing persons still coming in. Yet no deaths were reported other than Rex.

I sat in a small waiting area, while Isabel was led into another room to identify the body. I was sweating and anxious, staring at the colorful vintage posters of idyllic destinations—Roma, Sicily, Positano—as if this were a travel agency. I tried not to think of the lacerated abdomen, the clumps of blood, now dried and crusted, in his silver hair. I never saw Graham's body after they pulled me from the water. His limbs mangled, his spine severed beneath the surf.

After Isabel confirmed the corpse belonged to Rex, we were led into a private room with a large window framing the lake. Even in the wake of catastrophe, forgoing a beautiful vista would be a bigger crime to the Italians. The detective stood as we entered, perched behind a wooden desk. He was a stately older man, his gelled-back silver-black hair tucked beneath a cap with a gold medallion. He nodded to the sergeant, who closed the door behind us as we sat down in front of the desk.

"So, signorina, why don't you tell me what happened last night," the detective began. "In your own words."

"It's hard to say," I said. "I slept in the villa last night, in Isabel's room, so I wasn't aware of what was going on outside."

"But you had been sleeping in the boathouse during your stay, yes?" he said, and I nodded. "So what caused you to suddenly change bedrooms?"

"Because it wasn't safe to stay directly on the water during the storm?" I answered.

The detective nodded, as if he couldn't argue with this obvious logic.

"And did everyone know that you slept in the villa?" he said.

"No, everyone was drunk by then, so I don't think they knew where I fell asleep."

"And what time did everyone go to bed, approximately?"

I looked at Isabel for an assist. "Around midnight," she offered.

The detective stroked his mustache, assessing who was covering for whom. I glanced at the table of Rex's waterlogged belongings: a phone, a wallet, my passport. And Damon's blazer. They must have collected it when they swept the boathouse for evidence.

"So you didn't hear anything unusual in the house?" the detective continued. "Or did you *see* anything unusual, perhaps?"

"I . . . I can't be sure," I stammered.

"It should be noted that her vision is severely impaired," Isabel stated.

The detective frowned, his thick black eyebrows like slanted hyphen marks.

"Is that true, signorina?" he said.

"Yes, from a bad accident," I said. "So even if I did see something, it can't be verified."

I leaned forward to show him my fixed pupil, then pulled back from the direct beam of the sun. He made a *hmm* sound, nodding at me.

"I see," he said. "As you know, the CCTV was down because the power was out. But the reason I ask is that a neighbor claims she saw not one, but *two* figures on the bridge last night. Do you have any idea who that other person could be?"

"Yes, she does," Isabel said firmly. "Tell them who you saw walking toward the bridge."

Isabel gave me an unflinching nod, a steely indictment beneath her eyes. I understood then, with a sharp twinge in my sternum, her ultimate objective. By incriminating Damon, betraying him to a criminal degree, I would be indelibly severing our romantic tie. It would be an irreparable act of treachery.

Then Isabel could swoop in to save him, securing Damon's indebtedness to her.

This was her final test of loyalty. My only chance of redemption lay in my response.

"Signorina, you must tell me," the detective implored. "Who might you have seen?"

I took a breath. "I think I saw Damon walking toward the bridge."

"Damon was an additional guest at the villa, *sì*?" The detective blinked.

"*Sì*, and he was at the villa with us last night," I said. "But at some point, he seemed to have fled."

The detective spoke to the sergeant in rapid-fire Italian, gesticulating with his hand, and the sergeant argued back defensively. Isabel was no longer looking at me, but staring vacantly out the window at the lake.

"And where is this man right now?" the detective continued.

I shook my head. "I have no idea. I heard his car take off late last night."

The detective leaned back in his chair. "But tell me, signorina, why would he go to the boathouse in the middle of the storm last night? Can you think of a reason?"

"He probably assumed I was sleeping there," I admitted. "So he was coming to visit me."

He frowned. "In the middle of the night?"

The detective opened his mouth to speak but then slowly pieced the story together.

"Ah, *sì*, I see, you were . . . how do you say, *lovers*?" he said with a small smile.

I nodded, kneading my scraped-up palms. Isabel kept staring straight ahead, her face as hard as stone.

"And did Signor Rex know about this, ah, arrangement between you two?" he asked.

"Yes, and he was very jealous. They even had a physical

altercation earlier in the evening," I noted. "So it's possible Damon ventured into the storm to see me, and then Rex followed him outside . . ."

"And then they got into a deadly fight?" he offered excitedly. "A crime of passion, yes?"

"Yes, exactly," I confirmed.

The detective squinted at me, drumming his fingers on the desk.

"*Bravissima*, signorina!" he said, clapping his hands. "That's a very dramatic story, but we have a report that this Damon was seen driving south earlier in the evening. So how do you explain that?"

I swallowed hard, my throat dry. Soon Damon would be swimming off a sun-baked shore, collecting watermelon seeds in his palm. His blazer as abandoned and discarded as I was now. I thought of our nights in the city, miles away, my education on the duplicity of stones. All the brilliant fatalities of color.

Though, in all that time, he never asked how I'd kill him.

"Signorina?" the detective said. "Do you have an explanation, or do you not?"

Isabel looked at me then, with a firm exhortation to honor our deal, yet beneath was a tremble of disappointment that made my heart sink.

"I know that he did it," I said. "I have proof."

The detective cocked his head. "How could you know if you did not see him?"

I instructed him to open the interior of the blazer. Reticently, the detective put on gloves, as if I was trying to obstruct justice, and tore open the seam. Inside was a small trove of contraband corals, little red ventricles as though ripped from my own chest. Later, I would learn that the superficial laceration in Rex's abdomen contained a small fragment of coral, the brittle tip snapping off and embedding in his skin. A coral cut, the fishermen called it, a common coastal injury. And though it did not kill him—it did not cause a fatal vascular injury—that red slice of stone was the guilty evidence of foul play.

"Buying and trafficking endangered coral is illegal here," the detective explained. "It is a very precious treasure in our country."

The phone rang, and the detective answered it. He nodded gravely, then looked at Isabel as if seeing her for the first time. When he hung up the phone, he straightened his uniform and cleared his throat.

"Signora, *mi dispiace*," he said apologetically. "I didn't realize who your husband was."

"Yes, he was very fond of our time spent here," Isabel said graciously. "Italy was a special place to him."

The detective sat back down, folding his hands with a conciliatory smile. "So perhaps we can discuss some sort of, how do you say, deal?"

Eventually, the detective agreed to release me and arranged for an officer to drive me back to the villa. But as I stood up and walked toward the door, I didn't feel relief, or even reprieve, but the wrenching cut of an invisible thread, the one that tied me to Isabel and Damon, unraveling my inner seams.

"Ah, signorina?" the detective said, and I turned around.

He was waving my passport in his hand. As I walked toward him, his eyes skimmed my scraped knees, registering the fresh abrasions. The scabbed marks of guilt.

"How did you hurt yourself?" He squinted.

I shrugged, taking the passport from his hand. "I have no idea."

By early evening, a few roads had reopened, but the damage would persist for months and years after I was gone, buried houses and fallen bridges left unrepaired. I was finally leaving, my flight scheduled for eleven that night. The hotel driver arrived to transport me to the airport; my suitcase, thankfully, was still in his trunk.

Before I left, I went in search of Isabel.

The villa was weighted with silence, the rooms preparing for a night of absence. In the kitchen, I found Maria chopping vegetables for a Bolognese; she hugged me and gave me a bag of parmesan flecks and green plums for my trip. Then I went upstairs. Isabel's bedroom door was ajar, a crease of copper light on the floor. I was about to call Isabel's name when I saw her kneeling before the open window. At first, I thought she was praying, hands clasped, rocking back and forth. But as I got closer, I saw she was crying. Clutching the photograph of her husband to her chest, the silk skin of her bathrobe rippling with silent sobs.

In all this time, I had never seen her cry like that, her sorrow spinning through me like a skipping stone. I wondered who she was mourning: Was it the death of her husband or the dissolution of a dream? Maybe we call it loss because we can never locate that part of ourselves again; the dead take it with them when they go. In its place they leave an unanchored self, stripped of its bearings.

"I came to say goodbye," I said finally.

Isabel turned around. Her eyes were red, a faint etching of lines more defined than they had once been.

"Why did you do it?" she said. "Why did you lie to me?"

I had no explanation for what I had done. My mind was roaring with a maelstrom of questions, ones that I burned to ask her: *Why did you save me that night? Did you see my body lifted over the cliff? Did you find my ring in the bloodbath? How did you know that I felt trapped in the car, in my life, but his death was the one thing I would never escape?*

I took a ragged breath, but the words stuck in my throat. Maybe I knew the answers would not bring me closer to the myth of closure, to the artifice of an ending.

"I trusted you so much that I couldn't see what was right in front of me," Isabel said.

"Forgive me, please," I said. "It's not who I am, it's not who I was."

"But it's who you became."

Isabel drew her robe tightly across her chest, as if a cold wind had blown through the room. Then she turned toward the window to face the sinking sun. I had wounded her, but no more than I had myself. I ran back downstairs, around the pool littered with broken branches and dead insects, and through the sunken garden to the waiting car. I climbed into the back seat and shut the door, my eyes filling with tears.

"You ready to head back home, signorina?" the driver asked.

"Yes," I said. "Let's go."

As we drove down the gravel path, pausing before the iron gate, I saw Damon. He was standing on the steps of the villa, looking down at me from above. I met his eyes, as fathomless as the lake after the storm, unaware of what was to come.

On the road below, two police officers got out of their cars and headed toward the villa.

Isabel emerged onto the balcony in her robe, her eyes now dry, a spoke of sun striking her face as she gazed down on us both. When Damon saw the police approaching, he said something to me that I couldn't hear or understand, though for years afterward I would imagine what it was, as if I had been left with more than a wordless end.

The gate finally opened, and I turned away to face the hot horizon. The sky was flushed with red, like all the stones I had come to know over the past few months: ruby, garnet, carnelian, spinel, and that one branch of coral, washed of blood, a small fire burning in my hand.

PART IV

30

Then autumn arrived, almost a year after my return, so I began again and again I began. I was back in the maid's room, back in New York. The days contracted, the darkness exceeding the dying light, until winter was nearer than summer had once been.

I hadn't spoken to Isabel since that last day in Italy, back in late August. We never acknowledged what had happened between us, the events leading up to our fatal complicity. For weeks I replayed that final scene, the triangulated composition of it, and speculated what had unfolded in the subsequent days. I imagined that Damon was released after a short stay in prison, the penalty settled by Isabel. But afterward, had they stayed in the villa together, just the two of them? Did they stay up late, drinking wine, while she disclosed the story of Rex's death? I assumed that she painted me as a traitorous woman, unfaithful to them both in the end.

It was also possible that Isabel spent those final nights alone, bereft in an emptied house.

The news of Rex's death came out a few days later. It was written off without suspicion, thanks to Isabel's artful hand. A few tributes quoting notable friends, saying it was a fitting way for him to go, the reckless rake, the irreverent bon vivant.

Like everything else, he was soon forgotten. Overshadowed by other news, elections, protests, the anxious blitz of modern life.

Sometimes I wondered how my life would have changed. If Isabel had not intervened, not once but twice; if she had not recharted the map of my misfortune. If my name had been inextricably tied to wrongful death, an immutable culpability. The perennial questions asked—addressed exclusively to women, as if we are at fault for the failings of men. But they were impossible to answer, just as it was impossible to reconcile the paradoxes of the dead. Graham had been buried with our secrets; there were things I was resigned to leave unresolved.

On nights I couldn't sleep, I would compulsively search for Isabel and Damon online, looking for traces of their continued lives. Occasionally, when a glossy photo appeared of them together—at a dinner or a party, though less frequent now—I would study them in the dark until my eyes burned. Like staring directly at the sun, willing the damage of light exposure. On the darkest nights, I fumed that I hadn't heard from Damon—not even to ask why I had turned on him. Or maybe he accepted the consequence of our actions. It was, after all, the game he had set in motion from the beginning.

But I knew, looking back, that I had always been the trespasser. Still, sometimes I missed them. I missed them in the way you ache for a faded memory, it is both alive and absent within you. Eventually, I stopped looking for signs. I stopped trying to pinpoint the moment that had pushed us all over the edge until the bridge could no longer hold.

As September bled into October, I grieved less for a future that might have been and tried to reconstruct the blank map of the present. The season pulled back its light, and I pulled back my longing for it. I walked around the reservoir at sunrise, the wild russet leaves dangling like hangmen. I accepted a screenwriting job adapting a Scandinavian erotic thriller about a ruinous affair, which seemed, if nothing else, relatable. I saw friends, I saw plays, sometimes I went to parties. I scheduled a follow-up with the neuro-ophthalmologist. I watched old movies with Sam. Life was quieter, but still the earth tilted away from the sun as it does each solstice, in spite of everything, and I was alright.

Then, one morning, I saw Damon.

The first chill of fall had arrived, erasing any last trace of summer. The air tasted of wet leaves. I was headed briskly toward the park, shivering beneath my coat from the last winter I had narrowly survived, and passed by Via Quadronno on 73rd to pick up a coffee.

There he was, standing in the window.

I stopped walking, suspended beneath the buttery shade of a ginkgo tree. His hair was all buzzed off, his summer tan faded. He had a tired, strained expression, impatiently shifting his weight as if carrying some burdensome thing. When he saw me, I held my breath. We stared at each other, separated by a pane of glass, by the sidewalk, by the impassable distances of longing. And I realized that whatever door I hadn't knocked on, whatever blizzard of night I hadn't seized, was no longer available to us. Or maybe it never had been. We render our lives in inflection points, we invent the fiction of a different outcome, yet, in the end, it might have led us to the same place.

Behind him, I saw Caroline. She was visibly pregnant, a chunky knit sweater taut around her stomach. She handed Damon a coffee, and he distractedly glanced at her, then back at me once more.

But I was already gone.

In the park, I walked by Pilgrim Hill. The old woman in the ratty raccoon coat was still there, sitting in front of a large wooden easel. She held the same palette in her lap, but the trees had changed. Candied cherry blossoms replaced with the somber passages of autumn, olives and ochres, rusted branches reaching toward a burnt umber sky.

"I love your trees," I said.

She scowled and looked up from her canvas. But then her scrunched, fuchsia mouth unfurled into a smile. "Thank you, my dear."

I smiled back. Maybe I couldn't see who I had become, but I was no longer peering into the darkness. I was looking up at the leaves, blazing like red comets, not yet ready to fall.

31

A few weeks later, I awoke in the maid's room to a bone-chilling dawn. It was dark out, a shiver of raw wind seeping through the unsealed air-conditioner vent. I didn't want to get out of bed, but I dragged myself to the bathroom.

Pulling my hair into a bun, I cracked open one eye in the mirror. I blinked several times, the soft focus of my reflection crystallizing into a different face. I squinted into the flickering bulb, then looked in the mirror again: my pupil constricted against the green sequin of my iris. I couldn't believe it. My bad eye almost looked normal. I palpated the hard knot of my scar and felt a sharp edge beneath the skin, like the tip of a knife trying to break the surface. I didn't know whether to laugh or to weep.

It was November: one year after the accident. The anniversary of Graham's death.

I sat down on the cold ridge of the tub, trying to catch my breath. And then I fell backward into the bathtub, releasing and sinking into the soft body of my suitcase. It was still here, as I was, unmoved but not unchanged. I lay like that for a long time, staring up at the ceiling until it was no longer dark. Graham would remain a part of my story, but he would no longer be trapped inside my body like the sliver of glass. An inclusion within a stone.

After a while, I heard Sam shuffling into the kitchen. He switched on the coffee machine and toasted his English muffin, ruffled the pages of the *Times.* The quiet rhythms of morning I had come to depend on.

"Slash?" he called out. "Are you awake?"

I could hear his slippers on the cracked wood, approaching the door.

"I'm in here," I said.

Sam came into the bathroom and looked down at me in the bathtub. His white hair was uncombed, and he was wearing faded plaid pajamas, a Christmas gift from a lover years ago. But he looked frail, his cheeks gaunt and ashen.

"Honey, I hate to tell you," he said, "but that tub hasn't worked since the Mets played the Polo Grounds."

"Which Bond Girl was that year?" I said.

"The very best one," he said.

Sam smiled, looming over me like a tomb. I sat up slowly, the blood rushing to my head. Dawn was straining through the window like black honey, letting the light pass through.

"Don't worry, Sam. I promise I won't live here forever," I said.

"And neither will I," he said, his voice hoarse. "But what I worry about is where you'll be when I'm no longer here."

"Please don't say that," I said.

"Alright, I won't say it. I'll just think it silently," he said.

Beneath his pajama top, I could see his scar, a red branch of stitches, where his own chest had been cleaved apart. One day soon, there would be no more old films and no more dinners together, no more nights just the two of us cocooned from the outside world. I tried to smile, but tears were slipping from my eyes.

"Who will ever love me again?" I said.

"Who won't love you?" Sam said.

"No, I think that's it for me." I shook my head. "I think I'm done."

"You'll have many more loves, Slash. This I know for certain," he said, taking a raspy breath. "Our scars remember the wound, but even the deepest ones fade with time."

Finally, Sam pulled me to my feet. I wrapped my arms around him, listening to the unhurried beat of his heart, as if it had no more reason to move fast.

"It's been a gift to live here," I said.

"Well, that cad never even gave you any jewelry, so I had to make up for it somehow."

I laughed, but I was crying now.

"Maybe we should get married," I said.

"Ah, I should be so lucky," he said. "Now, come on, Slash. Let me make you a little breakfast."

Sam wiped the tears from my cheeks, his eyes twinkling softly. For so long, life had seemed like an endless series of departures, from cities and seasons, my insoluble dreams, from splinters of myself that might never be recovered, yet each left space for something new and untold to arrive.

I took a breath, and then I stepped out of the tub.

ACKNOWLEDGMENTS

My deep and boundless gratitude to those who helped bring this book into the world . . .

To Margaret Riley King, who fearlessly believed in it from the beginning, many drafts and years ago, and never stopped fighting. Meredith Clark, and the HarperCollins team, who understood the dualities of this story and guided me through each stage (and title change) until the last. Paul Bogaards, champion extraordinaire, who came on board this wild ride with a bang and then some. Olivier Sultan, who had faith I could write more than dialogue, and Michelle Weiner, Olivia Blaustein, and Jon Cassir, my fierce CAA team who took the chance. Darren Trattner, who listened to and believed in me while we clocked too many steps to count.

To Daphne Merkin, who offered the shelter of her own maid's room in my darkest hour and continually challenges me to write about how "the desires of the heart are as crooked as corkscrews." Adam Rathe, who helps carry me through the chaos and always delivers the sagest advice, in art and in life. Jessica Whitaker, whose incisive notes, during our "despair walks" and on the page, pushed me to dig even deeper. Stellene Volandes, who expertly answered jewelry-related questions during our New York nights that kept me inspired. Christina McDowell, who assuaged my many creative crises and told me to keep going.

To Karyn Lyons, whose luminous painting *The Imposter* is the star of the cover—thank you for bringing this dream to life and granting me permission to use your brilliant image.

To the dear friends who generously provided escapist writing retreats, when I needed it most: Eleanora over the water in Rhinebeck and Italy; Kevin beside the Reservoir on 90th Street; and Jack Shear amid the sculptures in Spencertown.

To my loving family, Bebe, Mark, Evan, and Danielle, my earliest readers; especially Bebe, who always encouraged me to write a novel—even if it took me a decade to listen. And to Doug's wonderful family for their support during this process.

And to those who guided me in their painful absence. Mark Strand, beloved mentor, whose poetic voice resounded in my ear as I wrote, and who continues to infuse my life with his "weather of words." And James Williams, who left us in 2021, a loss that left such a gaping hole the only thing I could do was write through it . . .

Finally, to Doug, who invited me to finish a deadline at his desk, thinking it would be a month—and I never left. Thank you for your unwavering love and sensitive syntax, and all the hours and nights you listened to me read these chapters aloud. I'll always write next to you, not about you.